WOLF HUNT

PAIGE TYLER

sourcebooks
casablanca

Published by Sourcebooks Casablanca, an imprint of Sourcebooks, Inc.
P.O. Box 4410, Naperville, Illinois 60567-4410
(630) 961-3900
Fax: (630) 961-2168
www.sourcebooks.com

Printed and bound in Canada.
MBP 10 9 8 7 6 5 4 3 2 1

With special thanks to my extremely patient and understanding husband. Without your help and support, I couldn't have pursued my dream job of becoming a writer. You're my sounding board, my idea man, my critique partner, and the absolute best research assistant a girl could ask for.

Love you!

Prologue

Southern Idaho, 2012

"YOU REALLY THINK THEY'RE IN THERE?" JESS PARKER asked as they knelt in the heavy line of trees that ran the perimeter of the LaRouche farm, scanning the house in front of them with binoculars.

U.S. Marshal Remy Boudreaux's attention was focused on the biggest window along one side of the large ranch-style home. Lights barely illuminated the interior, but he could see enough to know there hadn't been any movement since he and Jess had started watching the place fifteen minutes ago.

He pulled the binoculars away from his face and grinned at his partner. "I haven't seen them, darlin', but my instincts are screaming at me that all three of those scumbags are in there."

Remy normally would never call a fellow marshal *darlin'*, but considering that he was in love with this particular one, he figured it was okay.

Jess grinned back at him because she flat-out adored his N'Awlins accent, though he could just barely make out her expression in the darkness. Even so, that little smile dazzled him. It was one of the things that had attracted Remy to the tall redhead in the first place, convincing him to throw caution to the wind, blow off every rule in the U.S. Marshal handbook, and get into a romantic relationship with her.

"You know I always trust that instinct of yours," Jess said. "How are we going to handle this?"

Remy turned back and scanned the farmhouse where the LaRouche family—Tammy, Jack, and their three kids—lived. From the outside, nothing seemed amiss. Just another summer night in the rolling wheat fields of southern Idaho. But it felt like the hairs on the back of his neck were standing on end. Something was definitely going on in there, and he was damn sure it had to do with the three murderous prison escapees they were looking for.

"Let's move closer, so we can get a better look," he said softly.

Before he could move, Jess reached out and grabbed his shoulder. When he turned to look at her, she leaned in and kissed him. It wasn't a long kiss, but there was definitely heat. They'd only been sleeping together for a couple of months, but the passion between them burned with a fire hotter than Remy had ever experienced.

"Be careful," she whispered after she pulled away. "Those three assholes are dangerous. There's no way in hell they'll willingly go back to prison."

Then Jess was moving, pulling out her Glock and skulking toward the side of the farmhouse. Remy drew his own sidearm and followed, watching as her lithe, athletic body moved through the night ahead of him.

He hadn't needed Jess's reminder that the men they were after were dangerous. He'd read the transcripts from their trials, seen the prison records, talked to the other inmates at Leavenworth who'd had dealings with them. These three men were beyond evil.

No one knew how Conrad Neal, Joshua Cobb, and Walter Ramirez had even managed to break out of the Leavenworth federal penitentiary in Kansas. As far as anyone could tell, the men had been in their cells before lights-out, but when the sun came up, all three were gone. Remy's job wasn't figuring out how they'd managed to escape, it was tracking down the men and putting them back in prison.

Neal was likely the leader of the trio of escaped convicts. His record indicated he had a high IQ and a charismatic personality. Unfortunately for him—and the rest of society—he was also possessive as hell and had an out-of-control temper. He'd beaten three men to death in a bar in Oklahoma simply for smiling at his girlfriend. One of those men had been an off-duty FBI agent, hence Neal's 118-year term in federal prison.

Cobb had been convicted of multiple charges of murder as well, along with rape and arson. The son of a bitch thought he wouldn't get caught if no one could recognize the woman he'd attacked, so he'd murdered her, then burned down her house, assuming all the evidence would disappear. But the fire he'd started in Oregon had spread across the border into Washington, resulting in the destruction of dozens of homes and the deaths of three more people, including a firefighter. That had earned him a life sentence in Leavenworth.

Ramirez might have been the scariest. A doctor for the Veterans Administration in Arizona, Ramirez had invited male patients over to his house for private treatment sessions and then experimented on them. He was serving a life sentence as well.

When Remy and Jess reached the side of the house,

he cautiously peeked in the window overlooking the kitchen sink. At first, he didn't see anything, but then he caught sight of Ramirez sitting in the shadow-shrouded living room, smoking a cigarette and watching TV. There was a teenage boy sitting beside him, tied and gagged, staring at the television.

Shit.

Remy was right. Again.

Everyone else on the task force had thought Remy and Jess were wasting their time running all the way out to Idaho on a crazy hunch. But ever since he could remember, Remy had listened to his gut. So while the rest of the marshals focused on the various friends, pen pals, and visitors the three convicts had been in contact with over the past year, Remy and Jess had been busy tracking down the one person suspiciously absent from Neal's life since his incarceration—his former girl-friend, Tammy Andrews, or rather Tammy LaRouche, now that she was married.

Tammy hadn't testified in Neal's defense. In fact, she'd never shown at his trial. She hadn't visited him in prison, called him, or even written him any letters. The poor woman had been so traumatized by the whole ordeal in the bar that she'd simply walked away from Neal and never looked back.

Some people might consider that a betrayal. According to an inmate Remy had spoken to at Leavenworth, Neal was one of those people.

"If someone does him wrong, Neal will remember it for the rest of his life and do whatever it takes to get revenge on that person," the inmate had said. "He's one vindictive son of a bitch."

Beside Remy, Jess was on her cell phone with the local PD, requesting backup. He hoped this town had a SWAT team, because they were going to need it. When she hung up, they slowly moved around the outside of the house, hoping to pin down exactly where Neal and Cobb were hiding.

They were a few feet from the back door when a woman's scream cut through the humid night air. A split second later, there was a crashing sound, followed by coarse laughter and another terrified scream.

Remy's gut clenched. Going in on their own was insanity, but he and Jess had no choice. Their backup was at least twenty minutes out. They couldn't wait.

He glanced at Jess, hating the idea of her going in there. If she was simply his partner, he wouldn't have given it a second thought, but she was more than that to him. There was no way in hell she'd ever let him go in alone though.

"Watch yourself in there, okay?" he whispered.

"You too," she said softly.

Taking a deep breath, Remy led the way to the door, then grabbed the knob and turned it. Once inside, he and Jess quickly moved through the kitchen toward the living room, where he'd seen Ramirez and the boy.

The kid was still sitting there, bound and gagged, but there was no sign of Ramirez. Remy gave Jess a nod. As one, they checked the rest of the room and the hallway beyond, covering each other at the same time.

Another scream came from the back of the house. Remy immediately headed down the dark hallway toward the sound, Jess at his heels. Charging into a room with three armed fugitives who'd already shown a willingness to kill and as many as four possible hostages was definitely in the category of Bad Ideas. There were so many ways it could go wrong, he couldn't even count them all. But he didn't have a choice.

When he got to the door at the end of the hallway, he lifted his foot and kicked it in. The only lights on in the large master bedroom were two small bedside lamps, but even in their dim glow, the scene that met his eyes was horrific. Time seemed to slow to a crawl as he took everything in, his head trying to make sense of what he was seeing.

Jack LaRouche was tied to a big armchair that had fallen over on its side in the corner, his head hanging loosely to the side, blood from his battered and bruised face running down to stain his flannel shirt and the light-colored carpet.

Tammy was lying on the bed, shallow slash marks across her face, her brown eyes filled with horror as she reached her bound hands toward where Cobb stood near the footboard with a girl who couldn't have been more than ten in his grip.

Ramirez was standing casually in the corner near the husband, a sick smile twisting his ugly face, a knife in one hand and an automatic pistol in the other. There was no sign of Neal or the LaRouches' third child.

Muttering a curse, Cobb lunged forward and scooped up a big .357 revolver that Remy hadn't even seen near the bed. Remy leveled his weapon and started to squeeze the trigger only to freeze as Cobb ducked behind the girl. There wasn't any way Remy could shoot Cobb, not without hitting the girl.

Shit.

Remy had half a second to come up with a plan before Cobb and Ramirez started shooting. Knowing Jess would take care of Ramirez, Remy charged Cobb and the girl he was using as a human shield.

He felt the first bullet hit him somewhere to the right of his belly button, then another higher up on his chest. He was wearing a lightweight Kevlar vest under his shirt, but the first round hit well below the bottom, going right through his stomach. As painful as that shot felt, it was the one to the chest that worried him more. His preference for increased mobility, which meant he sacrificed protection by wearing the lighter Kevlar, had just bitten him in the ass. The ballistic fibers of the vest had failed to stop the fast-moving .357 round. The pain in his chest hadn't been the hammer punch it should have felt like if the damn vest had done its job. Instead, it felt like he'd been stabbed with a hot poker.

Gritting his teeth against the pain, Remy leaped at Cobb and the girl. She cried out as Remy slammed into them. They all went down in a tumble of arms and legs, hitting the floor hard. Remy grabbed the barrel of Cobb's gun and shoved it toward the ceiling. Then, making sure the girl was out of the way, he fired a round point-blank into the fugitive's head.

Remy immediately rolled to the side and came up on his knees, aiming his weapon at the spot where Ramirez had last been standing. At least that's what he attempted to do. He succeeded for the most part, but his right arm wasn't very steady and he was moving slower than usual.

Thankfully, Ramirez lay on the floor, unmoving. Jess stood beside the convict, staring at Remy in horror. Fighting a sudden wave of dizziness, he looked down and saw the blood covering his stomach. Okay, maybe he was hurt worse than he'd thought.

He lifted his head to tell her that he was okay, but the words stuck in his throat. As he watched, blood slowly seeped through her blouse on the upper left side, just above the line of her vest. Oh God, she'd been hit too. And she was bleeding really badly.

He was so focused on Jess that he almost didn't realize Neal was coming out of the bathroom with the LaRouches' other daughter clamped against his chest. Before Remy could react, the man lifted his gun and shot Jess three times.

Remy swung his weapon on Neal at the same time the girl jabbed her elbow into the man's gut. Neal lost his grip on her for only a split second as she fought to get away, but it was enough time for Remy to get a shot off.

The round wasn't well aimed—neither Remy's arm nor his vision was steady enough for that—but it hit Neal in the shoulder, allowing the girl to get away. Remy squeezed the trigger and didn't stop until his Glock ran out of ammo and Neal lay dead on the floor.

Remy dropped his weapon and pushed to his feet, but his legs didn't seem to be taking requests at the moment, so he had no choice but to crawl over to Jess instead. It was less than ten feet, and yet he was gasping for air by the time he reached her.

He ignored the lack of oxygen and the blackness threatening to engulf everything around him, focusing on Jess and her beautiful face. She was bleeding now from more places than he could ever hope to stop, but he tried all the same, pressing one hand to the wound in her chest and the other to a gash in her neck. Then he leaned forward and rested his forehead against hers.

"I told you to watch yourself," he whispered.

Unbelievably, her blue eyes fluttered open and stared up into his. "I'm...sorry."

He shook his head, trying not to cry but unable to stop the tears. "Stop it! It's going to be okay. I know it in my gut, and like you always say, my instincts are never wrong. Never!"

Jess smiled at that. A moment later, her eyes closed and she was gone.

Remy closed his eyes too, tears streaming down his face. Even as his heart broke in his chest, the pain in his body slowly began to fade. It wouldn't be long now. At least he and Jess were leaving this fucked-up world together.

Chapter 1

New Orleans, Louisiana, Present Day

REMY DIDN'T REALIZE HOW MUCH HE'D MISSED NEW Orleans, but as he walked down Bourbon Street basking in the ambience of his hometown, he remembered why he loved it so much. To make it even better, he was getting the chance to show it off to the most important people in his life—his pack mates. SWAT officers-slash-werewolves Max Lowry, Jayden Brooks, and Zane Kendrick took in the bright lights, crowds of partying people, a variety of music coming from nightclubs on either side of the street, talented street performers all around them, and the unique combination of scents hanging in the air with a mix of curiosity and excitement.

Remy's mouth twitched. Yeah, New Orleans had that kind of effect on people.

Gage Dixon, their boss, pack alpha, and commander of the Dallas SWAT team, had sent the four of them to New Orleans to cross-train with the local tactical unit, the city's term for their SWAT teams. At the same time, four officers from NOPD SWAT would take part in a weeklong exercise in Dallas. While Gage and the guy who ran NOPD SWAT had become friends when they worked together in Dallas years ago, they still had to handle the whole thing carefully, both here and in Texas. Cross-training with cops who weren't werewolves meant hiding their abilities, so Gage had made his expectations extremely clear.

"Don't run too fast, lift anything you shouldn't be able to, or let your tempers get away from you, and whatever you do, no claws, fangs, or frigging glowing eyes," Gage had reminded them before they'd left.

A year ago, Gage would never have considered letting them do something like this, but he and the Pack had changed a lot since then. Not only were they better at controlling their abilities, but they were also a lot more trusting of the outside world now. Having so many guys find their soul mates recently probably had a lot to do with that.

"Is it always this wild here?" Zane asked as a group of attractive women passing by gave them long, lingering looks and dazzling smiles.

Remy chuckled. He wondered if Zane knew his British accent was always more noticeable when he was around the opposite sex. Probably. No doubt the former soldier from the British Special Air Service knew it made women go crazy.

"Yeah, it's always like this here," Remy confirmed. "New Orleans is a city that takes the concept of having a good time to a whole different level."

There was also a palpable tension in the air tonight that had absolutely nothing to do with the normal wild-party atmosphere of the city—the tropical storm brewing in the Gulf. While his teammates had probably picked up on the nervous energy percolating around them, they most likely didn't know the cause. But Remy knew from growing up here and living through Hurricane Katrina in 2005.

Not that anyone was comparing Tropical Storm Ophelia with Katrina. It was a much smaller, weaker storm than Katrina had ever been, and if the talking heads on the Weather Channel were to be believed, the storm was destined to disintegrate into a tropical depression and do nothing more than drench the Texas coast with a couple inches of rain. That sucked for places like Houston, which had gotten more than its fair share of rain lately, but was a serious blessing for New Orleans.

Even with everyone saying Ophelia wasn't going to be a repeat of Katrina, and that the levees, floodgates, and canals protecting the city would be fine, there was still an underlying current of fear in the city. Some of it was because many of the same people saying Ophelia wasn't a threat were also the ones who'd said there was *almost* no chance Katrina would hit the city. People might have forgiven those weather experts, but no one had forgotten.

The thing that really had the city walking around on proverbial eggshells at the moment was the fact that Katrina had forced everyone to accept how vulnerable the delta city was to almost any kind of storm. New Orleans was a unique city because it was essentially an island surrounded by large lakes to the north and east, the Mississippi to the south, and wetlands to the west. Even worse, most of the city was below sea level. In fact, parts of it, like the infamous Lower Ninth Ward, were three or four feet below the water surrounding New Orleans.

Despite knowing another big storm could drown the city again, maybe worse than the first time, people chose to stay anyway, making an uneasy peace with all the water surrounding them. So while Ophelia churned slowly through the Gulf trying to figure out where it wanted to go, people went about their business, working, laughing, and having a good time—but they also had their TVs turned to the Weather Channel and the prognosticators trying to predict how strong the storm would become and where it would go. And they made plans just in case.

"Where do we go first?" Max asked excitedly. "This place is like one huge, awesome party."

Remy did a double take when he saw the iridescent gold rimming Max's blue eyes. Damn, the city's energy was already starting to get to the guy. Not surprising. Max was the youngest guy in SWAT and the newest werewolf in the Pack. He'd gone through his change barely four years ago and was still getting a grip on his inner wolf. Sometimes things slipped out a little.

"Max, your eyes are glowing," Brooks said, nudging him in the shoulder. "Dial it back a bit, dude."

Unlike Max, Brooks was completely in control and probably had been from the day he'd become a werewolf. A former fullback at LSU, he was one of the few members of the Pack who could do a full shift to his wolf form without breaking stride or even a sweat. Remy had only been able to completely shift once and that was after Gage and Brooks had spent hours talking him through the process. It had been painful as hell and not something he looked forward to ever doing again.

Muttering a curse, Max closed his eyes for a moment and took a deep breath. A few moments later, he opened them again. "Better?"

Brooks nodded when he saw Max's eyes were back to their normal color. "Good to go."

"Sorry about that." Max ran a hand through his perpetually messy, dark hair. "I'm not sure what the hell that was about. That hasn't happened to me in months."

"Don't worry about it." Remy laughed, slapping the other werewolf on the shoulder hard enough to break bones in a normal person. "No one is going to notice glowing eyes on Bourbon Street. Hell, down here, I doubt they'd even care if you sprouted fangs. Gage would go apeshit though, so you'd better not. As far as where we go first, it doesn't matter. You can't go wrong down here. Let's start on the left side of the street and stop anywhere that catches our attention."

"Sounds like we have a plan." Brooks grinned, his teeth a flash of white against his brown skin. "Let's have some fun."

Remy let Zane and Max lead the way as the four of them headed down the sidewalk toward the first club, a blues joint that already had a crowd of people moving in and out of the large, wide-open door. Zane headed to the bar for drinks while Remy and the other guys staked out some standing room space near a support column by the door.

Loud blues music and dancing people filled the club in equal measure, creating a rush of memories that brought a smile to Remy's face. Damn, it had been a long time since he'd been here. He quickly did the math and realized it had been five years since Gage had found him in a club in the French Quarter doing his very best to drink himself to death.

He was just tugging on that particular memory,

relieved that it didn't bring him as much pain as it used to, when an unusual and extremely tantalizing scent caught his attention. He whipped his head around to stare at the door, sniffing the air. His nose was okay, certainly nothing special like some of the other werewolves in the Pack. It made him wonder why he was picking up this particular smell so clearly.

There were a lot of overwhelming scents down on Bourbon Street. Sweat, booze, perfume, cigarette and cigar smoke, moldy wood, drugs, sex—you name it. All that made it hard to discern anything else around him. This particular scent was different and it demanded his attention.

"Hey, you okay?" Brooks asked.

Brooks was one of his pack mates blessed with a good nose. Remy turned to the big guy and motioned toward the open door.

"Do you smell that?" he asked.

Brooks sniffed. "I smell a lot of things. Which one are you talking about?"

"That flowery, spicy scent coming from outside."

Brooks sniffed again. Beside him, Max did the same. A moment later, they both looked at him and shook their heads.

"I don't smell anything like that," Brooks said. "Is it a trace scent or more concentrated?"

Remy breathed deeply through his nose and almost got weak-kneed. What was more, he actually started getting a boner. *What the hell?*

"Yeah," he managed. "You could say it's concentrated." He glanced at Brooks and Max. "You guys are screwing with me, right? You seriously can't smell that?"

"Smell what?" Zane asked as he appeared beside them carrying four plastic cups of beer.

Remy ignored him and the beer, which was saying a lot. He really liked beer. But the idea of taking a big gulp right then didn't interest him at all. He didn't have a clue what the hell he was smelling, but he damn well knew he needed to find out what it was. He'd go nuts if he didn't.

"I'm going for a walk," he said.

Zane and the other guys followed as he tracked the scent out onto the street. At this time of night, it was closed to vehicles and packed with people. He was big and muscular, so most of the crowd avoided him, which was good, since his mind was too preoccupied to worry about running anyone over.

"Hey!" Zane called out. "You want your beer?"

"No, you keep it," he said, too focused on the scent to care.

"Sweet," Zane said as he and the other guys followed. "More for me."

The scent led Remy on a much longer chase than he thought possible. As strong as it had been in the club, he was sure he'd find the source right outside the doors, but he'd already gone five blocks and the scent was still getting more intense. That was pretty frigging hard to believe.

The trail led him into a bar and grill, where the scent was powerful enough to make him think the person had spent some time there, then to a live music club. The scent wasn't quite as concentrated there, so she probably hadn't stayed there very long. He could understand why. The music had been loud, and not very good.

It wasn't until he was back out on the street with

Max, Brooks, and Zane still in tow that he realized he
was following a woman.

He tried to tell himself it was insane. He'd smelled thousands of women since becoming a werewolf. Hell, maybe
tens of thousands. None of them had ever possessed a
spicy, flowery scent this delectable. Not even close.

Remy walked faster. What kind of woman could
generate a scent so powerful it gave him a hard-on the
moment he caught a whiff? The curiosity was killing him.

He was vaguely aware of his pack mates talking to
each other, but he didn't pay too much attention to what
they were saying. Something about betting on the hair
color of the woman he was tracking down. He briefly
wondered how they knew it was a woman, since they
couldn't seem to smell her scent, but then decided that was
a stupid-ass question. He was Remy Frigging Boudreaux.
If he was putting this much effort into tracking down a
scent, anyone who knew him would realize there had to
be a woman on the other end of the line. He would have
never gone through this much trouble otherwise.

Remy wasn't sure how long he followed the scent,
but the next thing he knew, he was walking into a night-
club with a steady dance beat throbbing out of every
hole, crack, and pore of the building. In bloodhound
mode, he headed straight to the second floor, moving
like an arrow shot through the crowded, noisy room
until he was standing in the middle of the dance floor
full of gyrating bodies.

Right there, dancing with her back to him in a group
of four other women, was the source of the scent that
had dragged him halfway across the French Quarter.
This close, her fragrance was damn near overwhelming.

If he wasn't such a gentleman, he probably would have leaned forward and licked the small portion of her neck that was exposed every time her long, black hair swung aside. If she smelled this good, he could only imagine how she tasted.

The thought was enough to nearly bring him to his knees.

He was trying to figure out the best way to initiate a conversation—tapping her on the shoulder and saying he'd been tracking her scent for blocks might come off as a bit stalkerish—when the woman turned to face him.

Maybe she'd sensed him behind her, or perhaps it was because her friends had stopped dancing to stare over her shoulder at him. Either way, when she spun around, Remy swore his heart stopped beating for a second.

It was dark on the dance floor and the flashing strobes were bright enough to practically blind him, but it didn't matter. The light-brown-skinned beauty would have stood out in any light. Hell, she would have stood out in complete darkness too.

He was still taking in the smoking-hot curves, perfect skin, and exotic amber eyes when a realization struck him so hard he almost stumbled backward.

He *knew* her. Not in the biblical sense, though that was obviously one hell of a shame. He'd known her back in high school when she'd been a skinny, awkward teenager who never seemed to look anywhere but at the ground.

She was a lot different now—understatement there—and easily the most beautiful woman he'd ever seen. Now she possessed a confidence that made it hard to look at anything but her. Even with all the changes, he would have known her anywhere. He hadn't talked to her since high school graduation, but they'd been friends and probably would have been more if he hadn't been such a chickenshit back then.

"Triana?"

Remy didn't expect her to recognize him. While she'd grown from a girl into a woman, he'd grown from a boy into a werewolf. He looked a lot different than he had in high school.

Triana's eyes widened. "Remy, is that seriously you? I can't believe you're here!"

Grinning, she threw her arms around him. His went around her automatically, holding her close. He was shocked at how good she felt against him—good as in *let's go find a room somewhere or a dark corner or, hell, the backseat of the nearest car*.

At the same time, his mind spun as he tried to understand what the hell was going on. Could he have subconsciously recognized his old friend's scent? Okay, maybe. But that still didn't explain why she smelled so good or why her fragrance had pulled him so frigging hard in her direction. He'd never felt anything like it in his life. The animalistic urge he'd had to track her down didn't fit with any concept of friendship he recognized.

And neither did the erection he had going on in his jeans right then. That was definitely not the way people greeted old childhood friends. Crap, if he didn't do something quick, this was going to get really frigging embarrassing.

He pulled away and gave her a smile. "We probably shouldn't be wasting this music. You want to dance some before we go find a place where we can catch up on old times?"

—∿∿—

Triana Bellamy didn't mind when Remy's big, strong hand glided down her back to tease the curve of her bottom as they danced. Nor did she complain when his muscular, jean-clad thigh occasionally slipped between her legs to press against her in the most delicious way through the little black dress she wore. Instead, she focused on the pounding rhythm of the music and enjoyed being with the sexiest man she'd ever seen.

Besides, it wasn't like Triana wasn't getting just as naughty as he was. In fact, she should have probably received an honorary police badge considering the way she'd been frisking his body the whole time. Not that there was a woman on the planet who would blame her for wanting to give Remy a pat down. The guy was seriously built.

Triana lived and worked in Houston but was back in town for the week visiting her mother and hanging out with old friends. When those same girlfriends had stopped dancing to stare at something over her shoulder a little while ago, Triana had feared the worst. She'd turned around terrified she'd find some drunk tourist with a facial tattoo and gumbo breath standing there. Instead, it had been the guy she'd crushed on all through high school looking better than any man had a right to.

Remy had always been fit and muscular as far back as she could remember, but now it looked like he'd grown four inches and added at least fifty pounds of pure muscle. But even more amazing than the physical changes was the whole animalistic-sex-appeal thing he had going on. He exuded it like a cologne.

Then there were his gorgeous hazel eyes. When the colored strobe lights reflected off them at just the right angle, it was like they were actually glowing. It made him seem like some kind of hungry predator. Damn, that gaze of his did all kinds of crazy things to her insides.

Truth be told, there had always been something about Remy that did it for her, even before she'd understood what the heck that meant. But now there was something about him that was impossible to resist. If she knew her friends, they'd been staring at him because they all wanted to jump him. Well, they were all going to have to get in line behind her.

As they danced to one song after another, Triana smiled as she remembered what it was like growing up with Remy. They'd been fourteen when their parents had met at her late father's jazz club on Frenchmen Street. Even though they'd been from drastically different walks of life, they had formed an immediate friendship, and it wasn't long before they were having dinner at each other's houses all the time. She and Remy became close too. When they weren't hanging out doing homework together, they were talking about what they wanted to do when they were older.

But even though she'd always had a crush on him, they'd never dated, partly because they had moved in different social circles. He liked sports, while she was into all kinds of science and math activities. However, the bigger issue was that they'd both been afraid getting involved would screw up their friendship.

After they'd both gone to college, she'd tried keeping in touch with Remy through her parents, but life had somehow gotten in the way and she'd lost track of him. She'd thought about him a lot since they'd both gone their separate ways though, and there were times when she'd daydreamed about what could have been if they actually had gotten together.

Now, as if to prove the world really was a small place, she'd bumped into him after all these years. Her mom—who believed in stuff like that—would probably tell her the spirits or her guardian angel or the fates had taken a hand in her life and guided Remy to her side. Triana didn't buy any of that, but if she was lucky enough to run into a man this sinfully hot, she wasn't going to waste the opportunity.

Flashing her a grin, Remy spun her around, so her back was to him, wrapping his muscular arms around her waist and pulling her close. They swayed in time to the music, and Triana rested her arms on his, letting her fingers tease the well-muscled biceps left exposed by his snug-fitting T-shirt. She couldn't tell which was sexier: the way he rubbed up against her bottom, or the way he tilted his head and buried his face in the curve of her neck and breathed deep. Both were arousing, but she finally decided on him nuzzling her neck. It made her think he couldn't get enough of her. What woman wouldn't like that?

As he twirled her around to face him again, she realized that their friends weren't on the dance floor anymore. Her girlfriends had been dancing and flirting with his friends outrageously ever since Remy and the other guys had gotten there. Triana looked around, wondering if they'd left without telling her and Remy.

"They slipped out onto the balcony a little while

ago," he said, leaning over to put his mouth close to her ear, making her quiver. "You want to head out there?"

Triana would have preferred to dance with him for the rest of the night, especially if it involved him wrapping his big arms around her and burying his face in her neck again. But she thought she should probably check on her friends. Besides, she had about a million questions for Remy, and she wouldn't be able to ask him on the dance floor.

So she held his hand and let him lead her through the crowded club toward the doors. It was definitely nice having someone his size when it came to creating a path. Even though Remy was polite as could be, people naturally got out of his way.

Between the music coming from inside and the noise from the street below, it was still rather loud on the balcony, but the fresh air was a welcome relief. She hadn't realized how hot it had been on the dance floor. Then again, that probably had more to do with whom she'd been dancing with.

Triana had no problem finding Remy's three friends. Even when they were sitting at a table, as they were at that moment, they were easy to pick out of the crowd by their mere presence. Kim, Nora, Whitney, and Deanna, on the other hand, were nowhere to be found. She kept her curiosity at bay as Remy made introductions.

"Triana Bellamy, I'd like you to meet my friends and coworkers. Max Lowry," he said, pointing out a hunky guy with brown hair, twinkling blue eyes, and one of those devious-little-boy smiles that made you think he was always up to something. "The one with the British accent is Zane Kendrick," Remy added, pointing at a

good-looking man with dark hair and eyes the color
of chocolate. "He's not really a stuck-up snob; he just
sounds like one," Remy said in a lower voice, as if he
was trying to share a secret.

Zane chuckled and leaned forward to shake her
hand. "Try to ignore Remy when he speaks. It's not his
strong suit."

She laughed. Oh yeah, Zane had an accent for sure,
and it was sexy as heck. No wonder Kim had taken an
immediate liking to him. Those two had been slow dancing for most of the night, even when everyone else had
been moving to a much faster beat. Triana worried about
that for a second. Kim had recently broken up with her
longtime boyfriend and it wasn't a stretch to say that the
girl was still in free fall. It was one of the reasons they'd
gone out tonight—to make sure Kim didn't sit at home
and mope. Triana had always trusted her instincts about
guys though, and right then, she wasn't getting a bad
vibe from Zane. Besides, she liked to think that Remy
wouldn't hang out with a guy who was a jerk.

"And this is Jayden Brooks," Remy said, drawing her
attention to a dark-skinned Adonis with the most amazing
blue-gray eyes she'd ever seen. When he stood to shake
her hand, she realized he was even bigger than Remy.

"Everyone calls me Brooks," he said in a low, reso-
nating voice she didn't have any problem hearing over
all the noise. "By the way, in case you were wondering,
your friends made a run to the ladies' room. They said
they'd be right back."

*No doubt to figure out how they're going to divide
you three hunks between them*, Triana thought—because
Remy was definitely hers.

"I'm just taking a shot in the dark here," Zane said as she and Remy sat, "but I'm guessing you guys know each other."

Triana smiled. "Yeah, we do. We went to high school together here in New Orleans. I can't believe we ran into each other."

"Huh." Zane's mouth curved. "I never realized Remy went to school. We all just assumed he grew up in the swamps and learned how to read and write from talking with the animals."

Remy snorted. "Funny."

Triana was still laughing at that remark when Kim and her other girlfriends showed up. One look at their freshly applied makeup told Triana they'd disappeared to the ladies' room to make sure they looked their best for Remy's friends. Kim claimed the seat beside Zane, while Nora, Whitney, and Deanna gathered around Max and Brooks.

A little while later, a waitress came over to take their drink orders. While her friends flirted with the guys, Triana leaned in close to Remy.

"Last I heard, you were with the Jefferson Parish Sheriff's Office," she said. "Do you still work there?"

He shook his head, the neon lights from the streets below reflecting off his eyes and making them look like they were almost glowing. "I was at the JPSO for a while after college, but now I'm on the SWAT team in Dallas. The guys and I are in town for some cross-training with the local PD."

She blinked. The Dallas SWAT team, huh? That would certainly explain why Remy and his friends were all so well-built. Considering how attractive they were, she could only guess the SWAT also went out of their way to hire hunks.

Triana sipped the rum punch she'd ordered. "How long are you going to be in town?"

She hoped it wasn't only a day or two.

"A week," he said with a smile that made her think he could read her mind. "We just got here this morning."

She returned his smile. "As it turns out, I'm in town for the week too."

He lifted a brow. "You don't live in New Orleans anymore?"

She shook her head. "I moved to Houston after college."

She was in the middle of explaining where she worked when Kim scooted her chair over and nudged her shoulder.

"Why don't the two of you get out of here and go catch up?" her friend said in her ear. "It's too loud to even think in this place."

As much as Triana would have liked to be alone with Remy, she didn't feel right bailing on her friends. "I promised you a girls' night out. I can't take off on you."

Kim laughed. "Don't be silly. It's not every day you run into a friend from high school—not one like Remy anyway. Go! And don't worry. I'm sure Zane can keep my mind off Shawn."

Shawn was Kim's ex, the jackass who'd dumped her two weeks ago. Triana leaned over and hugged her friend. "Okay, but call me if you change your mind."

Kim nodded, then gave Remy a wave and slid her chair closer to Zane and the others. Triana had to admit, her friend looked comfortable with the Dallas SWAT

officer. Kim was smiling more than she had since Triana
had gotten back into town.

Triana looked at Remy, who'd been waiting patiently
during the conversation. "You ready to get out of here?"

He gave her a sexy smile. "Lead the way."

Chapter 2

FIVE MINUTES LATER, THEY WERE WALKING HAND IN HAND down Bourbon Street, taking in the sights and finally able to talk without having to shout. It felt completely natural holding his hand, like they'd been dating for months.

"You were saying you work in the Houston crime lab?" Remy prompted, bringing her back to the conversation they'd been having in the club before Kim had interrupted them.

Triana nodded. "Technically, it's called the Harris County Institute of Forensic Sciences, but that's such a mouthful that everyone calls it the crime lab. I do trace-evidence analysis there."

It looked like Remy was about to say something, but he had to hesitate as an older couple came dancing down the center of the street wearing nothing but the tiniest of swimsuits. Triana would have liked to say that was uncommon, but it wasn't. Bourbon Street brought out all kinds.

Remy steered her around the half-naked couple, not even batting an eye. "You went to LSU for chemistry, right? How'd you end up in Houston?"

"They have a great intern program, and I got a chance to go there during my senior year. One semester in the lab and I was hooked. It took a little while to get a job there, though. I had to end up going to Alabama to get my master's in forensic science first, but I've been working there for four years now." She tucked her hair behind her ear with an embarrassed smile. "You probably think it's nerdy, but I love it."

Remy shook his head. "Nah. I've worked with the people from the Dallas ME's office a couple times, so I understand the hard work that's involved in your job. I think it's cool. I'm just surprised your mom let you go to Alabama. I would have never in my life imagined that."

Triana laughed. "Yeah, it was a tough sell convincing her I needed to go there. She finally agreed, but only after I vowed never to attend an Alabama football game. I also had to promise to walk the other way if I ever crossed paths with Nick Saban."

Remy thought that was hilarious, but Triana wasn't joking. Her mother had never taken kindly to Coach Saban leaving LSU, and then coming back into the college ranks and coaching for rival Alabama was an unforgivable crime.

"So you're in town visiting your mom?" he asked as they passed by a trio of musicians playing jazz on the sidewalk. There was a crowd gathered around listening, and Remy leaned over to toss a five-dollar bill in the hat sitting on the curb, giving a wave to the performers in passing.

"Yeah," Triana said. "I try to come back and spend time with Mom as often as I can. I don't like her being by herself so much in that big apartment above the shop now that Dad is gone."

Remy was silent for a while. "I was sorry to hear about your father. Sorry I didn't make it to the funeral, too. I only heard about it through the grapevine months after the fact."

Triana nodded, having to take a breath before answering. It had been over two years since her father had been murdered, but sometimes it still felt like yesterday.

"You don't need to apologize. Mom was amazing, pulling everything together as fast as she did, but there were a lot of people she couldn't reach. I wish I could have been more help to her, but I was a complete mess."

Remy stopped and tugged her close, wrapping his arms around her right there in the middle of a throng of passing people. "Hey, you had every right to be a complete mess. You'd just lost your dad. I know how close you two always were."

Triana rested her cheek against Remy's muscular chest and closed her eyes. The warmth from his body seeped into her, comforting her down to her very soul. She had gotten most of the tears out a while ago, but his touch had a few more leaking out. Remy was right. She'd had a special relationship with her dad. He was so big and gruff that he'd frightened a lot of people. And yeah, he'd been known on more than one occasion to wade into brawls at his club and break them up all by himself, whether the people involved were armed or not. But he'd always been a gentle giant to her. She missed him like crazy.

Triana could have stayed in Remy's arms just like that for the rest of the night, and reluctantly pulled away with a small smile. If Remy noticed she had to wipe a few tears from her face, he didn't call her on it.

They started walking again, and she squeezed his hand a little tighter now than she had before. They strolled along in comfortable silence for a bit before

Remy got around to asking the question most people usually brought up at some point.

"Did they ever catch the person who did it?" he asked tentatively, as if he dreaded continuing to talk about the subject. "Or even come up with a motive?"

"No. To both questions," she said with a shake of her head. "At first the police thought it was a robbery gone wrong, since they found him on the floor in the middle of his club, but there was still money in the register behind the bar and in his office. They didn't even touch his wallet."

"I talked to one of my friends at the JPSO shortly after I got the news," Remy said softly. "They didn't want to get into the details, but they implied the attack had been very...violent. Was there any thought that maybe it was personal?"

Her dad had been shot multiple times, so yeah, *violent* was one way to put it. "That's the current theory, not that it has helped much. Dad came from a rough background before he met Mom. There were probably quite a few people who didn't like him. The police found a lot of blood at the club that wasn't Dad's, too, but they were never able to figure out whose it was."

Remy looked at her in surprise. "They're not working on it anymore?"

She shook her head. "One of the detectives calls my mom every once in a while and tells her they're still trying, but I don't expect much now."

Which was why Triana had been paying a private investigator to look into the case for the past five months on the off chance he could find something to jump-start the investigation. She was tempted to mention it to Remy but decided against it. In her experience, most cops didn't think much of private detectives, and she really didn't want to get into an argument with Remy.

"Well, for what it's worth," he said, "I always liked your father. He loved you and your mother, and he didn't take crap from anyone."

She laughed, putting thoughts of the PI away for now. "That he didn't."

"How's your mom doing?"

"She focuses on the business," Triana said. "The shop is doing as well as ever, maybe even better than it's done in years. I'm sometimes shocked at how much money people will spend on this voodoo stuff, but it seems to make her and her customers happy, so who am I to say anything about it?"

They were about to turn off Bourbon and onto Ursulines Avenue, which would ultimately lead them to her mom's shop, when they came upon another scene that was unfortunately all too common in New Orleans and displayed the dark side of the city. Paramedics were pushing a skinny, young girl of about seventeen out of a club on a gurney toward an ambulance parked along a side street. There was an oxygen mask covering the girl's face, so it was hard to see much in the way of features, but she looked drawn and gaunt, and her skin was unusually pale.

"What happened?" Remy softly asked someone in the crowd.

Triana didn't need to hear the answer. She'd seen it often enough here and in Houston to have a pretty good idea.

"Drug overdose," a woman told Remy. "Meth. The stuff going around lately is a lot stronger than some people are used to."

Before she and Remy left, Triana heard three other bystanders talking about how dangerous the new crystal meth that had been flooding the streets lately was.

"The stuff used to be cooked up in bathtubs by mom-and-pop labs," Remy said as they continued down the street. "But now the Mexican cartels have gotten involved with large-scale operations selling crap that's ten times as pure. People don't recognize the difference and end up overdosing. We're seeing a lot of people winding up in the hospitals in Dallas from this stuff."

"Houston too," Triana agreed. "Between this new meth and the recent influx of heroin overdoses, it's driving a complete shift in how our department is handling drug users. We're finally doing more to get them into treatment, instead of just tossing them in jail. But sometimes it seems like it's a losing battle, when there's so much of the stuff flowing in."

They walked in silence for a while, the mood somber after what they'd just seen on top of the earlier conversation about her father. This part of the street didn't have as many lights as where they'd just been, and Triana subconsciously moved closer to Remy. If she'd been alone, she would have quickened her step, but she felt safe with him.

"What happened with your parents?" she asked, glancing at him. "They came to Dad's funeral, but they weren't together."

"They split up when I was in college." Remy shrugged. "I don't know what the problem was. Neither of them would ever talk to me about it. Maybe it was empty-nest syndrome or something like that. They tried to get back together when I was working with the JPSO, but in the end they got divorced and moved to opposite sides of the country. Mom wanted to be closer to her family in New York State and Dad took a job in San Diego. It had gotten pretty nasty by that point, and I made the decision to stay the hell out of it. We still talk on the phone on holidays and birthdays, but I don't see either of them too much these days."

"I'm sorry to hear that," she said. "So did you move to Dallas and join the SWAT team because you wanted a change of scenery?"

He shook his head. "While I was looking for a change of scenery about that time, that's not when I moved to Dallas. I was a U.S. Marshal for three years after I left the JPSO."

Triana did a double take. "Talk about burying the lead. U.S. Marshals do witness protection stuff, right?"

"That's one of their primary missions, but I mostly hunted fugitives. Maybe it's a Cajun thing, but I've always been good at tracking people down."

"Okay, that sounds more than dangerous and exactly like something I could see you doing. Why'd you leave the Marshals?"

For a moment, something that looked like pain flashed across Remy's handsome face, but it disappeared too quickly for her to be sure. When he looked at her, there was nothing but hunger in his hazel eyes. "It's a long, complicated story best told while both of us are in a warm bed, preferably with our naked bodies twined around each other."

Heat pooled between Triana's thighs at the casual remark. While they'd gotten a little naughty dancing, this was the first time he'd given her any indication he hoped they'd end up in bed just as much as she did. The image made her whole body hum with anticipation.

That was what happened when you finally got another shot at a guy you should have made a move on over a decade earlier.

She gave him a sexy smile. "That might be arranged."

It wasn't until they were another two blocks down the street that Triana realized Remy had smoothly avoided answering her question about why he'd left the Marshals. She would have brought up the subject again, but she suspected he'd only sidestep it. Something told her he didn't want to talk about why he'd made the career change.

So instead, they chatted about lighter topics such as the TV shows they watched, foods they liked, and places they'd visited since graduating from high school. Triana was having so much fun, she was disappointed when they finally reached her mother's voodoo shop and the apartment over it. Even though it was after two in the morning, she didn't want the evening to end yet.

"The shop hasn't changed much, but do you want to come in and look around anyway?" she asked hopefully.

He grinned. "Yeah. I'd like that."

Triana unlocked the door, then closed and locked it behind them quietly, so she wouldn't wake her mom. When she turned back around, Remy was already walking around the dimly lit shop, taking in the shelves upon shelves of knickknacks that had mesmerized her since childhood. The overhead lights were off, so the red, green, and purple neon tubes that edged the display windows were the only source of illumination, but it was more than enough to guide her steps as she moved to

Remy's side. She watched as he picked up the various dolls, candles, beads, tarot cards, potions, books, and other trinkets that filled the store. For such large hands, he handled everything with a surprisingly gentle touch.

"Everything is exactly the same as I remember it." He turned to smile at her, a warm glint in his eyes. "Well, not everything. You've changed quite a bit."

The heated way he looked at her made her tummy quiver. "Really? How so?"

Remy took her hand and tugged her closer. The tips of her nipples grazed his muscular chest, sending tingles spiraling through her. "I tend to remember you as a shy, somewhat awkward girl who was all knees and elbows back then."

She laughed softly, a little embarrassed. Yeah, that was a pretty good description of her when she was in high school. She had been what her mom called a late bloomer, so everything had changed her freshman year in college, when her body had made up for lost time.

"And now?" she asked in a near whisper.

He bent his head until his face was so close to hers that she could feel the warmth of his breath on her skin. His left hand came up and found her hip, slowly gliding back and forth across the silky material and heating the skin underneath.

"And now, you definitely aren't shy, you move like a cat, and all those knees and elbows have turned into some serious curves I'd love to explore, since I'm smart enough to know what I want."

She blushed at hearing him put all that into words. "No one's stopping you."

The glint in his eyes flared brighter for a moment as

the neon lights caught them. Then, one of Remy's hands was in her hair and he was kissing her. A moan involuntarily escaped her lips as his mouth came down on hers and his tongue slipped inside. He tasted so delicious she couldn't help it.

She slid her hands up the front of his shirt and grabbed his shoulders, squeezing hard as she pulled him even closer, urging him to kiss her harder.

Remy must have understood what she was trying to say because the hand in her hair tightened possessively and his tongue teased hers more aggressively. At the same time, his free hand moved around from her hip to her lower back, fitting her against him so firmly she could feel every ripple and bulge in that perfect body of his. And one of those bulges suggested he was enjoying the kiss just as much as she was.

Triana melted against him, surrendering to a kiss she'd been fantasizing of for over a decade. She'd heard women talking about going all weak-kneed from a great kiss, but she'd never experienced it or even believed it. She believed it now. If Remy hadn't been holding on to her so tightly, she was sure she would have collapsed to her knees right there in front of him.

Isn't that an interesting thought?

She whimpered as Remy's hand slid down her back to cup a nice handful of cheek and squeezed. How had he known she loved having her bottom played with?

Jumping in bed with a guy after a few kisses wasn't something she would ever consider, but Remy wasn't just some random guy. He was the guy she'd crushed on all through high school, someone she considered more than a friend even if they hadn't seen each other in years.

Besides, he was like no one she'd ever kissed before. Good heavens, he had her stomach doing flips and barrel rolls!

Triana was on the verge of asking Remy if he wanted to sneak upstairs to her old room when he pulled away so suddenly she almost fell over. She'd thought for a moment he must have read her mind, but then she realized he'd stepped back to put a disturbing amount of distance between them. At the same time, he reached down to rearrange the front of his jeans, which suddenly seemed too tight for him.

She opened her mouth to ask him what was up when a creaking sound on the stairs behind the cashier counter startled her.

"Triana, is that you down there making all that noise?"

Her eyes widened even as Remy gave her an apologetic smile. He'd pulled away because he'd heard Mom coming downstairs. Damn, he must have some seriously good ears. No shock there. The rest of him was frigging awesome, why not his ears?

She ran her hands over her little black dress as she heard her mom coming down the last few steps. It was a good thing, too. The dress, which was already short, had crept up and would have flashed a load of skin. From the knowing grin on his face, she imagined Remy might have had something to do with that.

Her mother wasn't a prude by any means, and Triana wouldn't have been embarrassed if she'd found her kissing a guy. But still, it was better to avoid the whole issue. Her mom was going to be shocked enough to see Remy as it was.

"Yes, Mom, it's me," Triana said. "And look who I ran into on Bourbon Street."

Her mother reached the bottom of the stairs, grumbling about how Triana expected her to see anything with the lights off. When her mother flipped them on, Triana was shocked to see her standing there with a baseball bat over her shoulder like she'd been about to bean whomever she'd heard down here.

Tall and slender, her mother was a graceful woman in her sixties with a spring in her step and dark, curly hair she always wore tied back in a scarf.

Her mother's eyes widened when she saw Remy, but then a warm smile spread across her face.

"Oh Lord! Remy, is that you?"

Her mother set down the baseball bat, leaning it against the wall, then hurried across the shop in a way that made Triana think she already knew the answer to that question.

"Yes, Mrs. Bellamy, it's me," Remy said with a laugh, stepping forward to give her mother a hug.

When her mother pulled away, she looked Remy up and down with a sharp eye. "Goodness, look how much you've grown. What the heck have you been eating, entire cows? And stop calling me Mrs. Bellamy. It's Gemma."

Remy chuckled. "I'll try, but you've always been Mrs. Bellamy to me, so I'll probably screw up a few times. I'm sorry we woke you up. Triana was showing me around the shop."

Her mom threw a glance her way, a knowing look in her dark eyes. "Just showing you around the shop, huh? With the lights out?"

Remy didn't even bat an eye. "We left them off so

we wouldn't wake you up. The glow of the neon in the display windows is more than enough to see by."

The smile tugging at the corners of her mother's lips suggested she knew Remy was full of crap. "Uh-huh."

"Remy is a police officer in Dallas now," Triana quickly said before her mother could ask what else they'd been doing down here in the dark, though it was obvious she already knew. "He and three of his fellow officers are in town for training, and I was lucky enough to run into him in a club. I just turned around and there he was."

Her mother arched a brow, studying Remy thoughtfully. "You just walked into a random club on Bourbon Street and ran into Triana by pure chance? That's... amazing."

Remy's mouth curved. "Right place at the right time, I guess."

"Maybe," her mother agreed. "Or perhaps the fates took a hand and made sure you two ran into each other tonight."

Triana stifled a groan. She might have known it was simple, random luck that Remy had found her in the club, but her mom took this destiny-and-fate thing seriously. While Triana didn't buy into any of that stuff, she also never mocked her mom for believing in it.

"Where are you boys staying while you're in town?" her mom asked suddenly, catching Triana completely off guard.

"The DoubleTree over on Canal Street," Remy said. "The department was able to get a really good deal on the rooms, which is the only reason we're not stuck in a cheap motel out by the airport."

The DoubleTree was a nice place and close to a lot of the big attractions near the river, but it was also on the far side of the French Quarter from the shop. Triana winced as she realized Remy was going to have a long walk back tonight, unless he called a cab. Her mother must have been thinking the same thing because she frowned.

"Why don't you and your friends stay here while you're in town?" her mother suggested. "I have plenty of space, and it will save your police department some money."

Triana blinked. Okay, she hadn't expected that. Inviting Remy to stay was one thing, but letting three guys she'd never even met was out of character for her mother, to say the least.

Remy seemed surprised too, but he recovered quickly. "I appreciate the offer, Mrs. Bellamy—Gemma—but my commander expects us to use the rooms he put all the work into getting for us. Besides, we'll be stomping in and out at all hours of the day and night. We'd only wake you up all the time."

Her mother sighed. "I understand. But if you change your mind, tell your friends they're more than welcome."

Remy thanked her again and assured her he would keep her offer in mind.

Triana knew Remy was simply being polite. He might be willing to stay there, especially after the kisses they'd just shared, but she was betting his friends preferred having their own hotel rooms in the event they needed a place to take any girls they picked up. Considering how her friends had flirted with them at the club, needing the privacy of a hotel room was an extremely good possibility.

Her mom chatted with her and Remy for a few more

minutes before announcing she was going back to bed. "It's good seeing you again, Remy. I hope you make time to stop in a few nights and have dinner with Triana and me while you're here."

"I will," he promised, glancing at Triana. "In fact, I think I might be spending quite a lot of time here."

Triana couldn't help noticing the tingle of excitement that ran through her at the thought of spending time with Remy.

"Oh, and you don't have to rush off, Remy," her mother said before disappearing up the steps. "You can turn off the lights and look around the shop for a while longer if you like."

Remy chuckled as they listened to the bedroom door close. "Your mother is amazing."

"Yeah, she is, isn't she?" Triana agreed with a smile. She reached out and slipped her fingers into the waistband of his jeans, tugging him closer. "So, would you like to look around the shop for a while longer…with the lights on this time?"

He grinned, wrapping his arms around her and lightly touched his lips to hers. Triana moaned and buried her fingers in his short, dark-blond hair, intending to yank him down for a serious kiss, but before she could, he pulled away.

"You have no idea how much I'd like to spend the whole night kissing you," he said softly, his eyes blazing with hunger. "But the first day of cross-training starts in a few hours."

It was the same thing she would have done in his position, so Triana was surprised at how disappointed she was that he had to leave.

She forced herself to be mature and nod. "I understand. I had fun tonight."

"Me too," he said with a smile. "How about I stop by tomorrow after training? We can go out to eat or dance or just hang out and talk, if you want."

She liked the sound of that. "It's a date."

Chapter 3

REMY STRODE DOWN THE EMPTY HALLWAY, MAX, BROOKS, and Zane at his heels in tight formation. When he reached the stout wood door at the end, Remy nodded his head rapidly three times, then quickly moved aside, making room for Brooks to come through with the battering ram.

Brooks slammed the thirty-pound cylindrical piece of metal into the door directly below the knob, shattering the wood and sending pieces of the lock flying. The moment it was open, Zane reached out and pulled Brooks back from the doorway, where the momentum of the ram's swing had left him a sitting duck. Remy darted into the room, Max right behind him, each of them covering their respective quadrants. It was something they'd done so many times in training that it was as familiar to them as breathing.

By the time Brooks and Zane entered the room behind them, he and Max were already motioning that the space was clear. Remy gestured toward a door on the far side. As they approached it, Remy holstered his standard-issue SIG Sauer .40-caliber pistol and swung his tactical shotgun off his back. If the lock on this second door was as strong as it looked, the battering ram would probably bounce off.

Okay, probably not with a werewolf of Brooks's size handling it, but the goal wasn't to draw attention to themselves. It was to get through the house quickly using the most efficient breaching techniques available.

In the SWAT world, if you were worried about the lock being reinforced, you ignored the lock and went after the hinges.

Remy's teammates took an extra step back as he pressed the barrel of the shotgun against the door, where the lower hinge was attached, and fired three shots into it. Without pausing to check the effect of his first shots, he repeated the process at the top and middle of the door, shredding most of the area along the edge. Pointing his shotgun upward, he kicked in the door, then hauled ass out of the way as Max and Brooks slipped through to clear the room beyond.

Shots immediately rang out as Max and Brooks handled the targets inside. Remy had his shotgun back over his shoulder and was drawing his sidearm when Brooks silently motioned that the furniture-filled room was clear and pointed toward a door on Remy's right.

This one was heavy-duty metal, like something you'd see on the outside of an industrial warehouse. It wouldn't normally be an issue for a werewolf to get through it using simple brute force, but he knew Gage would be pissed if they did that, so Remy went for plan B.

While the other guys covered him, he moved toward the door, reaching into the demo bag on his hip for the breaching charge he'd put together before coming into the building. Remy pulled the paper off the peel-and-stick back of the charge and shoved it against the door, in between the knob and the jamb, then unspooled the wires of the electric detonator he'd already hooked up to the firing device and gave Brooks a nod. The big man double-checked to make sure the other three members of the team were safely away from the charge and returned his nod.

Remy immediately flipped the cover on the firing device and pressed the red button, then spun around, putting his back to the door. The sound of the blast reverberated throughout the room, the force of it vibrating through him as plastic fragments peppered the back of his tactical vest and cargo pants. By the time he turned around, the dead bolt had been torn apart and the metal door was open.

Zane and Max stormed into the cloud of acrid smoke left in the charge's wake, firing at the targets set up in the room beyond. Remy and Max had just followed them in when a voice rang out over the speaker in the top right-hand corner of the room.

"Cease fire! Course complete."

Silence descended over the shoot house as Remy and the other guys complied with the command.

"You got through there in twenty-two seconds. That's what I call frigging impressive as hell," the man's voice came through the speaker again. "Now get out here and tell us how the hell you did it."

Remy chuckled and holstered his weapon, then led his teammates to the back door of the shoot house and out into the early morning sunshine, where Lieutenant Drew Thompson and the rest of the New Orleans SWAT team were waiting for them. The twenty men and two women had watched the whole thing on the monitors and were regarding them in admiration.

"Okay, so spill," Drew said.

Tall with blue eyes and salt-and-pepper hair cut

military style, Drew had come up through the ranks on the Dallas SWAT team with Gage, and when Gage had been named commander, Drew had moved to New Orleans. According to Gage, Drew hadn't been pissed or jealous Gage had gotten the job but had simply wanted to be in charge of his own team. They'd parted as friends and had stayed in touch.

"What we just did in there might look good, but some of that stuff would be impossible to do on a good portion of the calls our team in Dallas handle," Remy said. As one of the more experienced breachers on the team, he'd volunteered to lead the training in this area. "The three breaching methods we demonstrated—the battering ram, shotgun breach, and explosive charge—all come with advantages and disadvantages."

Remy walked over to a long table set up with all kinds of tactical breaching gear, stopping beside the battering ram that was similar to the one Brooks had used to take down the first door. "The ram is the simplest method to get through most doors, but it leaves the person using it standing in the middle of the doorway defenseless because they don't have a weapon out."

He moved farther down the table to a shotgun that was identical to the one on his back and held it up. "This can deal with doors that have been reinforced along the lock or hinge side, but it also exposes whoever uses it to someone firing through the door. Worse, the ammo you use, whether it's buckshot or slug, will keep going and could hit civilians." He placed the rifle on the table. "The same goes for the explosive breaching charge— it's going to throw fragments everywhere when you initiate it. So, for either of those methods, you'd better know what's on the other side of the door you're going through, or you're going to end up injuring, or killing, the people you're there to save."

That wasn't anything the cops on the NOPD SWAT team didn't already know. It wasn't difficult to find a SWAT officer who didn't live in fear of going through a door expecting to find a bad guy with a gun and instead finding a four-year-old in their pj's.

"We're going to spend the rest of the morning breaching all kinds of doors," Remy continued. "But we're not only going to worry about getting through the obstacles. We're also going to learn where the fragment debris from different breaching techniques goes and how dangerous it can be." He walked along the table until he came to a cardboard box filled with red balloons. He took one out and held it up. "You pop a balloon, it means you injured or killed a hostage or a teammate. Whoever pops the most balloons buys a round of beer for everyone."

That earned Remy a couple groans, some chuckles, and more than a few grins. Every SWAT officer appreciated learning a new skill, but they also loved a little competition—especially if the loser ended up having to buy the winner beer.

"All right, you heard the man," Drew said. "Let's break up into teams and get to work."

Remy was soaked with sweat by the time training ended just in time for a late lunch. As he and his pack mates sat at a picnic table behind the NOPD SWAT facility, drinking Gatorade and talking about the plan for that afternoon's training, he realized he'd forgotten what the humidity down here on the river was like. It was so hot and sticky it was hard to believe there was a tropical storm still sitting out in the Gulf meandering around like a lost two-year-old.

But humid or not, it had been a good morning of training. On the downside, they'd probably blown through the SWAT unit's entire budget for wood, building supplies, and training explosives for the quarter, but they'd learned more about breaching in one morning than they probably had in the past two or three years. You couldn't put a price tag on that.

Remy and his teammates had planned to run out and grab lunch at the nearest restaurant, but Andy told them to hang around because they were cooking up something special in the facility's kitchen. If Remy's nose was right, that something special was sausage and crawfish gumbo with a side of rice and corn bread. He sure as hell didn't mind waiting around for that.

"We're going back to Bourbon Street tonight," Max said between gulps of Gatorade. "You in?"

Remy shook his head. "Nah. I'm getting together with Triana tonight."

Brooks grinned. "Triana, huh?"

"Yeah," he said, trying to downplay his interest in her. He told himself it was so the guys wouldn't rag on him, but it was more than that and he knew it. Introspection wasn't his thing though, so he wasn't going to waste brain cells thinking about it. "I figured we'd go out and get something to eat, catch up on old times."

"Good for you," Max said from the other side of the picnic table. "Considering the way you were able to pick up her scent and track her halfway across the French Quarter when none of us could even smell it, she's obviously special. You'd be stupid not to go after her."

Self-preservation made Remy stomp on the figurative brakes. "Whoa, slow down there. I might have crushed on Triana back in high school, but I don't have any interest in doing anything more than hanging out and talking."

Max, Brooks, and Zane stared at him as if he were a pig wearing a Rolex. Remy suddenly felt like shit for lying his ass off. And if the frown on Brooks's face was any indication, the guy knew he wasn't being honest.

He and Triana were going to hang out and talk, but that sure as hell wasn't the only reason Remy wanted to see her tonight. The thought that they might be doing a lot more than catching up on the good old days had not only kept him from getting any sleep last night, but it had been buzzing through his head all morning too. He wasn't sure how the hell he'd managed to focus on training.

Even after spending most of the evening with her, he still couldn't believe the woman Triana had become. He'd been around his share of beautiful women, but none had affected him the way she did. She was so dazzling he could barely breathe when she smiled at him. Her scent was so intoxicating he'd walked around with a hard-on the whole night. And when he'd kissed her, he'd damn near lost it and shifted right there in her mother's shop. If she'd been wearing a Little Red Riding Hood costume, he would have been more than ready to play the part of the Big Bad Wolf and eaten her up on the spot.

Walking away from her last night had been one of the hardest things he'd ever done. Not that leaving had helped very much. It had been a long walk across the

French Quarter, and yet he barely remembered going back to the hotel. When he'd gotten back to his room, he lay there and dreamed about her as the few remaining hours of night waned. He'd have sworn he could still smell her scent from halfway across the city, and it had nearly been his undoing. It had taken everything in him not to climb out of bed, run back to the shop, and make love to her as the sun came up.

He'd been with Triana for half the night and he already had it bad for her. Yet here he was, trying to tell the guys it was no big deal. And they weren't buying it. Hell, it probably didn't help that every one of them could hear his heart rate elevating simply from thinking about kissing her.

"Really?" Brooks said, eyeballing him like he knew exactly what was going on. "Sure seemed like a lot more than that. If I had to guess, I'd say it was like the two of you had an immediate, almost magical connection. After all the crazy stuff we've seen in the last year, you don't think there's a chance she could be *The One* for you?"

Panic shot through Remy. *The One* was that one-in-a-billion soul mate who existed for every werewolf out there. Even though they were supposedly as hard to find as hens' teeth, five of his teammates had already met their mates in the past year. The odds said something like that should have been impossible, but it had happened anyway. Now, most of the other members of the Pack were essentially looking behind every tree and around every corner, wondering if their soul mates were going to show up at some point.

Remy wasn't one of them.

He'd found love already. As far as he was concerned,

he was *one and done*. He was completely fine hooking up with women who caught his fancy, but he never let things progress beyond that. There was no denying he and Triana had some serious chemistry going on between them, but that was a far cry from being soul mates, mythological or otherwise. Just hearing Brooks say the words *The One* made him feel like he was going to be ill.

"Hell no!" he said vehemently. "It's nothing like that. Triana is just a friend. Period…dot…end of sentence."

Across from Remy, Brooks regarded him with a knowing look. He knew Remy was hiding something for sure. Some of the more mature werewolves in the Pack, like Brooks and Gage, were walking lie detectors. By picking up on subtle changes in heart and respiratory rate, body scent, and even random muscle twitches, they could tell when other people were trying to feed them a line. Brooks almost certainly knew Remy was talking BS, but thankfully he didn't call him on it.

Zane, on the other hand, wasn't so reserved. "Did you stand too close to the breaching charge when it exploded this morning? Because unless you have a concussion, I have a hard time believing the words coming out of your mouth. I've never seen you not go after a woman you're attracted to, and don't try to convince us you're not panting like a hound for Triana. I saw you two dancing—and smelled you. Pheromones don't lie."

Remy considered arguing, but then figured he'd not only lose, but probably embarrass himself too. There was no way in hell he was going to sit here and have a discussion about the scent he might put off when he was aroused. That was simply not a conversation he wanted to have. So, he went in a completely different direction instead.

"Yeah, okay, I'm attracted to her. So what? Triana has been a friend for a really long time. I don't want to mess up that friendship."

Beside him, Zane nodded. "I can understand that. But I should probably point out that you and Triana weren't exactly dancing like friends last night—at least, not like any friends I've ever danced with."

Remy snorted. "That's because you're too uptight and British to know how to relax and have a good time. Friends in New Orleans dance like that all the time."

"That's a load of crap," Max said. "Zane and I are friends, and we weren't dancing like that last night."

Remy looked back and forth at his two pack mates. "Maybe you should. You two would look good together."

Max chuckled. "Yeah, but that's because I look good with anyone. Unfortunately, I don't think I'm going to get a shot at him. For reasons that are beyond me, Triana's friend Kim seemed to take a liking to Zane. I don't think she's going to let anyone else get near him the whole time we're here."

Desperate for any topic that would get his pack mates' attention off him and Triana, Remy jumped on it. "Now that you mention it, I did notice you and Kim were getting close. You do realize she's on the rebound, right? You sure you want to get in the middle of that?"

Zane swigged some Gatorade. "Kim and I aren't getting into anything. We danced and snogged a bit, but mostly all we did was talk. She's not looking for anything serious but admitted she wouldn't mind hanging

out with someone who'd help take her mind off her ex
for a while. I graciously agreed to do that. We're two
intelligent adults with no hidden agendas. She's looking
for a distraction, and I'm cool with that. She's funny,
easy to talk to, and sexy as hell. And before you ask, no,
she's not *The One* for me."

"How do you know that?" Max asked.

"You have talked to Gage and the other guys who
found their mates, right?" Zane countered. "According
to them, they knew they'd found *The One* before they
ever kissed. It might have taken them a while to realize
what it was, but it was there. Based on that, I can state
with certainty that Kim isn't my mate."

Max and Zane were still arguing about that and the
possibility you could meet your soul mate and not even
know it when Drew came out of the main building.

"Is lunch finally ready?" Remy asked the NOPD
SWAT commander with a grin. "Hope so, because I'm
starving."

Drew didn't return his smile. "Gumbo's made, but
unfortunately it's going in the fridge. We've been called
in to support the Narcotics Major Case Squad. They
need backup to serve a high-risk search warrant on a
target so sensitive they couldn't even talk about it over
the phone. But if it's the guy I think it is, this one could
get ugly. The four of you feel up to doing some real
SWAT work instead of just training for it?"

～◆～

Triana frowned at the chaotic mess of voodoo dolls on
the huge table in the middle of her mother's shop—what
was left of them anyway. Sometimes when the tourists

came through, it seemed like a hurricane had hit the place. Things were everywhere.

"Mom, I think you need to make some more voodoo dolls," Triana shouted toward the back room, where her mom was doing her thing. "The big tour group from New York that came through yesterday just about wiped you out."

"Already on it," her mother called.

Triana couldn't help smiling. Her mother was amazing. Most of the voodoo shops in town bought their stuff from overseas these days, but not her mom. While the T-shirts and knickknacks were from out of town, her mother hand made all the authentic voodoo items like the spells, oils, herbs, charms, candles, dolls, and gris-gris bags.

"So when was the last time you heard from this PI you're paying so much money for?" Kim asked, dragging Triana's attention back to the subject they'd been discussing before the critical voodoo doll shortage had been identified.

Kim had taken off from work to hang out with Triana and help restock the shelves and straighten up the place.

"It's been five weeks," Triana admitted with a shrug. "But he warned me this could take a while. The case was ice-cold by the time I hired him, and the detective who handled the case hasn't exactly been very interested in talking to a private investigator about what he learned, probably because he never learned a damn thing."

"So you're getting nothing out of this guy but a bill?" Kim attempted to reattach a voodoo doll's arm that had been savagely ripped off. After a couple of attempts, gave up and instead simply ripped off the other arm in what Triana assumed was an effort to make the doll look symmetrical. "How long are you going to keep paying the guy?"

"I have no doubt he's probably milking me for everything he can get, but I have to try something. I can't let the man who murdered my dad get away with it…not without at least trying to find him."

Kim hid the dismembered voodoo doll in the back of the pile. Triana took note of where it was, so she could dig it out later. Kim was a great friend but lousy at stocking shelves.

"I know," Kim said. "All I'm saying is that you need to watch yourself. There are people in the world who will see your loss as their gain. Just be smart, okay?"

"I will."

Triana understood what her friend was trying to say, but at the end of the day, she didn't care about the money. If there was even a minuscule chance of finding the person who killed her father, she'd pay any price.

They worked in silence for a while, and as much as Triana tried to prevent it, her mind went to that dark place it tended to go whenever she thought about how much she missed her father and how much she hated the person who'd taken him away.

Kim tossed her blond curls over her shoulder and turned to her, one hand on her hip. "All right, enough of this depressing stuff. I'm not going to let you get into a funk over this. Time to change the subject."

"Okay." Triana pasted on a smile for her friend's benefit. "What do you suggest we talk about to lighten the mood?"

Kim grinned, her green eyes dancing. "Why don't we talk about Remy and the way you two were getting down and dirty last night?"

Triana laughed. If Kim had been looking for a topic that would brighten her mood, she'd definitely picked a good one. It was impossible to think about Remy and not smile.

"We weren't *getting down and dirty* last night," she insisted as she put the last doll in place. "We were just dancing."

Kim gave her a dubious look. "Please. There were some wicked-hot sparks flying off you guys. I thought you and Remy might burst into flames right there on the dance floor. You sure there was never anything between the two of you in high school?"

"No, there was never anything between us, but I always wished there had been," Triana said, unable to keep the wistful tone out of her voice. "Man, did I have a serious crush on him back then."

Her friend's lips curved. "I can definitely see why. The guy is a hunk."

"He's definitely a hunk, all right—and then some."

Triana smiled, remembering the feel of all those muscles under her fingers as they danced…and kissed. She'd been so aroused after Remy had left her mother's shop last night, it had taken almost an hour for her body to return to normal. Just thinking about those kisses had her tummy quivering all over again.

"How the heck did you let a guy like that get away in high school?" Kim asked. "Especially since it's obvious he's completely enamored with you."

A warm blush crept into her cheeks at the thought of

Remy being attracted to her. "That's the funny part," she admitted. "Remy wasn't like this in high school. I mean, he was definitely hot, but nothing like he is now. It's hard to even stand beside him without getting turned on."

"Damn," Kim breathed. "If you got turned on simply from standing beside him, I can only imagine what it was like when you guys were dancing. I'm surprised you didn't orgasm right there in the club."

Triana stifled a moan, then threw a quick glance at the back room to make sure her mother was still in there before giving Kim a grin. "Me too."

"When are you seeing him again?" Kim arched a brow. "You are seeing him again, right?"

Triana laughed. "Duh! Of course I am. We're going out tonight." Crap, the other day she'd promised Kim they'd go see a movie tonight. How the heck could she have forgotten that? "Oh God. I completely forgot you and I had plans. I'll call Remy and tell him we need to do dinner another night."

"Don't you dare!" Kim said. "Remy's only in town for the week. I know you think I'm falling apart since Shawn dumped me, but I'm fine. Really."

Triana wasn't sure she believed her friend. The jerk formerly known as Shawn had dumped Kim on the same night she'd expected him to pop the question. Any woman would have been thrown for a loop after that.

"Kim, you and Shawn dated for four years," she said gently. "You have every right to be down."

"I was for a while," Kim admitted. "Worse, I was down on myself because I thought the whole breakup was my fault. But after we left the club last night, Zane told me something that put everything into perspective."

"What's that?"

"He pointed out that Shawn walking out had nothing to do with me," she said. "It was one hundred percent about Shawn and his inability to grow up and accept our future together. Zane made me realize I wasn't the reason Shawn left. Shawn threw away what we had because he's an immature coward."

Triana knew there was a reason she'd felt good about leaving Kim in Zane's company. Then something Kim said earlier caught her attention.

"So…wait a second. You and Zane left the club together?"

Kim's smile was dreamy. "Yeah. We walked around the Quarter until four o'clock in the morning, talking… and making out a little. We could have easily ended up in bed, but we didn't. It was fun hanging out with a guy who's so comfortable in his own skin that there's no reason to rush anything."

The comfortable way Kim implied there could have been sex surprised Triana a little. She didn't expect Kim to even be interested in jumping into bed with a guy so soon after breaking up with Shawn.

"Are you planning to sleep with Zane?"

Kim shrugged. "Maybe. If it feels right. Is there any reason I shouldn't? We're two consenting adults with no other commitments. As much as I cared about Shawn, and still do, he left me. I don't even know where he is right now. And Zane isn't seeing anyone at the moment." She straightened a voodoo doll. "We talked honestly about it last night. If we sleep together, it will be plain and simple, no-strings sex with no expectations. I'm thinking at this point in my life that might be the very best thing for me." She smiled. "I'd be lying if I said the idea of a little rebound sex with someone as perfect as Zane isn't awfully tempting."

Triana stood there, stunned to complete silence. In one night, her confused, hurt, and devastated best friend had been transformed into a completely different person after simply spending an evening with a handsome guy she'd just met. Triana had been trying to console her since getting into town and hadn't gotten anywhere.

"What about you and Remy?" Kim asked.

Triana shrugged. "We'll probably grab dinner someplace, then walk around the French Quarter. Maybe go dancing."

Kim smiled. "Sounds like fun, but that's not exactly what I meant. I was asking if you're going to sleep with him. You know, make up for lost time and all that."

Triana opened her mouth to reply, but then realized she didn't have a clue how to answer what should have been a simple question. She was attracted to Remy. Okay, understatement there. She'd come damn close to dragging him up to her room last night. The intensity of the sensation would be scary if it wasn't so intoxicating at the same time.

But now that she was out of his hypnotizing presence—and thinking more clearly—she was glad nothing had happened last night. She wasn't the type to jump into something with a guy without thinking it through. She had her love of all things scientific to thank for that. It made her cautious, linear, and kind of practical. None of those made a woman want to jump in the sack with a guy she'd crushed on in high school, especially one who was only going to be around for a week.

"Earth to Triana," Kim said, waving her hand in Triana's face. "I wasn't asking you to do calculus in your head. Stop thinking so much all the time and just go after the guy you've wanted since you were old enough to have those kinds of thoughts. From what you just said, you and Remy had it bad for each other all the way back in high school, and if what I saw last night is any indication, it's obvious the spark is still there. Why don't you take a leap of faith and see where the heck it takes you?"

Triana gave her a look. "You're honestly saying you think I should jump in the sack with him and not worry about what happens when he goes back to Dallas and I go home to Houston?"

"That's exactly what I'm saying. Just treat this next week as a chance to make up for all that time you wasted back in high school." Kim grinned. "Worst case, you have a week of unbelievable sex. Because trust me, after watching that man move on the dance floor, there's no chance in hell he isn't an Olympian between the sheets."

"And best case?" Triana prompted, figuring she already knew where Kim was going with this.

Kim's smile broadened. "Best case, you two fall madly in love and figure out the three-and-a-half-hour drive from Dallas to Houston isn't that much of an obstacle to overcome. Heck, who knows? Maybe you get so swept up in each other that you chuck it all and run off to live with Remy in Dallas."

"Or he could chuck it all and run off to Houston to live with me," Triana countered with a laugh.

"Exactly!" Kim said. "Now you're talking."

All Triana could do was shake her head. After everything Kim had been through with Shawn, she was thinking Triana and Remy were going to have some kind of storybook romance. Her mother would be thrilled if that happened. She hadn't said as much, but Triana knew her mother wanted her to find something special, like her mother had found with Triana's dad.

Triana wasn't sure if Remy was that guy, but maybe Kim was right about going with her feelings and seeing where it led. Like Kim said, worst case, there'd be some great sex involved. What kind of girl turned her nose up at that?

She opened her mouth to tell Kim she'd let things take their natural course with Remy when the bell on the door to the shop tinkled.

Triana turned to see an older man in a white linen suit and fancy dress shoes shamble into the shop. He looked around the store with an air of disdain, but his expression brightened when he saw her and Kim. Triana wasn't fooled for a second. She knew a bullshit facade when she saw it. This guy was full of it.

He walked over and extended his hand. Even though she didn't want to, Triana shook it nonetheless. She regretted the decision when she got a palm full of cold, clammy hand. Ick, she hated men with limp, sweaty hands. Then she caught sight of the man's buffed and polished nails. Crap, his manicure probably cost more than her shoes. That was the final nail in the coffin as far as she was concerned.

"Kenneth Murphy, attorney with Taylor and Burr," the man said in an officious tone. "Is your mother in?"

A shiver ran down Triana's back. She'd never seen this man in her life, yet he obviously knew her. How else had he known to ask for her mother?

She opened her mouth to ask him as much when her mom stepped out of the back room and leveled a piercing stare at the man.

"You didn't need to come here, Mr. Murphy. I already told you over the phone that I couldn't help you."

The man gave her mother another fake smile. "I completely understand, Mrs. Bellamy. But I thought that if we talked in person and you took a look at the offer I'm making, it might change your mind."

Reaching into the inside pocket on his suit jacket, Murphy took out a sheet of paper, unfolded it, then held it out. It was a drawing of a necklace in the shape of a wolf's head. "It's a copper pendant, and the eyes of the wolf are made of yellow topaz."

Her mother didn't say anything. Instead, she stood with her arms crossed over her chest, an irritated look on her face.

"As I mentioned when we talked on the phone, my client is offering a very reasonable sum of money for a trinket such as the one I'm describing," Murphy said.

"And who is this client of yours, Mr. Murphy?" her mother asked in an icy voice.

Triana frowned. Her mother was never abrupt or cold with anyone. If her mom didn't like this guy, there was a reason.

The man gave her a syrupy smile. "He prefers to remain anonymous in this transaction, but I can assure you, Mrs. Bellamy, I'm fully authorized to negotiate on his behalf. As I said, five thousand dollars is a very reasonable offer."

Triana did a double take. That wasn't chump change for a shopkeeper who sold voodoo merchandise to tourists and some of the locals. That kind of money could pay the taxes on this place for a year, maybe more.

"That's very generous," her mother said. "But as I told you over the phone, I don't have any necklace like that in my shop."

"Of course you don't," Murphy said in a tone that made Triana think the man thought her mother was lying. "But perhaps you know where my client could find one exactly like it—and I do mean exactly."

"I'm sorry, Mr. Murphy, but I can't help you," her mother said in a tone that brooked no compromise.

Triana was confused. She remembered her father wearing a wolf-head pendant just like the one Murphy was looking for. She'd even played with it as a child when he'd held her in his great big arms. He'd never taken it off. And she did mean never. No way had her mother gotten rid of it.

"Perhaps if the offer was more substantial, it might help your memory?" Murphy proposed sweetly.

Her mom smacked that idea down like a june bug. "Apparently I haven't made myself completely clear. Let me do so now. There is no necklace like that anywhere in my possession, but even if I did have it, I would never sell it to you or this anonymous client of yours. Please leave and don't come back here again. Good day, Mr. Murphy."

The man's face turned red as he glowered, but her mother returned his glare with one of her own. Triana thought for a moment she might have to step in and do something, but to her surprise, Murphy sullenly gave her mother a nod, then turned and walked out of the shop.

Triana opened her mouth to ask what all that had

been about, but her mother had already disappeared into the back room and closed the door.

"That was weird," Kim said.

"That's one word for it," Triana agreed.

Chapter 4

REMY'S BACK THUMPED AGAINST THE INTERIOR WALL OF THE operations van as the vehicle made a right turn off the main street, then bounced a little as it crossed some train tracks. He closed his eyes and visualized the map that had been taped to the whiteboard during the tactical mission briefing. Crossing those tracks meant they'd just turned off Chartres and were only a couple of blocks from the river. In a few minutes, they'd reach the docks, the cargo ship, and the warehouse owned by a man named Aaron Lee.

Remy had already been familiar with the name before sitting through the briefing that Drew and the lead detective from the narcotics squad, Lorenzo Claiborne, had conducted earlier. Remy had run across Lee's name more than a few times when he'd worked in the sheriff's office years ago. The man had been a long-standing criminal fixture in the city, a heavy hitter in nearly every illegal activity going on along the Mississippi River. Drugs, prostitution, gambling, fencing stolen property, protection rackets—the man was into all of it. Remy thought for sure someone at the local, state, or federal level would have been able to pin something on the man a long time ago, but clearly Aaron Lee was too good a criminal for that.

If the informant Detective Claiborne and his narcotics crew had inside Lee's operation was right, all that was about to change. Because they were about to serve a warrant on one of Lee's ships just in from Mexico, which was supposedly carrying over three hundred pounds of high-quality crystal meth. If they found that stash of drugs, Aaron Lee was finally heading to prison.

Serving search warrants on drug operations was always a risky job, which was why SWAT was so frequently asked to go in the door first. Going up against a man who'd been running his drug operation for decades made it even worse. With a shipment of "ice" having a street value of close to five million dollars, Lee was bound to have dozens of heavily armed men covering the ship and the warehouse. The chances of this operation turning into a shoot-out were extremely high. But with the memory of that young girl on the ambulance gurney from last night still fresh in his mind, Remy knew there wasn't any other way to do this. They couldn't let a shipment this big make it onto the streets of New Orleans, or the girl he and Triana had seen would be just one of many people ending up in the hospitals—and the morgue.

Remy watched as his pack mates and the NOPD SWAT officers checked their gear and weapons again, then went over the plan one last time. As they murmured softly to each other, his heart began to beat faster. Around him, everyone else's did too. But while Remy's and his pack mates' did so out of excitement, that wasn't the case with the cops on the NOPD SWAT team.

The officers he and his pack mates had spent the morning training with knew they were going up against people who had no qualms about shooting cops. To be blunt about it, the men and women on the NOPD

SWAT team had no way of knowing if they were even going to be alive an hour from now. Their adrenaline was pumping because they were nervous, even a little scared. Remy didn't hold that against them. They were only human.

That limitation didn't apply to Remy and the other members of his pack. Getting shot wasn't that big of a deal for them. Werewolves could survive just about any kind of wound imaginable, as long as it wasn't to the head or the heart. Getting shot hurt, sure. But knowing you weren't going to die from it tended to give the Dallas SWAT team a completely different outlook on danger—it probably wasn't an outlook a mental health professional would approve of, but it was definitely unique.

Remy and his pack mates were amped up because this was the shit alpha werewolves lived for.

He knew he'd never be able to explain the concept to a normal person, but feeling that surge of adrenaline when his werewolf senses went on hyperalert, experiencing the tension that rippled through his body as his inner wolf attempted to come out to protect itself... There was no better feeling in the world. For an alpha werewolf like him and the Pack, it was the feeling of being alive.

"We're approaching the west gate. Thirty seconds out," Detective Claiborne's voice came through over the radio in Remy's ear. "Drew, you ready on the east side?"

"Roger that," Drew replied. "Gate personnel in position. The operation is a go. Move in."

"Weapons hot," Brooks murmured.

As one, the charging handles on eight M4 carbines

were yanked back and released, loading the weapons with a familiar and soothing clatter. At the same time, Remy felt the operations vehicle accelerate. He pulled down his ski mask along with everyone else.

Lee's warehouse complex had a tall fence around the entire property, with two gates, one to the east and the other to the west. Both of them were normally secured with locked chains. Now that Drew had given the word, two other members of the team dressed in plain clothes would be heading toward the gates with small explosive charges ready to blow the locks. The timing would have to be perfect, though—too early and they'd alert the people on the ship they were coming, too late and the operations vans would smash into the gates.

The driver of the operations vehicle Remy was in backed off the gas a little. No doubt he was worried the gate wouldn't be open when they got there. But a moment later, the driver floored it, and they were racing through the gate so fast Remy bounced off the seat as they crossed over the entrance bump.

Remy tensed, ready to move the moment the operations vehicle came to a stop. It was only about a hundred feet across the west gate parking lot. Any second now, the driver would swerve to the side and they'd exit out the back of the van. Then, he and the other members of the Dallas SWAT team, along with the NOPD officers, would head for the cargo ship moored at the dock. While Remy and his pack mates began sweeping the ship, NOPD SWAT would head to the ship's bridge to make sure no one tried to start the engines.

While all this was happening, Drew's team would move into the warehouse from the east and gain control of the structure. Lorenzo and his men from the narcotics squad would hang back until the whole area was initially secured; then, they'd come in with dogs and personnel to do the detailed search for the drugs.

Remy was still visualizing exactly how much ground he and the others would have to cover to get to the ship when the truck slid sideways and Brooks shoved the doors open. Then he stopped thinking and started moving, jumping out of the truck and running for the southwest corner of the building and the ship docked just beyond it. He told himself to hold back a bit, so he wouldn't blow past the NOPD SWAT officers, but that was damn hard to do when every instinct he had screamed at him to go as hard as he could, to attack ferociously before Lee's people had a chance to react.

Off to Remy's left, the warehouse was a giant metal structure with lots of rust and even more dents. Outside of it, pallets of steel oil pipes and heavy-duty equipment for drilling platforms out in the Gulf were scattered haphazardly along their path. It was almost as if someone had gone out of their way to convince people this was a legitimate warehousing operation.

Just ahead of him, Remy could make out the wide, slow-moving expanse of the Mississippi lined almost entirely with docks along this part of the river. He reached out with his senses, straining to pick up any sight, sound, or smell that would indicate Lee's people were about to start shooting at them. To be truthful, he'd expected to run into resistance by this point. That they hadn't didn't make him feel any better. In fact, it worried the hell out of him. You could never trust criminals who didn't play their proper roles.

As he raced around the building, Remy got his first real look at the coastal merchant vessel tied up at the pier. It wasn't as huge as some of the container ships that plied the waters of the Mississippi, but it was still large enough to hide a football field in, not to mention a buttload of armed thugs.

Still not running into a single person—armed or otherwise—he and the others reached the metal gangway attached to the side of the ship and raced aboard. Remy's gut told him something was off here, but they had no choice except to keep going.

The four NOPD SWAT officers peeled off and headed toward the rear of the ship and the elevated bridge positioned there, while Remy and his pack mates split up into pairs and headed down into the cargo hold. Even though they moved fast, they covered each other the whole time. While they weren't worried about getting shot, it was a standing wager in the Pack that the first wolf who got hit would have to buy the beer for the next team cookout. The pain of getting shot might not be a big deal, but the pain of buying beer? Now that was excruciating.

Remy ducked through a rounded door, then moved down a flight of stairs, Max on his heels. Somewhere off to the right, he heard Brooks and Zane moving along an adjacent set of stairs. As they descended, he let his eyes shift to see in the rapidly darkening depth of the ship. One level down, and it was already getting dark as midnight.

Coastal vessels like this one were true multipurpose workhorses, with some parts of the hold set aside for neat pallets of anything from computers to clothing to food, other areas designed for loose storage of grains or coal, and still other spots where tractor-trailer-sized containers could be placed and locked down. Down in the hold, a regular human could quickly get turned around in the dark, bewildering maze of partitioned spaces and the confusing corridors created by the cargo itself.

Remy wasn't worried about that for himself or his guys, no matter how dark it was. Their werewolf senses made up for their lack of experience in places like this. His biggest concern was that they'd get into a running gunfight in the middle of a ship full of who knew what kind of hazardous cargo. Having the ship burn down to the waterline because some idiot accidently started a fire in a hold full of coal wasn't what they were looking to do today.

But as they moved farther down the stairs and into the first section of loose cargo, it quickly became apparent there wasn't going to be a gunfight, running or otherwise.

"Guys, I'm not picking up any active scents down here," Brooks whispered. "No one has been in this part of the ship for at least a half hour or so. That doesn't make a damn bit of sense."

Remy cursed silently. Something was definitely off with this raid. It was like there was no one home, which was crazy since the ship was obviously still fully loaded. There should have been tons of people down there, prepping the stuff for off-loading. Not to mention the fact that there should have been some armed guards protecting the drugs that were supposed to be here.

He and his pack mates weren't the only ones thinking there was something wrong. The four NOPD officers who had split off and headed for the bridge came on the radio with a status report, saying the bridge was secure and that even though the captain and several of his men had been there, they hadn't resisted.

"Same in the warehouse." Drew's voice was terse in Remy's earpiece. "There were two guards on duty, but they were just sitting at a table playing cards when we came in. I swear, it was like they knew we were coming."

A moment later, Lorenzo came on and announced he was bringing the drug dogs in, but Remy already had a sinking feeling it was going to be a waste of time. Either the drugs had never been here, or somehow Aaron Lee's people had known the police were coming and had gotten the drugs out before they'd even arrived.

"Guys, over here," Brooks said.

Remy looked up to see Brooks standing near an open door in the darkness on the far side of the cargo hold. No doubt it led to a storage room, but from the look on Brooks's face, it wasn't pallets of potato chips that had attracted his attention.

As he got closer, Remy picked up the slight chlorine-like chemical smell coming from the room. This was where the drugs had been hidden.

Remy stepped past Brooks into the room and followed his nose over to the far wall. Eyes narrowing, he looked closer and realized one section of it was a removable panel four feet high and three feet wide. He ran his hands along the edges until he found the cleverly hidden grips. Grabbing hold of them, he moved the section of wall away.

The chlorine-like odor wafted out, stinging his nose and making his eyes water. Meth was a simple chemical formula, so it could be difficult to pick up sometimes. In theory, the smell could belong to any of a hundred

different industrial compounds. But a person didn't go
to all the work of creating a hidden storage compartment
on a ship to conceal pool cleaner. Combine a chlorine-
like odor with a secret contraband space and you get a
meth shipment.

While the compartment was big enough to hold three
or four large duffle bags, it was empty now.

"They knew we were coming," Zane said from behind
him. "Bloody bastards moved the crap right before we
got here."

"Put the wall back," Brooks said. "We'll let the dogs
find the hidey-hole."

Remy replaced the section of wall with a muttered
curse. He'd hoped like hell they'd be able to take down
Aaron Lee and his operation. In some stupid way, Remy
had convinced himself that sending Lee to prison today
would set things right with the poor young girl who'd
overdosed the night before. Unless they had better luck
in the warehouse, they were going to have to wait a little
longer to take down the scumbag.

Remy and his pack mates spent over two hours down
in the cargo hold helping Lorenzo, his narcotics team,
and the drug dogs with their search. As expected, the
K-9 team alerted on the back wall of the equipment
room, finding the empty hidey-hole. Lorenzo was just
as disappointed as Remy and his pack mates had been,
especially when a thorough search of the rest of the ship
turned up absolutely nothing. The warehouse had come
up clean so far too.

"I don't know how, but that son of a bitch Aaron Lee

knew we were coming," Lorenzo said as they headed out
of the ship to meet up with Drew. Stocky, with close-
cropped black hair, the Hispanic police officer looked
like he was ready to blow a gasket. "The asshole saw
this coming from a mile away."

Lorenzo was probably right, considering that when
they stepped off the ship, they had found a large black
Cadillac parked in front of it with Lee and a couple of
his goons leaning casually against the fenders.

From what Remy remembered, Aaron Lee had grown
up working the docks of the Mississippi. Even though he
must be approaching his late fifties and there was some
gray in his otherwise dark hair, the man was still built
like an ox. He had the bearing of an extremely confident
man and the aura of a criminal who'd thumbed his nose
at the police in New Orleans longer than most of the
cops on this scene had been alive.

Seeing the arrogant glare Lee threw their way as they
approached him, not to mention his slow and relaxed
heartbeat, Remy could understand how the man had
maintained his grip on the city's criminal enterprises for
so long. It was obvious the guy had absolutely no fear of
the law. Hell, it wouldn't have come as a shock if they'd
discovered the man was a complete psycho who didn't
even know how to feel fear.

"Ah, Detective Claiborne," Lee said, giving Lorenzo
an insincere smile that was somehow able to convey
both amusement and violence. "I should have guessed it
was you violating my civil liberties."

Lorenzo's eyes narrowed. "No one is violating your
civil liberties, Mr. Lee. We have a search warrant signed
by a judge."

"I saw." Lee's lip curled. "One of your fellow jack-booted thugs waved that little piece of paper in my face. Signed by Judge Thibodeau, wasn't it? Isn't he running for reelection soon? Seems like a strange campaign plan, sending police to harass a potential voter like myself."

Lorenzo crossed his arms over his chest. "We're not here to harass you. We're conducting a search for illegal drugs."

On either side of him, Lee's goons let out derisive chuckles. Lorenzo had shown Remy and the other SWAT cops photos of Lee's personal-security-slash-lieutenants during the mission briefing, and while both men wore similar amused expressions on their ugly mugs, the two couldn't have been more different.

There was Shelton Quinn, a muscle-bound guy easily as big as Brooks. The man had a shaved head and a couple tattoos showing on his arms and neck that looked like they'd been done in a prison or someplace equally primitive. According to Lorenzo, Quinn specialized in physical intimidation and breaking everything from kneecaps and heads to spirits. From the looks of him, it was obvious the guy spent a good portion of his life in the gym, though the sour scent coming off him seemed to indicate at least some of those gains were the results of steroids or something more exotic.

The other guy, Chad Roth, was whipcord lean with wiry muscles he liked showing off under a tight athletic shirt. His dark hair was trimmed close to his head, with three parallel lines etched in it above his right ear. The man seemed to have a thing for gold earrings, too. He had three in each lobe that glinted brightly against his dark-brown skin. It wasn't the unusual hairstyle or the earrings that caught Remy's attention though. Instead, it was the man's calculating eyes. As he watched, the thug scanned every cop in front of him—not in a quick, shifty manner, but with an intent look that told Remy the man was memorizing every detail he took in.

When Roth got to Remy and his pack mates, his eyes narrowed at the sight of the DPD patches on the front of their tactical vests. He locked gazes with Remy, staring straight at him. Remy stared back.

Lorenzo had said Roth was the smarter of the two lieutenants, and even though he'd only been associated with Lee's organization for a few years, it was likely he'd take over running the show someday, assuming Lee ever stepped aside.

Remy listened with half an ear as Quinn ribbed Lorenzo about how the search for drugs was going, asking if maybe the cops needed some help looking, since it was obvious they didn't know what the hell they were doing. All the while, Aaron Lee stood there with a smile on his face, letting his lieutenant have his fun with the narcotics detective.

Roth slowly slid his gaze from Remy, casually taking in Max, Brooks, and Zane. Remy watched the man's open perusal, trying to understand the funny vibe he was getting off the guy. Whereas Lee was calm and serene inside, sure the cops weren't going to get anything off him, and Quinn was a pile of juiced-up energy, getting off on his chance to stick it to the cops, Roth wasn't putting off anything. He wasn't merely calm; he was shut off. Like a dead man walking. Remy had never experienced anything quite like it and couldn't help but wonder if maybe it meant the guy was a cold-blooded serial killer.

"Search as long as you like, Detective Claiborne," Lee finally said, interrupting Quinn's fun. "You're not going to find anything, but you can be sure that my lawyers will be talking to the city about the damage you've done to my property, as well as the amount of income lost waiting for you and your cop buddies to finish here. I wouldn't be surprised if some of the reimbursement came out of your paycheck."

Lorenzo's jaw tightened, but he didn't say anything as Roth opened the back door of the Caddy for Lee. Before climbing in, Lee turned to regard Remy and his pack mates thoughtfully before looking at the narcotics detective.

"I always thought you and your people were incompetent, Detective Claiborne, and bringing in outside muscle isn't going to help you pin something on me." Lee's mouth twitched. "Not unless they can sniff for drugs better than your dogs."

With that, Lee climbed into the backseat of the car. Roth went around to the passenger side while Quinn got behind the wheel.

As he started the engine, Quinn gave Remy and his pack mates an amused look. "Ruff, ruff, little doggies. Ruff, ruff."

Beside Remy, Max growled under his breath. "You wouldn't be laughing if I sank my little doggy fangs in that steroid-filled ass of yours," he said as Quinn drove away.

"You can bite his ass if you want," Remy said softly. "Me? I'm going for his fucking throat."

Chapter 5

THE SUN WAS JUST GOING DOWN AS REMY HEADED TO THE voodoo shop to pick up Triana for dinner. He still couldn't stop seething about how badly the raid had gone. They'd stayed at the docks for another three and a half hours after Aaron Lee had left, checking every little nook and cranny of the warehouse and the cargo ship. As Lee had predicted, they'd found nothing. And while the drug dogs had alerted on several places within the warehouse, they hadn't found any actual crystal meth. It was frustrating as hell, too. Not only because they knew Lee had slipped the meth out shortly before they'd gotten there, but also because the man had been so damn snide about the whole frigging thing.

Lorenzo had promised them this wasn't over, that Lee would have to store the meth somewhere in the city until he could get around to breaking it down into smaller packages.

"Breaking that much ice down and stuffing it into baggies is going to be a slow process," the detective added. "My informant will get word to us soon, I can promise you that, so keep your phones on. When we get the next warrant, I want to move fast."

Remy prayed Lorenzo was right, but he wasn't holding out much hope. Lee hadn't gotten where he was by being sloppy.

He shoved those thoughts away as he opened the

door to Gemma's shop. The one thing he didn't want
to do was ruin his evening with Triana because he had
a bad taste in his mouth over failing to bust Aaron Lee.
He'd been looking forward to spending time with her
all day. The moment he walked inside and breathed in
Triana's scent, it was like a heavy, wet blanket lifted
off his shoulders. Everything seemed lighter and he
found thoughts of Aaron Lee and his freaky lieutenants
fading away.

"There you are," Gemma said, coming out from
behind the counter to give him a hug. "I was worried
that if you didn't get here soon, Triana would primp
until she passed out. That girl has been working it in
front of that mirror upstairs for nearly two hours."

"Mom!" Triana scolded from the top of the stairs.
"Don't tell him that."

Gemma laughed, her dark eyes dancing as Triana
started down the steps. "Why not? I'm just subtly letting
Remy know how much effort you put into this date, so
he makes sure to properly show his appreciation."

Remy laughed, but the moment Triana's bare legs
came into view on the staircase, her smooth, light-brown
skin flexing as she carefully descended each step in her
heels, the sound caught in his throat. The sight of her in
the flowing yellow sleeveless dress was enough to ramp
his heart rate up to the danger zone. Combined with her
long, wavy hair, smoky makeup, and flowery perfume
that accentuated her natural scent, the complete package
was almost enough to make his heart stop beating alto-
gether. *Damn, damn, and double damn!* Right then he
was as sure as heaven above that he'd never met another
woman as beautiful as Triana Bellamy.

She held his gaze as she sidled over to him, her head cocked to one side, the tip of her tongue just touching the center of her upper lip. All at once, her heart sped up and her body put off the most delicious aroma on the planet. It was the same scent of arousal that had surrounded her last night as they'd kissed. The mere hint of it made him go hard in his jeans. The idea of saying the hell with dinner and heading straight for "dessert" was suddenly the only thing he could think about. His fingers itched to scoop her up and carry her back upstairs. He might have done it, too, if Gemma hadn't spoken.

"Cold shower, anyone?" she asked, a knowing smile curving her lips.

Triana blushed. "Mom!"

Gemma only laughed as she went behind the counter.

Even though Triana still smelled as delectable as before, her mother's words had achieved their desired effect. The trance Remy had been in was broken, and while he was still aroused as all hell, at least he was back in control. Another minute and he would have been panting.

Remy took a deep breath, then cautiously walked over to Triana, moving slowly to make sure he wouldn't go all wolf and jump on her. Fortunately, while his hard-on definitely seemed to approve of getting closer to the object of its affection, nothing crazy happened.

Unable to resist touching her, he ran his fingers down her arm. "You ready for dinner?"

Triana nodded, casually intertwining her fingers with his. Remy stifled a groan. Damn, even that simple touch felt good. A little voice in the back of his head suggested his intense reaction to something as vanilla as holding hands probably meant something significant, but he shoved it back in the cluttered closet of his mind, and it shut up.

"Definitely," Triana said, completely missing the fact that he was temporarily caught up in a distracting internal dialogue. "I'm starving."

He motioned toward the door. "After you," he said, enjoying the way her hips swayed as she walked in front of him.

"Good night, Mom," Triana said over her shoulder as Remy opened the door for her. "I'll probably be out late, so you don't need to wait up."

Gemma laughed. "Have fun, you two."

Triana's hand found Remy's again as soon as they were out on the sidewalk, and he tugged her a little closer so he could enjoy the way their arms brushed against each other as they walked. Neither of them said anything for a while, instead simply enjoying the pleasure of being in each other's company. Considering how keyed up he'd been just a few minutes ago, it was kind of amazing how relaxed he was now that he was with Triana. Sexually aroused, yes, but pretty chill other than that.

"The weather is so perfect tonight," she finally said. "It's hard to believe that stupid storm is still out there in the Gulf."

"Tell me about it," Remy said. "I checked the weather before coming to pick you up. Ophelia barely moved more than a mile today and the so-called experts still don't have any idea whether it will keep moving toward Texas or turn toward Louisiana. At least it's not getting any stronger, which is good. But as far as where it will make landfall, they're pretty much in wait-and-see mode."

Triana smiled at him. "Well, at least we know she's not coming this way tonight, so there's nothing to get in the way of our dinner date."

He paused midstride to lean in for a quick kiss that ended up being not all that quick as he got a taste of her lips. His cock hardened even more at the slight hint of her tongue, and he had to remind himself that they were on a public street. If they hadn't been, he might have been tempted to pin her up against the nearest wall and go exploring under that flowing yellow dress.

"Absolutely nothing to get in the way of our dinner date," he agreed after pulling away to get his breath back.

They walked along again in silence for another block or so until Triana spoke. "Speaking of dinner, are we going anywhere in particular?"

"I made reservations for us at Muriel's, if that's okay with you?"

She gave him a sidelong glance. "I'm not going to complain if you want to take me to Muriel's, but you know we don't have to go somewhere that fancy, right?"

He smiled. "I know. But I thought since this is kind of a reunion dinner, it should be kind of special. Like you."

Triana's lips curved. "Remy Boudreaux, you got all smooth on me in your absence, didn't you? You realize flattery really will get you everywhere, don't you?"

He chuckled and nudged her shoulder with his. "Promises, promises."

"Actually, it is a promise. But I think you already knew that."

Remy felt his jeans tighten uncomfortably and his

heart rate climb back up at the heat in her gaze. Damn, she was going to drive him insane before they even made it to dinner.

"So, how was your cross-training with the local SWAT team today?" Triana asked, as if she wanted to tease him by making him think about normal crap instead of what she might be promising.

He stuck a crowbar in the recesses of his mind and forced it to change gears. "Training was good, though it was cut a little short."

"What happened?" she asked as they turned down a side street and headed toward Jackson Square. "Nothing bad, I hope?"

He shook his head. "No, nothing like that. NOPD SWAT got called out to support a search warrant on a drug operation, and we went out to help them. It ended up taking the entire rest of the day."

Triana's eyes widened in alarm. "Wait. I thought you were just here to do some training. You went out to serve a drug warrant?"

Remy heard her heart thump louder in her chest, this time for all the wrong reasons, and he realized he probably should have kept that piece of reality to himself. Triana might be involved in law enforcement back in Houston, but that didn't mean she was okay with all aspects of it.

"It wasn't anything crazy," he said, hoping to downplay any danger. "An informant said a shipment of meth was coming in on a boat, but by the time we got there, the guy had already moved the stuff. It was all a big waste of time."

That seemed to mollify her somewhat, but she was

still regarding him seriously. "You might be doing more of these kinds of things while you're here in New Orleans…going out on real calls?"

"It's my job."

"I know," she said quickly. "I just thought you'd be doing training this week. I mean, I didn't even think you'd have jurisdiction here in New Orleans."

"My boss took care of all that before we came," Remy said. "He didn't want us put in a position where we needed to do something and not have the authority to do it. There was a lot of paperwork, but we're completely legit in the city for this week. But I promise you, my guys from Dallas are the best SWAT officers in the country, and we always take care of each other."

Triana thought about that for a while. "This is probably going to sound stupid, but you're always careful, right?"

He nodded. "Yes. And like I said, our number-one rule is to always watch out for each other."

She relaxed a little at that, but her heart was still beating a little faster than normal and he could feel the tension in her body. He regretted bringing up the drug raid, but there was no way to take it back.

They continued for another block in comfortable silence before Triana surprised him by asking for more details about what the raid had entailed. Remy took his time and laid out not just what he'd done today, but also what a typical search warrant operation was like. He stayed away from details she didn't need to know, like the fact that they'd been trying to take down Aaron Lee. Triana listened carefully but also asked a lot of pointed and intelligent questions.

Remy was showing her how he and his guys

communicated during operations using nothing but hand signals when they passed a club with bright, shiny lights and a gaudy sign advertising open mic karaoke every night. Apparently, the sign wasn't lying, since Remy could already hear the most god-awful voice butchering "Beast of Burden" by the Rolling Stones. It was one of the rare times in all his years as a werewolf that Remy was sorry he had such good hearing. The noise coming out of the open door was actually painful to listen to.

But it wasn't the crap sound from the place that made him stop and take a second look. He was sure he recognized the club, though he wasn't sure why it was familiar. Then it struck him. It wasn't the appearance of the building—it was the address. He looked up and down the street a couple times to be sure, because it had been eight years since he'd seen the place last.

"Hey. Isn't this where your dad's place, the Jazz Joint, used to be?" Remy asked, sure he had to be wrong.

He remembered going to her dad's club for dinner when he was in high school and had always thought the place had a cool, laid-back vibe. Nothing like this garish mess they were standing in front of now. The reputation of the club had been so good that well-known jazz musicians would show up all the time just for a chance to play there. But with the bellowing coming out the door combined with the cheap signage, he couldn't imagine any respectable musician even wanting to walk on the same side of the street as this place.

Triana nodded sadly, not looking at the karaoke club as they walked past. She even tugged his hand a little so he'd quicken his pace as they moved down the street, clearly unwilling to spend any more time than necessary near the place that occupied where her dad's old club had been.

Remy could understand that.

"After Dad's death, Mom tried to keep it going," Triana said, and Remy could almost taste her grief on the air. "Sort of in his memory...you know? She tried to get a partner, but no one was willing. Some people didn't like the idea of working in a place where such a horrible murder had happened. Others simply pointed out that it simply wasn't going to work. Dad didn't just run the Jazz Joint; he was its heart and soul. Without his charisma and energy, the old building seemed like an empty shell. The people who used to play there wouldn't come back. Mom said it was because the magic was gone."

Triana fell silent as they crossed a street. Her father's murder had been two years ago, but it was obvious the pain was as raw and upsetting as if it had happened yesterday. Remy squeezed her hand, trying to let her know without words that she didn't need to talk about it but that he was there for her if she wanted to.

Rufus Bellamy had always been such a larger-than-life character—big, strong, loud, loving. Remy remembered him as this huge guy with muscles he'd gotten working on the docks of New Orleans as a young man, humping cargo and loading ships. He'd had a wild head of shaggy blond hair and a mustache to match. Everyone knew Rufus had lived part of his life on the wrong side of the law, but in a city like this, that wasn't necessarily the stigma it might have been in other parts of the country.

The man had been out of that life for a while by the

time Remy had met him. As far as Remy was concerned, Triana's dad had been a faithful husband and loving father. But at the same time, Remy understood where Rufus Bellamy had come from. He loved to laugh and have fun like anyone else, but he was also a man no one wanted to mess with unless they wanted to know what it felt like to be beaten to a bloody pulp.

It was hard to believe that a man as powerful and full of life as Triana's father was gone. He'd been a rare kind of person.

"Mom finally ended up selling the club," Triana said after a few blocks. "While neither of us wanted to keep the place after my dad's murder, it still sucks seeing the jazz club he poured his heart and soul into become a karaoke bar. It's almost like blasphemy."

"After hearing whoever was singing as we walked by the place, I agree," Remy said. "But I'm pretty sure your dad wouldn't be that upset. As I recall, he used to get up and sing with some of the musicians who came in…and he was pretty awful. That never kept him from doing it, though. I think he'd be fine with people singing in his old club as long as they're having a good time."

Triana stared at him for a moment, then a big smile spread across her face. "You know something, I think you're exactly right. Don't tell Mom I said this, but if Dad ever came back as a ghost, I could imagine him standing up at that karaoke mic, butchering songs with the best of them."

They laughed at that image, and before long, they were telling each other all the stories they remembered about Rufus Bellamy—and there were a lot of them.

By the time they reached Muriel's over on Saint Ann, Triana's mood had lightened considerably and they were back to the playful, sexy banter that had started off their date.

With its red brick and white wood trim, the two-story building on the edge of Jackson Square known as Muriel's Bistro was a beautiful structure. The building on the corner of Saint Ann and Chartres had been in existence in one form or another practically since the founding of the city, and the owners of the restaurant had invested a lot money into lovingly restoring the place to its mid-1800s grandeur.

The best thing about Muriel's—beyond the amazing food, of course—was the ambience. There was something about the blend of mid-nineteenth-century French charm, the New Orleans mystique, and the Southern hospitality that really worked for this place. How many other restaurants maintained a reserved table for a ghost? It was true. The place kept a table set with wine and bread for the ghost of Pierre Jourdan, one of the restaurant's previous owners.

Remy didn't miss the way men's heads turned to follow Triana as the hostess led them across the main red-and-yellow-decorated dining room and seated them at a table for two in the back corner. While he was surprised at the spike of jealousy that rushed through him, not to mention the animalistic urge to turn and snarl at the gawkers, he couldn't blame the men whose gazes were drawn to Triana's hypnotic beauty. He certainly was as well.

The hostess took their wine orders, then mentioned the name of their server and left them alone. Even though the dining room was crowded, the alcove where they were seated offered them a little privacy. Not that it mattered. Triana was so alluring it was like there was no one else around.

"So, what are the other guys from Dallas up to while you're out wooing me tonight?" she asked with a sparkle in her eyes.

He chuckled. "Wooing? Is that what I'm doing? I thought I was taking you out for dinner."

She flashed him a smile. "I could have had dinner at home. I came out with you tonight because I'm expecting much more than food."

Remy felt a crazy vibration start in his gut at the teasing, playful look she gave him. Gaze locked with his, she licked her full lips, tracing her nimble tongue over them in a gesture that was innocent and sexy at the same time. The heat that had come with that earlier vibration spread from his stomach in a distinctly southerly direction. Sitting this close, it was impossible to miss the pheromones rolling off her—or to be immune to them.

That's when he knew the night was going to be very special.

"Are you the kind of woman who likes to be wooed?" he asked, his voice sounding a little deeper as his inner wolf attempted to come out and play. He casually looked over at his fingers where they rested on the table to make sure his claws hadn't slipped out. Thankfully, they hadn't.

"All women like to be wooed and charmed and appreciated," she said softly, tilting her head and looking at him in a way that made his inner wolf growl a little louder in hunger. "If the man doing those things is the right man."

He grinned. "I hope I'm the right man."

Triana leaned forward a little. "Well, if it helps, you're definitely on the right track so far."

They were forced to put their flirting on temporary hold as their server arrived to introduce herself and deliver their glasses of wine. The woman gave them the standard pitch about house specials and chef recommendations, but since he and Triana were more interested in each other than in dinner, they ignored all the appetizers, soups, and salads and headed straight for the main entrées. He ordered the filet of beef while Triana chose the sautéed salmon. It wasn't like they could go wrong with anything they picked because everything was good there.

"You never did answer my question," Triana reminded him after the waitress left. "What are your friends up to?"

Remy sipped his wine. "They said something earlier today about heading to the French Quarter again."

"You're not sorry we didn't go out with them, are you?" she asked teasingly. "We could always give them a call and meet up with them later if you want."

His mouth twitched. "No, thanks. I'm good. Don't get me wrong. I'm closer to the members of my SWAT team than most people are with their families, but tonight, I'd much rather spend time with you instead of them."

"Good answer. You really are skilled at this wooing thing," she said with a smile. "But I have to admit, you have me intrigued. I saw the way you guys acted with each other last night, so I could already tell you're tight with them. You obviously spend a lot of time with them outside of work."

"Yeah, I hang out with them a lot," he said, trying to figure out how to put what he wanted to say into words that made sense. It wasn't like he could tell her he was a member of a wolf pack that spent just about every waking minute together. "The men and women on our team are kind of like a family—closer than most families, actually. It's kind of hard to explain, but doing the job we do tends to make for a pretty tight bond."

Triana regarded him over the rim of her wineglass. "There are women on your SWAT team? Do I need to be jealous?"

"I don't know," he said, unable to resist teasing her. "Are you the kind of woman who gets jealous at the idea of a man she's seeing working with another woman?"

She hesitated, seeming to think about it. After a moment, she frowned thoughtfully. "Normally, I'm not. But in this case, I find myself feeling somewhat... possessive."

While there was a part of him that felt a trace of alarm at what Triana's jealousy meant, a more practical portion was quick to point out he'd been a little *possessive* himself a few minutes earlier when half the guys in the dining room had twisted their heads around like Linda Blair in *The Exorcist* to follow Triana's movements across the room. What was good for the goose was good for the gander, as his grandmother used to say.

As to what all that jealousy meant, he and Triana were sexually attracted to each other. The primitive part of them that wanted to get naked and nasty was sure to express itself in other ways, such as in her knee-jerk jealous reaction to him working with women and his desire to bite the men who were ballsy enough to stare at her ass.

"Well, in this case, you have no reason to feel *possessive*," he told her. "There's only one woman on the Dallas SWAT team and she's off-limits. Beyond the fact that I think of her as a sister, she's in a serious, committed relationship with another member of the team. They'd probably be married by now if it wasn't for the fact that they have to hide their relationship from the brass."

Triana did a double take. "Wait a second. Two members of your SWAT team are sleeping together and the rest of you are covering for them?"

He shrugged. "Yeah, pretty much."

Their food came then, interrupting their conversation. Remy was glad, because he definitely didn't want to get into the fact that the only woman on the Dallas SWAT team was in a relationship with her own squad leader. For someone like Triana, who worked in the law enforcement community, that little detail might be difficult to accept. It wasn't as if he could tell Triana that bonding with one's soul mate threw all the normal rules of society straight out the window.

Remy speared a piece of steak with his fork and tasted it. As he'd expected, the food was amazing. Triana seemed to approve of the salmon she'd ordered as well, if the little moan she let out was any indication. As she nibbled another piece of fish off her fork, Remy discovered he enjoyed watching her eat. He was as orally fixated as the next guy, and seeing her lips close over the fork and her mouth move as she slowly chewed was an erotic experience.

Then again, almost anything Triana did would probably be a turn-on, considering he seemed to have it rather bad for her at the moment.

She must have seen him staring at her lips as she chewed, because she gave him a sultry smile. "Are you watching me eat?"

He contemplated denying it but changed his mind. What would be the point?

"Yeah," he admitted. "I hope it doesn't make you uncomfortable. But you have a very sensual mouth and I have a hard time watching it move without thinking all kinds of things I shouldn't be."

"That's a pity," she murmured, returning her attention to her salmon and field pea succotash.

"What's a pity?" he asked, hoping she'd clarify her words. "That I find your mouth so sensual, or that I have completely naughty thoughts when I watch it move?"

Triana lifted her head to look at him, then slowly and carefully ate another bite of fish, clearly savoring it. When she finished up by licking her lips, he was relatively sure everyone in the dining room could hear the thump his hard-on made as it smacked the underside of the table.

"I think it's a pity you don't feel comfortable enough with me to talk about those naughty thoughts," she said as she sipped her wine. "I'd enjoy hearing every one of them in slow, exquisite detail."

Remy's fingers tingled and he quickly slid his hands under the tablecloth to hide the fact that his claws had slipped out. Damn, this woman was dangerous. He flexed his fingers a few times until his claws retracted. *Crisis averted—for now at least.*

"I guess I'll have to be bolder, then," he said. "I'm sure that by the time we have dessert, I won't be able to keep my thoughts to myself anymore."

Triana smiled. "Good, because I thought we could go to Café du Monde for beignets and coffee after dinner. I just love the way that powdered sugar sprinkled over the top of them gets absolutely everywhere."

That vivid image of her covered in powdered sugar was almost enough to have Remy calling for the check. But he resisted, knowing this night of extended verbal foreplay was only getting started. He might have a difficult time walking with an erection, but he had no problem stretching the evening out, if for no other reason than the anticipation would make the end of the night even better. So, as difficult as it was for him to think about anything other than the image of Triana covered in powdered sugar, he did his best to move the conversation toward another topic.

"In a blatant and obvious change of subject, how do you like living and working in Houston?" he asked, spearing another piece of steak.

Triana laughed but otherwise didn't bat an eye, smoothly shifting gears from sultry to casual with the agility of a Ferrari—she'd always possessed a quick and clever mind, even back in high school.

"Well, there's no one in the crime lab sneaking around sleeping together, so it's not as exciting as your team, but I still enjoy it," she said with a smile. "It's extremely satisfying being able to use my science background to do something meaningful."

"Do you ever get a chance to go into the field and work an active crime scene?"

He'd seen techs collecting evidence in the field in Dallas all the time, but he didn't know much about how crime labs were organized in other police departments.

She shrugged. "Sometimes. We have a team of trained crime scene investigators who do most of that work, though. I've had the chance to go out a few times, when there was something special the police wanted us to check for or if investigators wanted us to actually conduct a test in the field. But to tell the truth, I prefer the safe and cozy confines of my lab. Call me a wuss, but I'm an analyst, not a cop."

Remy laughed. "That's not being a wuss. That's being smart."

They talked some more about the kind of work she did before moving on to other personal topics, such as where she lived, what she did for fun, and what her social life was like.

"Is that your roundabout way of asking me if I'm dating anyone?" she asked in a playful tone.

He put on a shocked expression even though she was right. He hadn't intended to ask her something like that, but it had kind of slipped out.

"Of course not," he lied. "I would never ask anything so personal. I'm just concerned you might be one of those scientist types who's always getting so wrapped up in their work that they forget to take care of themselves."

The smile she gave him made him think she wasn't buying it. "Well, that's really sweet of you to worry about me like that, but you don't need to. There's a lawyer in Houston I see on and off. It's nothing serious, but he keeps me from getting too wrapped up in work."

Remy couldn't help wondering if she was messing with him just to get a reaction. Well, it worked. He and Triana were merely hanging out for the week while they were in New Orleans, and yet he was bothered by the idea of her with another guy. Feeling a little spike of jealousy when anonymous men watched her walk across the room was one thing, but getting pissed at a man she might or might not be seeing, even on and off, was insane.

Maybe so, but the sensation was there, and it was frigging real. Suddenly, he was sorry he'd asked her the question in the first place. It had been better not knowing.

"What about you?" Triana asked, setting her fork and knife on her empty plate. "Is there anyone back in Dallas you see now and then to get your mind off work?"

Alarm bells went off as Triana's flirty tone changed to something more serious. He realized he was about to step into a potential minefield and there was nothing he could do about it.

"Me?" He shook his head. "No, I'm not really seeing anyone seriously at the moment. In fact, I haven't been on a date in a long time."

Remy held his breath, expecting Triana to call him out. It wasn't that he was lying. He honestly hadn't been on a date in years—but that was only because he tended to limit his social contact to women who didn't use the word *date*. *Hookup* was probably a better term to go with, though he doubted Triana would appreciate the difference.

"Good answer," she said with a smile. "Ready for those beignets now?"

———

As they walked out of Muriel's and headed for Café du Monde, Triana's legs felt a little wobbly. So okay, she was turned on. She supposed an hour and a half of nearly nonstop flirting could do that to a girl. She'd gone out with guys who could talk a good game before, but nothing like Remy. Bottom line, the man possessed a way with words that made her think he could make her panties wet simply by reading a dictionary to her.

Between his clever banter and smooth-as-honey voice, she was ready to skip dessert and head straight to the nearest available horizontal surface. Heck, she wasn't even sure if the horizontal part was a definite requirement. She could think of a few standing positions that might work just as well.

It was only a short walk to Café du Monde, but they took their time anyway, slowly strolling hand-in-hand along the edges of Jackson Square, admiring the artwork set out for sale along the sidewalk. Triana discovered she and Remy had similar taste in art, both of them drawn to bold colors and strong lines. She wasn't surprised. It was becoming more obvious to her with every passing moment that there was a serious connection between her and Remy. A few days ago, she would have said the idea was crazy, but right then, she had to admit maybe her mother was right. Maybe the magic of New Orleans had had a hand in bringing her and Remy together after so many years apart.

From the moment Remy had picked her up that night, Triana had felt the crazy sexual spark that seemed to exist between them growing brighter. Within seconds of coming downstairs, she'd gotten all warm and tingly. From that point on, every touch, every heated glance, every innuendo-filled sentence had only turned her on more. Right then, she was more aroused than she'd ever been in her life. As turned on as she was, she could almost believe Remy could actually give her an orgasm without ever touching her. In theory, something like that shouldn't be scientifically possible. Then again, science couldn't explain just how perfect Remy Boudreaux was, either.

As they stopped to admire another street vendor's artwork, Triana glanced at Remy, unable to help herself. With that dark-blond hair, those expressive hazel eyes, and his square jaw with just a hint of stubble, he was more attractive than any man she'd ever met, not to mention had a body that was so well-built it was practically sinful. He was also fun to hang out with, interesting to talk to, and unbelievably charming. Individually, any of those qualities would have been enough to make Remy amazing; but beyond all of those, there was something else about him that made her want to swoon like the Southern belles of olden days. She couldn't quite put her finger on what it was or even understand it. All she knew for sure was that Remy was perfect for her.

Café du Monde was open twenty-four hours a day, seven days a week, and since it was a popular tourist attraction, it was usually also extremely crowded. However, in what had to be the strangest customer service concept on the planet, they expected people to find their own tables. There were multiple entrances into the covered seating area with signs everywhere pointing that out. Yet, while many locals walked in and found their own tables, most of the tourists found a line and got in it. Fortunately, the lines weren't too long at the moment, so Triana didn't feel too bad about grabbing a table while the tourists stood there waiting for someone to tell them what to do.

The moment she and Remy sat, a waitress came over to grab the plates, mugs, and money left by the previous customers, then took their orders.

"Two orders of beignets," Remy said to the waitress, then looked at Triana. "Hot milk?" When she nodded, Remy finished their order. "Two coffees. One *au lait*, one black with sugar."

The waitress nodded but didn't write anything down. No notepads or menus at Café du Monde—it wasn't that kind of place. After the woman left, Triana couldn't help smiling at Remy. "So you like your coffee strong, black, and sweet, huh?"

He returned her smile with a sexy grin. "I'm not even going there."

She laughed. He was no fun. She'd really wanted to tease him about the connection between his taste in coffee and women. She rested her forearms on the small table and leaned closer. "I'm surprised you agreed to come here for dessert."

"Why are you surprised? I love this place."

She shrugged and reached out to trace a finger over one of his bulging biceps, enjoying his sudden intake of breath. Not only did it let her know that he liked it when she touched him, but it also made his pecs flex under his shirt.

"It seems obvious you work out a lot." She ran her finger down the rolled-up sleeve of his button-down, along his strong forearm, all the way to the top of his big hand. "I thought you might worry about blowing your diet and all."

He chuckled, flipping his hand over so fast she didn't see it move, capturing hers and caressing it casually with his thumb. "Are you kidding? I'm a cop. I practically live on doughnuts."

She lifted a brow, seriously doubting that. "Yeah right," she laughed. "Next, you'll be telling me you have Dunkin' Donuts on speed dial."

Triana was pretty sure he hadn't eaten a doughnut, or any other kind of junk food, since high school. His kitchen probably didn't have anything in it but whole grains and protein shakes. She was okay with that, especially if it gave him a body like the one he had.

"As a matter fact…" Remy let the words trail off as he glided the fingers of his other hand up and down her forearm. His touch made her skin tingle everywhere—and she did mean everywhere. She would have squirmed in her chair, but he was holding her hand too firmly.

Did he even realize how much she enjoyed what he was doing? Probably not. Guys could be so oblivious.

"So you're not worried about your diet at all, huh?" she managed.

The light from the streetlamp outside caught his eyes, making them glint gold. "Something tells me I'm going to be working off a lot of calories before the night is over."

She lifted an eyebrow. "Really? Are you going jogging or something?"

Triana couldn't help teasing him just a little. Verbally fencing with Remy was such a heady turn-on.

"Or something." His mouth quirked. "I'm not sure exactly what I'll be doing, but I have no doubt it will be strenuous, get my heart rate going, and probably last most of the night."

"That sounds like a lot of exercise."

He gave her a slow, sexy grin. "When I exercise, I like it to last for a very long time."

The thought made Triana's breath catch. Oh yeah, Remy could definitely flirt better than any other man she'd ever met.

"Maybe we can exercise together, then," she murmured softly. "I love a long, exhausting workout myself."

Remy opened his mouth to say something, but the waitress appeared with a tray of beignets and cups of coffee. Café du Monde apparently owned stock in powdered sugar because they absolutely drowned their doughy treats in the stuff. Some might consider it a ridiculous amount of sugar. Triana thought it was perfect.

As she and Remy ate, they talked about how much Remy and his teammates from Dallas actually worked out. He claimed they maintained the bodies they had with as little as two hours of exercise per day.

"Sometimes we lift weights when there isn't much going on around the compound," he added. "But that's pretty rare."

True to his word, Remy ate all three of the beignets on his plate and two of Triana's. She gladly let him, because while he supposedly didn't have to work very hard to look the way he did, she certainly did. If she was going to be *exercising* later, she didn't want to do it on a full stomach. Besides, if she'd be getting naked with a man who looked like Remy, she wanted to measure up.

She'd finished the last of her beignet and was sipping her coffee when Remy smiled and motioned at her mouth.

"You have a little powdered sugar on your lips," he said.

She blushed. Of course she did. It was impossible to eat beignets at Café du Monde and not get sugar everywhere. She quickly grabbed one of the little paper napkins the waitress had given them and patted it over her lips, then gave Remy an embarrassed smile.

"Better?"

"Not quite," he said. "Here, let me."

She expected him to reach over and dab at her lips with a napkin. Instead, he leaned over and kissed her. Not one of those sweet, innocent, we're-in-public kind of pecks, but one that made her quiver all over.

Triana slid her fingers into his short hair, pulling him closer and returning the kiss with all the passion and arousal that had been building the entire evening. She moaned softly as Remy's tongue slipped into her mouth. The sweetness from the sugar and beignets along with the spice from the coffee and chicory all mixed with his unique masculine flavor, and the combination was intoxicating.

When he finally lifted his head, he hesitated just a moment to swipe his tongue over the corner of her lips, making sure he got all the powdered sugar off. Not that she cared why he did it. By then she was so aroused she was ready to climb onto his lap and devour him.

Triana gripped the edge of the table, holding on to it for dear life as she fought to get herself under control. She'd never been kissed like that before, and while she wasn't completely sure if it was possible to orgasm from a kiss, it was pretty darn close.

"So, did that do it?" she asked softly, and she sure as hell wasn't referring to getting all the powdered sugar off her lips.

Remy's hazel eyes glinted. "Yeah, it did. Are you ready to get out of here now?"

She smiled. "Finally. I thought you'd never ask."

Chapter 6

TRIANA DIDN'T REMEMBER MUCH ABOUT THE WALK ACROSS the French Quarter with Remy. She vaguely recalled stopping along the way to make out a few times. Okay, maybe more than a few. Overall, she was very proud that she was able to keep her hands mostly to herself until they reached his hotel. Her willpower gave out on the elevator ride up to his fourteenth-floor room. The moment the doors closed on the lobby level, she was in his arms kissing him.

Remy buried one hand in her hair even as the other slid down her back to pull her closer. She sighed as his hard-on pressed against her tummy through their clothes. It made her feel insanely good knowing she was getting to him the same way he was getting to her. She wanted him so badly right then it hurt.

Refusing to be a passive player in their game, Triana reached up and twisted her fingers in his hair, yanking his mouth down harder onto hers, tangling her tongue with his and giving as good as she got. As they kissed, she let her free hand roam over his shoulders and down the front of his shirt, thrilled at the feeling of his strength under her fingers.

In the space between two heartbeats, Remy urged her backward until she was up against the wall of the elevator. His hardness was even more evident in this position and she moaned at the thought of what he would look like naked.

The hand that had been on her back moved slowly down her hip, until it was sliding up and down her right thigh, teasing her little yellow dress up higher and higher. Remy could have yanked the thing off if he'd wanted and she wouldn't have stopped him.

But just as she felt the tips of his warm, strong fingers on the bare skin of her thigh, the elevator suddenly stopped with a ding. She barely had time to understand what was going on before Remy pulled down her dress and broke the kiss, then spun her around so she was standing in front of him. A moment later, the doors slid open and an elderly couple stepped onto the elevator. The couple smiled at them, thankfully oblivious to what had just been taking place a few seconds earlier.

She waited for the couple to press the button for their floor, but they merely stood there as the elevator went up. That was when she realized the couple was riding up to the fourteen floor with them. At the same time, it also dawned on her that Remy had positioned her in front of him to hide his erection, which was currently poking her in the bottom.

She probably should have been on her best behavior since there was another couple around, but she couldn't resist teasing him a little by pressing her ass against his obvious arousal. Then she wiggled a bit to make sure he wouldn't miss it.

Remy let out what sounded suspiciously like a growl. It was soft and his nose was buried in her hair, but she heard it. Judging by their expressions as the doors of the elevator opened on the fourteenth floor, the older couple heard it too. They quickly exited and turned left, while Remy took Triana's hand and urged her to the right.

His room was at the end of the hall. One fast swipe of the key card and they were inside. Remy locked the door behind them and flicked on the lights, then pinned her against the nearest wall.

"You are so naughty," he murmured, his mouth tracing along her jaw, driving her crazy and making her tremble all over.

"I know," she breathed. "I couldn't stop myself. For some reason, I don't seem to have much control over myself when you're around."

He pulled back and looked at her for a long moment, then flashed her a sexy smile. "I can't say that's a bad thing, necessarily, at least from my perspective."

Triana opened her mouth to say something witty in reply, but his warm mouth came down on her neck and started to nibble before she could. She rested her head back against the wall with a moan, then quickly bit her lip as she remembered they were in a hotel full of people. She was going to have to keep the noise to a minimum.

Remy clearly wasn't going to make it easy on her, she thought, inhaling sharply as he nipped her shoulder with his teeth. Okay, she'd never had a guy do that before. But as tingles of pleasure rippled through the rest of her body, she decided she'd been missing out.

She wasn't sure when Remy got his hands on the hem of her sundress, but one moment he was doing crazy things to her neck, and the next he was dragging the material over her head. He was even able to get her tiny purse off her shoulder without tying her up in it. Before she knew it, she was standing in the entryway of his hotel room wearing nothing but her skimpy bra, a tiny pair of panties, and her strappy high heels.

She was about to make a comment about him being as smooth at undressing her as he was at talking, but the words got stuck in her throat when she caught sight of the hunger on his face. He looked like he wanted to eat her up.

She started to reach behind her back for the clasp on her bra, more than ready to get completely naked in front of him, but Remy caught her hand.

"Not yet," he said. "I want to look at you."

She should have been self-conscious standing there against the wall in her underwear while a guy ogled her, but the way Remy gazed at her, drinking her in like she was the most beautiful woman in the world, made her believe she actually was.

Locking eyes with her, he stepped closer and leaned one hand against the wall beside her head. A playful smile curving his mouth, he lifted his free hand and traced a finger down her half-naked body, starting at her neck, then gliding along the edges of her delicate bra, before skimming over her taut abs to tease the waistband of her panties. She sagged into the wall, her body pulsing all over from his touch.

When Remy finally took her hand and led her over to the bed, Triana realized she'd never been more ready to sleep with anyone.

She generally followed a basic rule when it came to having sex with a guy. It wasn't as rigid as one of those three-date things, though. She simply liked to get to know a man before letting sex cloud the situation.

But she had known Remy long before running into him at that club last night. In some crazy way, it was like she'd been waiting for this moment since high school. The idea that they needed to slow down and take their time was silly. If anything, she was kicking herself for not looking Remy up years ago. If she had, she could have been with this amazing guy all along.

When they stopped by the bed, Triana unbuttoned his shirt, dragging it out of his pants at the same time, then tossing it aside. Remembering how he'd gazed at her earlier, she took her time admiring the perfection that was Remy Boudreaux.

Damn, he was sinfully gorgeous.

Triana moved closer, slowly running her hands over his thick pecs, sculpted deltoids, and oh-so-lickable abs, then back up again. She slowed so she could examine the tattoo on the left side of his chest. He was so tall that it was practically at eye level for her. The tattoo was a shaggy-headed wolf with intense eyes. Above the wolf, the word *SWAT* stood out in strong, bold letters. Even though she knew very little about tattoos, she knew enough to recognize that this one was exquisitely done.

She leaned forward to trace her lips along the lines of the wolf-head tattoo, smiling as his muscles trembled in response to her touch. Clearly he liked it when she did that. She'd have to make a note of it.

While the SWAT part of the ink was self-explanatory, she wasn't quite sure what the wolf represented. She opened her mouth to ask him what the deal was with it when she caught sight of a scar on the right side of his chest, almost directly above his nipple. There was a star-shaped indentation in the middle with three long, straight lines radiating from the center of it.

As she moved closer—disguising her inspection by kissing and nibbling along the way—she realized the lines had tiny, almost imperceptible dots on either side of them. Working in a medical examiner's office, she immediately recognized the dots as marks left by surgical staples.

She was tempted to ask him when the injury had occurred but decided against it. Now was definitely not the best time to discuss a subject like that, not when they were in the process of getting naked and naughty.

Setting her curiosity aside for the moment, she focused her attention on the man in front of her instead of his scar. That wasn't difficult to do. Remy was absolutely mesmerizing.

Gliding her hands down his abs, she got her fingers in his belt and began unbuckling it. He helped, kicking off his shoes and shoving down his pants.

She was pleased to see that his legs were just as muscular and sexy as the rest of him. In fact, there wasn't an inch of him that wasn't hunky. If the bulge in his underwear was any indication, things were only going to get better.

With a groan, Remy tugged her close and kissed her, his mouth making her dizzy as his hands slipped around behind her to undo the hooks on her bra. The garment went sailing and then she was reveling in the sensation of her sensitive nipples rubbing against his muscular chest.

She was so busy moaning against his mouth she almost missed it when his hands slid down her back and skimmed her panties over her hips. If it wasn't for the wetness grazing the inside of her thighs as the tiny scrap of material fell to the floor, she probably wouldn't even have known she was completely naked.

Remy's big hands returned to her ass, squeezing and massaging, making her whimper. She pulled away to look at him. "Okay, full disclosure time. I really like when you touch my butt."

He gave her a wicked smile as he tightened his grip on her bottom. "I'll definitely keep that in mind."

Drunk from his kisses, Triana melted against him, loving the feel of his strong hands exploring her body. But as he teased her breasts, then went back to caressing her ass again, it occurred to her that she was being selfish. How fair was it for her to be getting all the attention, while Remy's poor shaft was still trapped in his underwear? It was time to give him as much pleasure as he was giving her.

Pulling away, she dropped to her knees in front of him. Without a word, she hooked her fingers in the waistband of his boxer briefs and carefully slid them down over his erection. It took a little work, since they clearly hadn't been intended to contain everything Remy was packing. But with care and patience, she was finally able to set him completely free.

After she had his underwear all the way down his thighs, she took the opportunity to sit back on her heels and take him all in. Remy's cock was long, thick, and more beautiful than she could ever have imagined. It throbbed and pulsed in front of her, and as she watched, a glistening little bead formed at the tip, beckoning her forward.

Triana reached out and wrapped her fingers around

the base of his shaft, rubbing her hand up and down his length a few times before leaning forward to take him in her mouth.

Remy let out what sounded like a growl as she dipped her head, taking him as deep as she could. She moaned in appreciation as his masculine essence coated her tongue. She'd never tasted anything like that in her life... It was almost intoxicating in its effect on her.

She slid her mouth up to the tip, then back down, alternating between deep-throating and quick little butterfly flicks of her tongue along the underside of his sensitive head. Remy slid his fingers into her hair, urging her on.

Triana had intended to simply tease him to show him just how much she enjoyed all the things he'd been doing to her, but now that she was down there, she didn't want to stop. The idea of getting to taste all of him was definitely enticing, especially since she'd get to make him hard all over again. Was there anything not great about that?

But as she tightened her hand around his shaft, working it up and down in rhythm with her mouth, Remy apparently decided he wasn't going to let her have her way. One moment, she was kneeling on the floor with him in her mouth; the next, he was tugging her to her feet and spinning her around to face the bed. A split second later, he wrapped her big, strong arms around her, trapping her against his chest...and his extremely hard cock.

She stilled as she felt his hardness pressing against the top of her ass and lower back and pulsing with arousal. Slowly turning her head, she looked over her shoulder, catching sight of him out of the corner of her eye. Her breath caught at the hungry, almost predatory look on his face. She'd been going to say something witty about how it was impolite to interrupt a woman while she was working, but one look at the expression on his face changed her mind.

Foreplay was over, and things were about to get very serious.

"There are condoms in my purse," she whispered softly.

Remy nodded but made no move to let her go. Instead, he glided one hand up her belly to cup her left breast while the other moved around to slip between her legs.

Triana let her head fall back against his chest, gasping as he began to tease her nipple and clit at the same time. Her body's response to his touch was immediate and intense, catching her completely off guard. A few little circles of his finger on that most sensitive part of her anatomy made her tingle like crazy. The way he squeezed her nipple and massaged her breast only made the sensation that much more intense, and within moments, she felt like she was on the verge of coming.

But just as she was about to climax, Remy stopped. She opened her mouth to complain, but before she could say anything, she felt a hand on her shoulder, nudging her forward until she was bent over at the waist. She automatically placed her hands on the mattress, which put her in the most provocative position possible.

Triana threw a glance over her shoulder to see Remy regarding her with a serious smolder in his eyes. If she hadn't known any better, she'd have thought they were about to glow.

She gave him a sexy smile. "See something you like back there?"

The corners of Remy's mouth edged up. "Definitely."

Stepping closer, he trailed a hand up her outer thigh, then along her right hip, and across the curve of her bottom. He traced his fingers over each cheek, making her skin tingle and her legs tremble. Soon enough, the light caresses became a sensual massage, and she let out a husky moan.

Behind her, Remy chuckled softly. "You weren't kidding when you said you liked me to touch your ass, were you?"

All she could do was shake her head. Between the light, teasing caresses and firm, possessive squeezes, words were beyond her right then. And when Remy wasn't doing either of those things, he'd slip his fingers down to play with her pussy. He was teasing her so much she was surprised she wasn't a puddle on the floor already.

Triana was so caught up in the pleasure of the moment that she barely realized he'd slipped away to grab the condom until she heard him tear the foil wrapper. She glanced over her shoulder, watching as he got himself ready. She wondered for a moment if she should climb up on the bed, but the hunger in Remy's eyes as he looked at her gave her all the answer she needed. He wanted to take her just like this, and that was exactly what she wanted too.

Stepping up behind her, Remy got a tight grip on her hips, holding her steady as he positioned himself at her wet opening. He moved carefully, almost gently, making sure she was completely ready for him as he slowly slid in. She gasped as his thickness spread her wide, making her legs tremble and her body quiver.

"Yes," she breathed.

Instead of plunging deep, Remy pulled out a little, giving her several short, almost tender thrusts, going deeper each time. While it felt spectacular, it was also a sweet torture. Triana bit her lip to keep from screaming in frustration. She'd been ready for him since they'd walked into the room and she was in no mood to be treated gently.

Triana reached back with one hand, trying to grab his hip and encourage him to thrust harder, but Remy chuckled and caught her wrist in one of his big hands, gently but firmly pinning it behind her back, continuing his slow movements.

"Patience, Triana," he murmured softly. "We're just getting started."

She threw him an exasperated look over her shoulder. "I thought you would have remembered from back in high school that I've never had patience with anything."

"Then it's a good time to start, because I'm not rushing this, no matter how much you want me to," Remy told her.

Since words weren't going to sway him, Triana went with another tactic—shoving back unexpectedly and sending his cock nice and deep.

Remy groaned. "You are so bad."

He released her wrist so he could grip her hips in both hands again. Then he slid out a little. He probably thought he could control her movements better that way.

"Maybe you just bring out the bad in me," she said, planting her hands firmly on the mattress and thrusting back again.

With his strong hands grasping her hips, the move didn't work as well this time, but it was still enough to sink another inch or two of his hard shaft inside her, eliciting another groan from Remy. He tightened his hold on her hips, trying to keep her under control.

Like that was going to happen.

Triana opened her mouth to tell him as much, but all that came out was a gasp as he slid out and plunged back in, burying himself fully inside her and touching places she hadn't even known existed.

That felt ah-mazing.

"So, you think I bring out your inner bad girl, huh?"

Remy's voice was low, almost rough, in her ear, and she realized that he'd leaned over when she hadn't been paying attention. She'd been so focused on the overwhelming sensations racing through her that she hadn't even felt him move. But as his warm breath stirred her hair, she felt goose bumps spring up all over her body.

"Yes," she told him softly. "It's all your fault."

He chuckled. "Well, if that's the case, maybe I should see just how bad you can be."

Triana didn't answer. She had no idea what he meant by that, but she was more than willing to find out.

Straightening up, Remy jerked his cock out and plunged all the way back in, thrusting so hard that his hips smacked against her ass with an audible sound. Triana cried out her pleasure, clutching the blanket as he began to pound into her over and over so deliciously hard that stars sparkled behind her closed eyes.

Her body wasn't simply tingling now. It was ablaze. It wasn't just the feel of his cock inside her, though that was definitely enough to make her lose her mind. There was also the erotic sensation of his strong hands holding her captive and the sting of his hips smacking against her ass, not to mention the animalistic sounds Remy made. All of those things came together to shove her toward an orgasm that she instinctively knew was going to be more powerful than anything she'd ever experienced.

When her climax finally hit, it wasn't gradual and it wasn't tame. It was like a tidal wave, and for a moment, Triana feared it might wash her away. But at the same time, she reveled in pleasure so overwhelming and pure that she nearly cried at its beauty and intensity.

The crest peaked, then rose even higher, going on and on until her arms gave out and she was forced to bury her face in the blanket and cry out as her body spasmed in pure bliss.

She lost track of time for a while. Hell, she lost track of everything. But at some point after her orgasm subsided, she felt Remy slide out and pick her up in his arms.

She got her bearings back about the time her ass came down on something hard. She looked around and realized she was sitting on the low dresser on the other side of the room from the bed. Remy was standing between her spread legs with a hungry expression on his face that told her they weren't done yet. Triana glanced down and saw that he was still hard.

He scooted her to the edge of the dresser and spread her legs wide, moving closer at the same time. The dresser put her at the perfect height for him to stand there and slide in. Even better, in this position, they'd be able to gaze into each other's eyes the entire time.

Damn, he was good.

Remy's eyes never left hers as he lifted her legs a bit, so he could get his cock exactly where he wanted it, then nudged himself inside until he was once again buried deep. Her breath hitched. This position felt so completely different than being bent over the bed. Triana wrapped her legs around his hips and locked her ankles together behind his back, squeezing him tightly and pulling him in even more.

He didn't thrust right away. Instead, he slid his hand into her long hair, brushing it away from her face and tracing the edge of his thumb along her jawline.

"Do you have any idea how gorgeous you are?" he whispered softly.

Triana could only shake her head, overwhelmed at the sincerity in his eyes. She had never felt more beautiful in her whole life than she did at that moment.

He leaned forward and kissed her, his mouth capturing hers, then trailing along her jaw and over to her ear as he began to pump in and out of her pussy in a gentle rocking motion.

Even though she'd just had the strongest orgasm of her life not more than five minutes ago, Triana quickly discovered that her body was ready for more. Even these slow, measured thrusts were enough to make her tingle all over again.

Remy took his time, his hand tightening in her hair as he closed his mouth over hers and kissed her nearly senseless. She gave as good as she got, sometimes letting her tongue tangle with his, other times nibbling his neck and shoulder, something he seemed to like if the sounds he was making were any indication.

All at once, Remy began to move faster. Triana

gripped the front edge of the dresser and tightened her legs around his waist, holding on for dear life as the dresser thumped against the wall of the hotel. *Please let the room next door be empty*, she prayed. She really didn't want this moment interrupted.

She was in heaven as another orgasm approached, but then her entire definition of heaven was readjusted when Remy reached down and grabbed her ass with both hands, then jerked her a few inches off the dresser and pounded into her.

When Remy buried his face into the curve where her neck met her shoulder and said her name long and low in her ear, that trumped any orgasm high she'd ever had— even the one she'd experienced a few minutes ago.

She felt Remy tense inside her, felt his hands grip her ass harder as he poured himself into her. Something melted inside her then. She couldn't really describe it any other way, but she knew this moment was going to be special for the rest of her life.

It was a bizarre and likely lust-induced feeling that made absolutely no sense. Yet she was sure of its significance all the same.

Remy half groaned, half growled, slamming into her a few more times and extending both of their orgasms just a little bit further. Knowing she was giving him as much pleasure as he was giving her brought tears to her eyes.

They stayed like that for a long time, neither of them saying a word, before Remy finally carried her to the big bed. As he set her down on it, something told her they weren't going to be doing much sleeping in it that night. That was more than fine with her.

Chapter 7

TRYING TO FOCUS ON ANYTHING AT FOUR THIRTY IN THE morning was difficult enough, but trying to pay attention to what the weatherman on the TV was saying about Ophelia while Triana was lying in his bed naked made it damn near impossible. One look was all it took to remind him of the night they'd shared.

Dinner at Muriel's had been amazing and the beignets at Café du Monde had been even better. But while those things had been spectacular, they took a backseat to what happened after they'd come back here. Flat out, he'd never had a night like last night. He'd slept with plenty of other women before but never with a woman like Triana. Even now, he tried to find words to describe their connection and failed.

Simply put, she clicked with him sexually like no one else ever had. She was energetic, enthusiastic, adventurous, and insatiable. It was like they were a perfect match, and if it wasn't for the fact that he had to get to the NOPD SWAT facility early, the two of them would probably still be making love. How the hell had he missed such a remarkable woman when she'd been right under his nose all those years ago? He must have been blind—or stupid.

"Do these people seriously get paid for this?" Triana asked. She was on her side, her head propped up on one hand, a corner of the bedsheet strategically covering absolutely nothing. "The guy just confessed to not having a clue what the storm's going to do."

Remy couldn't answer the question. He was standing there with a toothbrush sticking out of his mouth, staring, so he tore his gaze away from Triana's display of sexy brown skin and attempted to focus on the TV.

In a way, he kind of felt sorry for the people responsible for predicting where Ophelia was heading. As far as Remy could tell, this storm wasn't following the rules. It was still wandering aimlessly in a westerly direction, but mostly it seemed to be stuck. The only thing the weather experts could say for sure was that the storm was getting stronger. Other than that, they were baffled.

The hell with the frigging weather. Remy had to get to work, storm or no storm. Going into the bathroom, he rinsed the toothpaste out of his mouth and shoved the electric razor around his jaw for a bit before heading back to the bedroom so he could rummage through the dresser for underwear and socks. Since it happened to be the same dresser he and Triana had made love on last night, it was difficult to think about something as mundane as socks, but he forced himself to focus before he got too hard to put on his damn underwear.

Triana didn't make it any easier, choosing that particular moment to stretch, rolling around on the bed and arching her back like a kitty.

Stifling a groan, he turned his back on her, then dragged a pair of uniform cargos out of the closet and pulled them on. At least they were looser in the crotch than the jeans he'd had on last night. He pulled on the standard, dark-blue DPD SWAT T-shirt, then his socks and boots.

His car keys were in the room safe, but it took a while to find his wallet and room key card, which were on the floor by the front door. How the hell had that happened?

He patted the front right pocket of his cargos, realizing he was missing something. Frowning, he went in search of the jeans he'd been wearing the night before. Where the hell had he kicked them?

Triana laughed as he got down on his hands and knees and pulled them out from under the bed. Getting to his feet, he dug through the pockets and immediately found what he was after—a small, tan bag made out of chamois material and tied with a complicated knot at the top. A series of runes and letters were inscribed on one side of the bag. Well, they used to be. Now the marks were mostly faded.

"I can't believe you're still carrying the gris-gris bag my mom gave you," Triana said, coming up on her knees and leaning forward to peek at it.

Remy slipped the good luck charm in the right pocket of his uniform pants. "I never go anywhere without it."

Her eyes widened. "You've been carrying it every day since Mom gave it to you the day we graduated high school?"

He hesitated, almost telling her there had been a three-year period when he'd been in the Marshals that he'd gotten out of the habit. But that was too long of a story to get into—and too depressing. So he fibbed a little.

"Pretty much. Yeah."

Triana eyed him skeptically. "You don't believe in all this voodoo magic stuff, do you? You're a cop. You know better than anyone that there's no magic out there. There's just good guys, bad guys, and science."

He chuckled. Triana had always been into the science behind everything. If she couldn't see it or prove it with an experiment, she wasn't much for it. She'd always humored her mother about the stuff Gemma sold at the shop, but she'd never bought into it.

He shrugged, wondering what she'd do if she figured out he was a werewolf. Probably draw blood and look for a cure. "Don't be so sure of that. Take it from me, the world is a lot stranger than you might think. The moment you're sure you've seen it all, you run into someone who will prove you wrong."

Remy expected her to laugh, but instead, she looked thoughtful. "Funny you should say that, considering the guy who showed up in the shop yesterday."

"What guy?" he asked, checking his duffel bag to make sure he had all his tactical gear as well as another uniform to change into if he needed it.

Triana sat back on her heels with a sigh. "Same whack job lawyer looking for the necklace with the wolf head my father used to wear all the time. Apparently he represents some rich guy who wants to remain anonymous and offered my mom five thousand dollars for the thing."

"Whoa."

Remy remembered the necklace Triana was talking about, but he was pretty sure it wasn't worth anywhere near that kind of money.

"Yeah, no kidding." Triana gracefully climbed out of bed and padded over to him. "The funny thing is, Mom claimed she didn't know what necklace the guy was talking about."

"You think your mom has the necklace and just doesn't want to sell it?" he asked, trying to distract himself from the fact that Triana was still gloriously naked.

She shrugged, which did rather amazing things to her perfect breasts. "Maybe."

"Is that so surprising? I mean, it was your father's. I imagine it's probably important to your mother for obvious sentimental reasons."

Triana nodded. "Oh, I get that part. Hell, even if it wasn't, I wouldn't want her selling to the guy, because he came off as an arrogant prick. No, the part that struck me as strange was why someone is willing to spend that much money on a necklace, not to mention send a smarmy lawyer to be his mouthpiece."

Remy opened his mouth to reply, but Triana chose that moment to stand up on her tiptoes, wrap her arms around his neck, and kiss him. He'd already been aroused simply from being near her sexy, naked body, but the moment her lips touched his and he got a taste of her, he went from semi-erect to hard as a crowbar. He put his arms around her, fitting her more tightly against him. Damn, she was a walking, talking aphrodisiac.

"So, what do you have planned for today?" she asked, smiling up at him. "More training?"

What she was really asking was whether he'd be going out on any more drug raids. Remy knew he probably should have been honest and told Triana that was always a possibility, but he couldn't do that to her. She was obviously relaxed and happy after last night and there was no reason to bum her out.

"Yeah," he said casually. "We ran the training yesterday, so today the local guys are up. I think they plan on demonstrating some new room-clearing techniques based on a three-person team."

Triana nodded, though Remy could tell she had no idea what he was talking about. She seemed relieved he wasn't going to be putting himself at risk today. That was good enough for him.

"Well, have fun…I guess." She kissed him again, making him burn with the need to taste even more of her. "You want to get together tonight?"

He grinned, sliding his hands down her back until he had a handful of ass cheek in each. Her bottom should have been listed as a New Orleans work of art. It simply defined perfection.

"That's a clown question, and you know it," he told her. "I'm up for anything you might have in mind."

She rubbed her tummy against the hard-on hidden in his uniform pants. "Yes, you are, aren't you? But I was actually talking about going out to the French Quarter again. I blew off a night out with my girlfriends last night and was hoping you'd be willing to come out with us so I could make it up to them while still spending time with you too."

"Works for me," he said. "My teammates probably wouldn't mind coming, if that's okay with you?"

Actually, he wasn't really sure about that last part, but if he needed his pack mates to pull wingman duty, they'd do it.

Triana smiled. "It's a date then." She nodded down at his crotch. "You sure there isn't something I could do to help you out with that before you go to work? I can work fast when I need to."

He groaned at the visual and almost gave in, but then

resisted the urge. If last night proved anything, it was that once they got going, they didn't want to stop.

"You don't know how much I'd love to, but if I don't get downstairs, the guys are going to come banging on the door." He caught a stray curl from where it rested against her breast and twirled it around his finger. "Rain check."

She looked disappointed but nodded.

"Feel free to stay here and catch up on some sleep if you want," he said. "I'll put the Do Not Disturb sign on the door."

"I probably will." Triana grimaced. "This is a crazy time to be getting up for work anyway."

Before she let him go, she pulled his head down once more for another kiss, this time slow and passionate.

"By the way," she said softly, "in case you didn't notice, last night was fantastic—and I don't just mean once we got back here to your room. Cross my heart, I've never had a better date in my life."

Remy weaved a hand into her hair and tugged her in for a kiss that he hoped spoke volumes about how much he agreed. "Best. Date. Ever."

"Something tells me tonight will be even better," she said.

Smiling, Triana turned and headed for the bathroom, putting a little extra wiggle in her walk as she went—probably to punish him for leaving without taking her up on the offer of a quickie.

"Later, sweetie," she said over her shoulder.

Remy watched her ass until it completely disappeared from sight, then grabbed his duffel bag and left the room.

Halfway down the hall, he stopped in midstride as he realized how painful it was to leave Triana. His inner wolf shouted at him to go back, even if only for one more kiss. Damn, he'd known the sexual chemistry between them was intense, but it was stronger than he knew—more powerful than anything he'd ever felt before. He supposed that was what happened when you finally made love with the girl you'd been crushing on since high school.

Giving himself a mental shake, he started down the hall again.

Remy smelled the guys waiting for him long before he reached the elevators. Max, Brooks, and Zane were standing there with knowing looks on their faces.

"Good night?" Max asked as he pressed the button for the elevator.

"Good enough," Remy said noncommittally.

Brooks snorted as the elevator doors slid open. "Dude, you are so full of shit."

Triana left Remy's hotel room and headed toward the diner on Magazine Street a little after nine that morning. While the sky might have still been bright and clear, the threat of the storm in the Gulf was starting to have a visible effect on the inhabitants of the city. It was hard to put into words, but she could feel the tension in the air as people walked along the sidewalks a little bit faster, smiled a little bit less. People were getting worried, and it was starting to show.

She stopped in the entryway of the crowded restaurant, looking for Marcus Bodine, the private investigator she'd hired, and spotted him sitting at a booth in the back, eating breakfast. She wasn't sure how he knew she was there, but he glanced up and made eye contact the moment she walked in, motioning her over.

She'd just gotten out of the shower when Bodine had called, saying he wanted to meet with her as soon as possible. He had something she needed to see. Triana barely remembered putting on her dress, she'd moved so fast.

Weaving her way through the tables, Triana slid into the booth on the other side of the table from Bodine and flagged down a passing waitress.

"Coffee and whole wheat toast," she said.

While the diner made a delicious breakfast, her stomach was too jumpy to consider anything heavier. For the first time in months, there was a chance she'd finally learn something about the man who'd killed her father.

"Sure you don't want something else to eat?" Bodine said. "My treat. I swear I won't even add it to the expense report."

Triana almost laughed. So far, the PI had added everything to his expense report. The last one had had an entry for thirty-five cents, the cost of the parking meter outside the coffee shop he'd stopped at for a bagel while on the way to his office to email her the report.

"Toast is fine," she said. "What do you have?"

Short and stocky, Bodine had a touch of gray in his curly brown hair, and dark eyes that didn't miss a thing. He reached down into the messenger-style bag beside him on the bench and came out with a thick yellow envelope. Without a word, he shoved it across the table at her.

She started to open it, but he shook his head. "Not here. If anyone sees you reading that, it would lead to a lot of awkward questions."

Triana was so curious her fingers itched, but she resisted the temptation to assume Bodine was being a drama queen and instead put the envelope on the seat beside her.

"What is it?" she asked.

He went back to eating his Creole Slammer, a big mess of eggs and hash browns smothered in crawfish étouffée. She loved her city's down-home cooking as much as the next girl, but there was no way in heck she could eat something like that this early in the morning.

"It's the entire case file the NOPD has on your father's murder," he said. "And I do mean the *entire case file*, including the coroner's death investigation report."

If she'd thought her fingers had been itching to see it before, it didn't compare to how eager she was now. She'd been asking the NOPD for a copy of the file for over a year and hadn't gotten so much as a return phone call. Apparently, it wasn't something the police preferred to hand out, especially when the case was technically still open.

"How'd you get it?" she asked Bodine. She wasn't quite sure if it was illegal to have a copy of a full, unabridged police report in New Orleans, but she didn't think anyone would be thrilled about it.

Bodine didn't even look up from his plate as he shoveled eggs onto his fork. "I stole it. When you get a chance to read it in private, you'll notice the actual crime scene photos have been sealed in a separate envelope. It's my suggestion that you skip that part

of the report. Take my word for it, you don't want to
see them."

She nodded, forcing herself to suddenly take interest in the coffee and toast the waitress had just deliv-
ered to avoid thinking about what might be in that
sealed envelope.

"Any information you think is of particular interest?"
she asked as she sipped her coffee.

Bodine glanced at the nearby tables like he was worried the NOPD had suddenly started following him.
But after a few moments of surveillance, he must have
decided the risk was low enough because he nodded.

"Several items. In no particular order," he said
quietly, "first, the detective running this case should
probably be fired. Outside of the generic walk-around-
the-block-and-ask-if-anyone-heard-anything type of
questions, he's done nothing. My personal opinion is
that as soon as they saw your dad's old rap sheet, they
wrote this off as criminal-on-criminal violence and let
the case sink."

Triana immediately felt her face flush with anger. Her
father had never hidden the fact that he'd had a shady
background growing up or that he'd been in tangles with
the law back when he was younger. But all that had been
more than two decades ago. Everything had changed
after she and her mother were in his life. Didn't a man
get any credit for turning his life around?

Still, as mad as she was, Triana knew that Bodine
hadn't told her anything she hadn't already figured out
on her own. She'd known the police hadn't tried very
hard to find her father's killer, but it still hurt to have
it confirmed.

"There were a few random notes in the file about some people thinking your dad had pissed off someone dangerous in the days or weeks right before his death, but nothing specific," Bodine continued. "I'm going to dig into that angle a bit more."

Triana didn't say anything as she nibbled on her breakfast.

"The most interesting tidbits were found in the autopsy report," Bodine added, scraping up the last of his breakfast with a piece of toast slathered in so much butter that it left yellow streaks behind on the plate. Triana had to wonder what this guy's blood pressure and cholesterol averaged on a normal day. "There was also blood at the crime scene that wasn't your dad's—two distinct blood types beyond his—and lots of it. The coroner stated it was arterial, probably from the carotid based on angle and distance of spray. Unfortunately, there were no hits in CODIS or the Louisiana DNA databases."

Triana looked up in surprise. "Dad was attacked by two people?"

Bodine shook his head. "More than that. The coroner was of the opinion that the amount of blood at the scene indicated both of those people would have bled out in something like twenty or thirty seconds. But their bodies weren't at the scene, meaning there were at least three attackers and that whoever was left removed the bodies of the two who'd been killed. Why the hell someone would hang around to drag off their bodies but not the body of the person they'd killed is frigging beyond me. The coroner's theory is also supported by the fact that ballistics showed three distinct large-caliber automatics used on your father. None of the weapons were found at the scene or anywhere nearby, though."

"Three people shooting large-caliber handguns in the middle of the night and no one heard a thing?" she asked in disbelief. "It's not like Dad's club was in the middle of nowhere."

Bodine shrugged. "My guess is that they used silencers, which is kind of scary, since it likely means that these men were professionals. Common criminals don't walk around the street carrying silenced weapons."

Professionals, huh? Something else the NOPD detective had never mentioned to her and her mother. "They were professionals, but Dad was still able to kill two of them?" She felt a completely stupid sense of pride at that. Her dad had gone down swinging, the way he'd always told her to face any obstacle life put in front of her. "I didn't know he'd even kept a weapon at the club."

Bodine looked around the diner again, making sure no one was eavesdropping on their conversation, then lowered his voice. "That's where things get interesting. Those men weren't shot. The coroner and crime scene techs were sure of that. The only guns fired in that club belonged to the men who attacked your father. There was blood found on the tips of all of your dad's fingers though, implying that he ripped the men's throats out with his bare hands. I have to admit, that conclusion makes me wonder if the crime scene techs didn't mess something up during the collection. I know your dad was big, but I'm not buying the idea that he was able to rip two people's throats out while getting shot multiple times."

Triana wasn't so sure of that. Her dad had never been

one to mess with. As much as she loved him, she knew he was ornery enough to do something like that.

"So, is there anything else the police didn't tell me about my father's death?" she asked, not sure what to do with all the information she already had.

"Actually, there is."

He hesitated as the waitress came by to drop off the checks. True to his word, Bodine grabbed hers and paid for it. Triana reminded herself to check the next expense report just in case. She waited while the PI calculated the tip down to the sixth decimal place. When he finally looked up at her, his expression was cautious.

"To tell the truth, I have no idea what to make of this last part, but it's strange, so I think it's something we should dig into," Bodine said. "When you read the report, I'm sure the chemical names will mean more to you than they did to me, but bottom line—someone pumped your father full of animal tranquilizer just before he was shot. Again, I'm not sure how they're connected, but the report said the levels would have been lethal to a human in minutes. Essentially, someone tried to poison your dad to death before they shot him."

Chapter 8

"HOW BAD DO YOU THINK THIS IS GOING TO BE?" REMY asked the room in general. Talking about the upcoming ass-reaming had to be better than sitting around stewing over it.

"On a scale of one to ten?" On the other side of the table in the small NOPD headquarters conference room, Lorenzo's mouth tightened. "I'm figuring about a twelve, maybe even a thirteen since I'm feeling so lucky today."

Remy looked at Brooks, then Drew, hoping one of the other SWAT officers might offer up something to give the narcotics detective a little hope. But both men were sitting there with the same tight, concerned expression on their faces.

Okay. That must mean this meeting with the captain of narcotics major case squad and the assistant district attorney responsible for prosecuting Aaron Lee, if the man ever saw the inside of a courtroom, was going to be just as awful as Lorenzo feared. Not that Remy expected anything less after the absolute catastrophe of a morning they'd had at the freight storage warehouse owned and operated by another one of Lee's shell companies.

Remy and his pack mates had barely walked into the SWAT facility that morning when Drew stuck his head out of his office and said they had a call. He hadn't given them any details, just simple instructions to get their gear ready, load up the operations vehicle, and roll. Not that Remy needed much in the way of details to figure out they were going after Aaron Lee again. That was the only reason Drew would have been so mum about the whole thing.

Drew had given them an extremely basic mission briefing en route to the warehouse. According to their narcotics informant, the crime boss had the crystal meth stored in there and intended to start breaking it down today. Since Drew and Lorenzo didn't want to risk the operation getting compromised again, they'd accelerated the normal timetable for a raid like this as well as limited the number of people involved. They'd hoped by moving fast and light, they'd hit Lee's warehouse before word of the raid leaked out to the man.

Unfortunately, it hadn't worked that way.

Remy had known there was something wrong before he'd even kicked in the back door of the warehouse. The approach to the structure had simply been too easy, the lack of exterior guards was a blaring alarm that they were walking into a setup. His inner wolf had gone into alert mode, sure there were going to be shooters in the place waiting to mow them all down the moment they stepped inside.

Drew had sent his teams into the warehouse through multiple entry points, much the same way Remy would have done if he were running the show. They'd even blown out two windows, so they could get officers into the rearmost storage areas, where they were sure the drugs were being held. But there hadn't been any drugs in the place, even though Remy was able to pick up a clear scent telling him the crap had been there no more than an hour ago.

Even more embarrassing than the absence of meth was the obvious fact that the people running the warehouse had known they were coming. Instead of the normal bustling crew of twenty or thirty men that should have been working, there were only a handful of men who claimed to know nothing about the drugs.

On the bright side, Aaron Lee and his lieutenants hadn't shown up to crow at them. But on the not-so-bright side, Drew and Lorenzo had gotten a call about twenty minutes later, telling them to come downtown to police headquarters and to bring Remy and Brooks with them.

Remy felt bad that Drew and Lorenzo were in hot water, but he was also a little worried about why he and Brooks had been pulled into this mess. They were merely visitors here. No way in hell was he going to let the NOPD brass try and lay this shit sandwich at their feet.

He swiveled around in his chair as the door to the conference room opened. An older man with captain bars on the shoulders of his uniform and a name tag that read *Barron* walked in, followed by a harried-looking guy in a suit and tie that had to be the ADA. One look at him and Remy could already tell they weren't going to get along.

Captain Barron walked over and shook each of their hands. "You must be Senior Corporal Brooks and Officer Boudreaux. I'm Corey Barron. Thanks for coming down to talk to us." He motioned at the lawyer. "This is ADA Russo. He'd like to ask a few questions and see if we can get to the bottom of our current predicament."

Barron gave Russo a nod, then took a seat at the table beside Brooks. Russo didn't sit. Instead, he swept a glare over all of them.

"You realize that I've gone to Judge Thibodeau twice now for warrants, right? And that in order to get the one signed this morning, I had to go over to his house before sunrise with one of his clerks in tow and wake the man and his wife up?" He scowled at Lorenzo. "Do you know how much I hate waking up a judge at six o'clock in the morning? Do you?"

When Lorenzo didn't answer his question, Russo took a deep breath and ran his fingers through his tousled blond hair. "Thibodeau wasn't real keen on going up against Lee to begin with, so I had to talk him into it. He's coming up for reelection soon, and Aaron Lee can bury him easily enough if he wants to. But I'd promised him we had a solid source inside the old man's organization. I can't imagine the judge puts much stock in my promises now, seeing as we're oh-for-two on these damn raids. I swear, I don't know what's worse, the fact that Judge Thibodeau will probably shoot me the next time I walk into his office, or that I can forget about ever getting another search warrant signed by the man."

Remy wasn't generally fond of lawyers, and Russo was working his way steadily higher on his list of disliked people. So it wasn't really his fault he couldn't hold his tongue. "Since I've been shot a few times before, I think having the judge shoot you would be worse than having to go find another judge to sign your search warrants. But then again, maybe that's just me."

He opened his mouth to add that Russo getting shot might not be such a bad thing if the ADA could convince the judge to shoot him in some noncritical part of his anatomy like his ass or his brain, but beside him,

Brooks laid a hand on his arm and squeezed until the bones started to creak.

Russo glared at Remy but didn't say anything, much to Remy's disappointment. Instead, the lawyer turned his attention to Captain Barron.

"You'd think this day couldn't get any worse, right? Wrong," the ADA said. "Want to know what I get to do next?"

No one answered this question either, but Russo didn't seem to notice. He stood there, jaw clenched, his heart beating so fast Remy thought the lawyer was going to blow a gasket. *Shit, this guy needs to take up yoga or something.*

"I get to spend some quality time with Mr. Lee himself," Russo said, his heart thumping even harder. "Yeah, that's right. He is on his way here right now with his entourage of lawyers. They want to talk to me about why they shouldn't be suing the department for property damages and harassment. And guess what? The DA has left me to deal with this on my own. You want to know what he told me? *You're the one who wanted to go after the big fish. Guess you better figure out how to reel him in on your own.*" The ADA shook his head. "The man is flat out going to offer me up as fish bait if this goes wrong. And right now, it's going pretty fucking wrong. I mean, shit, guys, did you have to blow out his fucking windows?"

Russo grabbed a chair and quickly sat down, like he'd suddenly run out of gas—or might faint. His face did actually look a little pale. Remy almost felt bad for him. Not that bad, of course, since the guy had almost certainly jumped on this case because he saw some future value to be gained if he could take down a criminal as big as Aaron Lee. Political careers in this city had been started on far less. Now the weather vane was turning the other way and poor ADA Russo realized that maybe he'd made a serious tactical error.

"What the hell happened, Corey?" Russo finally asked, sounding totally defeated as he sat there pressing his fingers to his temples and making circular motions. "You said you had a man on the inside of Lee's organization. I get why you don't want to tell me anything about him, but I have to ask—is this informant incompetent or did he just get paid off?"

Captain Barron shook his head. "The leak is not our informant. They've been in the old man's organization for three years now and are in a position to know exactly what Lee is doing. This person is risking their life for us. There has to be someone in the NOPD or the DA's office who's selling us out to Lee."

Russo considered that for a moment, then pinned Remy and Brooks with a calculating look. "How do we know it's not the SWAT team you brought in from Dallas? It can't be a coincidence they've been on both operations and they've both gone bad." His eyes narrowed at Remy. "In fact, didn't you used to work in one of the local parish sheriff's offices a while back? For all we know, you've been in Lee's pockets for years."

Remy snorted. "Yeah, that's right. I orchestrated this entire SWAT cross-training exercise that took months to set up so I'd be in town just in time for Drew to send me out on a mission I had no idea I'd be allowed to go on, so I could tell a criminal I was on the way to bust him. Wow, that's fucking brilliant. Tell me, Russo, how many cases have you won? With an intellect like yours, you must be up to, what? Two or three by now?"

Russo jumped out of his chair to charge at Remy, who was already on his feet and ready to meet the asshat halfway. Brooks and Lorenzo quickly put themselves between Remy and the man. Not that the ADA looked too serious about taking a swing at Remy, now that he'd seen how much taller and bigger Remy was.

"That's enough," Captain Barron said sharply. "We're wasting time here, Russo. It's extremely unlikely that one of the SWAT officers from Dallas is our leak. They simply didn't have access to enough information to compromise either operation."

Russo looked like he wanted to argue, but then finally shook his head in disgust. "I know. But if it's not them, what the hell are we going to do? How do we find this leak and plug it?"

"I've asked the public integrity bureau to look into the situation, but the chances of them finding anything in the near term is unlikely," Barron said.

The NOPD Public Integrity Bureau—or PIB—was similar to the internal affairs division in Dallas. The fact that Barron was willing to turn this effort over to the cops in the PIB meant he was serious about finding this leak. But like he said, it would take time.

"What's the plan if the PIB can't find the leak in the next day or two?" Remy asked.

The captain sighed. "If we can't plug the leak before our informant sends us another tip, I'm pulling them out."

Lorenzo swore. "Dammit, Captain. We've been after Lee for years. We'll never get this close again."

"Don't you think I know that? I won't risk our

informant, not even for Lee." Barron got to his feet. "If you want to put Aaron Lee away, then you need to figure out a way to do it fast—without exposing our source."

Giving them a nod, the captain walked out of the room.

Remy noticed the captain had been careful to never mention the gender of their undercover informant throughout their entire conversation, or whether the person was a cop or not. His promise to pull the informant rather than put them at risk was something Remy could appreciate.

No sooner had Barron walked out than a uniformed officer stuck his head in the open door. "Mr. Russo, those people you've been waiting to talk to have arrived. They're in the interrogation room at the end of the hall. And by the way, the deputy superintendent will also be sitting in on the meeting."

Russo's face turned a few shades paler, but he nodded. "Okay. I might as well get this over with."

As the ADA left the room, Remy wondered if the man was even going to make it through the meeting with Lee and his lawyers. Russo's heart was pounding like a drum.

"You guys want to listen in and see what Lee and his lawyers have to say?" Lorenzo asked. "It might be interesting."

Remy doubted that but nodded anyway. "Why not? If nothing else, it'll be fun to see Russo squirm."

It turned out that watching Russo get grilled by Aaron Lee and six of his high-priced lawyers wasn't fun at all. In fact, it was kind of painful to see. From where he stood behind the one-way glass with Brooks, Drew, and Lorenzo, Remy winced as Lee and his lawyers eviscerated the ADA.

Russo tried to trip him up, but the old man was too good. Lee wouldn't have said anything incriminating even if his lawyers hadn't been there. The worst part of having a front row seat to the whole thing was watching Lee gloat about the fact that the police hadn't found anything to arrest him for and never would. He was even threatening to sue the NOPD and the city of New Orleans for everything he could get. The man was thumbing his nose at the ADA like it was all a game to him.

Beside Remy, Drew let out a snort of disgust. "As long as Lee has someone inside the department, we're never going to get close to him. Even if the informant is able to get word to us on where Lee is keeping the meth, the son of a bitch will know we're coming before we get there."

"Then why do we keep chasing our tails by trying to play whack-a-mole with this guy and his stash of crystal meth?" Remy asked. "Isn't there a way we can get a step ahead of Lee and hit him someplace he's not expecting? Where does he run his business from? I mean his legitimate business, not his shell companies."

Drew shook his head. "He's got a big old plantation to the west of Kenner, up near the lake. Everyone in this city knows he's got more incriminating evidence there than we have in our entire NOPD evidence warehouse."

Remy remembered driving around that part of the shores of Lake Pontchartrain when he was younger. There were some pricey properties up there. "If everyone knows, why can't we get a warrant for that place?"

It was Lorenzo who answered. "Never going to happen. He's too well connected with the right people in this city and even more in Kenner. The fact that we've gone after him twice and missed both times would make it even harder."

Remy ground his jaw as he continued to watch Russo flounder in his battle of wits with Lee. They needed to do something completely different, or the next raid would end up the same as their first two. Worse, it might end up with them finding the narcotics squad's informant dead in a swamp somewhere.

He turned away from the carnage in the interrogation room to look at Lorenzo. "I know my guys and I are outsiders here, but what if I told you I had a plan that had a good chance of taking down Aaron Lee and keeping your informant alive?"

The narcotics detective regarded him thoughtfully. "What kind of plan?"

"The kind that involves you not telling anyone but Brooks, Drew, and me the next time your informant calls with information, then letting us run the operation," Remy said.

Lorenzo flinched. "I don't think Captain Barron would ever go for that."

"That won't be a problem since a key part of the plan is not telling him either."

It was almost one o'clock by the time Triana got to her mother's shop. She hadn't been able to wait to read the police and coroner's reports Bodine had given her, so after leaving the diner, she'd hopped off the streetcar at the Tulane station and run across the street to the public library. At that time of the day, it hadn't been hard to find a quiet cubicle out of the way to review the files.

Even though she'd pored over thousands of reports like this in her job, it had been difficult to read these. This wasn't just a random murder. This was her father's. But she'd forced herself to push the emotions aside as much as she could and focus solely on the facts in the reports.

She'd hoped the file would provide some details she might be able to dig into with her forensic skills, but there had been no unusual hairs, fibers, trace evidence, or even fingerprints found at her father's club. Like Bodine had said, the blood of the two attackers her father had apparently killed was not in the system, and the bullet casings didn't come back as related to any other reported crimes.

She'd hoped the animal tranquilizer used on her father might be a different story. Xylazine was a sedative and analgesic used for horses and other large animals. The coroner had found several large, deep puncture marks on her father's body, indicating he'd been hit multiple times with a dart gun of some kind. The dosage used on her father had been extreme, and the coroner estimated that nearly fifteen milliliters of the stuff had been dumped into his body. That would have been a lot for a full-size horse. For a human—even one as big as her father—it would have been fatal in minutes.

But even though Triana had never heard of anyone using xylazine on humans in regard to murder, it appeared no one had done anything with the information. She'd read through the reports several times and found no record that the coroner or detective in charge of the case had checked with ViCAP or any other state criminal database to see if something like this had happened before.

Triana had called a friend at the crime lab in Houston

and asked the woman to check for other murders involving the use of this drug. Her friend had been curious, wanting to know if this had anything to do with her father's death, but when Triana said it wasn't something she wanted to get out to the rest of the lab, her friend had promised to keep it quiet.

It was entirely possible that the reason there hadn't been a note in the file about a ViCAP check was because the coroner had done his job and hadn't found anything, but it wouldn't hurt to check again, if for no other reason than it would give her something to do while Bodine was digging into the angle that her father had pissed someone off right before his death. Bodine promised to let her know if he learned anything and asked her to do the same.

As Triana walked into the shop, she couldn't help smiling when she saw her mom behind the counter, tying up gris-gris bags and putting price tags on them. Her mother looked up and returned her smile.

"So you finally decided to come home, huh?" she teased.

Triana laughed. She'd texted her mom earlier that morning, before her meeting with Bodine, and again before stopping at the library. So it wasn't like her mother hadn't known where she was and that she was safe.

Walking over to the counter, she set down her purse and the envelope so she could help with the gris-gris bags. She absolutely loved the smell of the combination of herbs and spices her mom put in them.

Her mother glanced at her as she reached for another bag. "Since you spent the night with Remy, that must mean your date went well."

Triana's first instinct was to say it was wonderful and that they had a great time, but she caught herself. Her mother was as much her friend as her parent, and if there was one person in the world she could tell about her date with Remy—minus the part about them sleeping together—it was her mom. Besides, if she didn't talk to someone about Remy and how much she liked him, she was sure she would explode.

But wanting to talk about Remy and actually getting the right words to come out were two completely different things. Especially because her head was still swimming with everything she'd been feeling. Thankfully her mother didn't rush her as she tried to get her thoughts together.

Finally, she took a deep breath and opened her mouth, hoping the right words would somehow find their way out. "It went extremely well. I can honestly say that I've never been with a man so charming, engaging, relaxed, confident, or so…"

"Attractive?" her mother finished.

Triana grinned. "Yes. Without a doubt, Remy is the most attractive man I've ever seen, much less dated. The funny thing about it is that I don't think Remy knows how incredibly handsome he really is. I saw at least a dozen women trying to catch his eye when we walked into Muriel's and he didn't even notice. He never looked at a single one of them. In fact, he never took his eyes off of me the entire night."

Her mother's lips curved. "Why would he? Remy's as smitten with you as you are with him."

Even though Triana appreciated her mother's analysis of Remy's feelings, she couldn't help laughing. "Mom.

No one uses the word *smitten* anymore. And even if they did, I'm not sure I'd say I'm smitten with him. It's a little too early for anything like that."

Her mother lifted a brow. "What word would you use then, if not *smitten*?"

Triana opened her mouth, all ready to try to put the crazy feelings that had been zipping back and forth through her head all morning into a single, simple word. She failed.

"I don't know," she finally admitted. "What I'm feeling right now is too complicated to fit into a single word or even a whole bunch of words. All I can say for certain is that I've never been with anyone like Remy. I can't stop thinking about him."

"You seem to have done a decent job of saying how you feel right there," her mother said. "And whether you want to admit it or not, you *are* smitten with him."

Triana knotted the ribbon on the gris-gris bag she was working on. "I can't be smitten with him. That would mean I'm falling for him, and that would be certifiably insane considering we've only gone out once."

Her mom laughed. "First off, I think you get a little credit for being friends with Remy in high school. It's not as if you just met the man two days ago, you know. Even if you had, there's nothing crazy about falling fast. It simply means fate put you in front of the man you were meant to be with. There's nothing insane about that. In fact, it's magical." When Triana looked skeptical, her mother continued. "If it makes you feel any better, the exact same thing happened when I met your dad."

Triana looked at her mother in surprise. "It did?"

She knew how her parents had met, of course, but she didn't know it had been love at first sight.

"It did," her mom said. "I knew there was something special about him the moment I saw him. Neither of us felt the need to play games. Your father asked me to marry him a week after we met, and I said yes."

Triana stood there so stunned she wouldn't have been surprised if her mouth was hanging open. She'd thought her parents had dated for months, maybe even years, before deciding to get married—the way normal people did. The idea that her mother and father had fallen in love in a week was crazy hard to believe. But she had to admit it was also interesting. Her parents had been the most in-love couple she'd ever seen. If it was possible for that kind of love to happen in days, maybe this thing going on with Remy wasn't so insane.

Chapter 9

REMY COULDN'T UNDERSTAND WHY TRIANA NEEDED TO GO back to her mother's apartment above the shop to change before they headed out to the French Quarter to meet up with everyone else that night. As far as he was concerned, the form-fitting navy-blue dress she was wearing, with a slit that showed off plenty of thigh, was just fine with him. But she insisted it wasn't sexy enough for Bourbon Street or the kind of dancing she had in mind.

Not that he really cared what they did. After the day he'd had, he simply wanted to spend some quality time with Triana. If that meant watching her change clothes for an hour, he was definitely okay with that. Actually, in terms of quality time, he couldn't imagine anything better than watching her take her clothes off over and over again.

After spending another hour down at NOPD headquarters, he, Brooks, and Drew had headed back to the SWAT facility, hoping to get back to the training they had planned out for the day. It hadn't worked out that way. Instead, they'd sat in the briefing room the entire afternoon talking to officers from the Public Integrity Bureau and filling out statements regarding when they had learned about the raids and with whom they had talked during the time period from that point until the actual raids had taken place.

If there was anything Remy hated more than lawyers, it was paperwork. And the PIB truly loved their paperwork.

It had been easy to put all that frustration and stress behind him the moment he'd picked Triana up for dinner, though. Being with her made all the crap he and the SWAT team had been dealing with the past two days fade into the background. He didn't have a clue how she did it, and by and large, he didn't care. If it meant being able to put thoughts of Aaron Lee and his damn crystal meth out of his head for a few hours, he was willing to accept it without a lot of analysis.

When they'd gone to a nearby diner to grab an early dinner, Remy quickly discovered it didn't take a fancy restaurant to enjoy himself with Triana. He'd had a simple seafood po'boy sandwich and a bowl of soup but had enjoyed it as much as the expensive cut of meat he'd had last night. They'd sat in the booth and chatted about inconsequential stuff like how the Saints were looking this year and whether LSU was going to fire their football coach. He found it didn't matter what he and Triana talked about. He simply loved hearing her velvety, soft voice.

They were half a block away from her mother's shop when Remy heard the sound of strident, angry voices coming from that direction. He didn't recognize the man, who was saying something about this being the last offer Gemma was going to get. But he definitely knew the woman. It was Gemma, telling the man to get the hell out of her shop.

Tightening his hold on Triana's hand, he picked up his pace the last twenty feet or so, jerking open the front door. The second he stepped inside, his senses went on alert and he gently pushed Triana behind him.

There was a slick-looking man in a fancy suit standing in front of Gemma, berating her for being a stubborn old woman. The man's attitude and clothing screamed lawyer, and Remy instinctively knew it was the same jackass Triana had mentioned to him that morning. But it wasn't the lawyer or his condescending voice that had Remy's fingertips and gums tingling. It was the three large brawler types the lawyer had with him. Remy recognized professional thugs when he saw them. They had noses that had been broken multiple times and scarred knuckles, not to mention wore cheap, loose-fitting sports jackets that allowed them to move easily as well as conceal a weapon.

All eyes turned toward him and Triana as the little bell above the door tinkled, announcing their presence.

"Mom?" Triana said hesitantly from behind him. "Is everything okay?"

Gemma turned, relief on her face. "Of course. Mr. Murphy—or rather the person he claims to be representing—seems to have taken a sudden interest in my little voodoo shop. He offered to buy the whole place, including all the merchandise inside it and the apartment above it, for a ridiculous amount of money."

Remy was focused on the three toughs, who'd started to spread out and move toward him, but out of the corner of his eye, he saw Triana's startled expression. She was obviously stunned and more than a little confused.

"You're selling your shop...your home?" she asked softly.

Gemma shook her head. "Good heavens, no. I was

just telling Mr. Murphy, for the second time, that the shop isn't for sale, when you came in. Unfortunately, he's a little hard of hearing."

Murphy glared at her. "Mrs. Bellamy, insult me all you want, but the offer my client is making is very fair. And as I've said more than once, it's not an offer you're in a position to refuse."

It was impossible for Remy to miss the threat in the man's words. He didn't imagine Gemma had either. But Triana's mother didn't bat an eye. Instead, she folded her arms and looked at the lawyer like he was an errant two-year-old having a tantrum.

"Yet here I am, refusing your offer nevertheless." She looked at Remy. "Could you please be a dear and escort Mr. Murphy and his friends out of my shop? This conversation is over."

"My pleasure," Remy said.

Two of the lawyer's thugs immediately stepped forward to block his way while the third moved over to stand near his boss. Remy wasn't in the mood to toy with these guys, not after they'd come in here and tried to intimidate Triana's mother, but with Gemma and Triana standing there, it wasn't like he could cut loose and go all werewolf on them. Unfortunately, he was going to have to restrain himself.

So, instead of tossing both men across the room like he wanted to, with two fingers, he poked the first guy in the sternum hard enough to crack the bone and make the man stumble back a few feet. A split second later, the man fell to the floor, gasping and fighting for air.

Remy spun around just as the second guy took a swing at his head. Remy brought up his hand, catching the thug's fist in midair and stopping it a few inches from his face. Then he squeezed. Not as hard as he could but hard enough to end the fight quickly. The sound of the bones in the man's hand cracking was probably loud enough for Triana to hear over by the door.

The guy wailed in pain, his knees giving out as he collapsed to the floor. Remy squeezed the man's hand a little harder before he let go, just to make sure the asshole didn't develop any silly ideas about getting back up.

Out of the corner of his eye, Remy saw a flash of movement and turned to see the third man coming his way, his hand behind his back like he was reaching for something. Remy didn't know if it was a knife, a gun, or some other weapon, but he wasn't going to let the man get it the rest of the way out.

Unable to contain his inner wolf any longer, Remy snarled low in his throat, an animalistic warning that would be unmistakable to even the dimmest bulb in the box. The idiot coming at him must have been at least a little brighter than that because he stopped in his tracks, his hand still behind his back.

"You might want to reconsider your plan," Remy warned. "Because if that hand comes out with anything in it, you're going to learn just how far out of your weight class you really are."

The guy stared at him for a moment, then glanced at his two buddies where they were lying on the floor rolling around in pain before finally eyeing the lawyer, who was paler than his white linen suit and obviously not going to be of any help.

Shoulders slumping, the man's hand slowly came out from behind his back, empty.

"You want to call the police?" Remy asked Gemma as he continued to keep his eyes on the third man.

"No," she said.

Remy frowned. "You sure? These guys threatened you."

The lawyer opened his mouth to say something, likely full of bullshit concerning the legal threshold for establishing the conveyance of a threat or some other crap that Remy really didn't care to hear. Remy glared at the man, letting his eyes flash gold for a split second. The old man swallowed his words and looked like he might do the same to his tongue.

"I hate lawyers, so don't talk," Remy said. When it was obvious the man was smart enough to keep his mouth shut, Remy turned to Gemma. "You sure about not calling the police? What if these guys come back?"

Gemma's mouth curved. "I think they've gotten the message. This shop and the things in it are *not* for sale. Is that understood, Mr. Murphy?"

When the lawyer nodded, Remy motioned with his head toward the door. He didn't like the idea of not calling the police, but he understood Gemma's reasoning. She wanted these people gone and probably thought he'd scared them enough to keep them away for good. He hoped she was right.

But as the lawyer and the uninjured thug helped the other two jerks off the floor and out the door, he couldn't miss the angry looks on their faces. They'd been embarrassed, and they were pissed. Remy had a bad feeling this might not be the last time he saw them.

Then he caught sight of Triana standing by the door, watching the men hobble out. She hadn't said a word or even moved the entire time the confrontation had taken place, but now her heart was thudding like a drum and she was breathing fast. She was scared to death, and if the way she was looking at Remy was any indication, what she'd just seen him do likely had as much to do with her fear as the fact that a bunch of lowlifes had threatened her mother.

———ᴧᴧᴧ———

Triana decided she must be in shock. She wasn't even sure how she'd gotten upstairs, other than a vague recollection of Remy steering her that way.

She hadn't even realized Murphy was at the shop until Remy had tightened his hold on her hand and practically dragged her there almost faster than her feet could move. Triana's stomach had clenched the moment she'd seen that creepy old lawyer and his scary friends. The fact that they were there trying to intimidate her mom was obvious, not to mention terrifying. Those three men were big, and they looked like they were eager to hurt someone.

"Do you want me to make you something to drink?" Remy asked softly as they sat down at the kitchen table. "Tea, maybe? Or something stronger?"

Triana shook her head. "No, I'm okay. I just need time to process everything. It all happened so fast."

Fast was an understatement. One moment, her mother had been talking about the lawyer making an offer for the shop and everything in it, and the next, Remy was beating up Murphy's goons. The entire thing couldn't have lasted more than a minute, but while Triana had been freaking out, her heart thundering in her chest as she tried to understand why they hadn't called the police, her mother had acted like a brawl in the middle of her shop wasn't a big deal.

After Murphy and his crew left, her mom had gone about her business while Triana stood there gaping like a fish out of water, saying she was heading out to attend an emergency meeting of the local shop owners about coordinating preparations for the storm in the event it turned in New Orleans's direction. Then her mother gave her and Remy hugs and told him to bring his friends over for dinner tomorrow night, before flipping over the closed sign and walking out.

Triana tucked her hair behind her ear with a trembling hand. "Are you sure it was safe to let Mom go out there on her own? What if those men are waiting somewhere out there?"

Remy reached across the table and took her hands in his. She couldn't help noticing how small hers looked compared to his and that they'd stopped shaking the moment he touched her—as if he was some kind of security blanket she liked to hold on to.

Triana cringed a little at that admission. She might work for a crime lab that supported the Houston Police Department, but clearly she wasn't built for tense situations. She'd been worthless down in the shop.

"Those men are currently on their way to the nearest emergency room," Remy assured her. "They have no interest in anything beyond pain relief at the moment."

Triana supposed she could believe that. She was pretty sure she'd heard bones break when those two thugs had tried to get in Remy's way. She had no idea how he'd done it, but maybe it had something to do with his SWAT training. Hopefully those goons had been scared off for good. The idea that they might come after her mother at some point when Remy wasn't there scared the crap out of her.

Regardless of what Remy said, something told her there was a good chance those men, or others like them, would come back. And she and Remy would both be going back to Texas soon.

"All that stuff about buying the shop is BS," she said quietly. "While I'm sure Murphy and whoever he's working for would be thrilled to get his hands on this place—it's worth a thousand times what Mom's family paid for it back in the day—the offer to buy it is about the necklace my father wore. I guess they thought she'd take one look at the amount on the check and forget about taking the necklace with her when she moved."

Remy gently caressed her hand with his fingers. "But you knew your mom wouldn't sell, right?"

Triana nodded. "Deep down, yeah. This place has been in her family for a long time. It's where all her memories are, especially those she made with my dad."

She smiled as she thought about the conversation she and her mother had earlier, when she'd told Triana she'd fallen for her father the moment they'd met.

"What?" Remy asked softly.

She shook her head. "Nothing. Just something Mom told me today about her and Dad. It was a special memory she has of him and this place and is yet another reason she'd never sell the shop. Not voluntarily, anyway."

"And she's not going to have to," Remy said firmly. "If Gemma has any more problems with these people, my guys and I will go pay Murphy a visit. We may look like poster children for Officer Friendly, but trust me, we can be very persuasive when we want to be."

She laughed. She was sure that if Remy or any of those other big cops from Dallas showed up at Murphy's office, the guy would probably flee the city within the hour. She hoped it wouldn't come to that, but she felt better knowing Remy would do something personally if those jerks threatened her mother again.

"I can see you being very persuasive, considering how quickly you handled those guys downstairs earlier," she said. "Speaking of which, how were you were able to push them around so easily? I know you have training on your side, but those men were nearly as big as you."

He chuckled. "It's my experience that size rarely matters as much as people thinks it does. Most of the time, it usually comes down to locating that one sensitive spot on the other person, then knowing what to do with it when you find it."

Triana lifted a brow. "Are we still talking about how you handled those goons downstairs?"

He gave her a sexy half smile, and she realized he'd been playing with her, trying to get her to stop stressing over the stuff she'd seen downstairs. It was amazing how he could be so in tune with her emotions and what she needed at any particular moment.

She was still thinking about that and all the stuff her mom had said about falling fast simply being a way of knowing you'd found the right person you were meant to be with, when Remy suddenly pushed back his chair and stood, tugging her to her feet.

"Come on," he said. "I'll show you what I mean."

Curious about what he meant by that, Triana let him guide her across the kitchen and through the living room, into the short hallway that led to her old bedroom. Her heart began to beat faster all over again, but now it was for a different reason.

Remy stopped and turned so suddenly she almost ran right into his chest. Before she could move, he put a hand on her shoulder and gently nudged her up against the wall in the hallway. Her pulse skipped a beat. It was kind of crazy how fast he could get her going.

Triana thought he was going to kiss her, but instead of capturing her mouth with his, he stayed where he was, one big hand on her shoulder pinning her to the wall.

"Now imagine that I'm one of those thugs from downstairs," he said. "What do you do?"

She stared up at him, sure he was kidding. That was definitely not the image she wanted in her head right then. "Is now really the best time for a lesson in self-defense?"

"Something else you'd rather be doing?" he asked, a knowing smile teasing the corner of his mouth.

"Yeah, there is."

"Great," he said. "Then show me what you'd do and we can move on to that something else you'd rather be doing."

She considered trying to distract him with a kiss, but the firm set of his jaw dissuaded her. He was serious about this. Sighing, she gazed up at him, trying to imagine what she could do if a man as tall and muscular as Remy were pinning her to a wall like this. After a moment, she shrugged.

"I guess I would punch the guy."

"Where?"

She looked at Remy like he was speaking a foreign language. "Where?"

"Yeah," he said. "Where would you punch me?"

She lifted her hand and balled it into a fist, then gently rested it on the side of his strong, sexy, scruff-covered jaw. That's where everyone got punched in movies. "Here?" she asked.

He frowned. "Not unless you want to break your hand. Remember what I said earlier about finding that one sensitive spot on the other person?"

She couldn't resist a teasing little smile. "And your sensitive spot would be…?"

His mouth quirked. "There's the obvious one, and if you can kick or knee a guy there, it will definitely work. But if all you can do is punch, there are other places just as sensitive."

"Like?" she prompted, hating the idea that she might need to know this kind of stuff.

He pointed at a spot just below his sternum, right in the center. "There's the solar plexus. A hard strike to this area will definitely knock the wind out of someone and give you time to run." He tapped his index finger to the side of his head. "A punch to the temple is going to hurt your hand, but it will temporarily stun most people. If you don't think you can hit a person there hard enough, grab the top of the ear and yank. That will definitely take the fight out of the toughest bad guy. However, if you only have one chance to hit a person and it's life or death, aim for the throat, and punch as hard as you can. At the very least, it will give you time to get away."

Triana leaned against the wall, praying she was never in a position to have to do any of the things Remy had showed her. She wasn't sure she'd be able to.

"Okay," he said softly. While he still towered over her, his expression was less serious than it had been before. "Self-defense lesson is over for the evening. Sorry I spoiled the mood we had going on there, but with what happened downstairs earlier, I felt it was something we needed to talk about, and I didn't want to let it wait."

She nodded. "I understand. And you didn't spoil the mood."

His smile told her he was fully aware she was fibbing her butt off. "Why don't you change and we'll get out of here? Everyone is probably wondering where we are."

When Remy took a step back, she grabbed his hand, pulling him back. He gave her a questioning look, but before he could say anything, she stood on tiptoe and kissed him.

"Thank you," she whispered.

"For what?" he asked.

"For being more worried about me and my safety than you are about getting naked with me. It sounds like something any guy would do, but trust me when I tell you, it isn't. Most men are so focused on what's important to them that they'd never tell a girl something she really needed to hear, no matter how badly she needed to hear it, if it got in the way of what they wanted."

He chuckled, looking a little embarrassed at the compliment. "That's me—Sir Remy Lancelot, your knight in shining armor."

"Actually, that's exactly what I'm starting to think you are," she said.

Before he could say anything else self-deprecating and humble, she pulled him down for another kiss. And this time, she did it forcefully enough to convince him he definitely hadn't spoiled any mood.

Triana knew she had him when his hands went around to cup her bottom and tug her hard against him. She could already feel his cock hardening in his jeans as his tongue slipped into her mouth and tangled with hers.

Her body immediately responded to his touch, desire spiraling through her to coalesce between her thighs. Clearly, it took very little on his part to get her going. If the hard-on in his jeans was any indication, she was good at getting him going too.

That's why it surprised her when Remy lifted his head and took a step back. "I really was serious about what I said earlier. If we don't get moving, we're going to be late meeting up with everyone at the club. I know you really wanted to go dancing."

She slid one hand down to the front of his jeans, caressing the bulge she found there. "I definitely want to go dancing, but that doesn't mean we can't have a quickie first."

Remy's beautiful hazel eyes glinted, reflecting every ray of light in the hallway. "A quickie, huh?"

She tugged at his belt, unbuckling it. "I told you this morning that I can work fast when I have to, so I guess the real question is, can you?"

"Tell me you have a condom nearby." His voice was a husky whisper, making her legs quiver. "Then you'll see how fast I can work."

Triana expected to find Remy naked and in her bed by the time she ran back from grabbing the condom out of the purse she'd left on the couch, but instead, he was standing in the hallway, his T-shirt still on and his jeans down around his ankles, his gorgeous hard-on at the ready. Okay, he really did intend to work quickly. She could handle that.

As difficult as it was to do, she resisted the urge to drop to her knees in front of him and instead helped him get the condom on. The moment she had that extremely enjoyable task done, she reached for the hem of her dress, ready to yank it over her head. She never got the chance because Remy pressed her back up against the wall and shoved the dress up to her waist. Excitement rushed through her at the idea of making love with most of their clothes still on. There was something so urgent and primal about it.

She hooked her fingers in her panties so she could push them down, but Remy grabbed her hands and pinned them to the wall above her head with one of his. "I'll get those for you."

Triana gasped as she felt something sharp graze the skin along her hip. A moment later, there was a tug and a ripping sound, then the remnants of her panties were flying through the air. She wondered briefly where the heck he'd hidden a pocketknife, but then he released her wrists to nudge the underside of her chin, tipping her face up to his. At the same time, the fingers of his other hand traced along the folds of her pussy, making her gasp.

"How did you get my panties off like that?" she whispered.

Remy flashed her a grin, then pressed his lips to her neck. "SWAT magic," he murmured in her ear. "You don't have a problem with a little magic, do you?"

She opened her mouth to reply, but the words came out as nothing more than a moan as his mouth did amazing things to the sensitive skin of her neck while one of his fingers slipped inside her. "Well, I was planning to wear those panties tonight when we went out dancing," she finally gasped as his finger wiggled around, making her wetter by the second.

"I guess that means you'll just have to go out tonight without any panties," he said with a deep chuckle. "What a shame."

Triana whimpered. Like she needed another visual to get her more excited. The thought of going dancing without wearing anything under her dress was scandalous and something she never would have done with anyone but Remy.

She was about to tell him as much, but he chose that moment to slip his finger out of her wetness. Getting a firm grip on her hips with both hands, he lifted her up and pinned her against the wall. She didn't have time to wonder how he was able to hold her there so effortlessly because in the next breath, he buried himself deep inside her.

She gasped loud enough to be heard out on the street as he moved his hands to the underside of her ass and thrust into her urgently. All she could do was wrap her arms and legs around him and hold on for dear life as he took her harder than anyone ever had. She'd never been with a man so strong, so animalistic...so perfect.

As she buried her face against Remy's strong shoulder while she came, Triana couldn't imagine not being in his arms for the rest of her life.

Chapter 10

TRIANA HAD BEEN SURE HER MOTHER HAD LOST HER MIND when she'd set three big cast-iron pots on the stove that morning to make dinner for Remy and his friends.

"It's just the four of them. You know that, right?" Triana said as she helped her mom chop mountains of peppers, onions, celery, and herbs. "They can't eat this much jambalaya, or we'll have to roll them down the steps."

"Don't worry about that," her mother laughed. "Something tells me those boys are going to show up here with an appetite."

It turned out her mother had been right. Remy and his three friends had oohed and aahed in appreciation of the aroma coming from the kitchen before they'd even gotten upstairs to the dining room. And once they'd started eating, they hadn't messed around. They'd put away more of the thick, spicy stew than Triana would have ever thought possible. And that was on top of the huge tray of corn bread they'd demolished. How the heck could guys who looked like they did eat like that? Triana put on weight just watching them.

"You have to give me this recipe," Max told her mother as he inhaled another piece of corn bread, then helped himself to seconds—or whatever it was called when someone ate six bowls of anything. "I have to make this the next time I'm running the grills at the cookouts we have at our SWAT compound in Dallas."

"I'll write everything down for you," her mother promised. "If you're making it on a grill, you'll have to watch the heat and stir it constantly, or all the rice will sink to the bottom and burn to a crisp."

Sitting there at the table in a dining room that had started feeling way too lifeless since her father had died and listening to her mom share jambalaya cooking tips with Max made Triana smile. She hadn't realized it until now, but Remy and his friends reminded her a lot of her father. She couldn't quite put her finger on why she thought so exactly. None of them looked like him or acted like him. They simply had a presence that struck her as familiar. She was almost certain her mother felt it, too, which was probably why she was having such a good time.

Triana was still thinking about that when she realized Remy was looking at her in a way that had her stomach doing backflips. Their eyes locked, and while everyone around them was laughing and talking, she and Remy simply shared a moment alone in a room full of people.

There was no denying it. She was falling for Remy— hard. Even though she'd known him since high school, she'd only been seeing him romantically for three days, but she already wanted to spend time with him after they both went back to Texas at the end of the week. Dallas and Houston were only a few hours' drive from each other. If she and Remy wanted to, they could make it work.

If anyone had told her she'd have these kinds of

thoughts about a guy so soon after getting involved with him, she would have told them they were crazy, then tightened the straps on their straitjackets herself and called for a pickup wagon. But it wasn't crazy. She'd never met anyone like Remy, and no matter how much she got of him, she always found herself wanting more.

Part of it was the amazing sexual chemistry between them. There was no denying that. She loved sex as much as the next girl, but with Remy she didn't just love it—she *craved* it all the time. That quickie in the hallway last night had been amazing and probably should have left her satiated for days. Instead, after a couple of hours dancing with him at a club on Bourbon Street, she'd dragged him back to his hotel room for another round of lovemaking that probably qualified as an out-of-body experience.

Even more than the sexual cravings, there was something about being with Remy that made her happy. Whether they were walking quietly hand in hand down the street or chatting about the storm in the Gulf and where it might end up, Triana found herself feeling the way she imagined people felt when they were in love.

Loud laughter pulled her attention back to the conversation, and as she gave herself a mental shake, she swore from the knowing look Remy gave her that he somehow knew what she'd been thinking. It wouldn't have surprised her. She already thought he was some kind of superhero with powers and abilities far beyond that of mortal man. How else could he be so amazing?

"Cooper wanted to do something special for his new bride to show her how much he loves her, but he also wanted it to be something she would never see coming in a million years," Max was saying, and it took Triana a moment to figure out they were talking about one of the other guys on the Dallas SWAT team who'd recently gotten married. "So he got the whole team together and we came up with a choreographed line dance to the song 'Howlin' for You' by the Black Keys."

"Let's just say there's a reason most of us are cops and not dancers," Brooks said with a pointed look at Zane. "The whole thing was supposed to be sexy, but it ended up being hilarious. Everly, Cooper's wife, practically passed out she laughed so hard."

Triana's mother smiled. "And you all danced?"

"Only because we didn't want to let Cooper down," Zane said. "But since I have absolutely no rhythm, I mostly stood there looking cool and snapping my fingers to the beat."

Triana wasn't so sure of that. She'd seen Zane and Kim dance together last night, and he seemed to have plenty of moves as far as she could tell. She opened her mouth to say as much, but Max already had Zane on his feet and was attempting to show him how to do the dance they'd done at the wedding. Despite what she'd seen last night on the dance floor, it turned out that Zane honestly didn't have any rhythm. Then again, he didn't have any music to work with so that could have been part of the problem.

"You gotta loosen up those hips, dude," Brooks said in between laughing. "You dance like you have a stick shoved up your butt."

Zane tried, he really did, but it was hopeless. Triana laughed so much she almost fell out of her chair. If she stayed and watched the British SWAT cop try to dance any longer, tears were going to start running down her face and that would just make a mess of her makeup.

"I'm going to get the dessert," she said to Remy. When he made as if to join her, she shook her head. "Stay. I'm just going to slice the cake and bring it out. Hang out here and make Mom laugh some more."

In the kitchen, Triana took the big chocolate cake out of the fridge, then grabbed plates from the cabinet. When her mother had frosted the layer cake earlier, Triana had been sure most of it would go to waste, considering how much jambalaya she'd made. But after seeing those guys in there eat, she figured there wouldn't be a crumb left.

As she sliced the cake, Triana wondered when she should bring up the idea to Remy of continuing their relationship long distance. She was so distracted, she hadn't even realized she'd cut herself with the knife until she felt a sting along one side of her left index finger.

Crap.

She jerked her hand away from the cake, afraid she was going to get blood on it. She'd barely gotten her hand under the faucet so she could wash it off and see how bad it was when she felt someone beside her. She turned to see Remy standing there, a look of concern on his face.

Damn, he was quiet for someone of his size. She hadn't even heard him come in.

"Let me see how bad it is," he said, taking her hand and pushing it under the faucet, then gently washing away the blood.

Triana opened her mouth to tell him it was nothing and that she could take care of it, but the words got stuck in her throat at the worry on his face. She glanced at her finger, thinking maybe the cut was worse than she'd thought. But it wasn't bad at all. In fact, it was a little nick less than half an inch long and not as bad as some paper cuts she'd had. You wouldn't have known that from the care Remy took tending to the cut. He washed it out with soap and water, then put pressure on it to stop the bleeding, while drying the rest of her hand with a towel.

"Where does your mother keep her Band-Aids?" he asked.

She was going to tell him that she could get it, but one look at his face changed her mind. "On the lower shelf of the linen closet in the hallway."

Triana expected him to go get it, but instead, he stood there holding her finger tightly, his expression thoughtful. While she certainly enjoyed him holding her hand, she was a little confused at the same time. They certainly couldn't stay like this for the rest of the night.

She opened her mouth to point out that everyone was probably waiting for dessert when Zane walked in with the box of Band-Aids. The British SWAT officer didn't say a word but simply set the box on the counter, then walked out.

Triana stared after him.

"How did he…?" she began, but the words trailed off as Remy opened the paper wrapping of the Band-Aid and applied it to her cut.

"Thanks," she said. "I never thought of first aid as romantic, but now I see I was wrong."

He arched a brow. "Romantic, huh? I've never thought of it that way, but maybe I have a different definition of the word than you do."

Triana raised up on tiptoe and kissed him, wrapping her arms around him to pull him close. "Does that fit your definition of romantic better?"

Remy nodded, giving her another kiss, this one long and lingering. Her body quivered in response, and she glided one hand down to caress the bulge in his jeans.

"Think anyone would noticed if we slipped into my room for a quickie?" she asked teasingly. "I promise not to make too much noise."

He chuckled softly. "As tempting as that is, I think someone might come looking for us."

She let out a dramatic sigh. "You're probably right. Promise to make it up to me later?"

He kissed her again, making her weak in the knees. "Count on it."

"So, now that the locals are gone, are you going to tell me what the hell has been occupying that so-called mind of yours?" Max asked.

Remy frowned across the table at the younger werewolf. He and Max had joined some of the NOPD SWAT team for lunch after Drew and Brooks had put an early halt to the morning's training so they could make that afternoon's work more difficult. Since there'd been fifteen of them, the waitress had shown them to a back room reserved for parties, but now that the other cops had left, he and Max had the place to themselves.

"Nothing," he lied.

Max snorted. "Bullshit. You were so preoccupied during training this morning that you tossed a 180-pound body dummy over your shoulder and hopped an eight-foot-high chain-link fence like it wasn't even there. Gage told us not to do crap like that."

Remy opened his mouth to deny it, then stopped himself. Maybe he had done something that stupid. He wasn't sure. The morning had been kind of a blur. In fact, he barely remembered any of the combined physical fitness and tactical movement training Drew had put together for them. It wasn't his fault. The training, which consisted of humping heavy gear and rescue dummies, climbing buildings, and shooting pop-up targets, hadn't been very challenging. Unfortunately, that had left him with lots of time to think about other stuff—like Triana.

"Did anyone see me do it?" he asked.

Max waited until the waitress dropped off their second orders of burgers and fries and left the room before answering.

"No. No one saw you do it but Brooks and me." Max reached for the bottle of ketchup. "So what the hell is bothering you?"

Remy glanced out the window at the light drizzle coming down. That morning, the weather experts had announced that Ophelia had changed direction and was now moving along a more northerly track. While New Orleans wouldn't get hit with the worst of the storm, it would still get wet. The outermost rain bands of Ophelia had started coming ashore an hour ago, dropping rain all the way from Mobile in the east to Lafayette in the west.

"I'm just worried about this thing with Aaron Lee," Remy said, turning back to Max. "It's been two days and we haven't heard anything from the informant in his organization. For all we know, the guy—if it is a guy—could be dead by now."

"I hear ya." Max dumped half a bottle of ketchup on his plate, completely drowning his waffle fries, then took a big bite out of his cheeseburger. "How's everything going with Triana?"

Remy cringed. He should have known Max wouldn't buy his crap about the informant. While he was worried about the informant risking his, or her, life to put Aaron Lee behind bars, that wasn't what had his head spinning in circles. That didn't mean he wanted to talk about it though.

"Good," Remy said noncommittally as he focused on his food. He stayed away from the ketchup, preferring to taste the food he was paying for, not the free bottle of crushed tomatoes on the table. "We have a lot of fun together."

"You have a lot of fun together," Max mimicked, imitating Remy's casual tone. "Don't take this the wrong way, but what the hell is wrong with you?"

Remy ground his teeth. Did Max even have a filter on that damn mouth of his? "What do you mean?"

"It means you're full of shit," Max said. "I haven't been a werewolf long enough to know if you're sending out those signals that some of the others can pick up on telling them if you're lying, but I don't need to be a werewolf to figure it out. Don't tell me you haven't realized just how special Triana is, because the rest of us sure as hell have."

"I've already said we have a lot of fun together," Remy pointed out.

Max shoved a waffle fry in his mouth. "Yeah, I heard you the first time. If I didn't know any better, I'd think you're scared."

Remy gave him a sharp look. "Scared of what?"

"Scared that Triana is so special."

Remy shook his head. "It's not like that. Just drop it, okay?"

But Max didn't drop it. Instead, he reached across the table and poked Remy hard in the chest, making his chair slide back a few feet.

"It's not like that?" Max snarled, his eyes rimmed in gold. "Then maybe you can tell me how it is, because I'm not seeing it."

Remy stared at him. Like any newer werewolf, Max sometimes had control issues, but Remy had no idea why the guy was so pissed at him.

"Things with her are happening too fast, that's all," Remy said, pulling his chair in.

Max frowned. "What do you mean, it's happening too fast?"

Remy sighed, wishing he didn't have to talk about this but knowing Max would never let it go.

"I was thrilled when we ran into Triana in that club Sunday night," he said. "She's a beautiful, intelligent woman I enjoy spending time with, but I never wanted it to go beyond that." Max opened his mouth to say something, but Remy cut him off. "Unfortunately, it's too late for that, and now things are getting…strange."

Max downed another waffle fry. "Define strange."

"Remember when Triana nicked her finger with the knife last night?"

Max nodded. "Yeah. I smelled the blood the same time you did."

Remy sighed. "I knew she cut her finger before I smelled the blood."

Max frowned. "What? How?"

"That's where the strange part comes in. I knew it the moment it happened. I didn't smell it. I didn't hear it. I frigging *felt* it."

"What do mean, you felt it?"

Remy shook his head. "I know it's crazy. I was sitting there watching you trying to teach Zane to dance, then I felt a twinge of pain in my left index finger. I didn't even know what it meant, but I was up and heading for the kitchen anyway."

Max's eyes widened. "Okay, that's freaky."

"No kidding. And it's something that's been building since I saw her on Sunday night. Triana is getting under my skin like you wouldn't believe." Remy stared down at his half-eaten cheeseburger. "After I bandaged her finger, she asked if I wanted to go to her room for a quickie."

"I heard," Max said. "So Triana is wild. Nothing wrong with that."

"The problem is I'm finding it nearly impossible to say no to her," Remy said. "It's like I'm addicted to her."

Max grinned. "As addictions go, I think I could deal with it. Yeah, feeling things she feels is a little weird, but I'm still not understanding your major malfunction with this situation."

Remy cursed silently. Why did this have to be so frigging complicated? "When we got back to my room last night, we ended up making love for hours, and it was amazing."

"Is the malfunction showing up at some point?" Max interrupted. "Or are you just rubbing it in?"

"I'm getting to it," Remy snapped. "As Triana lay

there on my chest afterward, she whispered something I can't stop thinking about."

"What?" Max quipped. "'Worst sex ever'?"

Remy bit back a snarl. "No, you stupid dumb-ass. She whispered that this—us…her and me together—is something she could really get used to."

Max stared at him as if he was a pig wearing a Rolex.

"Damn, you're slow," Remy growled. "Max, we've been together for four frigging days and Triana is already thinking long-term. While I didn't exactly freak out, I definitely tensed when she said it, and I think she picked up on it."

"Shit," Max muttered. "You sure?"

Remy shrugged. "She didn't say anything else to me the rest of the night and didn't give me more than a quick kiss when I left the hotel room this morning. I didn't do it to upset her, but when she said those words, they set off alarms."

Not to mention made him want to run for the frigging hills. Even that might not be far enough to forget about Triana and the things she was making him feel.

Max didn't say anything. Instead, he seemed to be considering that as he ate the rest of his fries and wolfed down what was left of his cheeseburger. When he finally finished chewing, he wiped his mouth with a napkin and shook his head.

"Okay, I thought about it and I'm trying to understand where you're coming from, but I don't get it. You have a beautiful woman who's crazy attracted to you. She also happens to be an old friend, so she has that going for her too. Then there's the whole sexual-chemistry thing, and apparently she's already excited about the idea of a future with you. So, what the hell is the problem again?"

Remy cursed. "It's not that simple."

"It seems pretty simple to me," Max said. "You've found *The One* for you, so what's all the drama about? You're like the sixth member of the Pack who's found theirs in the past year. Seven, if you count Khaki. I'm not really sure if that counts as one or two since she fell for Xander, and I already took him into account. Now that I think about it, I'd count her in the total number, since she's part of the Pack now."

Remy ignored the rest of Max's rambling babble. *The One*. Remy had avoided even thinking about that term over the past few days, telling himself there was nothing more going on between him and Triana than an old friendship and some epic sexual chemistry. There was a part of him that had known he was lying to himself, of course. But he did that a lot, and was completely okay with it.

Now, he couldn't avoid the obvious anymore. The thought that Max was right and Triana was almost certainly the one-in-a-billion soul mate he was destined to be with for the rest of his life started a panic attack like nothing Remy had ever experienced. One second he was hyperventilating, and the next he was starting to shift.

They might have been in the backroom of the restaurant, but there were probably forty people twenty feet away, and there he was completely wolfing out. His fangs and claws extended, his facial bones reformed, his nose began to push out, and every muscle in his body started to twist and spasm as it attempted to assume a shape that sure as hell wasn't appropriate for his current environment.

If he hadn't been freaking out at that moment, Remy would have taken the time to wonder how it was possible for him to shift so fast. Unfortunately, he *was* freaking out, and all he could do was attempt to get a grip on himself, slow down his breathing, and shove the beast back inside its cage. But no matter how hard he fought, it wasn't working. He was going to completely lose it. Right there. Right then.

Remy was about to get up and launch himself out the window, praying he could make it into the wooded area behind the restaurant without anyone seeing him, when he felt a stabbing pain in his hand.

He looked down at his hands stretched out on the table in front of him, inch-long claws extending from the tips of each finger. The ring finger on his left hand had been dislocated at the second knuckle and now lay twisted to the side at a weird angle. As he tried to make sense of that, Max grabbed the pinky finger beside it and twisted that one too.

Shit, that hurt.

When the pain of the ligaments starting to give way finally broke through the panic racing through his body, Remy's control snapped back into place. His facial features returned to normal, then his fangs and claws retracted, and finally the long muscles of his legs and back calmed down and stopped spasming.

He popped his two fingers back into place as Max swiped a waffle fry off his plate. Remy resisted the urge to stab him with a fork.

"What the hell is up with you?" Max asked after all

Remy's parts were back in place. "I've never seen you lose control. Hell, I don't think I've ever seen any of the Pack lose it as bad as you just did. Well, maybe Carter, but he's always had issues."

Remy grabbed his iced tea and downed the entire glass in a few swallows. Then he sat there a while trying to get his heart rate back to normal when all it wanted to do was start racing all over again at the knowledge that Triana was *The One* for him.

He had a sudden urge to ask the waitress to bring in a couple of bottles of the strongest whiskey they had behind the bar, but decided against it. Not only would it look bad as hell to have a cop in a Dallas PD uniform sucking down booze with his lunch, but Max wouldn't have let him do it anyway. The idiot would probably sit there cheerfully breaking his fingers for the rest of the afternoon.

"I've been in love before," he finally said. "Her name was Jess, and she was my partner in the U.S. Marshals, back before I became a werewolf."

Max was so stunned he stopped, the waffle fries he'd stolen from Remy's plate halfway to his mouth. "No shit?"

"No shit," Remy confirmed. "I was naive enough to believe having a relationship with my partner wouldn't lead to trouble at some point. It was against the rules, but I was young, cocky, and thought I knew it all. I figured I could have everything I wanted without having to pay the price. It turned out I was wrong."

"What happened?" Max asked.

"We went after some assholes who'd broken out of the federal prison in Leavenworth and ended up trying to take them down without backup. My relationship with Jess made me lose focus at the wrong time. It got her killed and turned me into a werewolf."

On the other side of the table, Max stared at him. "That's it? You were in love, she died, and now you aren't interested in women anymore? Wait a minute. What am I saying? I've seen you go out with lots of women. Hell, I've never known you to not be with a woman."

Remy shrugged. "That's different. Sure, I like women—I'm an alpha frigging werewolf. It's just that I have no interest in anything serious with any of them. I let them know I'm in it for the fun and I only go out with women looking for the same thing. I rarely see any woman more than three or four times, except a select few. But those are special cases because both parties involved know it's just a sexual thing. We're both comfortable with the fact that we're using each other for sex."

Max shook his head as he pilfered more fries from Remy. "Damn. I'm a guy and even I think that's messed up. You've committed your life to a series of meaningless fucks because a woman you were serious about died in the line of duty? You can't really believe that Jess's death is on your hands. I don't know the particulars, but she probably would have died even if you hadn't been sleeping with her."

"But I was sleeping with her, and she did die." Remy held up his hands so Max could see his palms. "See that?"

"See what?"

"The blood."

Max lifted a brow. "Dude, maybe we can set you up with that shrink who talked to Cooper a while ago. He might even be able to text you her number, so you can call her now."

"I don't need to talk to a shrink," Remy ground out.

Max looked doubtful. "I think maybe you do, because there's no blood on your hands—figurative or otherwise."

Remy stared down at his hands. "That's funny, because I see it all the time." He pinned Max with a look. "Watch someone you love die in your arms when you could have done something to prevent it, then tell me there's no blood on your hands."

Max sighed. "Okay. You blame yourself for your partner's death. I get that. I hate to tell you this, but none of that matters. Because whether you want it to happen or not, Triana is *The One* for you. You're going to have to come up with a way to deal with that."

Remy didn't bother denying it this time, not even to himself. He shook his head in disgust at his own stupidity. The moment he'd seen Triana on the dance floor, he'd known there was something special there. He should have run the other fucking way then, but instead he'd convinced himself he could reach out and play with fire for a little while and not get burned by the werewolf legend that had bonded the other members of his pack with their soul mates.

He'd been wrong.

He wasn't sure if he wanted to laugh or throw up. Of all the guys in the Pack who'd been secretly looking forward to finding *The One* for them, it had happened to him, the one werewolf who'd been praying it wouldn't.

The irony wasn't lost on him.

Max sat there silently, apparently waiting for Remy

to wake up and realize there was nothing he could do about the situation and that he was simply going to have to accept it.

Panic punched him in the gut. After what he'd gone through with Jess, not to mention the aftermath, he promised himself he'd never get close to anyone else. The mere thought of going through the pain of seeing another woman he loved die in his arms was almost enough to bring another shift on.

"I'm not going to deal with it," he told Max. "This is my fucking life and I'm not going to let some stupid legend decide how I live it. When I go back to Dallas, I'm going without Triana."

Max regarded him thoughtfully for a moment, then snorted. "That's your big plan? You're going to stand up to this magical force from the cosmos that has been making some of the strongest werewolves in the Pack jump through hoops and just tell it to fuck off?"

"That's exactly what I'm going to do," Remy growled.

Max reached into his back pocket and pulled out his wallet, yanking out enough twenties to cover both their meals. It was only right, since the waffle-fry-stealing punk had eaten most of the food anyway.

After tossing the money on the table, Max gave him a curious look. "I've come to the conclusion that you have a frigging screw loose, so I've stopped expecting anything you say to make sense, but let me ask you one thing. What the hell are you so worried about?"

Remy swallowed hard. "I'm worried that I'll have to live every second of my life looking over my shoulder, worried a mistake I make is going to get Triana killed."

Max shook his head. "Yup, you're beyond mental.

Damn, Remy. Triana isn't Jess. She's not a cop; she's a scientist in a lab, complete with the funny white jacket and a magnifying glass. She's not in any danger."

Remy got up from the table and headed for the door, not even bothering to reply. Max wouldn't get it. How could he explain his gut was screaming that if he gave in and let Triana into his life, she'd be the one that would pay for his decision?

Chapter 11

TRIANA SAT AT A TABLE IN THE BACK OF THE CLUB ON Dauphine Street with Kim, both of them trying their best to ignore the skeevy way the guys at the bar were leering at them. It was still early in the afternoon, and probably two or three hours before the normal evening crowd started trickling into the underground speakeasy to drink their fancy cocktails and listen to the blues musicians strum their instruments in the joint's almost cave-like ambience, but that hadn't stopped the half-dozen professional drinkers at the bar from starting early—or taking a marked interest in them.

"This guy is showing, right?" Kim asked softly.

Triana glanced at her watch. The man she and Kim were waiting to meet was already ten minutes late. Ten minutes wasn't that late in this part of town, where it could take that long just to find a parking space, but with the guys at the bar eyeing her and Kim like they were candy in a vending machine, it felt a lot longer.

"He'll be here," Triana said firmly.

She had to believe that, if for no other reason than the fact that she'd dragged Kim all the way down here with her in the first place.

"You sound pretty convinced considering you don't even know the name of the guy we're supposed to be meeting," Kim muttered.

Triana couldn't argue with that since it was true. But

Bodine had promised the guy would be there, and she trusted Bodine. Mostly.

She was here for one simple reason—she'd opened that sealed envelope of crime scene photos Bodine had given her. Everything had changed the moment she'd seen them. She knew she shouldn't have looked, especially since Bodine had warned her against it, but she'd been digging through the rest of the files full of information on her father's death early that morning and the plain brown envelope had been lying there, bugging her. So she'd opened it and pulled out the photos.

She knew it wasn't as much the need to see if there was new evidence in there as it was the curiosity of not knowing. She hated not knowing stuff.

Part of her realized this sudden burst of curiosity probably had something to do with the fact that she didn't know what was going on with Remy. Last night had been strange. She'd first picked up on the vibe at her mom's place, during dessert. Remy had been looking at her, not with the interested, hungry expression she'd seen earlier, but almost with a distracted and distant one. She also noticed he hadn't laughed too much the rest of the evening either.

It had only gotten worse when they'd gone back to his hotel room. Yes, they'd made love, and it had been beautiful and amazing. But afterward, Remy had been tense and hadn't spoken more than a word or two as she'd fallen asleep on his chest. She was sure she'd done something wrong but had no idea what.

She couldn't help feeling Remy was pulling away from her all of a sudden. That had confused the hell out of her and left her sitting in her room at her mother's apartment trying to figure out what had changed. When she couldn't figure that puzzle out, she'd decided to work on another one instead.

Unfortunately, once she'd spread the photos across the top of the small desk in her bedroom, she'd realized why Bodine hadn't wanted her to see them. To say they were horrible was an understatement. She'd known her father had been shot multiple times, but she hadn't been ready to see the amount of damage.

She worked in an ME's office, so she'd seen horrible things before and had dealt with them. She told herself she'd be able to look at them in a detached manner, maybe see a clue the police and Bodine had missed. She could treat it like another case at work.

But this wasn't another case. This was her father, and it was different.

Tears in her eyes, she'd shoved the photos back in the envelope, never wanting to think of her father that way again, but it was too late. What she'd seen couldn't be unseen. She'd never forget what those men had done to her father.

She was glad her mother had been out shopping at the time because she'd cried for a long time after that. Later, the pain and tears had turned to anger, and she'd started seething. That was when she'd vowed she would catch the people who had murdered her father. Suddenly, she didn't want them in prison any longer; she wanted them dead. It was a horrible thing to think, but it was there, and she couldn't act like it wasn't.

That was also about the time Bodine had called and told her he'd spent the night talking with a guy who'd heard someone bragging about killing a "mean old man in a jazz club and putting a bullet right in his head." The man told Bodine it had been a while ago, but he still remembered the braggart clearly because the guy had been one big-ass dirtbag.

Bodine had a good description and was going to start nosing around for the guy. "A big blowhard like him shouldn't be too difficult to find. If he's bragged about it once right out in the open in a bar, there's a good chance he's done it other times."

That had seemed like a reasonable plan, but with thoughts of her father's violent murder still fresh in her mind, Triana said she wanted to meet the guy and talk to him personally. Bodine hadn't been thrilled with the idea, but she'd insisted, pointing out she was the one paying the bills.

Triana glanced at her watch again, then sighed.

"What's going on with you and Zane?" she asked Kim, hoping to distract herself from thoughts of how crazy it had been to come to a place like this to talk to a man who obviously hung out in bars with murderers. Kim could probably use the distraction too.

Kim smiled. "Nothing much. We mostly hang out and talk. He's easy to talk to, and I have to admit, I could listen to that sexy accent of his all day."

Triana considered asking exactly what her friend meant by *mostly* but then reconsidered. It was obvious that Kim was more relaxed than she'd been since Shawn the Jerk had left her. If Zane was responsible for that, she was fine with it, regardless of what they did or didn't do when they were together. Triana was just happy to see a smile on her friend's face again.

"Zane's figured out I'm not really in a relationship

place right now, that I'm rebounding and just need a way to get my frustrations out," Kim continued. "We make out a little, but nothing serious. I don't think it would be fair to Zane. He's too amazing to jerk around. Besides, I'm still in love with Shawn, even if he isn't in the picture anymore."

Triana tried to read between the lines of those last few sentences, still not sure if Kim and Zane were sleeping together, but something told her they weren't.

"How about you and Remy?" Kim asked. "Did you take my advice and use this week as a chance to make up for all that time you wasted back in high school?"

Triana smiled.

"I'll take that as a yes," Kim said. "So, are you guys going to be doing the long-distance-relationship thing then?"

Triana's smiled faded at that. Before last night, she would have said the two of them were definitely heading in that direction, but now, she didn't think so. The ache in her chest hurt so much she could barely breathe. It was her own fault. She'd let things get a little out of control, started feeling things for Remy way too fast.

"What's wrong?" Kim asked.

"Nothing." Triana pasted on a fake smile. "We've had a lot of fun this week, but I don't think there's a future between Remy and me."

Kim's eyes widened, but before she could say anything, movement near their table interrupted her. Triana lifted her head to see a skinny, gray-haired man standing there. The way he looked at her made her think he wasn't all there, and Triana was doubly glad she'd asked Kim to come with here. Even though she had no idea what Kim would do to help in a scary situation involving this man.

"Are you Triana?" he asked in a rough voice.

Triana nodded, sure he must be the guy she was there to meet. He certainly fit the part of a man who spent a large part of his life in a bar. His voice had that distinctive throaty rasp she imagined came from a lifetime of living off booze and cigarettes.

"That's me," she said. "Are you the person Marcus Bodine told me about?"

The guy nodded but didn't sit. Instead, he looked back and forth between her and Kim. "Marcus said you'd be here alone."

There was no question in the statement, just a simple declaration of fact.

"I didn't think it was a very good idea to come here alone, so I brought my friend," she said.

The man regarded them for a moment, then nodded. "Probably smart. This joint can get a little rough when the alcohol starts pouring." He glanced at the bar. "For some of these guys, it never stops." He pulled out a chair and sat down. "I'm Dominic. Marcus told me about how you're looking for the man who murdered your father. I told him everything I know about the guy I heard bragging about killing someone. It might have been your father or someone else, or maybe he just made it up. I know you probably want details, but I'm not sure what else I can tell you."

Triana really didn't know what kind of details she was looking for, but as a forensic analyst, she knew that sometimes the littlest clues made all the difference.

"Just tell me everything you remember from that

night," she said. "Sometimes, talking helps you remember stuff you thought you'd forgotten."

Dominic didn't look convinced, but he nodded. "I was barhopping that Thursday night. I remember because it was payday. It was also getting near closing time, around four o'clock in the morning maybe. Most of the tourist types were off the street.

"There were a bunch of rough guys at the bar in this one place. Can't for the life of me remember which place it was, though." He shook his head. "Anyway, these guys were telling stories to prove to each other they were a bunch of badasses. Most of the stories were lame, like punching some drunk guy who was already too tanked to see it coming.

"But then this big guy started telling this story about walking into an empty jazz club and killing an old man. A lot of people laughed at first, but they all stopped when the dickhead started adding details about how many times the old man was shot and where. It got really graphic, and by the time he was done, half the bar had emptied out. No one wanted to be anywhere near this guy. He smelled like ten kinds of crazy wrapped up in a bag of horse crap."

Triana swallowed hard. "Tell me exactly what he said."

Dominic hesitated but then did as she asked. By the time he was done, Triana was convinced the man had definitely been talking about her father. He even said the old man had growled. That was something her father did when he was mad.

"What did the man look like?" she asked Dominic. "Can you describe him?"

Dominic thought about it for a while. "Like I said,

he was a big man. I mean, the guy had muscles on top of muscles. He had a tattoo on his arm too—a ship's anchor, I think."

Triana glanced at Kim, wondering if her friend was thinking the same thing she was, that maybe the guy had been a sailor or worked on a ship. New Orleans was a port city, so there were a lot of sailors. But how many would fit this guy's description? He sounded like a man who'd stand out in a crowd.

"Have you ever seen him again?" Triana asked.

Dominic shook his head. "No, ma'am."

Regardless of what he looked like, Bodine would still need a lot of luck to find him, Triana thought.

"Did you recognize anyone else who'd been at the bar that night, someone who might know who this guy is?" Kim asked.

The question seemed to catch Dominic off guard, but after a moment, he nodded. "Yeah, actually I'm pretty sure I've seen some of those guys around before. They're a group of us regulars who live in the bars of this town."

Triana tried to keep herself from getting too excited—and failed. "Do you think you could talk to some of those other guys, see if they might know the name of this big man?"

Dominic looked concerned. "I don't know about that. I understand you wanting to find this guy if he was the one who killed your father, but I wasn't intending to get involved like that."

"I can pay you," Triana said quickly.

At the mention of money, Dominic's whole demeanor changed. "How much?"

She pulled out her purse, digging through it under the

table until she came up with eighty-seven dollars. She shoved it across the table at him. "This is all I have on me, but if you find this guy, I'll give you five hundred more."

That must have convinced him because he nodded, quickly scooping up the money. "If you give me your number, I'll call as soon as I find out something."

Triana wasn't thrilled to be handing out her number to a random stranger, but if this worked, she'd happily get a new phone number.

Five minutes later, she and Kim left the bar and were walking down the street, glad that the on-again, off-again rain had decided to stop for a while. As she turned toward her mother's shop, Triana quickened her pace until she was practically running. This was going to work; she could just feel it. She was going to finally find the guy who murdered her father.

She was still thinking about that possibility when Kim brought her crashing back down to earth a few minutes later.

"Okay, I came with you to see that creepy guy, and I really hope something good comes of it, but right now I want to hear about you and Remy," her friend said. "Why do you think you guys don't have a future?"

Triana sighed. Even though she didn't want to talk about it, the words came tumbling out on their own and she told Kim everything, starting with the night she and Remy had first slept together and finishing with what had happened last night. She hadn't intended to get emotional about the whole thing, but all her worries and doubts came rushing back to the surface, and before she knew it, she was crying. Not just for what she might have already lost, but for what now might never be at all.

———

Remy glanced over at Triana, where she sat in the booth across from him scanning the menu. He couldn't miss the fact that she seemed more subdued than usual. Her heart was beating a little faster than it usually did and she was putting off a weird vibe.

Then again, maybe it was the weather. It was making everything seem off. He looked out the big windows that overlooked Lake Pontchartrain. The rain and wind had gotten stronger throughout the day, making him think it had probably been stupid to drive all the way out to the far side of the lake for dinner. But he'd wanted to take Triana someplace quiet and private so they could talk. On the other hand, coming to a restaurant that was a thirty-minute drive from her mother's shop might not have been the best idea, considering the topic he planned to bring up tonight.

He hated to do it, but after the conversation he'd had today with Max, it was obvious that he needed to be honest with Triana and tell her where things were—or rather weren't—heading. The mere thought of telling her he wanted to stop seeing her was enough to make him want to throw up. He prayed she'd handle the breakup well. If not, he didn't know what he would do.

If he was lucky, Triana would be the one to suggest she wasn't interested in seeing him after they got back to Texas, so he wouldn't have to handle the chore.

What a completely gutless piece of crap he was.

Since he wasn't very hungry, Remy didn't really pay too much attention to the menu. His stomach was feeling a little tender anyway. A side effect of those burgers he'd eaten today at lunch, he supposed. He'd probably just get whatever Triana ordered. That turned out to be a seafood plate with shrimp, crabmeat, and steamed vegetables. It wasn't something he would have normally ordered, but it would do for tonight.

After the waitress left, an uncomfortable silence descended over the table. Remy searched for something to say, wondering where the easy connection that had existed between them the past few days had gone.

"Have you missed working with your team in Dallas this week?" Triana finally asked.

Remy's mouth edged up as he thought of his pack mates. Now that she mentioned it, he actually did miss them despite the fact that they could be irritating as hell sometimes.

"Yeah, I guess I do," he admitted. "I thought I'd enjoy some time away from the insanity that's our lives on the Dallas SWAT team, but now that I'm here, I kind of feel like I'm missing a part of myself, you know?"

She smiled. "Not really. I mean, I love my job at the crime lab, but outside of a few close friends, the only time I see most of them is during the annual Christmas party. I can't imagine being so close with my coworkers that I'd think of them as family. It must be pretty awesome."

He chuckled, feeling a weight dropping off his shoulders as the tension that had been filling the space between them melted away, reawakening their vibrant connection. Maybe he could put off the serious part of the conversation until he dropped Triana off at her mother's shop.

"It is." He couldn't count how many times his pack mates had covered his ass on the job, even taking bullets for him when necessary. "There's something special about knowing people will always have your back but will still call you out when you're screwing up."

She laughed. "I can't imagine you ever screwing up."

"We all screw up," he said. "The thing that's important is having people around that you trust enough to get you out of trouble when it happens."

She considered that for a moment. "If the rest of your team is like Max, Brooks, and Zane, they must be pretty incredible. You must have a million stories about them."

That was an understatement. But if he told her any, he'd have to censor some of the best parts. He couldn't have her figuring out the whole Dallas SWAT team was made up of werewolves.

Remy rested his forearms on the table and grinned. "Well, if you want to hear a funny story, I should probably tell you about Cooper first. He met his future wife in line at the bank right before the place got held up."

"No way!" Triana's eyes widened. "What happened?"

"He arranged a date, then kicked the crap out of the bank robbers."

"Whoa." Triana smiled. "How'd their date go?"

"Exceptionally well," Remy told her. "They met in June and got married two weeks ago."

"You're full of it," she said, smacking his arm. "You're making that part up."

As the waitress set down their plates, Remy promised her he wasn't joking. To prove it, over dinner, he went into greater detail about Cooper's whirlwind romance with his wife, Everly.

Triana laughed and asked lots of questions, saying it sounded insane but that she believed Remy. Before long, he found himself telling her about all the guys meeting their significant others, while leaving out all the werewolf stuff, of course.

A little while ago, he had wondered why he'd even brought Triana all the way out here in such crappy weather, and now he was beginning to think the tension he'd felt was all just a figment of his imagination. Hell, even his appetite was back. He'd absolutely demolished the plate of seafood in front of him.

"Wait a minute," Triana said with a laugh. "I think I'm picking up a theme with all these stories you're telling me. Is it me, or do most of them revolve around your teammates getting themselves into crazy situations with women they just met?"

Remy shrugged. "Yeah, I guess you're right. Relationships do seem to be the central theme of most of the insanity that's been going on lately."

She sipped her wine thoughtfully. "Speaking of relationships, do you mind if I ask you something personal?"

Remy's gut clenched as he wondered where she was going with the question. Nowhere good that he could think of. But it wasn't like he could say no, not without coming off weird.

So he nodded—and prayed.

"How is it possible that a guy as good-looking, sweet, and single as you hasn't gotten seriously involved with anyone yet?" Triana asked.

Remy felt his fingertips start to tingle, as if another shift was coming on. He forced himself to calm down as he tried to laugh off the question, not sure how to even begin to answer it.

"I guess I just haven't met the right person yet," he said.

Triana's gaze darted to him. Suddenly, he realized he'd left a lot of room for interpretation with that lame-ass answer. *Shit.* What if she assumed he was implying she was the right person? Which he supposed she was… just at the wrong time.

But Triana didn't bite one way or the other. "I think you're avoiding the question," she said. "Are you honestly telling me that with all of your teammates finding love in the most unusual of circumstances, you've never found anyone you thought might be the right person for you?"

Remy swallowed hard. He couldn't help thinking about what he'd had with Jess, but that wasn't anything he wanted to get into. He *had* wanted to talk to Triana about their relationship, though—or at least the relationship they couldn't have. Now was as good a time as any to do it.

"There was someone," he finally admitted quietly. "But that was a long time ago."

Triana looked stunned. "Did you love her?"

He nodded, unable to say the words.

On the other side of the table, Triana looked ashen. "What happened? Why didn't it work out?"

Damn, he didn't want to get into this. "It's something I'd really rather not talk about."

"Why not?"

Remy gripped the edge of the table, afraid if he didn't, he might shift at any moment. On the other side of the table, Triana regarded him curiously, and he knew he couldn't leave her hanging. He'd wanted her to understand there couldn't be anything between them, hadn't he? It was time to man up and say what needed to be said.

"It didn't work out, okay?" he said, his voice sharper than he intended. "It ended badly, and since then, I haven't been able to find anyone who could convince me to try again."

He cringed as he realized how harsh his words had been. That was nothing compared to how shitty he felt when he saw the pain in Triana's eyes. But what else could he have said? It was the truth. He didn't have it in him to open his heart up again, to get hurt again. Wasn't it better for Triana to know that now, instead of waiting until later when it would be even harder for her to take?

"So, there's no…" Voice trailing off, she looked down at her half-empty plate, blinking her eyes rapidly.

"No," he said softly. "There isn't."

Triana shook her head, then pushed back her chair and made a beeline for the door. Remy hastily tossed money on the table, running out of the restaurant to catch up to her. By the time he did, she was halfway to his car, oblivious to the rain soaking her pretty dress. He got the umbrella up and over her, but she didn't seem to notice that either. At least he could lie and tell himself the wetness he saw on her face was the rain.

As he got her in the car and walked around to the driver's side, he thought he might actually throw up.

The drive back into the city was long and painfully quiet, except for the constant *thump-thump* of the windshield wipers and the splash of the tires on the wet road. Remy tried to convince himself he'd done the right thing, but damn, if that was the case, why the hell did it hurt so much to see Triana simply shut down like she had? It was like someone had turned off a light bulb, leaving everything in darkness.

Chapter 12

Triana was reeling.

Remy might not have said the words, but in every way that mattered, he'd broken up with her. The fears that had been building in her heart since the night before had turned out to be true, and now it felt like something inside her was dying.

She didn't remember the drive back across the lake bridge, barely even noticed the rain drumming on the roof of Remy's car as they headed into the city. Heck, she didn't even realize they'd made it back to her mother's shop until Remy came around to help her out of the car and walk her to the door. At least it wasn't raining by then.

She looked down in confusion and saw that Remy was holding her hand. If they were over, she didn't need him walking her to the door or holding her hand. She started to pull her hand away when Remy stopped suddenly, his posture rigid and tense.

"Stay here," he said.

She opened her mouth to ask him what was wrong, but he was already running the last dozen feet toward the door of the shop so fast he was practically a blur. She was going to tell him the door would be locked, but she didn't get a chance as he jerked it open and disappeared inside. A moment later, she heard the sound of glass breaking.

Triana's heart lurched.

"Mom!"

Heedless of Remy's order to stay where she was, Triana raced for the door. She had no idea what the hell was going on, but her mother was in there. She'd be damned if she was going to stand there and do nothing.

She ran into the shop, absently wondering why it wasn't locked like it usually was. The interior was illuminated only by the glow of the lone streetlamp outside and the neon in the windows, and she skidded to a halt, trying to make sense of the blurs of movement she saw in the near darkness as well as the grunts, growls, and curses she heard. The only thing she knew for sure was that Remy was in there, and he was fighting with someone.

Triana took out her cell phone to call the police when the lights suddenly came on, making her vision sparkle with stars. When it cleared, the image that met her eyes was enough to almost make her want to turn off the lights again as she saw her mother coming out from behind the counter with her baseball bat at the ready and Remy facing off against the three big goons from the other day. Well, actually there were only two of them now, since the third was rolling around on the floor, groaning and cradling a cast-wrapped hand against his chest. The cast looked like it had been crushed in a trash compactor. The other two men were still coming at Remy hard though, and this time they were armed. Triana's heart almost stopped as she saw that one of the men held a gun, while the other held a long, wicked knife.

She hadn't realized her feet were moving in that direction until her mother yelled at her to stop. Every pair of eyes turned her way, immediately followed by the barrel of the gun.

All Triana could do was stare. Why was everything moving so fast, but she was moving so slowly?

There was a deep growl, then the sound of her mother screaming, followed by a blur of movement as Remy smashed into the guy with the gun so hard the man bounced off the wall behind him and the gun went skittering across the floor. But going after that guy left Remy with his back to the man with the knife, who used the opportunity to take a savage swing at him.

"Remy, behind you!" Triana yelled.

Remy ducked and swung around, bringing an arm up to block the knife. She watched in horror as the sharp edge of the blade sliced through his upraised forearm, slinging blood across the room.

Triana expected Remy to gasp in pain and drop to the floor, but instead, he stepped back and kicked the guy in the chest hard enough to send him rolling across the floor…and straight into her. She went down in a heap of arms and legs, punching and kicking at the man, terrified he might still have the knife.

Everything went crazy after that. There was shouting and swearing; then she was being pulled to her feet by someone really strong. She almost took a swing at the person until she realized it was Remy.

"Are you okay?" he asked urgently, his eyes full of terror as he gently ran his hands over her, apparently looking for injuries.

Triana couldn't answer him because all she could see and comprehend was the blood running down his arm.

He must have decided she was okay, because he

turned to go after the men now fleeing the shop. *Like hell*, Triana thought. There was no way she was going to let him go anywhere with his arm bleeding like that. Slapping one hand over the wound, she buried the other in the fabric of his T-shirt and refused to let go.

Remy let out one of those growls like her father used to, then tugged at her hands. "Triana, they're getting away!"

Triana held him tight, digging in her heels and refusing to let go. "You're bleeding!"

Remy opened his mouth to argue, but closed it again as her mom came over to put her hand on his shoulder. "Let them go, Remy. We know how to find them."

He clenched his jaw but nodded. Triana sagged with relief, only to tense again when she saw blood seeping out from between the fingers she had wrapped around Remy's forearm.

"We need to call an ambulance," she said, hearing a voice rising high in panic and realizing that it was hers.

Her mother gently peeled Triana's hand away from Remy's T-shirt, then did the same to the one clutching his forearm. "We don't need an ambulance, Triana. I have a first-aid kit in the back room. I can patch him up just fine here."

Triana released his arm, swaying a little on her feet, suddenly queasy. She'd seen a lot of blood in the crime lab, but none of it had come from someone she knew, much less a man she was falling in…

"Remy needs to go to a hospital, Mom. He needs stitches," she said.

Triana had taken enough first-aid courses in college to know that.

Her mom shushed her and steered Remy over to the counter. "He doesn't need a hospital or stitches. I used to fix up your dad after he'd get into fights down at the club. This is just a little scratch."

Triana stood there in disbelief as her mother disappeared into the backroom, coming out with a first-aid kit in a big green canvas bag that looked like something an army medic would use. Inside it were forceps, clamps, retractors, and even scalpels. What the heck was her mother doing with a setup like this?

Triana was even more confused at the calm, confident manner her mother displayed as she pulled out the various pieces of gauze and bandages she wanted. A moment later, her mother snapped on some gloves and went to work, apparently not fazed at all by the amount of blood or the deep cut. Then again, now that Triana looked at the wound more closely, she realized it wasn't nearly as bad as she'd thought. It wasn't even bleeding that much now.

She glanced at Remy to see that he seemed as surprised as she was by the sudden appearance of Dr. Gemma, Voodoo Medicine Woman.

"Maybe I should run down to the emergency room and get this looked at anyway," he said cautiously. "I'm sure it would make Triana more comfortable."

Her mom made a tsking sound as she wrapped the wound in a thick bandage as though she'd done it a hundred times. "You know as well as I do that you don't need stitches, Remy. Triana is a big girl, you know. She'll figure it out soon enough."

Triana frowned, wondering what the heck that meant, but before she could ask for an explanation, her mother announced she was done and began cleaning up. Triana moved to check the bandage, worrying there might be blood soaking through it, but Remy was already heading for the door.

"I'm going to pay our lawyer friend, Kenneth Murphy, a little visit," he said.

Triana started to follow him but then forced her feet to stop. "Remy."

He hesitated at the door for a moment before turning to look at her. She wasn't sure what she expected to see in his face. Maybe she was hoping there'd be some sign that what had transpired at dinner had all been some big misunderstanding.

There was no such sign, merely a closed-off expression convincing her she'd been right. What had started out so hot and fiery between them had already burned out.

"Be careful," she finally said, hoping he wouldn't do anything to the lawyer that would get him into trouble.

Remy gazed at her for a long moment, then nodded before turning away and walking out. With his departure, Triana felt another thread connecting them snap. The pain that caused hurt more than she could have ever imagined.

Turning, Triana walked past the counter and up the steps to her room, ignoring the look of confusion on her mother's face. She wasn't in the mood to talk at the moment.

Tears pooled in her eyes, running down her face as she sat down on the bed. She was never going to see Remy again and she wasn't sure she'd ever get over him.

The windshield wipers on Remy's Mustang were fighting a losing battle trying to keep up with all the rain pounding the glass as he and Max drove into the SWAT facility. Ophelia had strengthened into a Category 1 hurricane during the night, and weather experts were now predicting landfall would be around Lafayette, Louisiana, a hundred miles west of New Orleans. But the storm outside was nothing compared to the one raging inside his head. That particular tempest was definitely a Category 5 catastrophe.

He hadn't slept at all last night. Instead, he'd lain in bed staring at the ceiling with eyes that let him see every tiny detail in the darkness, wondering how things had gotten this messed up. He'd started spending time with Triana because she was a friend, she was beautiful, and he'd been attracted to her more than he'd ever been attracted to anyone in his life—even Jess. It wasn't supposed to be anything more than a week filled with fun.

But somewhere along the way, he'd been dumb enough to let things go too far, and now everything was screwed up because he'd done the one thing he never intended to do—fallen in love with her.

Last night had been an absolute train wreck. He couldn't believe some of the shit he'd said to Triana. He'd wanted to make her realize there wasn't going to be a future between them, but he'd never meant to hurt her. That was sure as hell what he'd done though.

It had been bad enough during dinner when he'd as much as come right out and said he'd been in love once and never wanted to be again. He'd seen how much that had hurt her. Hell, he'd felt the pain in his own heart just like he had felt the twinge in his finger when she'd cut hers. But then later, after the break-in at her mother's shop, he'd walked away from her even though he'd known how freaked out and scared she was. What the hell was wrong with him? Who walked away from the woman they cared about and left her to deal with all that fear and confusion completely on her own? That wasn't who he was, dammit. At least not the kind of person he wanted to be. He'd told her he had to leave so he could go after Murphy, but that was bullshit. He'd left because it had been too hard to look at her anymore.

Besides, chasing the lawyer had been a bust. The man wasn't at the office listed on his website, and when he'd gone to the man's home address—which he'd found after snooping around the office for a while—it was to find signs of a hasty departure.

Remy shook his head, trying to clear it, which was difficult to do with the way it was spinning.

It had never been like this before. He'd walked away from plenty of women in the past, and it had never been a big deal. With Triana, it was definitely a big deal. He'd never felt this shitty in all his life.

This morning had been even worse than last night. He didn't just feel shitty; he actually felt sick. Like he was going to throw up, which he hadn't done since he was a teenager. Werewolves didn't get sick. He'd told himself yesterday it had been the burgers, then the seafood, but if that was the case, why was he feeling so crappy now? He hadn't eaten anything this morning.

"Remy!"

Max's voice jolted him out of his reveries and he

looked over to see his pack mate regarding him in concern. That's when Remy realized they were almost at the SWAT facility. Crap, he didn't even remember the drive.

"Dude," Max said. "I called your name three times. You were frigging muttering to yourself like a psycho."

Remy opened his mouth to crack a joke about talking to himself being more entertaining than talking to Max when his friend leaned over to sniff him. A moment later, he sat back, making a face.

"Are you okay? You're putting off a strange scent I've never smelled before."

Remy scowled. "Is that your polite way of saying I didn't shower enough this morning?"

Max shook his head. "I'm being serious. You smell… I don't know…kind of sick or something. To tell the truth, you don't look so hot either. You're sweating and your face is pale. Do you feel okay?"

Remy was about to blow it off, because…well…he was a guy, and that's what guys did. But he knew it would be useless because Max was a guy too. His friend would keep poking him until Remy told him what the problem was.

"Not really," he admitted. "I didn't get much sleep last night."

"Because you were with Triana fixing things, right?" Max asked hopefully.

Remy ran a hand through his hair, then quickly gripped the wheel tighter when the front tires of the car hydroplaned a little as he drove through a big patch of standing water. This wasn't supposed to be a bad storm, but there were areas of this city that tended to flood any time there was more than a light shower. With this much rain, it was going to be ugly.

"I wish that was the reason," he said after a moment. "Unfortunately, it wasn't anything that enjoyable."

"That doesn't sound good," Max muttered. "What happened?"

Remy shrugged. "Triana and I went to dinner and the subject of relationships came up. Without meaning to, I kind of told her that I'd been in love once and didn't have any inclination to do it again."

Max didn't say anything for a moment. Based on how Max had reacted yesterday, Remy wouldn't be surprised if his friend punched him, regardless of the fact that he was driving.

"I know we talked about this yesterday and that you felt it could never work between you guys, but dumping her right in the middle of dinner?" Max blew out a breath. "That's pretty fucked up, even by your relatively screwed-up social rules of engagement."

Remy sighed. "I know. I cringed the moment the words were out of my mouth, but by then it was too late to do anything."

"That's bullshit," Max said. "Maybe you should have just nutted up and told her you're a chickenshit who's simply afraid to fall in love again."

Remy snorted. "Oh yeah, that probably would have worked. Unfortunately, since you weren't around to give me advice last night, I went with my own instincts, which seem to be rather impaired when it comes to Triana."

Max groaned. "Oh hell, what else did you do?"

Remy told him about the lowlifes at Gemma's shop and how he'd dealt with them, then the strange way

Triana's mother had behaved after seeing him sliced open, and, most important, the way he'd walked out on Triana afterward.

"Damn," Max breathed. "When you want to sabotage a relationship, you really go all out."

Understatement there. "Even though I thought I was doing it for the right reasons, I still went to bed last night feeling like a complete shit."

He pulled into the parking lot of the NOPD SWAT facility when Max hit him with a question that completely caught him off guard.

"You think that's why you're sick this morning? Because of the way you treated Triana last night?"

"I'm not sick," Remy said firmly. "I'm just tired."

As he parked in one of the visitor spaces at the end of the first row of vehicles, Max leaned in and gave him another sniff. "Could have fooled me. You don't smell right, dude. I think we should call Cooper."

Remy frowned. "Why the hell would we call Cooper?"

"Because he always knows what to do about this kind of weird shit. Besides, you remember how screwed up Cooper felt when Everly didn't want to have anything to do with him. Well, I think you're going through the same thing, except worse because this time you're the one trying to walk away from the person who's *The One* for you."

Remy wanted to tell him that was just about the dumbest crap he'd ever heard, but unfortunately, he couldn't tell Max he was wrong. None of the other members of the Pack who'd been lucky enough to find their soul mates had ever tried to resist the attraction. For all Remy knew, Max could be right. This crappy feeling in the pit of his stomach just might be his body's way of saying he was making the dumbest mistake of his life.

He remembered Max laughing at his big plans to tell the cosmic forces behind the legend of *The One* to fuck off. Maybe this was how the cosmos responded to dumb-ass plans like that.

Not that he intended on listening to his body. He might hate the way this was all going down, but he still believed separating himself from Triana was the best thing to do.

Remy was still thinking about that as he and Max walked into the SWAT facility. They hadn't even shaken the water off their rain jackets when Brooks and Drew met them in the hallway.

"Don't bother drying off. You're going right back out," Drew said. "We have reports of some of the streets in Bywater already starting to flood. I need you and Max to get over there with some of my guys to help people evacuate from the worst of the low-lying areas."

Remy and Max immediately fell into step with several of the local guys who passed them in the hallway and headed toward the back door. Going back out in the rain was fine with him. It would give him something to occupy his mind instead of thoughts of Triana. Because right then, that was definitely something he didn't want to think about.

Chapter 13

"YOU WANT THE T-SHIRTS TAKEN UPSTAIRS TOO?" TRIANA yelled toward the back room, where her mom was busy packing up all her herbs, powders, and potions.

"Yes," her mother called. "I want anything that can get water damage moved upstairs. That includes the T-shirts, books, dolls, and gris-gris bags."

Triana groaned softly. She'd known before asking what her mom was going to say. She eyed the two racks full of shirts, dreading the task of boxing them up and carrying them upstairs, but she understood why her mother wanted the stuff moved. Ophelia was coming in closer to New Orleans than anyone was comfortable with, and even though no one was predicting this part of the city would flood, there was always a chance they'd get water coming in under the door, which it did during bad summer thunderstorms on occasion. If that happened, they'd all be happy they put a little work into saving the shop's merchandise.

"Those T-shirts aren't going to pack up themselves," Kim said as she dumped a pile of empty boxes at Triana's feet.

Triana smiled. Her friend had shown up an hour ago, saying she'd known Triana and her mom would need some help getting stuff done. That was just an excuse. In reality, Kim had stopped by because she'd known Triana needed a friend this morning. Kim hadn't asked any questions about what had happened last night. Instead, she'd walked in and given her a big hug. Triana wasn't sure what she'd done to deserve friends like Kim, but she thanked God she had them.

She and Kim spent the next hour silently loading up the merchandise and moving it upstairs. It was physically demanding and monotonous, but at least it gave Triana something to focus on, instead of all the crap that had happened last night. She'd spent the whole time trying to figure out what had gone wrong between her and Remy and had nothing to show for it. When she'd gotten out of bed that morning, she'd decided she was done wasting her energy trying to figure him out.

Triana had just come downstairs for another load of books when she caught sight of a wet, bedraggled figure standing at the door, tapping softly on the glass. For one insane moment, she thought it was Remy, but the guy wasn't anywhere near as tall or as big. Her first instinct was to tell whoever it was they were closed, but then she recognized the face under all that dripping hair and realized the morning had just taken a strange twist.

"Kim, you have a visitor!" she yelled up the steps. "I think you might want to come see who it is."

Her friend came bouncing down the steps a few seconds later, a questioning looking on her face. "Who the heck comes to visit on a day like today?"

Kim stopped cold when she reached the bottom step and saw who was at the door. A dozen different emotions flitted across her face, including hope, anger, and disappointment. Pushing her blond hair back, Kim squared her shoulders and walked over to the door. Instead of unlocking and opening it, she stood there staring at her ex-boyfriend through the glass.

"What are you doing here, Shawn?"

The man Triana had met dozens of times remained solemn as the rain continued to drip off of him. "I was worried about you, with the storm coming and all. I wanted to make sure you're okay."

Kim didn't say anything for a long time, but finally she nodded. "I'm fine. Thanks for asking."

Shawn wiped water off his face. "Can we talk?"

Kim slowly crossed her arms and tilted her head to the side a little. "Sure. Go ahead and talk. I'm not stopping you."

Shawn lifted a brow, which was rather impressive considering he was about to drown under all the water cascading off the side of the building. "Could I maybe talk to you inside...out of the rain?"

Kim sighed, then turned and looked at Triana. "Could I have a second? This won't take long."

Triana nodded, already starting to back up the stairs. "Sure. Mom and I will be getting stuff packed away up here. Take all the time you need."

As she headed up the steps, she ran into her mother coming down.

"Shawn showed up," she said, stopping her. "Kim needs a little time alone with him. I figured we could do some stuff upstairs while they talk."

Her mom frowned. "We could, but then we wouldn't be able to hear what they're saying."

Triana gaped as her mother quietly slipped down another step before taking a seat. "Mom, you are absolutely horrible."

Her mother didn't answer. Instead, she motioned with her hand for Triana to join her. Against her better judgment, Triana sat down beside her.

Downstairs, Kim had let Shawn into the shop and he was currently apologizing, saying he'd been stupid to walk out on her.

"I don't really have an excuse beyond the obvious fact that I was scared about taking the next step with you," he admitted. "I got comfortable with the way things were and couldn't understand why anything had to change. Instead of listening to you, I lashed out, then bailed."

"Yeah, you did," Kim agreed. "So what are you doing here now?"

Triana heard a heavy sigh and a rustle of movement. Even though she couldn't see downstairs, she imagined Shawn standing there raking his wet, black hair back from his face in frustration.

"I went on a three-day bender after we broke up," Shawn confessed. "I figured since we were over, I was free to do anything I wanted, but I discovered pretty fast I wasn't nearly as free as I thought I'd be. I've spent the last three weeks thinking about you almost every minute of the day, realizing that I don't want to be free. I want to be with you."

There was silence downstairs, and Triana leaned forward a little to hear Kim's reply.

"What are you trying to say, Shawn?" Kim finally asked. "That you want us to go back to the way things used to be? That you want a do-over?"

"No, I'm not saying that."

Triana's shoulders slumped. She'd thought from

everything Shawn said that he'd come to his senses, but she guessed he was still a jerk. What the heck had he come here for?

Shawn sighed. "I'm not saying that because I don't want that. I know we can't ever go back to what we used to be, but being apart has given me a lot of time to think. Every happy memory I have from the past three years includes you, Kim. I'm pissed that it took us being apart—and a frigging hurricane in the Gulf—for me to figure that out, but I finally get it. I'm in love with you and I know that the only way I'll ever be happy again is if we're together. So, even though I know I don't have any right to ask this of you, I'm asking anyway. Will you give me another chance, not just to be your boyfriend, but to be your husband?"

There was another rustling noise followed by the distinct sound of a jewelry box opening. Triana turned and looked at her mother, who stared back. As one, they scooted down the steps on their butts until they could lean forward enough to see into the shop. The scene they found was exactly what Triana had imagined. Shawn was down on one knee in a puddle of water, a black jewelry box in his outstretched hands, a beautiful ring nestled in the box's velvet-lined interior. Kim stood in front of him, one hand over her mouth, shock and awe on her face.

The two of them stayed like that for so long Triana thought she might have to run down there and kick them.

But then Kim grabbed Shawn's hands, pulling him to his feet and kissing him. Triana thought she heard a few murmured words of love and acceptance, but she was too busy nudging her mother upstairs to be sure.

Kim called up from the bottom of the stairs a little while later. "I heard you two on the steps, so don't bother acting like you have no idea what happened down here."

Triana grinned and hurried downstairs, her mom right behind her. Kim was alone in the shop, a big smile on her face and a ring on her finger. Triana and her mother both hugged her and offered congratulations.

"I asked Shawn to go check on his parents and make sure everything is okay there," Kim said. "He's going to come back and pick me up later, so I still have time to help you two finish packing up."

Instead of moving over to pack another box, Kim pulled out her cell phone. "I need to call Zane and let him know Shawn and I are back together."

Kim didn't try and hide her conversation as she called the British SWAT officer, so Triana listened in while her friend told Zane about Shawn. Zane must have handled it well because Kim laughed at whatever he said. After hanging up, Kim came over to help Triana pack a box of voodoo dolls.

"That guy is so amazing," Kim said. "Zane actually said he's happy for Shawn and me, and I believe him. I'm telling you, if I wasn't already crazy in love with Shawn, I'd make a serious move on the man. Though something tells me it's going to take one hell of a woman to win his heart. That guy is one of a kind."

While Triana's mother disappeared into her workshop to finish in there, she and Kim got the rest of the more delicate merchandise moved upstairs.

"Okay, so what's the word on Remy?" Kim asked as they stood in the hallway making sure the stack of boxes was stable.

Triana told her about their date at the restaurant across the lake and what had happened afterward. "I assumed Remy was going to make the dumping official once we got back to the shop, but the break-in sort of got in the way. Not that it really matters. As far as I'm concerned, we're done."

Kim hugged her. "That sucks. Why'd he take you out to such a nice place if he was just going to break it off with you? Hell, he could have done it by a text and it would have been better."

Triana snorted. "No kidding."

She and Kim chatted about men in general and ass-holes in particular for a while, until Shawn came to pick Kim up. Kim hugged Triana again and told her to call if she needed to talk, then left with her new fiancé.

Triana was happy the two of them had worked it out, but she couldn't help comparing Kim and Shawn's relationship to her and Remy's. She told herself it was silly to contrast the two. Kim and Shawn had been together a long time and had merely run into a rough spot. She and Remy had only gone on a couple of dates and slept together a few times. It had never been anything more than that, and if she'd let herself think that, it was her own damn fault.

When her mom came down a little while later, Triana was staring out the window at the rainwater running down the street outside like a little river. Her mother walked over to put her arm around her.

"I know some stuff happened last night with Remy. Do you want to talk about it?"

Triana shook her head. "Not right now. Maybe later."

Her mom nodded. "Whenever you're ready, dear."

She pressed a kiss to Triana's cheek. "I'm going to check on some of our neighbors and see if they need any help. You should stay close to the shop. The weather people said it shouldn't get too bad out, but the winds will probably get worse over the next couple of hours."

Triana gave her mother a hug and told her to be careful, then locked the door behind her. She was wondering what she could do next to keep herself occupied when her cell phone rang. Her heart leaped, hoping it was Remy, but it quickly sank when she looked at the number and didn't recognize it.

She answered anyway, immediately knowing from the rough voice on the other end that it was Dominic. It kind of reminded her of a sink disposal chewing on gravel.

"My timing is lousy with this storm, but I think I've found the guy I heard bragging about killing your dad," he said. "I thought you'd want to know, even with the hurricane coming."

Triana was so stunned she almost dropped the phone, but she recovered quickly enough. "How'd you find him so fast? Where is he? Do you know his name?"

"Whoa, slow down, woman," Dominic said. "I haven't slept since we met yesterday, so one question at a time."

Triana took a deep breath and forced herself to calm down. "Okay, since you said you haven't slept since yesterday, does that mean you've been looking for this guy the whole time?"

"Yeah. I spent the entire night dragging my ass through every lowlife bar and dive in this city, and let me tell you, there are a lot of them. An hour ago, I met a guy who knew exactly who I was taking about. Said he'd heard this shithead named Shelton Quinn mouthing off about taking out this big dude who owned a jazz club and thought he was a real badass. Even described the same tattoo I'd seen."

Her hand tightened on the phone. "Quinn—that's his name? Do you know where he can be found?"

The guy laughed, a sound that quickly broke up into a fit of coughing. "I can do you one better than that, lady. Meet me on Royal Street near the old Architect Alley and I'll point him out to you."

Her pulse raced, eagerness warring with concern. She knew the place. It was in the Marigny, which was a really nice part of town. But getting there would mean driving down a lot of streets that were probably close to flooding by now.

"You want me to meet you right now, with the hurricane coming in?"

"Hell yeah, lady. How the hell else we going to do this?" Dominic demanded, clearly pissed she'd even asked. "I'm sitting here in my car right now, across the street from the warehouse I tracked this guy to. He walked in a few minutes ago, but I got no idea how long he's going to stay here. And I sure as hell ain't going to wait around until he comes out so I can get a picture. Besides, I found him; now I want the money you promised me."

Triana still hesitated. She wanted to catch the man who killed her father more than anything, but she was smart enough to know that going to the place where this guy might actually work probably wasn't too smart. Bodine would have a cow if he knew she was considering something like this.

"Shouldn't we call Bodine and let him know what you found out?" she asked.

"Lady, you can call anyone you want, but I'm expecting someone down here with my money in the next fifteen minutes or I'm leaving. I don't want to be out in this weather any more than you do."

Triana was tempted to tell him she didn't appreciate being threatened, but she resisted the urge. It would only chase Dominic away, and she sure as heck didn't want to do that. She needed the guy.

"Okay, I'll be there as fast as I can," she snapped. "But it's going to take me a bit. I don't keep five hundred dollars lying around in my couch cushions."

Dominic laughed. "You can pay me another way, if you want."

That thought made Triana want to yak. "I don't think so. I'll be there in fifteen minutes with your money."

Another throaty chuckle. "I thought so, but now it's twelve minutes. You done wasted three minutes talking instead of driving."

Triana swore and hung up. Twelve minutes didn't give her much time to stop at an ATM. She ran upstairs for her purse, calling Bodine on the way back down. Hopefully, she could get the PI to meet her. Unfortunately, he didn't answer. She quickly left him a message, giving him the address Dominic had provided.

"I'll call as soon I get something," she added.

Triana started to drop her phone into her purse, then hesitated. Maybe she'd call Remy too. He might not care, but still…

She dialed his number before she had a chance to think better of it. It went to voice mail. She considered leaving a message but then hung up. For all she knew, he was ignoring her calls anyway, and she refused to come off as pathetic.

Remy and Max walked into the main briefing room of the NOPD SWAT facility, soaked to the bone and squishing water out of their boots with every step. They'd spent the whole morning working the streets of Bywater, Saint Claude, and the Lower Ninth Ward, doing everything from shoving water-stalled vehicles off the roads to helping those living in the worst of the flood-prone areas get to higher ground. The rain was still coming down in buckets, and in a city surrounded by levees, that meant lots of flooded streets. But at least it was better than getting hit with the storm head-on.

Still, it had been a long frigging morning and he was beat, which was unusual, considering werewolves rarely got tired. He couldn't help wondering if maybe Max was right and his exhaustion had something to do with breaking up with Triana. It sounded crazy, but if that wasn't it, what the hell was it?

Remy figured he and Max would be out helping people for hours, but Brooks had called fifteen minutes ago and told them to get their butts back to the shop ASAP. He hadn't said why, but one look at Lorenzo standing off to one side of the briefing room, clearly tense as hell, not to mention the building outline drawn up on the whiteboard with access points and entrance routes marked all over it, and Remy knew why Brooks had told them to get back here. They were going after Aaron Lee again.

"Took you two long enough," Brooks muttered, not looking up from the Google Maps image of a big building spread out on the table in front of him.

"Sorry about that," Remy said. "There's standing water on almost every street in the city now and some of the wind gusts are strong enough to shove a vehicle off the road if you start to hydroplane."

"Whatever," Brooks said. "Get over here so we can bring you guys up-to-speed on the plan. Zane and the team Drew selected for the raid are almost finished loading up."

"We got the call from our informant?" Remy asked as he scanned the drawing on the whiteboard. From the size and layout of the building drawn there, it looked like another warehouse structure similar to the last one they'd raided.

Drew nodded. "A text actually. Our informant said Lee's people are in a warehouse on Royal Street where one of the Mardi Gras krewes stores their floats. They probably figure it will be safer to use a location that has no connection to Lee. It's going to take them a while to break down hundreds of pounds of meth, so we've got time to do this right."

"Are we still keeping everyone else in the dark about this?" Remy asked.

Lorenzo nodded glumly. "Yeah. I haven't told any of my people at major case or the DA's office. That means we're going in with no backup and no warrant. The warrant thing isn't a problem because our informant gives us plenty of probable cause, but this had better work out right, or Lee won't have to work very hard to get Drew and me fired. The NOPD will gladly do it for him."

That was a sobering thought. "What's the plan this time?"

He and Max listened as Brooks and Drew outlined the plan. It was relatively basic. They'd go in through all three entrances at the same time, hopefully catching whomever was inside completely by surprise.

As the two senior SWAT officers briefed them, Remy felt a shiver run down his back, making goose bumps break out along his arms. He saw Max look at him out of the corner of his eye, but he ignored it. How could he explain he just felt freaky all of a sudden?

"The only thing that will make this job complicated are all the parade floats in there," Drew added. "If these guys see us coming, we could end up having to chase them around in that big warehouse like rats in a maze."

Something like that wouldn't have concerned Remy if it had just been Pack werewolves on this operation, but with the guys from Drew's team involved, they had to worry about things getting out of hand quickly. The NOPD SWAT cops were good, but all it took was one lucky shot and one of the officers they'd been training with all week could end up dead.

As Remy followed Brooks and the others out of the briefing room, his legs suddenly gave out from under him as a wave of near-total panic swept through his gut, making him feel both weak and queasy. A second later, he felt a stab of pain lance through the back of his head, and he reached out to catch the doorjamb. The sensation was similar to something you'd feel if you were terrified, but that didn't make any sense. He hadn't been scared of anything since he'd turned into a werewolf.

Max grabbed his arm to keep him from falling. "What the hell, Remy? You okay?"

Remy nodded. "Fine."

Shaking off Max's hand, he strode out of the room, into the hallway. His friend fell into step beside him, concern in his blue eyes. "Maybe you shouldn't go on this mission."

"I'm good," Remy said, still trying to get a sense of where the sudden overwhelming sensations had come from, and more important, why he didn't feel them now. "I'm tired because I didn't sleep last night and I've been humping through cold water all day."

It didn't seem as if Max bought that any more than Remy did. His friend continued to regard him worriedly as they left the building and headed to the motor pool.

"Do you think this has something to do with breaking up with Triana?" Max asked.

Remy didn't even try to answer that one. Scowling, he climbed into the back of one the NOPD SWAT operations vehicles while Drew and Brooks headed for another. Max closed the door behind them.

Zane held out their tactical gear, and Remy focused on getting the stuff on as the truck drove out of the enclosure, wishing like hell he had a dry uniform. What if Max was right? What if his decision to walk away from Triana was causing all this weird shit to happen to him?

"Did Brooks tell you that Cooper and Alex are on their way?" Zane asked, holding on to one of the truck's equipment racks as the vehicle turned right at an intersection.

Remy was feeling a little out of it, so he wasn't sure

he'd heard that quite right. "No. Why are they coming here?"

Zane shrugged. "The NOPD SWAT guys who were in Dallas for training are coming back early because of the storm, so Gage sent Cooper and Alex with them in case the city needs some extra first responders."

Remy nodded. Even if the storm didn't get any worse, that was probably a good idea. Maybe they could give him some advice while they were here. While both men had found their soul mates recently, neither of their relationships had been smooth sailing. If anyone knew whether this crap he was going through had something to do with him breaking up with Triana, it would be Landry Cooper and Alex Trevino.

Chapter 14

TRIANA SAT IN DOMINIC'S BEAT-UP OLD CHEVY NOVA, staring through the rain-covered windshield at the big, white warehouse a couple of blocks down the street, wondering what the heck she was supposed to be looking at.

"How do I know there's anyone even in there, much less the man who killed my father?" she finally asked. "No one has come in or out the whole time I've been here."

"You've only been here a few minutes," Dominic said from beside her, his sleepy eyes locked on the front door of the Mardi Gras krewe warehouse. "It looks like you're just going to have to take my word for it unless you plan on getting out of this car and peeking in a window for yourself."

As terrifying as that idea seemed, it was starting to look better and better with every passing second. She'd already been in Dominic's Nova far longer than she wanted, certainly more than a *few minutes*. The interior of the ancient car smelled like booze, cigarettes, oil, and a few things Triana didn't want to imagine. She was also getting the distinct feeling Dominic was starting to think there was going to be something more to this arrangement than the payment of five hundred dollars for services rendered. He'd already asked twice if she'd like to go out for a drink—in the middle of a hurricane.

"Did you at least get a better look at the guy?" she asked.

He'd given her a rather generic description the other day when they'd met at the bar, so she hoped he could tell her more now.

Dominic regarded her suspiciously, probably afraid she was going to run off and find the guy without paying him the five hundred dollars.

"He's a big guy—six three, maybe 280 pounds. He looks like a frigging defensive end for the Saints." Dominic scrunched up his face as if trying to remember what the man had looked like. "He had a shaved head and a tattoo of a snake or lizard running up the side of his neck all the way to his ear. I think I already told you about the tattoo of an anchor on his right arm. Didn't I?"

Triana nodded. Okay, it didn't sound like she was going to miss this guy.

Before she could think about whether what she was going to do was a good idea or not, she reached for the door handle. A part of her wished Remy were there. It was hard not remembering how safe she'd felt with him. Of course, if he were there, she probably wouldn't be doing anything this crazy.

But Remy wasn't with her right then. If anyone was going to catch the man who murdered her father, it would start with her, and she wasn't going to learn anything sitting in that car. She'd just snoop around and look for a window, take a quick peek then bail. She'd be able to give a good description to Bodine; then he would be able to take it from there. She hoped. She only prayed she wasn't taking a crazy risk like this for no reason.

"Whoa, what are you doing?" Dominic squawked in his raspy voice, reaching out to grab her arm as she cracked the door and got hit with a gust of wind-driven rain. "Are you crazy? If I'm right, and I am, that guy in there is a stone-cold killer. Which means the people he's hanging out with are probably just as whacked. Why don't you just stay in the dry car and wait?"

Triana stepped out into the rain and looked back at Dominic, stunned to see genuine concern in his eyes. "I'm just going to take a quick peek. I'll be right back."

"What about my money?" Dominic asked urgently, and Triana had to wonder if perhaps that was where the man's sudden concern started and stopped. "If you get killed, I'm out five hundred dollars."

Triana reached into her purse, leaning into the car a bit so her bag wouldn't get filled with water, and dug out her wallet. She counted out $250 and gave it to Dominic. "Here's half. I'll give you the other half once I've seen Quinn."

Dominic opened his mouth to complain, but Triana closed the car door. Turning, she darted across the street and huddled close to the building, hoping the overhang would shelter her from the worst of the rain. She would have used her umbrella, but it was currently on its way to the French Quarter after getting ripped out of her hands by the wind when she'd first gotten out of her car and into Dominic's. Not that an umbrella helped much in this weather. The rain was coming sideways more than down.

When she reached the big white building Dominic had pointed out, she slowed, wondering how she should do what she needed to. She supposed she could always walk in the front door, pretend she was simply trying to get out of the weather. The problem with that approach was that Quinn might recognize her. If he'd known her father, that was certainly a possibility. That meant trying to peek through the glass in the door was a bad idea too. So instead, she turned down the alley that ran along the side of the big warehouse. While there were windows, they were all positioned too high for Triana to see into.

Ignoring her wet jeans and sodden sneakers, she continued along the building, stopping momentarily at the metal door sheltered under the cover of an aluminum awning. She put her ear to the door to see if she could hear anyone inside, but the rain and wind whipping against the aluminum walls and awning made that impossible. Holding her breath, she slowly turned the knob, doubtful that it would be open but figuring she should check anyway. As expected, the knob didn't budge.

She slipped out from under the awning, gasping as water ran off the building and poured down the back of her neck and under her raincoat. *Damn, that was cold.* She yanked the collar tighter, but it did no good. Frigid water slipped everywhere, making her shiver like crazy.

The back of the building wasn't as well-maintained as the side, with two overflowing Dumpsters, a handful of pallets leaning haphazardly against the back wall, and a bunch of trash-filled and rain-soaked cardboard boxes piled everywhere. Some of the boxes shook and skated around in the wind, and Triana imagined that all of them, and maybe the pallets too, would have blown away if they weren't on the wind-sheltered side of the building.

She eyed the back door and the wooden pallets leaning against the wall under the windows, wondering which one was the better option. Like the side door, she doubted this one would open either but decided to check it out before attempting to climb the pallets up to the windows. She wasn't the most graceful and athletic person at the best of times. In this wind, she might be taking her life in her own hands.

She was so surprised when the knob turned and the door opened that she almost fell on her face. Catching herself, she poked her head inside, praying she wouldn't find a bunch of scary people staring back at her.

When she caught sight of human-sized silhouettes standing there in the darkness, she almost let out an involuntary shriek. But then she remembered she was breaking into a Mardi Gras warehouse and got a grip on herself. Taking a deep breath, she looked around the darkened interior of the warehouse. Relieved no one seemed to be in that part of the warehouse, she slipped inside. She closed the door behind her, careful not to make any noise. Not that anyone was going to hear her. The noise of the rain hitting the metal roof of the warehouse made her wonder if this was what the inside of a kettledrum sounded like.

Triana moved forward cautiously, her heart beating a hundred miles an hour as the gravity of what she was doing started to settle in. She was in a warehouse in the middle of a hurricane with the man who'd most likely murdered her father. She wasn't a cop, she had no weapon, and the only person who really knew where she was at that moment was a career bar rat who'd probably already left with her money.

Maybe this wasn't such a good idea.

That thought didn't keep her feet from moving her forward through the darkness, weaving past the Mardi

Gras floats with their scary monsters, comic book heroes, and smiling mermaids.

She'd been to a lot of parades in this city and had seen thousands of floats, but being in this dark warehouse with them was just about the freakiest place she'd ever been. She was staring at one of the big demon characters, sure it was following her with its eyes, when she heard a loud voice up ahead. She froze, terrified someone had seen her. But then a second voice reverberated through the metal warehouse, and she realized it was two men arguing.

She followed the sounds of their voices, trying to hear over the drumming of the rain. The argument was getting more heated. She couldn't tell for sure, but it seemed like one of the men was saying that the other had sold them out.

Triana was so intent on hearing what the men were saying that she came around one of the floats and almost walked into the two of them. She pulled back just in time, hiding behind the corner of the float as she stared wide-eyed at the two men yelling at each other.

Without a doubt, one of the men was the guy Dominic had described. There couldn't be that many shaved-head monsters in this city. He was huge and scary-looking as hell. He looked like the kind of man who twisted the heads off of dolls just to hear little girls cry. She could easily believe he was a murderer.

The other guy was African American, smaller, with close-cropped hair and a couple of gold rings in one of his ears. He was just as tough-looking as Quinn, and his face was filled with rage as he stood toe to toe with the larger man.

"Don't try to fucking lie to me, Roth," Quinn said. "You should have realized we were onto you when we came here to break down the meth instead of the place we talked about last night. That's because we've known about you since yesterday."

Roth looked confused. "What the hell are you talking about?"

"You didn't think we'd notice there were only three people—Lee, you, and me—who knew which ship the drugs were coming in on and which warehouse we'd be storing them in afterward? Since Mr. Lee obviously didn't rat us out, that leaves you."

"Screw you, you fucking steroid freak!" Roth shouted. "Maybe you called the cops on us. Everyone knows you've been jonesing to take over Lee's territory. After running around behind him for years saying Mr. Lee this and Mr. Lee that, maybe you finally grew a big enough pair of balls to try and take him out."

Quinn went completely still, and Triana decided it was time to get out of there, before they started fighting. She had what she'd come for, confirmation of what this guy looked like. She had no idea what they were talking about or who Mr. Lee was, and she didn't care.

But before she could move, Quinn whipped a gun out from behind his back and shot the other guy in the chest at point-blank range. The noise was loud in the warehouse, but instead of echoing like she'd thought it would, the rain beating down on the metal roof seemed to immediately swallow it up.

Triana stood there in stunned disbelief as the smaller man slowly slumped to the floor, blood staining the front of his shirt.

The sound of footsteps coming toward Triana abruptly reminded her that she needed to get the hell out of there.

She turned to run but didn't get more than ten feet before Quinn grabbed her hair and yanked her backward. The pain was so intense, she couldn't help but scream. But like the gunshot, the sound was quickly drowned out by the rain pounding on the roof.

She struggled, but Quinn ignored her movements and spun her around.

"Well, I'll be damned," he sneered. "I have no idea what the hell you're doing here, but you saved me an assload of work. Mr. Lee called earlier and told me to find you. Now I guess I don't have to."

Triana had no idea why Mr. Lee wanted this walking pile of muscles to find her, but something told her it couldn't be good. Panic raced through her chest, threatening to make her heart explode. In a panic, she took a swing at Quinn, aiming for his temple like Remy had showed her, but her fist bounced off his skull like she'd just punched a brick wall.

Quinn laughed, then casually reached out and cuffed her alongside the head so hard her whole body went limp and her vision began to go dark. Before she could fall to the floor though, Quinn grabbed her arm.

"Do you think anyone heard that gunshot?" a man's worried voice asked from somewhere behind Quinn. "Should we pack up and move the drugs?"

Quinn glanced over his shoulder at the man. "No one heard the shot in this storm. And no, don't pack up the drugs."

"What about Roth?" the man asked.

"That piece of shit didn't have a chance to get a call off to the cops. I kept an eye on him to make sure of it," Quinn said. "Finish breaking down the ice, then get it to our distributors. Mr. Lee wants the stuff on the streets by the time the weather clears so everyone will have plenty of okie coke for their post-Ophelia parties."

As Triana stared down at Roth's body, she thought she saw the guy move…maybe. But she couldn't be sure because Quinn tightened his grip on her arm and shoved her toward the back of the warehouse.

"Time to get you to Mr. Lee's," Quinn said.

Terrified at the idea of going anywhere with Quinn, Triana did the only thing she could think of—she turned and punched him in the sensitive spot right below his sternum. She couldn't remember what Remy had called it at that moment, but she remembered him saying it could give her a chance to run.

Her fist connected solidly, sinking into Quinn's stomach so hard he gasped. His grip on her arm loosened and she jerked away from him, running for the back door. She prayed Dominic was still out there.

Triana made it halfway there before Quinn grabbed her by the hair again and yanked her back. She ignored the pain in her scalp, kicking and punching with all her might, aiming for his balls and anything else she could reach.

Quinn laughed. "You're almost as tough as that mule-headed father of yours. Before the son of a bitch bought it, anyway."

Hearing this piece of crap talk about her father—whom he'd murdered—made her fight harder, and she reached out and raked her fingernails down the man's face.

"Bitch!" he cursed.

Swinging her in a big circle, Quinn slammed her headfirst into the closest available object—that damn spooky red demon she'd seen on her way in.

The figure might have been made out of Styrofoam and papier-mâché, but it was still hard as hell. Stars burst across her vision as she felt herself go limp in Quinn's grip. Oh God, she was passing out. She wouldn't be able to protect herself if she was unconscious.

Don't pass out... don't do it.

Her head didn't seem to care about that, and Triana felt her legs turn to rubber as everything went black.

"The back door is already open," Zane said over the radio headset, his voice barely audible above the rain and wind. "Standing by to enter."

"Understood." Drew's voice was calm in Remy's earpiece. "Team two, status?"

Remy watched as Brooks wedged a thin crowbar in the doorjamb at the side board, waiting until his teammate nodded at him and the NOPD SWAT officers with them. They needed a crowbar for this breaching job since the heavy metal door was designed to open out. Any attempt to kick or blow the door inward would have likely failed.

"Team two at the side door," Remy said into his mic. "Ready to enter at your word."

The drive to this part of town hadn't been as long as they'd feared in the rain, and setting up on the warehouse had been fairly easy too. Nothing like a torrential downpour to keep gawkers at a minimum. In fact, they hadn't seen anyone the entire time they'd moved into position around the building.

Zane, Max, and three NOPD SWAT team members would take the back door while Remy, Brooks, and two locals would take the side. Drew and Lorenzo would lead the largest contingent of six SWAT officers in through the main door up front.

Drew was worried the warehouse was already empty, but Remy knew better. Even through the rain and wind, he could hear movement in the big warehouse. He'd tried to get close to the door to see if he could get a whiff of crystal meth in there, but the rainfall had wiped away any trace scents in the area. Hell, between the rain and wind, he could barely smell Brooks, and the other werewolf was standing no more than five feet away.

"We go in three," Drew's voice sounded in Remy's earpiece. "Two...one...go!"

Brooks wrenched savagely on the crowbar, wedging the jamb back and popping the lock. At the same time, one of the NOPD SWAT officers grabbed the door and hauled it open. Remy and the other SWAT officers with him swarmed into the warehouse, moving toward the front of the place, where his nose told him the drugs and people were located. Brooks and the rest of the officers swept around him, fanning out through the float-filled warehouse.

Hearing shouts from the front of the place telling him that's where all of Lee's people were, Remy immediately headed that way. But before he could take more than a couple of steps, two unexpected and powerful scents hit his nose and brought him to a complete standstill. One was blood; the other was Triana.

Remy knew he should keep moving toward the front of the warehouse with Brooks, but he couldn't. Instead, he followed his nose toward the back of the building, even as the other officers he'd entered with disappeared among the insane-looking floats. His heart thumped at a hundred miles an hour as he tried to understand how he could possibly smell Triana in there. It wasn't trace residue, as if she'd been there a while ago, either. It was recent. He didn't think the blood was hers, but the two scents were so closely intertwined, he couldn't know for sure.

Zane was kneeling on one side of a wounded man, calling for an ambulance, while Max was on the other side, slapping a field dressing over a bloody chest wound and applying pressure. Remy immediately recognized him as one of Lee's lieutenants, Roth. He'd been shot in the right side of the chest, and while the man's heart was still beating, it was getting weak. From the amount of blood that had been lost, Remy was surprised the guy was even still alive. Clearly, Roth was one tough son of a bitch.

Remy left Zane and Max to their tasks while he tried to figure out what had happened here and where Triana's scent was coming from. It was more concentrated on one of the floats, more precisely the one with the freaky-looking red demon on it, but she was nowhere to be found. There was at least one other scent he recognized as well, but his olfactory memory wasn't good enough to pinpoint exactly to whom it belonged. There were a couple of werewolves in the Pack who could ID any scent they'd smelled before, but he simply wasn't that talented.

Max must have picked up on his anxiety when Remy walked past him for the third time. "What's wrong?"

"Triana was here," Remy said. "Recently. Like, ten or fifteen minutes ago."

Zane and Max tested the air with their noses, then shrugged.

"I definitely smell a woman's scent, but I can't tell if it's Triana," Max said. "Since you know her a whole hell of a lot better than we do, I'll assume you're right. But why would she be here? More important, where is she now?"

Remy didn't get a chance to answer because Lorenzo chose that moment to come in. The narcotics detective's eyes widened.

"Shit!" Lorenzo dropped to his knees beside Roth and checked his pulse. "Dammit, Chad. I warned you not to take any chances, but you just had to keep pushing it, didn't you?"

"This is the informant?" Zane asked in surprise. "One of Lee's lieutenants? How the hell did you make that happen?"

"Chad's a cop," Lorenzo said. "He's been undercover in the New Orleans crime scene for the better part of six years. He was able to develop a reputation that gave him the chance to slip into Lee's organization about three years ago. It was risky as shit, but he knew this would be our best chance to put Aaron Lee away."

Remy suddenly realized why he'd gotten such a closed-off vibe from the guy when he'd seen him a couple of days ago. Chad had been living undercover for six years. The only way cops survived that long in the criminal underworld was by closing themselves off.

"The ambulance is on the way," Max said, crouching beside Lorenzo. "It's bad, but he just has to hang on until the EMTs get here."

Lorenzo nodded but didn't look hopeful. "In this weather? That could take a while."

Max and Zane nodded, but Remy couldn't listen anymore. Triana's scent was driving him insane, but not nearly as much as not knowing what the hell had happened to her. Why had she been here? Where was she now? Who had her? Was she in danger? The stress of not knowing the answers to those questions, and about a thousand other ones, was enough to make his fangs and claws start to come out.

Not knowing what else to do, he yanked out his cell phone to call her and saw that she'd called him forty minutes ago but hadn't left a message. Growling in frustration, he dialed her number.

"What the hell, Remy?" Lorenzo demanded, frowning up at him.

Remy didn't answer. Calling your girlfriend—*ex*-girlfriend—in the middle of a raid wasn't exactly standard protocol.

"Don't ask how he knows," Max said, "but someone very important to him was in this warehouse right before we got here."

Lorenzo asked Max how he could possibly know that, but Remy tuned them out. He couldn't deal with that right then.

Not surprisingly, Triana didn't pick up. Instead, it went to voice mail. He considered leaving a message, but his gut told him it would be a waste of time.

"She's not answering," he growled, shoving his phone away as his stomach did flips and barrel rolls. "Something is wrong. I can feel it in my gut. Triana was right here at the same time your guy was getting shot."

Remy had no idea how he knew it was true, but he did. That was the only thing that mattered.

"I need to know what the hell happened in this warehouse," he said, turning toward the front of the building.

Lorenzo got up to follow. "Good luck with that. Those guys we arrested are all professional criminals. They're going to lawyer up and not say a word to anyone."

Remy growled as he headed in that direction. "Who said I was going to give them an option?"

Zane stayed with the injured undercover cop, while Lorenzo and Max hurried to catch up with Remy.

He passed between the last of the Mardi Gras floats and found himself in a large open area at the front of the warehouse. Long folding tables had been set up along either side, with a third row running right down the center. From all the tools, paints, stacks of Styrofoam, and craft paper scattered around, this was probably the place new floats were made and old ones repaired. But now all the art supplies had been shoved to the side and the tables cleared. In their place were scales, boxes of plastic baggies, and lots of crystal meth. The crap looked like big shards of rock candy, so clear you could see through it.

But Remy ignored all of that and instead turned his attention to the ten men lined up near the partial wall that divided this area from the entryway and front door. They were all cuffed and seemed to be waiting patiently for someone to come and take them in for booking.

Lorenzo got around in front of him and put a hand on his chest in an attempt to slow him down. "Remy, you need to stop."

"Get out of my way, Lorenzo," Remy said in a low voice.

He was damn close to losing control, and he didn't need some by-the-book detective telling him to back off. He'd done everything he could to push Triana away, even though it had pained her and him, so she wouldn't get hurt. After all that, it looked like it had been a waste. Somehow, she'd gotten wrapped up with a bunch of scary people anyway. He had no idea what was going on, but she was in danger. He knew that deep down in his soul. He'd do whatever it took to find her and make sure she was safe—even if that meant going through the middle of a NOPD narcotics detective.

He shoved Lorenzo's hand away and moved to step around the man, but the idiot got in front of him again.

"Damn it, Remy," Lorenzo said. "One of my very best friends put himself undercover for six years to get Aaron Lee and now it looks like it might cost him his life. I'm not going to let you waste his sacrifice. All the people we arrested work for Lee, and by catching them with all these drugs, we finally have something to pin on him. This is going to get us warrants for his home and every business he's associated with. We finally have this guy by the balls and I'm not going to let you do something stupid that will get this arrest thrown out of court."

Remy locked eyes with the narcotics detective, his fingertips and gums tingling as his shift came on. Gage would be pissed as hell, but Remy didn't care. He was going to get his questions answered one way or another.

"I need to find out what the hell Triana was doing in this warehouse and where she is now, and one of these men is going to tell me," he said softly, not bothering to keep the rumbling growl out of his voice. "So unless you plan on shooting me, you need to move."

The detective's face went blank as he took a step back, but then he slowly reached across his body to grab the pistol holstered under his left armpit. Several of the NOPD SWAT officers who'd been standing there watching the exchange tensed, hands near their weapons. This was about to get ugly.

Remy flexed his fingers. Guess he was going to have to do this the hard way. He could take them all down before they put more than three or four bullets in him.

"Remy, you might want to wait a minute before you do anything stupid," Brooks's deep voice interrupted from the entryway. "At least until you talk to these guys outside. I think they can answer most of your questions without anyone getting shot."

Remy opened his mouth to ask his pack mate what he meant by that, but Brooks had already turned and headed for the door. He gave Lorenzo a quick look, then walked out without another word. The narcotics detective didn't follow.

Remy found Brooks and Drew standing outside the warehouse with two other guys. The rain had slowed to a slow drizzle at that point, but both men were already soaked.

"This is Marcus Bodine, a local PI," Drew said, motioning at one of the men. "And this is Dominic, one of his informants. They got here right after we went through the door." He turned his attention to the two men. "Tell Remy what you told us."

Remy stood there stunned as the PI told him he was working for Triana, helping her find her father's murderer. The private investigator talked like a cop, giving a short, concise rundown of the facts, including how

Dominic had heard someone bragging about killing a person in a manner consistent with the evidence in her father's case file.

Somewhere in the middle of Bodine's story, the ambulance showed up and the PI paused as the EMTs ran past them with a gurney and their gear.

"Triana insisted on talking to this witness directly," Bodine said after the EMTs disappeared inside. "When I set it up, I never dreamed she'd be stupid enough to try to track down her father's killer herself."

Dominic took over the story then, explaining how he found the man he'd heard bragging in a bar and had followed him here.

"I called her so she could get a look at the guy, Shelton Quinn, as soon as he came out of the building, but she got impatient and decided to go take a look."

Remy's gut clenched at the mention of Quinn. Shit, that was the other scent he'd recognized in the warehouse near Triana's. The first time he'd seen the big, muscular bruiser who worked for Lee, his werewolf instincts had told him the guy was no good.

"What happened then?" Remy asked.

Dominic swallowed. "I started worrying about her after a couple of minutes, so I got out of my car to see where she was. When I got to the back door, I figured I'd go in and try to talk her into coming out, when I heard a gunshot."

The guy's hands were shaking as he spoke, and Remy realized that going after Triana was probably the only heroic thing the man had done in his life, and it had terrified him.

"I froze for a second," Dominic said. "The next thing

I know, Quinn was coming out the back door with Triana tossed over his shoulder like a bag of wheat. I wanted to do something, but I ain't no hero—not against a guy that big. So I hid and watched as he tossed Triana in a blue BMW and spun out of here. Then I called Marcus."

"When I got here and saw the commotion and all the cops, I grabbed the first person I found and told him everything," Bodine said, gesturing at Drew.

Remy could hardly breathe. "Was she still alive when you saw her?"

Dominic scrunched up his face, like he was thinking hard. "I think so. He was handling her like she was. I mean, he didn't throw her in the trunk. And I didn't see any blood on her."

Remy wasn't too certain how much faith he had in Dominic, but he breathed a sigh of relief anyway.

"None of this makes sense," Brooks said. "Don't take this the wrong way, Remy, but assuming Quinn figured out Triana knew that he'd killed her father, why the hell would he go to the trouble of taking her with him? If he shot Roth and left him for dead, why not do the same to her?"

Remy didn't have an answer to that question. The fact that Quinn had taken Triana instead of killing her outright both gave him hope and scared the shit out of him at the same time. He didn't even want to think about her being in that psycho's hands.

Chapter 15

TRIANA CAME TO WITH A THROBBING HEADACHE AND THE strange sensation of someone tugging at her wet clothes. Her head hurt like hell and she was so out of it that it took a moment to force her eyes open. When she finally did, she saw Quinn's scratched and ugly mug a few inches from her face like he was going to kiss her. Then she realized he was tugging at her shirt, trying to undress her. She screamed and tried to shove him away only to discover she was sitting in a chair with her hands tied together in front of her and a rope around her waist holding her down.

"Get the hell away from me!" she yelled, twisting her upper body to get his hands off her shirt while clubbing at him with her tied-up hands at the same time.

Quinn laughed and backed away. "Relax. Damn, I was only loosening your wet clothes so you can breathe better. Figured I should make sure you're comfortable since you might be here a while."

That's when everything came rushing back—her stupid plan to slip into the Mardi Gras warehouse to get a look at the man who'd killed her father, Quinn shooting that other guy and roughing her up, then telling her he was bringing her to Mr. Lee.

"What do you want with me?" she asked in a terrified rush, hating to look scared in front of Quinn but too desperate for information to keep quiet. "Why did you bring me here?"

Quinn regarded her in silence, his expression so damn creepy it made her skin want to crawl off and go hide. Finally, he walked over and casually sat down in a chair that matched the one she was trussed up in and stretched his legs out in front of him, crossing them at the ankles. Triana looked around and realized she was in a study with books all around, a wall of fancy windows to one side and a set of heavy double doors to the other.

"Maybe I wanted to spend a little quality time with you, since you obviously went to so much work to find me and all," Quinn said. "That's why you were at that warehouse, right? Because you figured out I was involved in your father's murder?"

At the mention of her father, Triana was nearly overwhelmed with a wild urge to charge out of the chair and attack the monster in front of her. The only thing that stopped her was the fact that she was currently tied down to the aforementioned chair. Well, that and the knowledge Quinn could swat her down like a fly anytime he wanted. So she swallowed her anger and fear, and realized that while he hadn't actually answered her question about why he'd brought her there, he had let one thing slip.

He said that he'd been involved in her father's murder, not that he'd killed him. If he was as much of a braggart as Dominic had said, wouldn't he take credit for it, especially since he had her right in front of him?

"How'd you find me?" Quinn prompted when she didn't say anything. "Did someone help you?"

Triana knew he was fishing to see if there was anyone who might know she'd been kidnapped, and for a moment she didn't know how to answer. If she admitted there was a private investigator involved, would he kill her now and get rid of her body quickly? Or would he hesitate, afraid her disappearance would be traced back to him?

She had to say something though, or he'd simply kill her to be on the safe side. So she went with what she hoped was the least threatening answer and prayed Dominic had stayed around the warehouse long enough to see Quinn grab her, then called the cops. Part of her even hoped Remy and his SWAT teammates might be on the way to her at that moment. It was an insane thought, but she was scared and needed to grab hold of something to give her hope.

"I found you on my own," Triana said. "I spent months looking and finally talked to someone in a bar who said they remembered hearing a man brag about killing my father. They described you, so you were easy to find after that."

Quinn laughed, and she thought she saw relief on his face. "Yeah, I guess I am kind of easy to spot. Still, it's impressive you tracked me down. You really are like your father. He was too damn stubborn for his own good too."

The way Quinn looked at her as he spoke made her insides turn to mush.

"Are you going to kill me?" she asked, steeling herself for the answer.

He shrugged. "Probably at some point, but Mr. Lee has something he needs out of you first, so it's really up to him."

It was hard to sit there and not flinch at the casual way Quinn dismissed her death as a foregone conclusion. But she forced herself to focus on something else, anything other than what this man was planning to do to her.

"Who is this Mr. Lee and what does he want from me?"

"My boss wants that damn wolf necklace your father used to wear," Quinn said. "He tried to use a middle man to buy it from your mother, some stupid-ass lawyer named Murphy, but she wouldn't sell it."

Triana blinked. Quinn's boss was the rich client who'd hired that lawyer to harass her mother? All because of some necklace? That didn't make any sense.

"Murphy must have thought there was going to be some big payout if he got Mr. Lee the necklace because he sent some local muscle to your mother's shop to steal it last night. That didn't work either, so I picked the guy up at his house and drove him out to the river, where I put a bullet in his head." Quinn's lips curled. "As they say in baseball, three strikes and you're out."

Triana gasped. This psycho had killed Kenneth Murphy because he'd failed to get a necklace? He really was insane.

"Mr. Lee decided he was done playing around and told me to go pick you up," Quinn continued. "He figures your mother will trade the necklace for you. Between you and me though, after she shows up with it, I doubt either one of you will be leaving."

Triana refused to think about this man hurting her mom, knowing it would just make her fall apart. Instead she scoured her memories, trying to figure out if she'd ever heard of Lee before, but the name wasn't familiar.

"Why would Mr. Lee want my father's necklace?" she asked.

Quinn gave her a funny look, then shook his head.

"Shit, you don't even know, do you? You have no idea what your dad really was?" When Triana regarded him in confusion, he continued. "Mr. Lee is a powerful man who's getting a little long in the tooth. People are starting to nip at the edges of his empire because they don't believe he's strong enough to defend it himself anymore, and that pisses him off. He wants the necklace so he can turn into a werewolf."

Triana stared, not sure she'd heard right, but then she saw the serious look on his face and realized he actually believed what he was saying.

"You're insane, you know that, right?" she said. "There's no such thing as werewolves."

Quinn shrugged. "I used to think that too, until I saw your dad in action." He stood and paced in front of her. "I got so damn tired of hearing all those old stories about your father and what a badass he was, about him being strong and fearless. I knew most of the stories were bullshit. Like the one about him getting stabbed and yanking the knife out of his own stomach, or the one Mr. Lee used to tell about your father taking a bullet right in the chest for him, then chasing after the shooter for a mile until he caught him." Quinn stopped to look at her. "To me he was just another old man who ran a jazz club."

None of the stuff Quinn was saying made any sense. It sounded like the babbling of a crazy person. But one thing was obvious.

"You knew my father before you helped kill him?"

"Mostly by reputation," Quinn admitted. "He used to work for Mr. Lee too, before he decided to get married and start a family. I have to admit, he must have been one tough son of a bitch back in the day because he helped Mr. Lee build his criminal empire." He put his hands on his hips and shook his head. "Mr. Lee let him be for a long time—some kind of respect shit, I guess. Then the boss decided he wanted to sell drugs out of your father's club. But old Rufus said no, which put Mr. Lee in a difficult situation. He couldn't have people thinking he was losing control or getting too weak to deal with some club owner. So, my crew and I went down to your father's place late one night, planning to break some bones and teach him a lesson."

Quinn began pacing again, leaving Triana to track his movements.

"It didn't quite work out the way we expected," he said quietly, as if remembering that night. "Your father frigging changed in front of us. I'm not shitting you. I'm talking fangs, claws, glowing eyes, the whole nine yards. He turned into a fucking monster. I've never seen anything so impossible in my life." Quinn shrugged. "I was one of the lucky ones. I got tossed through a window and halfway across the street outside. I only cracked a few bones and sliced up some skin. My boys didn't manage so well. Your father tore them apart— literally. And Mr. Lee had a front row seat to the whole thing. Hell, he should probably be dead right now, but your father must have had a soft spot for him. Told him to drag his ass out of there and never come back."

Triana had already assumed Quinn was insane. But now, she didn't even have a word to describe how incredibly bonkers he truly was.

"That was the last mistake your father ever made," a man's voice interrupted from the doorway.

Triana turned her head to see a big man in his mid-fifties standing there with a hard expression on his face.

"You don't piss on an enemy and let them walk away," the man said as he stepped into the room and walked over to stand in front of her. "The funny thing about it is that it was your father who taught me that lesson." Lee studied her thoughtfully. "You look exactly like your mother when she was younger. You definitely have your father's eyes, though. And apparently his stubborn nature."

Triana didn't say anything.

"I thought it would be difficult to find the right kind of people to do the job I needed," Lee said. "But they aren't that tough to find if you're willing to spend the money. You just have to look for people who know how to take down someone who's hard to get rid of. If you want to kill a particular animal, you merely have to find the right hunter."

That's when Triana realized she was in even more trouble than she'd thought. Quinn might be a deranged murderer, but Lee was even worse. The man seemed as cold and dead inside as a vampire.

Suddenly, she hoped with everything in her that Remy and his teammates didn't come looking for her. She didn't want these people getting their hands on Remy or anyone else she cared about.

—∾∾—

Remy stood just inside the front door of the warehouse, staring out at the rain coming down again. Another band of the storm was moving through, bringing even more rain and wind than the previous ones. The weather report said it would be like this most of the night, as the eastern edges of the storm slowly passed over the city, though at some point the intermittent crap would be replaced with a nonstop downpour.

Lee's minions had been hauled away nearly thirty minutes ago, while the techie types had left just a short time ago with all their evidence, including the hundreds of pounds of crystal meth. Remy was glad to get all that crap finally under lock and key. If nothing else, keeping it off the streets represented a couple hundred people who wouldn't end up in the hospital or the morgue.

Remy rubbed his temples, trying to ease the worst headache he'd ever had in his life. The pounding was so intense it felt like his eyes were going to pop out of his head. Unfortunately, even that pain didn't distract him from the fact that he had no idea where Triana was or how he was going to locate her.

He wanted to go find her as soon as he'd heard Quinn had kidnapped her, but Lorenzo and Drew stopped him, pointing out that Lee owned property all over New Orleans and even more outside the city. There was no telling where Quinn might have taken her.

"What about his home?" Remy asked. "You said he has a big plantation home near the lake, right?"

Lorenzo nodded. "Yeah, up in Kenner. But that's just one of his houses. What are the chances Quinn took her there? Hell, for all we know, this thing with Triana might not have anything to do with Lee. It might just be Quinn covering up the trail of a murder he committed on his own."

Remy didn't even want to think about the part of that

Lorenzo had left unsaid—that Quinn might have killed Triana already. He refused to contemplate that, because if he did, he didn't think he could keep going. He would find Triana and get her back.

A voice in his head asked him what he'd do then regarding the way he felt about her.

One problem at a time.

"Dammit, you shouldn't have moved without a warrant!"

The shout came from farther back in the warehouse, sending an ice pick of pain lancing through his head. Remy growled, trying to tune out ADA Russo's incessant whining. The prick had shown up ten minutes ago, losing his mind over the fact that Lorenzo had moved against Aaron Lee without his involvement. Remy had known the man had only gone after Lee for the political gain, but it was like the lawyer couldn't accept that he'd finally won, even with the evidence on the way to lockup.

Russo was shouting again, some crap about probable cause this time. Remy did his best to shut out the rest. He'd heard the lawyer's complaints at least ten times already. How the courts would throw out the drugs and everything found in this warehouse due to a lack of probable cause. How that would destroy the link to Aaron Lee and prevent any sane judge from issuing search warrants for the man's home and businesses. How this had all been nothing but a big waste of time.

Remy was so tired of hearing the man's crap, not to mention Lorenzo's and everyone else's patient attempts to convince Russo the informant's tip was more than enough to support probable cause.

"Do you really think a judge like Thibodeau, or any judge for that matter, is going to accept the word of a career criminal like Chad Roth over Aaron Lee's?" Russo let out a short laugh. "Roth will simply come across as a snake who betrayed his own boss, thinking he could take over the operation once Lee was in prison. You'll get nothing based on that guy's word."

Remy's head was pounding so hard at the moment that he didn't care what Russo thought about nearly anything, but something about what the man had just said bothered him. Without being sure exactly what it was, he left the doorway and walked toward the back of the warehouse.

When he got there, Russo was babbling on about some stupid idea of not even attempting to pin the drug charges on Lee, insisting it would instead make more sense to charge the men they'd arrested at the warehouse and hope one of them flipped on Lee. Lorenzo must have thought that was insane because he was looking at the ADA as if the man had just grown a flipper out of his head. Drew's expression was pretty much the same, while Max, Brooks, Zane, and the local SWAT officers that had stayed behind were regarding the lawyer with frowns.

"How did you know Roth was the informant?" Remy asked, his concern with Russo finally taking shape.

Everyone, including the ADA, turned and looked at him in confusion.

"What?" Russo said.

Remy moved closer, gazing down at the lawyer. "You said that no judge would ever take the word of Chad Roth over Lee's, implying you knew Roth was the informant. It's a simple question. How did you know Roth was the informant?"

Russo continued to look confused for a moment, then shrugged. "I heard it on the scanner on the way over. The ambulance crew said Chad Roth was the informant and that he'd been critically wounded prior to the raid."

Remy eyed Russo for a moment, then glanced at Brooks. His pack mate simply gave a slow shake of his head, his eyes deadly serious. Just as he'd thought. Russo was lying. Remy opened his mouth to point that out, but Lorenzo spoke up first.

"The EMTs weren't given a name, and as far as they knew, he was just one of Lee's people injured in the raid. They definitely didn't know he was the informant. And they couldn't check his wallet for an ID, since I made sure I took it before they left. I wanted him admitted to the hospital as a John Doe in case Lee tried to come after him again."

Russo looked at each of them, sweat beading on his brow. "Then I must have heard it over the SWAT radio. Simple mistake."

"This operation has been on radio lockdown from the start. No one announced anything over the radio," Drew said.

Russo eyes narrowed. "Look, I heard it over one of the radio channels that Roth was the informant. Why the hell does it matter where I heard it since it's true?"

"Because if we're right, and you didn't hear about Roth over the radio, the only way you could have known he was the informant is if someone else told you." Remy crossed his arms over his chest. "Someone like Aaron Lee or Shelton Quinn."

Russo looked startled for a minute, then let out a snort. "Right. I've been in contact with Lee and his muscle-headed bodyguard because I desperately wanted them to know one of their own people was ratting them out to the cops."

Out of the corner of his eye, Remy saw Brooks shake his head again, letting him know the lawyer was still full of shit.

"Actually, I think that's exactly what's going on here," Remy said. "I'm sure Lee was thrilled when you passed along Captain Barron's comments about the informant being in his organization for three years. That must have made it pretty damn easy for Lee to figure out who it was."

"That's crazy!" Russo shouted, looking around at each of them as if he expected someone to help him. "You can't think that I would do something like that."

Remy shrugged. "We might not, but the investigators at the PIB certainly will, especially when I tell them what Roth whispered in my ear right before he passed out."

Russo's eyes stopped darting around to focus on Remy. "No one said anything about Roth making a statement. What did he say?"

Remy knew he was taking a chance lying like this, but he also knew the ADA was about to lose it. The man's pulse must have been pinging up around 150 beats a minute.

"We didn't say anything earlier because, honestly, we didn't really understand what he meant at the time," Remy said. "I mean, who wouldn't be confused when a guy in that much pain grabs your tactical vest and rasps out, *It's the lawyer*? Of course, now that you slipped up and established your connection to Lee, it makes so much more sense. I'm sure the PIB will agree. They're going to dig through your life with a microscope until they find the link between you and Lee."

Russo's eye widened as Lorenzo pulled his cuffs out. "No way." He held up both hands as if warding them off. "No way is the PIB going to make a case against me based on the dying declaration of a con like Roth."

"Probably not," Remy agreed. "But they'll certainly base it on the dying declaration of a police officer who spent the past few years undercover so he could get close to Lee."

Russo turned so pale Remy through the man was going to pass out. "Roth is a cop?"

Remy nodded as Lorenzo walked around behind Russo and put a heavy hand on his shoulder. "Yup. And I wouldn't pin too much hope on Roth not making it. He seems pretty tough to me. Not that it's going to matter to you. Whether it's conspiracy to murder a police officer or the actual murder itself, both will get you a needle in the arm."

As Remy suspected, Russo immediately spilled his guts the moment Lorenzo slapped the cuffs on him, saying he'd only helped Lee because the man had threatened him, that he would testify against Lee in court, and that he never would have gone along with the situation if he'd known Roth was a cop.

Remy didn't pay attention to the rest as Lorenzo and several of the local SWAT officers took the former ADA away. He'd stopped caring about Russo the moment he confessed. Now that they'd exposed the department's rat, he went back to worrying about Triana and wondering where she was. He pondered for a second if Russo might know something but dismissed that idea as ridiculous. Lee had used Russo. He sure as hell wouldn't tell the lawyer anything that might come back to hurt him. If Remy was going to find Triana, it was going to have to be by some other way—like a frigging miracle.

When his phone rang a few minutes later, Remy yanked it out so fast the threads on his pocket tore. He prayed it was Triana, but he didn't recognize the number. He thumbed the green button and held it to his ear. He'd been hoping for a miracle. Maybe this was it.

"Remy, thank God you answered," Gemma said. "I was worried I wouldn't be able to reach you with the storm. I need your help."

His heart sank. Damn. Gemma must have realized Triana was missing and was freaking out. What the hell was he going to tell her? "I'm a little busy right now, Gemma."

The moment Remy said her name, Max, Brooks, and Zane all turned to look his way. Remy considered keeping the truth from Triana's mother, thinking it would be easier on her. Gemma's husband had been violently murdered two years ago. She'd never be able to handle another blow this big.

But he couldn't do that. Not to Triana's mother.

"Gemma, I don't know how to tell you this, but we think Triana has been kidnapped."

Remy expected Gemma to immediately break down crying, but instead the older woman sighed.

"I know that already," she said. "Why do you think I called you? I know who has her and where she is. I need you and your friends to get her back for me."

Remy did a double take. Triana's mother knew she'd been kidnapped? His pack mates were clearly just as shocked if the way they moved closer was any indication. With their exceptional hearing, they'd obviously heard what Gemma said, even from as far away as they'd been standing.

"What do you mean, you know who has her?" he asked carefully, not wanting to imply that she didn't have a clue how bad this really was. "How could you know who has her? She was only kidnapped barely more than an hour ago."

Gemma snorted. "Because the people who took her called me wanting to make a trade."

Remy exchanged looks with his pack mates, seeing his own confusion reflected in their eyes. "I think you need to start at the beginning, Gemma, because this isn't making a lot of sense," he said. "Triana was kidnapped because she was trying to track down the man who killed her father. Why would he want to make a trade?"

The phone was silent for so long that Remy thought the connection might have been broken, but then Gemma's voice came back firm and strong and more than a little angry.

"Damn headstrong girl. So much like her father." There was another long sigh. "They want to make a trade because a man named Aaron Lee wants something he thinks I have, and he wants it very badly."

Remy was just getting over the shock of realizing that Gemma really did know everything that was going on, when it hit him—he knew exactly what was behind Triana's abduction.

"This is about that damn necklace that lawyer has been trying to buy from you all week, isn't it?"

"It is," she said softly. "Lee thinks the necklace will allow him to turn into a werewolf. Of course, he has a good reason to think that since the last man to wear it actually was a werewolf."

Remy was pretty sure his eyes almost bulged out of his head, and it had nothing to do with his headache. Even so, he was relatively chill compared to his pack mates. They looked like they were going to pass out.

"Um, Gemma," he murmured. He was desperately trying to understand what the hell was going on, but things were moving too fast. "You know that sounds a little crazy, right?"

Gemma sighed again, louder this time. "Remy, we don't have time for this. Yes, I know about werewolves. Yes, Rufus was one. And yes, I know that you and your friends from Dallas are all werewolves too. Alphas, actually. Which I have to admit caught me off guard, since it's very unusual to see multiple alphas able to coexist like the four of you do. Regardless, now that we have the werewolf crap out of the way, can we get back to the important issue of your going to rescue my daughter?"

Remy stood there dumbfounded, the phone pressed to his ear, his head swimming. "Um, okay. So you have this wolf-head necklace that can really turn someone into a werewolf, and Aaron Lee wants it?"

"Yes, he wants it. Unfortunately, even though I offered to give it to him in trade for Triana, I don't actually have it. It disappeared the night Rufus was murdered. I'd gladly give it in exchange for my daughter, especially since it doesn't have the power to transform a person into anything, much less a werewolf."

"Wait, hold on a second. I can't keep up with all this." Remy was so frigging confused right then, he didn't know where to start. "You said Lee knows the necklace can turn him into a werewolf. That's why he wants it."

"No," she replied in a calm, patient voice. "I said he *thinks* it can turn him into a werewolf, and since he has my daughter, I sure wasn't going to correct his error. In reality, the necklace was a voodoo spirit charm I made for Rufus before we were married. It was designed to help him control his animal rages."

Something clicked then about all the things he remembered about Triana's dad. The size, the mane of shaggy, blond hair, the way he was always so quick to anger, the reputation he had for getting into fights—and finishing them. There was only one kind of werewolf defined by that lack of control and violent behavior.

"Triana's father was an omega, wasn't he?" Remy asked.

"Yes, he was," Gemma said softly. "But he never lost control with Triana or me, not even once. He was the sweetest, gentlest, kindest man when he was with us." She paused. "I always thought a roving band of hunters had caught up with Rufus, but now I realize Lee must have figured out what my husband was and had his men kill Rufus."

"If he thought so little of your husband that he wanted him dead, why would he want a necklace he thinks could turn him into the same thing?" Remy asked.

"I don't know for sure, but as power hungry as Lee

has always been, I can only guess it's for the obvious reason—to make him stronger. A criminal like Lee only stays in power until someone bigger comes along. A man his age has to be thinking about extending his shelf life."

Remy was silent for a moment. "You told him you'd give him the necklace, even though you don't have it now?"

"Yes," Gemma said simply. "He wants me to bring it to his plantation house in Kenner. He was feeling gracious because of the storm, so he told me to be there in two hours."

"That doesn't give us a lot of time," Remy said, wishing he knew more about the plantation house Lee lived in. "How big is this property of his? Any idea what security is like?"

"I was there years and years ago, when Lee and my husband were on somewhat better terms with each other," Gemma said. "It's an extremely big place with a high security fence and a lot of wide-open space between the fence and the main house. If it's like it used to be, he probably has a dozen people working security for him, maybe more now that he's gotten older and has to worry about people coming after his empire."

Remy swore as he realized they'd have to hit the place while it was still daylight. "The storm will provide some cover, but getting across those open spaces in the daytime is going to be tough. If security sees us as we're moving into position, Triana is going to pay the price."

"That's why I'll be going with you," Gemma said, "to provide a distraction." Remy opened his mouth to say no way, but she cut him off. "Don't even start with me.

You four are alphas, and I know what alphas can do. But this is my daughter we're talking about, and I'm going to help get her back. You're going to need everyone focused on the front gate when you make your move, and I can make that happen."

"Gemma, it's too dangerous," he growled. "I'm not willing to risk your life to save Triana's. She'd kill me if something happened to you. I'll find another way."

"No, you won't," Gemma said. "I'm already on the way to Lee's house right now. You can either let me help you, or figure out how to rescue both of us."

Remy's response was equal parts cursing and growling. Shit, she was stubborn as hell. He could understand how Gemma could have been married to an omega werewolf. She was a frigging force of nature.

"Lee is expecting me," Gemma interrupted. "While I have his attention on me, you and your friends go in there and get my little girl out. I'm depending on you, and whether she knows it or not, so is Triana."

Remy ground his jaw but forced himself to calm down. "Okay. We'll do it your way. Just don't do anything stupid until we get there."

"I won't do anything stupid," Gemma assured him. "Just don't dawdle. I don't like the idea of my daughter in the hands of those monsters."

Neither did Remy.

"We'll get her out safely. I promise," he said.

Gemma gave him Lee's address, and while he didn't know that particular part of the lake area, he knew he could find it.

As he was about to hang up, Gemma stopped him. "I know alphas are tough, maybe tougher than my

Rufus was, but you need to be careful. At least some of Lee's people know about werewolves and how to kill them. It's the only thing that explains what they did to my husband."

Remy promised they'd be careful, even though it was a lie. He was going in there to get Triana back, no matter what he had to do. He didn't care if he lived through it or not.

He put his phone away, then checked to make sure his pack mates had caught all of the conversation when Drew walked up. "I didn't hear everything, but I heard enough to know that you're going after Lee. You aren't dumb enough to think that I'd let you go alone, are you?"

Chapter 16

TRIANA SAT TIED TO THE CHAIR IN THE STUDY, TEARS IN HER eyes as Quinn went into great detail about how her father had been murdered, while Lee sat in the chair opposite her, smiling.

She had no idea which of the men was more insane: Quinn, who seemed to get off on describing the killing, or Lee, who obviously enjoyed seeing the pain on her face. Either way, all she could think about was what it would be like to do the same thing to these two that they'd done to her father.

"There were five hunters in all," Quinn said. "They told me they never go out in teams of fewer than that. And every time they go out, they treat it like a military operation. Quick, efficient, and with one purpose—to kill every werewolf they find." His mouth curved into a sneer. "I got to go along to watch, just to confirm the kill for Mr. Lee. I have to say, I was impressed."

If Triana hadn't been so upset about her father, she would have been terrified there were people out there like Quinn and Lee who were so delusional they really believed this stuff enough to hunt down and butcher people.

"They were the coldest bastards I think I've ever seen in my life," Quinn said, shaking his head. "And that's saying a lot. But they weren't lying when they said they were efficient. Those boys really knew what the hell they were doing."

Quinn walked over to the window, looking outside at the rain pouring down beyond the broad balcony outside the study. Then he glanced at his watch, leaving her to wonder how much more time she had.

"They had this spray they put all over themselves and me," Quinn continued as he stared out at the rain. "I couldn't smell a damn thing, but they said it would mask our scents from a werewolf. I thought that was pretty cool. Then those five boys kicked in the front door and walked right into the club and started shooting. Two of them were carrying big old dart guns the size of an elephant rifle. The darts were full of some kind of animal tranquilizer they said would slow down your dad enough for the kill shot."

Fresh tears rolled down her face as she listened to the story of her father being treated like some kind of poor animal that didn't even matter.

"I don't want to hear any more," she begged. "Just stop."

Quinn laughed, turning to look at her. "But I'm getting to the best part. See, the two guys with the dart guns were like the junior team members. The other three—they were the real hunters. They all carried silenced weapons, and when the shooting started, they went for heart and head shots. I have to hand it to your father; he really was a tough son of a bitch. Even with five hunters getting the drop on him, he gave them the shit. Pumped full of enough tranquilizers to knock out an elephant and hit about half a dozen times, he still kept coming. He ripped out the throats of those two boys with the dart guns and was heading for another when the leader of the group—a big fucking dude with eyes that would make a shark piss its pants—stepped up

and ended it with a shot through your daddy's head."
He grinned. "Bam! From, like, two feet away. Fucking
brains went everywhere."

Triana was crying so hard she could barely talk,
but she forced out the words she needed to say. "You
people are insane. You killed a man—my *father*—not
a werewolf!"

Quinn only laughed. Lee, on the other hand, stood up
and walked over to stand so close to her that she almost
knocked over the chair trying to get away from him. Lee
leaned down even closer but then stopped, momentarily
distracted by a popping sound from outside. Quickly
dismissing it, he turned his attention back to her.

"Yes, we are insane, Ms. Bellamy," he said softly.
"Which is something I hope your mother takes into
account when it comes to giving me what I want.
Because if she doesn't give me that necklace, what those
hunters did to your father will pale in comparison to
what I'm going to do to you."

Looking into the man's cold eyes, Triana shivered as
goose bumps raced up her back. "Mom says she doesn't
have the necklace."

"She's lying." Lee turned away and walked back to
his chair, sitting again. "Quinn saw it on the body after
your father was killed. Your mother must have taken
it off before he was buried. I know it's not there now
because I dug him up to look."

Triana had thought she was done being shocked by
these men. She was wrong. They had actually dug up
her father? She was about to call Lee every foul name
she'd ever heard—and she'd heard a lot of them—when
his phone rang.

Lee answered, listening for a moment. Then he got to his feet, the smile on his face twisted into anger. "What the hell are you talking about? She's one old woman."

He clenched his teeth together so hard Triana thought he might shatter them. Even Quinn looked concerned.

"Yes, you incompetent idiot," Lee ground out. "I'll be right there. Don't let her go anywhere, or the next person getting shot will be you."

"Everything okay, boss?" Quinn asked when Lee hung up.

Lee scowled. "That was security. It seems that Mrs. Bellamy has arrived. She shot one of the guards at the front gate in the leg and is currently threatening to shoot the other two guards and throw the necklace in the swamp unless I come out and guarantee her safe passage to see her daughter."

Triana's heart started beating faster at the knowledge that her mother was here and actually going to come in. What was her mom doing? She couldn't think that a promise from a man like Lee meant anything.

"Don't you dare hurt her!" Triana shouted at Lee and Quinn as they turned to leave.

Ignoring her, Lee opened the heavy double doors and motioned to the men outside the room. "Get more security to the front gate; then bring the girl downstairs. Keep her quiet until I have what I need; then kill her."

Triana was still shouting at Lee to leave her mother out of this when two muscular men with bored expressions on their faces untied her from the chair and dragged her out of the room.

—◈—

"Lee and a large group of security guards are headed for the front gate in three SUVs," Drew announced over the radio earpiece secured in Remy's ear, speaking louder than usual so he could be heard over the wind and rain. "It appears Gemma shooting that guard did the trick. You've got your distraction."

Remy growled, not sure what frustrated him more — that Drew had forced his way onto this operation or that Gemma had gotten a gun somewhere. He pushed both thoughts from his mind as he and Max jumped the fence along the back side of Lee's property and ran toward the main house the moment they hit the rain-soaked grass on the far side. They had about four hundred feet of open ground to cover, which would have normally been a suicide mission any other day of the week. But with the distraction Gemma was providing and the rain coming down so hard it was tough seeing more than twenty feet ahead of them, Remy hoped they'd be okay.

His gut clenched with worry, Remy tried to ignore the sense of fear bubbling to the surface and put on all the speed his werewolf abilities could muster. Pushing himself that hard made his fangs and claws slip out too, but it was a small price to pay for the swiftness he needed.

Fighting the wind and avoiding the occasional piece of flying debris slowed him and Max down a little, but they still made it to the house in less than thirty seconds. They'd just reached the cover of the stacked stone wall that made up the back of Lee's ungodly expensive plantation home when Brooks's calm voice came across the radio.

"I'm in the garage and I'm picking up scents as well

as the sounds of movement on the far side of a set of double doors that lead into the house," he said softly. "Multiple males, one female. Standing by to move on your word, but this door is seriously heavy duty. It might take me a while to get through it."

Of course Lee has heavy doors connecting his monster garage to his monster house, Remy thought. *The asshole probably stole them from a frigging castle in Germany*.

"Roger that," he whispered softly around his fangs. His control was shot to shit at the moment, so he was having a difficult time getting them to retract. "Max and I are at the back and moving in to get a fix on Triana's location."

He and Max slipped around to the pool entrance, hesitating long enough to confirm there weren't any other guards back there, then snapped the lock on the french doors that led inside. The sounds of a TV show reached him at the same time Triana's scent hit him in the face, almost making him shift further.

Remy fought down the urge and stepped into the kitchen, only to freeze as a numbing cascade of sensations washed over him. Shit, it felt like someone had shoved him under a waterfall of human emotions. All at once he was hit with a painful pinching feeling around his wrists, a sense of dread that had his gut nearly heaving, and an overpowering fear that made his heart start beating so hard he thought it might burst.

Max grabbed his arm, concern on his face. *You okay?* he mouthed.

For a moment, Remy wasn't sure he *was* okay. He was having a hard time getting control of all the bizarre sensations bombarding him. He was drowning in a sea of emotions and feelings that weren't his own, and it was disorienting as hell.

"Remy, what's your status in there?" Drew called out over the radio, his voice jarring Remy out of the sensory overload loop he'd been stuck in. "Lee and his men are at the gate and if you don't do something soon, we're going to be in trouble out here."

Remy shook his head to clear it and crossed the immense kitchen, with its high-end cabinets and expensive granite countertops, toward Triana's scent. Drew and Zane were out front covering Gemma by themselves, and if the situation out there turned into a shoot-out, they faced the serious possibility of getting overwhelmed, especially if Zane had to hold back and not reveal his true nature to the NOPD cop they hadn't been able to dissuade from coming along to help. If Lee's men got past Drew and Zane, Gemma wouldn't stand a chance.

Max kept him covered as Remy slipped out of the kitchen, through a huge dining room, and down a long hall. He stopped just before an arched opening to the right of the hallway, not needing his nose or his ears to tell him Triana was nearby. He swore he could frigging *feel* her just inside the room beyond. The urge to run in there and save her was hard to get a grip on.

He took a breath and focused on what he knew he had to do—he had to think instead of acting out of instinct, as much as the werewolf inside might have wanted to.

Taking a deeper breath, he picked up Brooks's fainter scent. After getting himself oriented to the layout of the house, he realized the door his pack mate was waiting behind led to the room Triana was in. That was good.

It meant they'd be able to come into the room from two sides at once.

Remy dropped to his knees by the arched entryway, then closed his eyes and extended his senses. Normally a SWAT officer in this kind of situation would pull out a small hand mirror and use it to check out the room beyond, but that wasn't necessary when you were a werewolf.

Using his nose and ears, he was able to paint a picture of the number of people in the room and where they were located. He knew that Triana was on the right side of the room, while the four men inside were scattered around her in a loose semicircle. Based on their positions in the room, all four of the men seemed to be facing in some direction other than the entryway Remy was kneeling in. Another bit of good luck. He reached down and fingered the gris-gris bag Gemma had given him all those years ago. *Just keep working*, he prayed. *Just help me get Triana out of this.*

He leaned forward a little to get a quick visual, then jerked his head back. What he'd seen in that one second had confirmed what his other senses had told him. It also scared the hell out of him at the same time.

To the left side of the large, posh living room, two men stood by a short set of stairs that led to the heavy oak doors Brooks had described. Another man was standing in front of an expensive wide-screen TV, apparently intent on watching a guy with shorts, tattoos, and a shocking head of bleached-blond hair shove a whole burrito in his mouth on some kind of cooking show.

About twenty feet away, on the right side of the room, Triana was sitting on the couch, looking terrified. Her heart was hammering in her chest and her wrists were bound cruelly in front of her. The sight of her made his fangs shove out even farther. He wanted to kill every man who had dared to touch her.

Remy took a deep breath and forced himself to stop thinking about that as he considered the last man in the room, the one standing closest to Triana, a pistol held casually and comfortably in his hands. Remy's werewolf instincts told him this was the most dangerous man in the room. The way the guy looked at Triana made Remy want to storm into the room to protect her. But Remy couldn't do that, not with how close the man was standing to Triana, ready to shoot her.

He needed the man distracted long enough for him to either put a bullet in him or run into the room and get Triana out of there. And after a few seconds of thought, he knew exactly how to do it.

Getting to his feet, Remy took a few steps back, covering his mouth as he whispered into his radio mic. "Brooks, I need you to set a charge on the center of the double doors and blow them on my mark."

There was only the barest hint of hesitation on Brooks's part. As the senior officer on the team, Brooks could have nixed the plan, but Remy knew his pack mate wouldn't do that because the woman Remy cared about was at risk.

"The wood is going to frag," Brooks whispered. "Is Triana clear of the door?"

"She will be," Remy said firmly. "Be ready to go in ten seconds."

"Roger that," Brooks confirmed. "On your mark."

Remy motioned to Max, making sure the younger werewolf knew what they were doing and that Remy wanted him to focus on the man by the TV. Turning back to the entryway, he dropped to one knee and forced himself to relax. The man standing right next to Triana would be his responsibility. When the door charge blew on the left side of the room, the man would instinctively turn and throw up his hands to protect himself—it was a reflex reaction that couldn't be overruled. That would give Remy the time he needed to get to the man before he hurt Triana.

But for his plan to work, he needed to get Triana's attention—and pray she remembered those hand signals he'd shown her a couple of days ago. Because if either of those two things failed to happen, Triana would get hit by the door debris. The thought of the damage that would do to her was simply something he refused to think about.

Triana's pulse raced as she sat on the couch in Lee's living room. She was scared to death for her mom. What was happening outside at the front gate? Would the next ring of a cell phone mean these insane bastards had killed her mother and were about to do the same to her? With her hands still tied and four big, armed men surrounding her, she doubted there was anything she could do to stop any of this, but she sure as hell wasn't going to sit here and wait for it to happen.

She glanced down at the big coffee table in front of the couch, her eyes coming to rest on the decorative wooden bowl full of shells, glass beads, and colored sand. It seemed out of place. Lee didn't strike her as the kind of man who was into decorative anything unless it was arm candy. If she dumped out the stuff inside, the wood bowl might be heavy enough to bash someone's head in.

She turned her head slightly, trying to see exactly where the guy behind her was standing. If she moved fast, she could grab the bowl, swing it around, and hit the jerk with the gun. If that worked, she could get the weapon and use it against the other three.

It was insane, especially since she wasn't sure she could fire the weapon with her hands tied, even if she was lucky enough to get it. But it was a plan, and right now, she was ready to try anything.

As she reached toward the bowl in front of her, the strangest sensation she'd ever felt in her life came over her, almost taking her breath away. One second her heart was thudding in her chest and her whole body was shaking in fear, and the next, a feeling of deep calm washed over her.

Not understanding why she was even doing it, Triana glanced over her shoulder at the arched opening that led toward the back of the house. There, in the shadows of the leftmost side of the entryway, she saw something that made her eyes widen.

Remy was down on one knee, most of his face and body hidden by the frame of the entryway and the dark shadows cast by the lights in the living room. But she knew it was him. Even without seeing his face, she knew it was him. Relief swept through her, making her dizzy.

But at the same time, she felt a stab of fear. Was he here alone? Was he going to try to save her all by himself? Was he going to get himself killed charging into a room full of psychos? That thought was more terrifying than facing death herself.

Her first instinct was to shout at him to run, to save her mom and get out of there. But then she saw his hands move. At first she had no idea what he was doing. He had one hand up, his fingers splayed wide, while the other hand was horizontal to the floor. As she watched, one upraised finger went down, leaving four still up. Then another dropped, leaving three.

Her mind was transported to a happier memory, of the two of them walking through the French Quarter and him telling her how his SWAT teammates communicated with each other while on a raid by using hand signals.

Three fingers, now two.

He was counting down to something. The hand flat to the floor meant…oh crap, what did that mean?

As another finger dropped, she remembered.

Hand flat to the floor means get down!

Triana had a half second before the last finger closed into a fist to throw herself to the floor.

She'd barely hit the expensive wood when the room above her exploded in sound, smoke, and whistling debris. She heard grunts of pain and people falling, but then there was movement near her head, and even though the force of the blast had stunned her, she still turned around to see the man with the gun coming at her. There was blood running down the side of his face and he looked furious.

She tried to scramble away, but he was too close. He grabbed her hair and yanked her to her knees, the force of the motion twisting her neck so much she thought he might break it. She saw the gun coming up toward her head and realized she was going to die. She struggled, refusing to go like this with Remy so close and her mother in danger, but she knew it wasn't going to make a difference.

Then a snarling growl ripped through the room, making the man with the gun freeze. Triana twisted her head toward the sound, ignoring how much it hurt.

Remy charged toward her, covering the distance across the room in a blur as he moved faster than anyone she'd ever seen. Then she saw the claws, the long white fangs, and the glowing, yellow eyes, and a part of her mind insisted it couldn't possibly be Remy.

The guy with the gun hesitated for a moment, as shocked as Triana by what he saw. He seemed to be unsure if he should shoot her or the thing coming at him like a freight train. Finally, after a split second, he made up his mind and turned his gun on Triana.

That indecision provided Remy—or the thing she thought was Remy—all the time he needed. Triana screamed and tried to duck as the thing with the fangs and claws leaped straight at her, but the man still held her fast.

As Remy jumped completely over her, she heard a heavy thud and felt a slight tug in her hair as the man with the gun went down. There was another crash as Remy and the man hit the floor, then chaos reigned as the entire room seemed to go insane.

There was a loud pop of the man's gun going off, a blur of movement to her left as one of Lee's other men flew sideways through the air and smashed through the TV, and a huge shape at the far end of the living room that looked like Brooks throwing two men around like they were dolls. The man who'd been about to shoot her hit a bookcase, slamming into it so hard that part of the shelves collapsed.

Then Remy was down on his knees in front of her. The fangs and eyes she'd told herself must have been a construct of her fear-shredded imagination were still there, an unmistakable part of the man she'd spent the past five days with.

As they gazed into each other's eyes, the room around them grew quiet. His eyes glowed gold, making her wonder if all those flashes of light she'd seen so many times hadn't actually been a reflection at all. But even though they were a different color and were somehow lit from within, she still recognized them as Remy's eyes. She even saw the worry and concern there in their strange depths.

He reached out a hand toward her and she instinctively scrambled back on the floor away from him. She hated herself for doing it, hated the pain she saw in his eyes even more, but she couldn't have stopped herself if she'd tried. She was too confused to understand what was happening right then.

Triana wanted to say something, but no words would come. Outside, gunfire erupted, and she flinched. It took her half a second to realize the shooting was coming from the front gate.

"Mom," she breathed.

She pushed herself to her feet, but before she could take more than two steps, Remy was at her side, scooping her up in his arms. The next thing she knew, he set her on her feet beside Max.

"Keep her here with you," Remy ordered. Then, he and Brooks raced out of the room toward the sound of the gunfire.

Triana considered trying to dash around him for the

door, but then remembered the blur of movement that had come right before Lee's goon had crashed into the TV. Was Max like Remy? Some kind of freak with fangs and claws?

Afraid to think about it, she stood there as the shooting intensified outside, thinking about what she'd seen and praying her mother would be okay.

Chapter 17

WITH THE POWER KNOCKED OUT FROM THE STORM, IT WAS AS dark in her mother's shop as it was outside, but Triana barely noticed. She was simply too exhausted, physically and mentally, to care by the time they finally got home. She wasn't sure what she thought about having Remy and his SWAT teammates there, even if they had saved her life and her mother's. She felt horrible for even thinking like that, but she was so confused by everything she'd seen and needed time to figure it all out.

Not that how she felt seemed to matter at the moment, since not only had Remy refused to leave them on their own, but her mother had also firmly stated she wouldn't stand for any of the men driving back to their hotel at that time of night, not with the way the wind and rain was kicking up right then.

So the guys stayed downstairs in the shop, making sure the windows weren't going to blow in and water wasn't going to come rushing under the door, while Triana went upstairs with her mother, hoping to get her head around everything.

She sat at the kitchen table while her mom bustled around the kitchen, heating up soup on the gas stove and getting all the flashlights and emergency lamps out. Triana had no idea how her mother did it. The events at Lee's house had drained her like a battery. She couldn't even put in the effort to change out of her wet clothes.

Half of her exhaustion came from all the questions the police had asked her after the shooting had stopped. Triana was a little surprised the cops had even shown up, considering the storm was so bad, but she supposed a shoot-out involving automatic weapons didn't happen every day in Kenner, so police, detectives, and politicians had come out of the woodwork.

Following her mother's suggestions, she'd kept her statements brief and vague. Quinn had lured her to a warehouse in the Marigny by saying he had information relating to her father's murder. When she'd gotten there, she'd seen Quinn shoot another man; then, Quinn had knocked her unconscious and taken her to Lee's home. Lee and Quinn had confessed to arranging the murder of her father because he refused to sell drugs through his club. Lee had lured her mother to his home to clean up any loose ends; then, the SWAT officers had stormed the place and rescued her.

She stayed away from any mention of werewolves or questions that veered outside the boundaries of her narrow story line. Of course, those were the questions the Kenner PD were most interested in. Why had Quinn told her about her father's murder? Why had a team from New Orleans and Dallas SWAT come to her rescue? Where were Lee and Quinn now? Why were the men in custody claiming they'd been attacked by glowing-eyed monsters?

Triana's answer to those questions and all the others just as impossible to explain was a plain and simple "I don't know."

She didn't realize she'd been sitting at the table that long, but the next thing Triana knew, her mother set a big bowl of steaming soup in front of her, with a ham and cheese sandwich on the side. She didn't feel like eating anything, but her mom shoved the bowl toward her and pointed at it.

"Eat."

Her mother set a battery-powered lamp on the table between them, then sat across from her and began eating. "I'm guessing you have a lot of questions about everything you learned and saw today."

Triana dipped her spoon in her soup, then took her time nibbling on her sandwich as she tried to figure out where to start. It wasn't like she had to worry that her mother hadn't seen what Remy and the others were. According to the guards at the front who'd been arrested, the SWAT cops had tackled cars and thrown men through the air like they were horseshoes.

"Lee and Quinn said some really crazy stuff about Dad," she finally said. "I thought they were off their rockers, but then I saw…things…inside the house when Remy and his friends came to get me. Things I can't explain."

Her mother set down her sandwich and regarded Triana for a moment. "Finding out werewolves are real can be a shock for most people."

Triana wanted to tell her that she was talking crazy, that werewolves weren't real, that there was some other explanation. But she knew the time for doubt was over. Even though she was a scientist who liked her feet firmly planted in fact, she knew what she'd seen.

"So Dad was a werewolf?"

Triana couldn't believe those words had just come out of her mouth. If anyone at the crime lab back in

Houston heard her, they'd have tied her up in her own lab coat.

Her mother gave her a small smile. "Yes. In fact, it's how we met."

Triana couldn't even begin to make sense of that statement, but since she'd already climbed fully aboard the crazy train, she figured she might as well find a seat and get comfortable.

"What did his being a werewolf have to do with you guys getting together?"

"You remember that your grandma ran the shop before you were born, right?" her mother asked. At Triana's nod, she continued. "Well, your grandma had a reputation for helping a lot of unusual people in her day. As she got older, she passed that responsibility on to me. When people stopped by looking for help, I did anything I could to help them. Your father was one of those people."

"Dad came to you for help because he was a werewolf?" Triana asked.

She was a little surprised at that. Her father had always been a man who liked doing things on his own.

"Yes," her mom said. "But not quite in the way you think. You see, there are three kinds of werewolves—alphas, betas, and omegas. Your father was an omega, meaning he had some anger management issues. When he got mad, his inner wolf would come out, and he was worried that sooner or later, someone would get hurt. He lived in fear of that happening, so he came to the shop looking for something to help him stay in control."

Realization dawned on Triana. "The necklace!"

Her mother nodded. "Exactly. The wolf pendant was

a charm designed to ward off negative energies and rein-force positive energy."

"Did it work?"

Her mom tried not to look too smug. "I admit, it was one of my more inspired pieces. But while it was very powerful, I prefer to believe it was your father's love for you and me that kept him stable. After all, love is by far the most powerful force in the universe."

Triana dipped her spoon into her soup again. Clearly, the world was a far more complicated place than she had ever imagined. "Why didn't you or Dad ever tell me any of these things?"

"Why?" Her mother smiled gently. "Because you were always much happier studying your own particular form of magic. We felt no need to confuse you with ours."

Triana supposed she could understand that. She'd always been into science and had never bought into the voodoo stuff her mother did. She probably would have thought her parents were crazy if they tried to tell her about werewolves. Still, she couldn't help feeling saddened by that fact. While it was strange trying to reconcile the sweet, kind man she knew with the savage ferocity she'd witnessed that night, it felt like there was a part of her father she'd missed getting to know.

Triana went back to her soup and sandwich, partly because she wanted to eat while it was still hot, but mostly because she needed time to think about what she wanted to ask her mom next. Her first instinct was to ask if her mom had known Remy was a werewolf before tonight, but she pushed that aside until later. The whole subject of Remy was too painful to get into right then.

"Quinn implied Lee and Dad used to be friends," Triana finally said. "Is that true?"

Her mother sighed. "Unfortunately, yes. When I met your father, he was Lee's enforcer. Since he was an omega werewolf, he was very good at his job. To some degree, your father was the brawn responsible for building most of Lee's empire. But when he met me, that changed. I told him if he wanted to be with me, he couldn't be in that life anymore."

Triana smiled. She could definitely see her mom laying down the law like that. "How did Dad handle the ultimatum?"

"Better than I expected," her mother admitted. "But only because he loved me so much. When you came along, it reinforced the importance of what he was doing." Her lips curved. "The moment your father saw you for the first time, his entire world flipped upside down. He bought the club, settled down, and became an even better husband and a tremendous father. I was aware he still did an odd job for Lee on the side now and then out of some misplaced loyalty to the man, but by and large, he stayed on the straight and narrow."

Triana's heart ached at the memory of her father and how much she missed him right then. "Lee said he hired some people he called hunters to murder Dad because he wouldn't sell drugs out of the club."

Her mother closed her eyes for a moment. When she opened them again, they were wet with tears. "I'm sure that was the excuse he used to justify what he did. But in reality, I don't think Lee could ever forgive your father for walking away from him and leaving him weaker."

They ate in silence for a few minutes, the only sounds

in the dark room the clink of their spoons against the bowls and the low, deep voices of Remy and his friends drifting up the stairs. Finishing her soup, Triana pushed the bowl away and took a bite of the sandwich, chewing slowly. Finally, unable to contain her curiosity any longer, she tackled the big pink elephant in the room.

"So, Remy and his friends..." she whispered, half-afraid they'd hear her. "They're like Dad, aren't they?"

Her mother laughed as she finished the last of her soup. "Don't bother to whisper, dear. Werewolves have incredible hearing. If they've been paying attention, they've heard every word we've said."

Triana blinked. Of course they had incredible hearing. Why not? She glanced over at the kitchen counter where she'd cut her finger the other night—right before she'd asked Remy if he was up for a quickie. Had the other guys heard them? She blushed even as she wondered what other abilities they had.

"Yes, Remy and his friends are werewolves like your father," her mom said, bringing her attention back to their conversation. "Though technically, they're a little different because all four of them are alphas, the more dominant kind of werewolf. They're strong, heroic, and tend to attract a lot of attention everywhere they go. I haven't met enough alphas to know for sure, but something tells me they're all hunks too."

Triana laughed despite herself. Remy was definitely that. But then an image of claws and fangs flashed in her head, and she shuddered. Things between her and Remy had been falling apart before she'd learned he was a werewolf. She doubted learning something like this was going to help their chances of working anything out.

The thought made her stomach churn as if it wanted to reject the soup and sandwich she'd just eaten.

Her mother reached across the table and took Triana's hand in hers. "Hon, I know this is none of my business, so if you don't want to talk about it, I understand. But I'm a little confused about what's going on between you and Remy. A few days ago you were talking about falling for him, and now you're sitting up here in the dark with me while the courageous man who saved your life is trapped in exile downstairs. What happened?"

Triana shook her head. She couldn't talk about it right now. Besides, what could she say? That Remy had already been in love and didn't want to go there again? That she had no desire to be with a man who didn't want her? That she had no idea how she felt about a man with fangs and claws? It was more than she could put into words.

"I'm tired, Mom. I just want to go to bed," she said.

"Of course, go ahead." Her mother stood up with her and came around to her side of the table to hug her. "I love you, baby girl."

She hugged her mom back just as tightly. "I love you too."

Triana didn't bother with a flashlight as she headed for her bedroom, since she knew the way by heart. As she passed the staircase, she felt the same pull she'd experienced in Lee's living room. She stopped to look down the stairs and saw Remy sitting on the bottom step, an empty bowl and plate beside him, his back to her like he was guarding the entry to the apartment, guarding her and her mother.

As if sensing her, he turned his head and Triana

caught a glimmer of gold in the darkness. The urge to go downstairs, wrap her arms around him, and tell him how much she appreciated what he'd done for her and her mother was overwhelming.

She pushed the impulse aside and headed down the hall toward her bedroom. Walking past the place where she and Remy had made love a few nights ago brought tears to her eyes, and she hurried the last few feet to her bedroom.

The hot shower felt good but didn't do much to make her feel any better. Drying off, she dragged on a long sleep shirt and climbed into bed. She lay there, staring into the dark and listening to the wind and rain batter the window as she replayed everything that had happened that day over and over in her mind. It was difficult to reconcile the Remy she knew—or thought she knew— with the glowing yellow eyes, claws, fangs, growls, and violence she'd seen.

She tried to force herself to go to sleep so she wouldn't have to think about Remy anymore, but her stomach rolled like the dirty Mississippi, refusing to give her a moment of peace.

Remy and Max stopped at the NOPD SWAT facility to change into dry uniforms and get something to eat before they headed back out to help the city's residents recover from the storm. They'd been out since six that morning, helping deliver food and water to evacuation centers, clearing streets and storm drains of debris, and handling traffic control for the crews repairing downed electrical lines. The storm hadn't been as bad as it could have been, but it was still cloudy with occasional bands of rain moving through, and there were still a lot of people who needed help. It would have been rewarding work if Remy hadn't felt so crappy. His stomach was tied in a frigging knot and he was exhausted as hell.

He was walking past the main conference room when he caught sight of Lorenzo, Drew, Brooks, Cooper, Alex, and several of the local SWAT officers sitting around the table, shuffling though dozens of thick manila folders. Cooper and Alex had arrived in town around two a.m. and spent the night sleeping on the floor of Gemma's shop with the rest of them. They'd volunteered to come in this morning and help out the NOPD any way they could.

"I'm going to see if they have an update on Lee and Quinn," Remy told Max. "Grab me something to eat, will you?"

Max nodded. "Will do. I really doubt those two scumbags are hanging around the city, though. They were probably scurrying across the border into Mexico before the storm even passed."

While Max was probably right about Lee and Quinn not hanging around, Remy couldn't imagine Lee *scurrying* anywhere. Quinn, yes. But Lee? No way. The man would have some kind of well-thought-out and cushy evacuation plan already put into place for a situation like this. Something involving a fancy yacht or a private jet. Remy wasn't taking any chances. That's why he had Zane stay at Gemma's shop. If Lee decided to make one more run at Triana and her mother before leaving town, he was going to get a rude awakening.

"Any sign of Lee or Quinn?" Remy asked as he sat

down in the empty chair beside Cooper with an audible squishing sound.

On the other side of the table, Brooks glanced up from whatever he was reading. "You're going to turn into a fish if you keep getting this wet all the time."

"Yeah, no kidding," Remy said. "So, any word?"

Drew shook his head. "Nothing yet. But we have alerts at all the travel hubs and border crossings. They'll pop up on the radar soon, especially if they're together."

"On the bright side," Lorenzo said, "we've already started getting results back from the search warrants we served this morning. When we find Aaron Lee and Shelton Quinn, they'll both be heading to jail for a very long time."

That was great, but Remy would have preferred if he and his pack mates had gotten Lee yesterday during the shoot-out at the gatehouse. Unfortunately Lee and his muscle-headed bodyguard had jumped in their vehicle and hauled ass the moment they'd seen Remy and Brooks running at them faster than humans were supposed to. Then Brooks did his signature move and slammed his shoulder into one of the SUVs. Seeing a guy tackle a car would take the fight out of anybody.

After filling them in on the early results of the search warrants, Lorenzo told them Roth had come through surgery early that morning and would make a full recovery.

"Okay, I don't know about anyone else, but I could use something to eat," the narcotics detective said when he finished. "Let's pick this back up after lunch."

Everyone but Drew got up to join him. Remy stayed behind as well. To say he'd been frustrated yesterday when Drew had gone with them to Lee's house to rescue

Triana was an understatement, but when the questions had started coming hard and fast after the fact, he'd been glad the man was there. Drew knew people in the Kenner PD, knew who needed to get involved, and, most important, knew how to push the right buttons to keep the attention focused on Lee and Quinn and the fact that they'd attempted to kill an undercover police officer and had kidnapped Triana.

In the end, Drew had definitely kept Remy and his pack mates out of a lot of hot water—not just by smoothing the feathers that had been ruffled by having out-of-state officers conducting a raid in their city, but also by not saying anything about what he'd seen Remy and the other werewolves doing during the raid.

"I never did get a chance to thank you for everything you did yesterday," Remy said quietly. "You covered for us when a lot of people might not have."

Drew met his gaze across the table. "You mean the part where I didn't mention the fact that you guys are part of a pack of werewolves?"

Remy tried his best not to let his surprise show, but he was pretty sure he failed. He considered denying it, but what would be the point? Drew had obviously seen what they were. Brooks had tackled an SUV ten feet away from him. Still, it was a big leap from seeing something strange to calmly acknowledging they were part of a pack of werewolves.

Wait a minute…*part of a pack*?

Clearly, Drew knew more than it appeared.

"How long have you known about us?" Remy asked.

Drew leaned back in his chair. "I figured out back while I was still in Dallas on the SWAT team that Gage was different. I'd see him do things a normal person shouldn't be able to do. At first I thought he was juicing on steroids or something like that, but then I saw a blitzed-out junkie shove a piece of rusty rebar through Gage's thigh. He pulled it out like it was nothing. When I saw him the next day in shorts and a T-shirt at morning PT, there wasn't a mark on him. That's when I figured out it wasn't simply a case of better living through chemistry."

The NOPD SWAT commander fell silent as a group of his officers walked past the door with paper plates in their hands, the mouthwatering scent of sausage and crawfish gumbo following them.

"Not long after that, Gage took over the team and I noticed the new people he brought in were as unique as he was," Drew continued. "Gage was different, and the team he was putting together in Dallas was built with that difference in mind. I'm a good SWAT officer, and working with Gage made me even better, but I saw what he was trying to do. I knew I wouldn't be able to hang with those guys for long. When the opportunity to apply for this position here in New Orleans opened up, I moved on it, and Gage helped me get it. He did the same for every officer who ultimately transferred. I always appreciated that."

Remy considered that. "Going from what you'd seen to knowing about werewolves and packs still seems like a big leap."

Drew laughed. "That part I learned once I got here. You work in New Orleans long enough and you start learning all kinds of new things—if you're willing to open your eyes and see them. Believe it or not, werewolves aren't that weird compared to some of the stuff I've run into."

Remy wasn't sure what to say to that. This wasn't the direction he'd expected this conversation to go. "I have to admit, you're taking this way better than I think most people would."

Triana came to mind.

"Probably not any better than the average person on the street." Drew regarded him thoughtfully. "You should have more faith in people. Most of them would surprise you with how accepting they can be if you give them a chance."

Remy was still considering that when Drew stood up and announced he was going to go hunt down some of that gumbo he'd been smelling. Remy nodded, saying he'd join him later. He was wondering if he should change into a dry uniform before he did, when Cooper walked in with two plates of steaming food and plunked one down on the table in front of him.

"You should eat," Cooper said as he sat down across from him. "You look like shit."

Remy snorted as he opened the plastic-wrapped utensil set Cooper tossed him. "Thanks for that. Nice to see you too."

"Just pointing out the obvious." Cooper dug into his gumbo and rice like he hadn't eaten in a week. "You know me. Truth and sarcasm are just two of the many services I provide."

Remy chuckled as he slid his plate of food closer. You could always count on Cooper, the Pack's explosives expert, to interject a heavy dose of snark into any situation. The guy simply couldn't carry on a normal conversation without slipping in at least one smart-ass comment. Remy had no idea how his new bride put up with him.

He ate a big forkful of gumbo, then immediately decided he didn't want another bite. While the food looked amazing and smelled even better, it tasted like dirt. He shoved the plate away with a growl of frustration.

Cooper looked at him. "Max mentioned you weren't feeling so well lately. No appetite, huh?"

Remy shook his head. "Not really. I guess I've been pushing myself too hard and it's starting to catch up to me."

As lies went, it wasn't bad. In fact, it sounded so logical Remy almost found himself believing it. Unfortunately, Cooper didn't.

"Is that the line you're going with? That you're overworked?" Cooper said, not even slowing down in between bites. "You don't think the way you're feeling might have something to do with what's going on between you and Triana?"

"No," Remy insisted.

There was no way he was talking to Cooper about Triana. He was doing everything he could to put her behind him. Remembering the way she'd recoiled from him after the raid at Lee's home definitely helped accomplish that. It was obvious she couldn't even stand to look at him. Rehashing everything wasn't going to help.

"Really?" Cooper lifted a brow. "Because Max mentioned you started feeling sick when you decided to push her away."

"Max says a lot of shit he should keep to himself," Remy muttered, slamming his fist down on the table and growling loud enough everyone in the whole facility probably heard it.

He regretted lashing out immediately, but Cooper didn't seem fazed at all. Instead, he regarded Remy thoughtfully.

"Fear leads to anger," Cooper said softly. "Anger leads to hate. Hate leads to suffering."

Remy stared at him. Where the hell did Cooper get this stuff? It sounded deep as shit, but surprisingly, it actually made sense. "Did you just make that up?"

Cooper shook his head and ate another forkful of gumbo. "Nah, that was Yoda. But it seems to fit. It's obvious you're scared to commit to a relationship with Triana, and that fear is leading you down a path of one dumb-ass decision after another. You're feeling like this because you're making a mistake. And while the rest of humanity has the free will to make all kinds of dumb-ass mistakes, there are some decisions that are essentially out of a werewolf's hands, like who they end up loving."

Remy ground his jaw. He wanted to tell Cooper he didn't love Triana, but the thought of denying it made him sick. "So you're trying to tell me I have no say in this? That werewolves don't get to make a decision that's in the best interest of everyone involved? That I can't walk away from Triana if I know being with me is going to get her killed?"

His hands shook as he said the words, pain and queasiness radiating out from his stomach in waves. *This must be what it feels like to be a junkie trying to come down from a drug the body is sure it needs to exist.* That's what it felt like Triana was, something he needed in order to live.

Remy got a grip and pushed that thought away. Getting involved with Triana had already gotten her kidnapped and almost killed. He might carry a gris-gris bag, but in every way that mattered, he was cursed. If he gave in, something else bad was going to happen to the woman he cared for more than anything in the world.

No matter how crappy he felt at that moment, he wasn't going to turn his back on his promise to never let that happen again.

Cooper reached over and grabbed Remy's uneaten plate of gumbo. "Don't get me wrong," he said as he ate. "You have the free will necessary to walk away from Triana. It's just going to come with a price."

Remy gritted his teeth as a particularly bad spasm of pain rushed through him, almost making him double over. Shit, he'd been shot before and it hadn't hurt like this. He wondered if this might actually be something that ended up killing him. Then decided he didn't care.

"That's a price I'm willing to pay," he said.

"That's cool. Be a hard-nosed badass, then."

Cooper finished the second helping of gumbo, then picked up both paper plates and walked over to toss them in the trash can. A moment later, he came back and leaned down over the table, his face inches from Remy's. "There's just one thing you might want to consider as you're suffering stoically in your misery."

Remy looked up at the other werewolf, not liking anyone this close to his grill. "What's that?"

"What makes you think you're the only one hurting like this?" Cooper asked. "You ever consider that maybe the suffering goes both ways? Think about that."

Straightening to his full height, Cooper walked out of

the room, leaving Remy alone with his doubts, his fears, and his regrets.

Chapter 18

TRIANA SAT AT THE SMALL TABLE IN HER MOTHER'S KITCHEN, doing her best to eat breakfast, but the mere sight of the egg white omelet her mother had cooked made her feel ill. Out of the blue, a little voice in her head screamed out two words.

Morning sickness!

She told herself to chill out even as her pulse skyrocketed. No matter how queasy her stomach felt, she wasn't pregnant. For one thing, she and Remy had used protection every time. For another, women didn't usually get morning sickness so quickly. So, unless there was something about sleeping with a werewolf that invalidated the normal rules of conception, she was fine. Besides, she didn't only feel like this in the morning. She'd felt crappy since Wednesday night. It didn't escape her notice that she'd first begun feeling this way when things with Remy had fallen apart.

She had no idea exactly what that meant, but something told her it couldn't be a good thing.

"Is Remy still downstairs?" she asked.

Her mother came over to the table with two mugs of coffee and sat down at the table opposite Triana. The power was back on, which meant the coffeepot was functional, so her mother was happy. Triana picked up her mug and took a sip.

Her mom shook her head. "Remy left already."

Triana's stomach lurched. "He went back to Dallas?"

"No. Some of their pack mates came in during the night to help with cleanup efforts in the city. I made them breakfast before they left, and let me tell you, those boys can eat. We're out of nearly everything. I'm going to have to make a run to the grocery store later."

Triana nodded, her heartbeat returning to normal as she realized Remy hadn't left town yet. She really did have it bad for him. It was over between them, yet she was nearly having a panic attack at the thought of him leaving town without saying anything to her.

On the other side of the table, her mother regarded her with a knowing look.

"Is it that obvious?" Triana asked.

"That you're in love with Remy? Yes, that part's obvious. What isn't so clear is what the heck is going on between the two of you."

Triana picked up her fork but didn't eat. Instead, she pushed her eggs around on the plate, trying to figure out where to start.

"I think I fell in love with Remy when I turned around and saw him standing there that first night at the club," she said softly. "That might not sound like a big deal to you, considering how fast you and Dad got married, but for me, it was out there. I started thinking crazy things, like how I could see myself being with Remy for the rest of my life. I thought Remy felt the same way."

"But?" her mother prompted.

Triana felt tears burn her eyes. "But a couple of days ago, something happened. I felt this weird...*pop*...I guess you'd call it. Like the connection between us broke. I've never experienced anything like it, but I knew in my heart something had changed and that Remy was pulling away."

Her mom didn't say anything and merely waited patiently for her to continue.

"Then Thursday night at dinner, before we came back and found those men in the shop, Remy told me he'd been in a relationship a long time ago and that he wasn't interested in getting into another one. And just like that, it was over."

"Over?" her mother echoed in surprise.

Triana nodded.

Her mom frowned. "So, if it's over, why did he risk his life, and the lives of his pack mates, to come rescue you?"

Triana opened her mouth to answer but then closed it again. She honestly didn't know.

"Well, it seems obvious he still cares about you." Her mother regarded her over the rim of her mug. "When Remy told you it was over, did you tell him how you feel about him?"

Triana shook her head glumly.

Her mother laughed as she sipped her coffee.

Triana tried not to be offended, but she couldn't help it. Her heart felt like it was broken into a million pieces, and her mom seemed to think it was hilarious.

"I don't see what's so funny," she snapped. "I certainly don't feel like laughing."

Her mother did her best to stop but couldn't hide the smile that remained. "I know, honey, and I'm sorry. It's just that you're so much like me when I was your age and met your father. I told you I fell in love with him from the start, but what I didn't tell you was that there were times when we were dating that his brooding drove me crazy. I probably would have sent him and his fangs packing if it hadn't been for your grandma. She was able to see what we were both blind to—that we were in love with each other but too lazy to work for it."

It was Triana's turn to frown. "Meaning?"

"Meaning that loving a werewolf can be difficult. They're big and strong, but that only means their luggage is a whole hell of a lot heavier. It takes a good soul mate to help them figure out how to carry it all. And right now, you suck in the soul mate category, dear."

Her mom had always been blunt, but it was especially hard to hear her being so truthful when it came to Triana's relationship with Remy.

"Were you afraid of Dad the first time you saw him change into a werewolf?" she asked.

"No, but that was because he wasn't the first werewolf I'd seen." Her mother gave her a sympathetic look. "Did seeing Remy like that scare you?"

Triana nodded.

"You were in shock, sugar. That's normal."

That didn't make Triana feel any better. "Maybe, but you should have seen the look on his face when I backed away from him, Mom. I really hurt him."

"Just because Remy is a werewolf, that doesn't make him a monster. You know that, right?"

Triana nodded. She'd known that last night too—deep down, anyway—but that still hadn't stopped her from cringing away from him. She picked up her fork and played with her eggs again. "Was it hard to love Dad?"

"You remember the part where I said his brooding drove me crazy, right?" Her mother's eyes twinkled.

"Honey, your father grew up on the streets, for all intents and purposes, on his own, and didn't want anyone telling him how to run his life. I have to admit, I was stubborn too. There were a hundred times it could have all fallen apart, but it didn't because we stuck to it and made it work. We weren't perfect together, but we loved each other and recognized that we were better together than apart. And when you came along, we knew we'd done the right thing, because we were a family."

Triana thought about that for a while until an absolutely crazy thought struck her, something she'd hadn't considered at all since discovering werewolves existed and that her father was one.

"Since Dad was a werewolf, does that mean I'm going to be one too at some point? Is it hereditary, or is it passed through a bite, like in the movies?" She tensed as another thought struck her. "Oh crap, if Remy bit me anywhere while we were…you know…will that do it?"

Her mother shook her head. "A bite won't do it, no matter how hard Remy might have nipped you. And while it might be hereditary, there are a lot of things that have to happen, at the right time and the right sequence, before a person can go through the first change."

"What kind of things?" she asked, curious despite herself.

"From what I understand, a person has to have the werewolf gift inside him or her, then go through a horribly painful and traumatic experience. Usually something that nearly kills them," her mother said. "If they survive, their body starts the change. As far as I can tell, while the gift itself might get passed on to a werewolf's children, I've never seen it materialize in any of them, and I've talked to at least three dozen werewolves in my time."

Triana was still wrapping her head around that when her mom looked pointedly at her plate of uneaten eggs.

"You aren't hungry?"

"I don't have much of an appetite. I'm not feeling very well." When her mother gave her a worried look, Triana added, "It's not a big deal. I've been feeling under the weather lately. I'm probably just coming down with a cold from being out in the rain so much."

Her mother reached over to rest a hand on Triana's forehead. "When did you start feeling like this?"

"Since Wednesday night, maybe Thursday morning," Triana said. "Why?"

Her mom took her hand away with a sigh. "You're not coming down with a cold, baby girl. What you're feeling is the severing of the bond between you and Remy that you mentioned earlier."

Triana shook her head. "That doesn't make any sense, Mom. Why would breaking up with him make me feel like this?" She'd broken up with guys before and never felt ill from it.

Her mother gave her a small smile. "Because you might have something so much more special with Remy than you could ever have imagined. You could be *The One* for him, and vice versa."

The way her mom said the words made it seem significant, though Triana didn't understand exactly how.

"Legend has it that there's one person in all the world for a werewolf who can accept him for what he is," her mother continued softly. "For Remy, you're that person."

It sounded so magical, so transcendent, so…roman-
tic. "If that's true, how could Remy walk away from
what we had?"

Her mother's smile was sad. "Only Remy knows the
answer to that, my dear."

Triana sighed. "Which is your way of saying I should
find Remy and have that conversation about how we feel
about each other, huh?"

"It is," her mom agreed. "If you want to be in his life,
and you want him in yours, Triana, you need to fight for
it. If you love him, don't let him walk away or you'll
regret it for the rest of your life."

Getting up, her mother pressed a kiss to the top of
her head, then took Triana's plate and walked over to
the sink, leaving her to ponder how she was supposed to
fight for a man who had made it clear he wasn't interested in falling in love again.

—⁓—

Triana was poking voodoo dolls with a pricing gun,
wondering what effect the little plastic pieces might
have on future victims of the dolls, when the tinkling
bell above the shop door rang. She didn't have to turn
around to know it was Remy. She knew it was him
because she could *feel* him.

She set down the pricing gun and slowly turned
around. He stood just inside the doorway, looking as
bad as she felt. His eyes had dark circles under them
and his face was haggard. His uniform was dry though,
at least.

He gave Zane a nod, then looked at her. "Can we talk?"

Zane pushed away from the wall he'd been leaning

against, using his finger to mark his place in the book of spells he'd been reading. "I'll be outside."

"No, stay." Triana glanced at Remy. "Let's go for a walk. I've been cooped up in here all day."

While she loved her mother's shop, in all honesty, she could use some air. Even though it had stopped raining, Triana grabbed her coat, slipping it on before walking out the door Remy held open for her.

"Where to?" he asked.

"Nowhere in particular," she said. "Let's just walk."

Between the cloudy night, light fog, and nearly empty streets, it felt like she and Remy had the city to themselves as they walked past Jackson Square and headed toward Woldenberg Park. She used to love going there with her father when she was little to watch the street performers and jazz musicians, so it seemed somehow fitting she and Remy went there to talk. If nothing else, maybe her father's spirit could give her some insight into the workings of a werewolf's mind.

Despite the decorative lamps along the paved walkway, darkness shrouded the area, but they managed to find a dry seat on one of the park benches. For a while, they both just sat there, gazing out at the Mississippi River, watching the water go past. Triana had so many thing she wanted to say, but she wasn't quite sure how—or even where—to start. Beside her, Remy seemed to have the same problem.

"I'm sorry I scared you last night," he finally said.

"I'm sorry I was scared." She turned her head to look at him. "How did you become a werewolf?"

Triana held her breath, afraid to hear the answer. Her mother had said people who became werewolves had gone through a traumatic event that triggered the change. Loving Remy meant loving all of him, and that included his werewolf side. So while she didn't want to know what horrible thing had turned him into a werewolf, she *needed* to know.

He started to speak, then cleared his throat and began again. "It happened when I was a marshal. Remember the other night when I told you I'd been involved with someone?"

Triana *really* didn't want to know about the other woman in Remy's life, but she nodded. "The woman you said things didn't work out with, right?"

"Yeah." He took a breath and let it out slowly. "The reason it didn't work out is because I got her killed."

Whatever Triana had expected him to say, it wasn't that. "What happened?"

Remy stared out at the river as he told her how he and his partner/lover had tracked three escaped prisoners to a farmhouse in Idaho. To hear him tell it, his arrogance had not only been the thing that sent them into the place without backup or even a plan, but that had also gotten Jess killed and turned him into a werewolf.

Triana's first instinct was to point out that Remy wasn't responsible for his partner's death, that it had been the escaped convicts who killed her, not him. But she was sure other people had told him the same thing more than a few times. He still held himself accountable—maybe because he was the naturally heroic alpha her mother had told her about. He would always risk his life for others and always blame himself when he failed to save everyone.

"It ate at me for a long time. It still does in a lot of

ways, I guess," Remy continued, hunching over to rest his forearms on his thighs and stare down at the ground. "For months after her death, I kept wondering why she wasn't the one who turned into a werewolf instead of me. Why didn't she live and I die?"

Tears burned Triana's eyes. This story would have been sad to hear anyone tell it, but listening to the man she loved recount it was pure torture. She moved closer, wrapping her arm around him.

"I hated being a werewolf," he said, his voice rough with emotion. "Somehow, in my messed-up logic, it was the werewolf's fault for changing me instead of Jess. So, to get my revenge on the beast, I started doing dangerous, outrageous stuff in an effort to get myself killed. I went after every bad guy on my own that I could find, but no matter what I did or how many times I got shot, the werewolf wouldn't let me die."

The tears she'd been holding back ran down her face. The idea of a world without Remy in it was one she couldn't bear to think about.

"When the direct approach didn't work, I started drinking—a lot," Remy continued. "I couldn't stand what I was, so I figured I'd drink the wolf into oblivion every night. People who know about the subject will tell you that a werewolf can't get drunk because our bodies break down and eliminate toxins like alcohol faster than we can drink it." He snorted. "It's not something to brag about, but I disproved that particular piece of werewolf lore. We can get drunk; we just have to be committed to the task. Some guys walk into a bar and line up a bunch of shots, then knock them back one after the other. I did the same thing, except I'd line up full bottles of whiskey, then drain them one after the other until I was so drunk I couldn't see straight."

The image of Remy doing that to himself brought another rush of tears to her eyes. "What made you stop drinking?"

He turned his head to look at her, his mouth edging up at the corners. "Gage Dixon, the commander of the SWAT Team in Dallas and the alpha of my pack of alphas. He'd spent years tracking down werewolves who fit the mold of what he was looking for in a SWAT officer and found me. Between trying to get myself killed in the Marshals and drinking myself to death, I wasn't exactly the poster child for the Dallas PD, but Gage wanted me on the team anyway."

Remy had said the commander of the team was also the alpha of his pack—she assumed that meant he was the one in charge—which made her wonder how many werewolves beside Remy and his friends were in Dallas SWAT. But that was a question she could ask later. Right then, she was more interested in other things.

"What did Gage say to convince you to leave the Marshals and join SWAT?" she asked quietly.

Remy let out a short laugh. "It wasn't what he said—at least right away. It was what he did."

"What did he do?"

"He sat down on a barstool beside me and took away my last bottle of whiskey. I told him to go away and leave me alone, and when he didn't, I got pissed and took a swing at him. One thing led to another, and we ended up getting in a fight and destroying the bar. There wasn't a chair, table, or bottle that didn't get smashed to hell by the time we were done." Remy shook his head.

"I'm not too proud to say that he kicked my ass. Then afterward, he told me something that forced me to take a step back and realize what a dumb-ass I'd been."

"What's that?"

"He asked me a simple question. If Jess had lived instead of me, would I want her to kill herself? His words were like a punch in the gut because if things were reversed, I knew it was the last thing I'd want. I also knew it was the last thing Jess would want."

Sighing, Remy got up and walked over to stand near the railing. He gazed out at the water for a long time, saying nothing. Triana knew she should probably give him some space, but her mother's words about fighting for him echoed in her head. How did one battle a ghost, though? Taking a deep breath, she stood and went over to stand beside him.

Remy turned away from the railing to look at her, his eyes wet with unshed tears. The sight made her heart ache. The wind coming off the water whipped at her hair, and he reached out to gently push it back from her face.

"I'm sorry about what I said at the restaurant the other night," he said, his voice hoarse. "I never meant to hurt you."

She gave him a small smile. "It's okay. You may have moved on, but your heart stayed with a woman who died. I understand now why you can't fall in love."

He shook his head, his expression suddenly earnest. "That's not it. Yes, I was in love before, but that's not why I pushed you away. I was afraid if I got involved with you, let myself fall for you, the same thing that happened to Jess would happen to you. When Lee kidnapped you in the same warehouse we raided, I told myself I'd been right."

Triana cupped his face in her hand. "That wasn't your fault, Remy. I would have ended up going to that warehouse to track down my father's killer whether we ran into each other at that club the other night or not. You weren't the reason I went there, and you certainly weren't the reason Quinn grabbed me. If anything, I'm alive right now because we did run into each other. You saved my life, Remy."

"I know that now. Since Jess died, I've kept every woman at arm's length until you. I told myself I was doing it to protect them, but I was really protecting myself. I didn't want to go through that kind of pain again." Remy's mouth curved. "But while I cared deeply for Jess, what I have with you is different, Triana. More intense. When I saw you on the dance floor that first night here, it was like I found a part of my soul I didn't even know was missing. I know this is going to sound crazy, but I feel so connected to you that sometimes I experience things you're feeling, both physical and emotional. When you cut your finger the other night, I felt it. When Quinn knocked you unconscious in the warehouse, I felt it. When you were terrified Lee was going to kill your mother, I felt it. Last night, I felt your confusion and despair when you were upstairs with your mother. When you're in a room, I can feel you nearby. It's like you're a part of me."

Triana's pulse skipped a beat. "I can feel you, too."

He looked at her in surprise. "You can?"

She nodded. "Uh-huh. At Lee's house, I could feel you in the hallway outside the living room; then later at Mom's place, I could feel you downstairs. And when you walked into the shop tonight, I knew it was you before I even turned around. This must be what Mom meant when she told me about *The One*."

"She told you about that? What did she say?"

"That every werewolf has one soul mate out there who can love and accept them for what they are," she said.

Remy took her hands in his. "Can you love me... knowing what I am?"

Triana smiled up at him, tears of happiness filling her eyes this time. "I already do, Remy. I think I loved you from the moment I turned around and saw you on that dance floor. Discovering you're a werewolf kind of shocked me, I admit, but it doesn't change the way I feel about you. Nothing could do that."

It had taken her all night and most of the day to come to that conclusion, but underneath the claws and fangs, he was still the guy she'd crushed on all through high school, the guy she was in love with now.

He grinned, letting out a sigh of relief. "You wouldn't believe how good it is to hear you say those words. Even though I'm terrified of putting you in danger by loving you, I can't stop the way I feel. I love you, Triana. I think I have since freshman year of high school."

Cupping her face in his hand, he bent his head and kissed her. Triana glided her hands up the front of his shirt, one gripping his shoulder while the other found its way into his hair. Remy wrapped his free arm around her, pulling her tightly against him and making her wish they'd gone somewhere more private to have this conversation than a very public park. Then she remembered his hotel was only a short walk from the park.

She was about to remind Remy of that when he stumbled against her, almost making her fall. He lifted his head with a growl, his eyes flashing yellow as the tips of his upper canines extended.

"What the hell?" he muttered.

The sight of his fangs almost made her pull away, but she resisted the urge. She wasn't doing that to Remy ever again.

"What's wrong?" she asked.

He didn't answer but instead twisted around, reaching behind him with one hand as he looked over his shoulder. She gasped at the sight of the two darts the size of jumbo Magic Markers sticking out of his back. Her blood ran cold. *Oh God.* Those were tranquilizer darts, just like the ones used on her father. As she watched, another heavy dart slammed into Remy's back, shoving him forward and almost sending him to his knees.

"Pull them out," he growled when he couldn't reach them himself.

Cursing herself for standing there like an idiot, Triana grabbed one and tugged, but it was stuck. "It's too deep," she said. "If I yank any harder, I'm going to hurt you."

The growl he let out this time was closer to a roar, and she stared wide-eyed as his fangs extended farther. "It hurts already. Rip them out!"

Heart pounding, Triana wrapped her hand around the one closest to his shoulder and pulled hard. The end of the needle was barbed like a harpoon, ripping his skin and leaving a bloody, gaping wound in its wake. The sight of it was enough to make her feel sick.

"Do the same to the others," he ground out, his face contorted in pain.

She yanked the other two darts out as fast as she could, tossing them on the ground. Her stomach plummeted as she realized they were empty. She remembered Quinn telling her the hunters had used tranquilizer drugs to slow down her father for the kill shot. They had to get out of here—now. She opened her mouth to warn Remy, but he'd already grabbed her hand and was running toward the parking lot near Café du Monde.

They didn't get more than ten feet before two more darts slammed into Remy, one in his lower back, the other in the thick muscles of his upper left thigh. *Crap.* Without being prompted, Triana immediately pulled the one out of his back while he did the same to the dart in his leg. It didn't matter though, because both were already empty.

Remy took her hand again and dragged her across the train tracks toward the parking lot. On the far side of the street, she could see a few patrons and waitstaff moving around inside the café. Once she and Remy reached it, they would be safe.

They were almost there when Remy suddenly slowed, then stumbled, the yellow glow dimming from his eyes. Whatever drugs had been in those darts was taking effect.

"Come on!" she urged. "We just have to make it across the street."

Remy growled and nodded, shambling forward.

Triana tugged on his hand, fearing another dart—or worse—would come at him any second. But they were moving too slowly. They weren't going to make it across the parking lot, much less all the way across the street to the café.

"Help me!" she shouted, waving her free arm wildly in the air, hoping someone would see them.

She was so focused on the people across the street she didn't see the van careering through the parking lot until it screeched to a stop in front of them. For half a second she thought whoever was inside was there to help, but then the side door slid open and she saw men with guns.

Remy lunged at them with a savage growl, but the guns popped a few times and he immediately went down.

"Remy!"

Triana tried to keep him from falling, but he was too heavy for her, and she couldn't keep him from tumbling all the way to the pavement. Then she saw a dark stain spread across the front of his shirt. She'd thought the men had dart guns, but they'd been pistols with silencers.

Three men jumped out of the van, rushing at her and Remy. She tried to shove them away, but one of the men got his arms around her from behind and tossed her in the van. A moment later, the other two flung Remy in beside her. With the amount of blood he'd already lost, there was no way he could still be alive. The thought that he might already be dead tore her heart in two. All she could do was pray the werewolf who'd refused to let Remy die so many times before would allow him to survive now.

The side door slammed and the vehicle took off with a squeal of tires, throwing Triana toward the back of the van. Rough hands caught her and jerked her to her knees. She turned, ready to take a swing at whomever it was. Her eyes went wide when she saw Quinn.

He blocked her fist with his hand. "Well, shit, girl. Long time no see."

Triana screamed and launched herself at him. She'd rip him to pieces with her fingernails if she had to. But he only grinned and caught her by the throat like she was a toy, slamming her head against the inside wall of the van. Stars exploded in her vision and her body went limp as she collapsed to the floor beside Remy.

Oh God, not again.

The last thing Triana heard before losing consciousness was Quinn's arrogant laugh.

Chapter 19

REMY KNEW HE WAS STILL ALIVE BECAUSE HIS HEAD WAS pounding like a drum. He stifled a groan, grimacing at the pain. Shit, his mouth tasted like he'd been eating dirt. He took a breath—or tried to, anyway. Damn, he could barely breathe. Or move. What the hell was wrapped around him?

As he fought to open his eyes, memories rushed back—being in the park with Triana, kissing her, getting shot with frigging tranquilizer darts, and running. Then a van screeching to a stop...and men with guns. They'd shot him and grabbed Triana.

The image of Quinn knocking her unconscious snapped Remy out of the haze he'd been trapped in. Lifting his head, he lunged forward.

He didn't make it very far. Actually, he didn't make it anywhere.

With a growl, he looked down and saw a heavy chain wrapped around his bare chest and arms, not only binding him, but also holding him off the floor so he was barely touching the metal decking beneath him. He glanced up to see the chain disappearing into the darkness above him, when he heard someone laugh.

"Looks like someone just figured out how fucked he really is."

Quinn's amused voice echoed in the ship's cargo hold. Based on the familiar scent, it was the same vessel

Remy and his pack mates had searched on that raid earlier in the week.

Remy looked over to see Quinn standing to one side
in the near darkness of the ship's hold. Aaron Lee was
beside him, his arms crossed, a curious expression on his
face. Behind him were two more of his goons that Remy
vaguely remembered from the shoot-out at the front gate
of Lee's home.

He paid little attention to the men. The only person
he cared about was Triana. She was sitting on a pallet
of bags filled with grain half a dozen feet away. Remy's
heart almost stopped when he saw that she was alive.
Then he smelled the blood, saw it streaked through her
hair and staining the left shoulder of her rain jacket. He
growled long and low. He was going to enjoy killing
every single one of these men.

Remy searched her face, looking for any other signs
of further injury, but all he saw was a mix of relief and
concern in her beautiful blue-gray eyes.

"Amazing," Lee said, moving closer to study his
chest. Or more precisely, the two bullet wounds that
should have been fatal but had instead closed over
already. "I knew Rufus had taken a bullet in the chest
before, but I never dreamed a werewolf could recover so
quickly from such an injury."

Letting out another growl, Remy lifted his legs and
kicked out at Lee's head. The older man quickly backpedaled. Not that it mattered. The angle had been all
wrong anyway. If not, the son of a bitch would have
been eating through a straw for a few months—if Remy
didn't kill him first.

Lee glared at him for a moment, then nodded at

Quinn. Lee's enforcer grabbed Triana by the arm and jerked her to her feet. Remy snarled, straining against the chains holding him, but the frigging things didn't so much as creak.

Smirking, Quinn pulled out a hunting knife from the sheath at his belt and pressed the blade to Triana's neck.

"Try something like that again, and I'll have him slit her throat," Lee warned.

Remy stilled. He had no idea what Lee had planned, but he was going to have to bide his time until he could figure out how to get out of these damn chains. He didn't know how he was going to do that, but he swore he would. And when he did, the only issue would be which one of the men died first.

Lee stepped closer again, and this time Remy was forced to let him. The man examined the wounds on his chest before going around to do the same to the ones on his back. Remy didn't point out that the healing wouldn't be nearly as impressive if either of the bullets were still inside him. A werewolf's body couldn't heal itself properly if foreign material was still in the wound. The outer skin would still close over in an instinctive attempt to keep from bleeding out, but the soft tissue and bones would never reknit, resulting in a hell of a lot of pain.

"You've lived a very violent life, I see," Lee said as he finished a complete circuit and came to stand in front of Remy again. "You've been shot, what? A dozen times?"

"Something like that," Remy ground out, wondering once again where the hell this was going.

Lee leveled his gaze at him. "You're going to turn me into a werewolf, or I will do things to your woman that you couldn't imagine in your worst nightmare."

Remy stared at him, stunned into silence. His heart dropped into his stomach. Lee would kill him and Triana the moment he figured out Remy couldn't do what he wanted.

Shit.

He was trying to come up with something he could say to Lee to either delay what was about to happen or, better yet, turn the tables on the madman, when Triana interrupted him.

"It's a curse," she said quietly. "In his blood."

Remy gave her a sharp look, wondering what Triana was doing. Quinn was still holding on to her, the knife dangerously close to her neck. But she didn't look at Remy. Instead, her gaze was fixed on Lee.

"A curse?" Lee laughed. "Now I know you're full of shit. I don't believe in any of that crap."

"You don't believe in them, yet you're okay with a man becoming a werewolf?" she said. "Why do you think he and my father came to the voodoo shop in the first place? They came because they wanted a way to break the curse."

Lee regarded Triana suspiciously for a moment before pinning Remy with a look. "Is this true?"

Remy still wasn't sure what Triana's plan was, but at least she seemed to have one, so he went with it. "Yes. I didn't know what was happening to me or even what I was. I thought Triana's mother could help me."

Lee turned to Triana again. "You said it's in his blood. If I inject myself with it, will it turn me into a werewolf?"

"No," she said. "The only way a werewolf can turn a person is to bite them."

Lee paled, and for the first time, Remy heard the man's heart beat a little faster. He shook his head. "There has to be another way."

"There isn't," Triana insisted. "The curse has to be passed through a bite, just like in the movies."

Lee considered that for a moment, then jabbed a finger at her. "You'd better not be lying to me, or you're dead."

Triana didn't flinch. "You might want to rethink that, since you'll need my help to survive the change. Especially if he has to bite you more than once."

Lee's eyes narrowed. "You're just saying that to save your neck. And his. Why the hell would he need to bite me more than once?"

"This isn't science, you know," she shot back. "It's voodoo magic. If you want to be a werewolf, you're going to have to keep both of us around."

Remy finally realized what Triana was doing, and he had to admit, it was brilliant. She'd created a situation where Lee couldn't kill either of them, not if he wanted to become a werewolf.

As inspired as the deception was, Remy was even more impressed with how convincing Triana sounded. For a woman who'd told him several times she didn't buy any of this magic stuff, she was doing one hell of a good job selling herself as a voodoo priestess. Even though Remy knew how werewolves worked, he liked Triana's version better.

Lee looked at the two other men in the hold. "Get me something to stand on."

When they brought over a wooden crate, Lee stepped up on it and rolled the sleeve of his dress shirt to his elbow, exposing his forearm. "Go ahead and bite me. And when I say let go, you'd better do it or Quinn will take great pleasure in scooping an eye right out of her pretty head."

Remy only growled in answer. He was tempted to suggest a bite to the neck would work better, but he doubted he'd get Lee to go along with that. He had no idea what was going to happen after he bit Lee, but he prayed Triana had something in that clever head of hers that would get him out of these chains.

Lee glanced at the two men who'd brought over the crate. "Be ready to shoot him if he doesn't let go." He shoved his arm in front of Remy's face. "Well, get on with it."

Remy eyed Lee for a long moment, then opened his mouth, letting his fangs slowly extend to their full length of an inch and a half. Lee went as pale as a ghost at the sight, but Remy didn't give him time to change his mind. He clamped his teeth down on Lee's forearm so hard he hit bone. He'd never bitten a person before, but then again, up until now, he'd never had a desire to. Sinking his teeth into Lee was satisfying as hell, though. The wolf inside wanted out to tear the asshole to pieces.

Remy ignored Lee's order to stop, immersed in the feeling of a rippling sensation spreading over his body as every muscle spasmed. He had no idea why it was happening, but he was shifting. The only other time he'd managed a full shift, it had hurt like a son of a bitch. This time…not so much.

Little by little, the chains around his chest loosened.

"I said, let the fuck go!" Lee shouted, punching him. Remy would have ignored him, but then he heard

Triana whimper in pain and knew he couldn't do anything to risk Quinn hurting her. He retracted his fangs and pulled away, resisting the urge to rip Lee's forearm off.

Lee stumbled off the boxes and over to Triana, holding his bloody arm out to her. "Is this deep enough? You'd better tell me it is because it hurt like hell."

Triana looked at the wound. "I think so. We'll only know for sure if you change."

"When will that be?" he demanded, wrapping his other hand around his arm, trying to stanch the flow of blood.

"It could be a few minutes or a few hours," she said. "I don't know."

"You'd better not be lying to me." Lee cursed. "Someone get me something to stop the bleeding, and hurry the hell up!"

Remy only half listened as Lee rambled on about how much his arm frigging hurt. He was too busy trying to breathe through the muscle spasms making his whole body shiver. Luckily, Lee's men were so focused on bandaging his arm they didn't notice the chains around Remy's chest slip another inch as his torso tried to morph into its new shape. If he kept shifting, there was a good chance he'd be able to scramble his way out at some point.

Keep distracting them a little while longer, Triana.

He felt the bizarre sensation of fur slowly sprouting on his back, when the sound of gunfire erupted from somewhere outside the ship.

"What the hell is that?" Lee demanded at the same time one of his men yanked out his cell phone and shoved it to his ear.

The man listened for a moment, then his eyes widened. "It's the cops," he told Lee as he hung up. "There are at least a half-dozen of them. Looks like SWAT."

Lee cursed. "Quinn, bring her." He turned to the other two men. "You come with us," he said to one of them, then looked at the other. "You shoot him in the head."

The bastard didn't hang around to see if everyone followed orders, but instead ran for the exit.

Triana screamed, fighting against Quinn even as Remy struggled against the chain binding him. When it held fast, Remy struggled harder, but that only served to slow down his body's transformation. He growled in frustration. It took every ounce of willpower to force himself to relax and let his body finish shifting while Quinn wrapped his arms around a struggling Triana and carried her up the metal stairs at the far end of the cargo hold.

Remy hadn't realized how far his face had shifted until the man Lee had ordered to kill him stopped dead in his tracks, his eyes widening in fear. He lifted his pistol, trying to aim, but his hands were shaking so badly he couldn't hold the thing steady. Remy took advantage of that, lunging at the guy with a ferocious snarl.

Scared shitless, the man backpedaled and squeezed the trigger. The bullet zipped past Remy and ricocheted around the hold a few times before thumping into something behind him.

While the man stood there in shock, Remy's shoulders cracked and popped as he shifted further. A few more seconds and he would be free.

Abruptly, the sensation of Triana moving farther away hit him. *This is taking too long, dammit.* No matter how terrified Lee's henchman might be, at some point he'd get his act together and put a bullet through Remy's head.

As if reading Remy's mind, the man squared his shoulders and came closer, pointing the suddenly much steadier weapon right at his forehead.

With his feet on the floor now, Remy wasn't nearly as defenseless as he looked. He brought his right leg up, catching the man's arm with his booted foot and sending the pistol flying. The man was so busy trying to see where the weapon went he never saw Remy's boot come up again and catch him under the jaw.

Remy slipped out of the hoist chain and hit the floor at the same time Lee's goon did. He immediately jumped to his feet, ready to go at the guy again, but the man was out cold.

Turning, Remy headed for the stairs, but barely made it two steps before his legs gave out as the wolf completely took over his body.

Remy wasn't sure if it was the urgent need to go after Triana, or if he was simply more accepting of the transformation this time. Either way, the full shift came fast, bones breaking and reforming, muscles tearing and reshaping to cover a new, sleeker shape.

Getting out of his pants proved to be a challenge since wolves didn't have opposable thumbs, and he was forced to roll around on the floor like a drunk puppy to get out of the things. Luckily, his boots and socks just fell off.

Finally free, Remy raced for the stairs, amazed at the acceleration he was able to get out of this four-wheel-drive version of his body. Then he hit the steps and nearly broke his frigging neck as his legs went out from under him. It was a lot easier to speed up in this body than it was to slow down, but he got his long legs back under him and scrambled up the stairs, through the serpentine maze of corridors and out onto the deck.

Triana was already in a car speeding away from the dock by the time Remy got topside. Ignoring the shootout between Lee's men on the deck of the ship and his pack mates on the shore, he headed for the gangway, slamming into anyone who got in his way. His presence freaked the hell out of Lee's men, and several of them jumped overboard to avoid him.

Remy leaped off the gangway and headed for Chartres Street, veering east as he quickly covered ground. He wasn't following any of his usual senses because he couldn't see where they were taking Triana and he couldn't smell her. But the connection he had to her told him he was headed toward her.

A wolf of any size running down the middle of New Orleans was sure to gain attention. A wolf his size was going to make people lose their minds. But he couldn't do anything about it. He only hoped the darkness and the rain would keep people off the streets.

He'd just turned and headed toward the bridge that would take him to the Lower Ninth Ward when his ears picked up a quiet rapid-fire thumping sound. He turned his head to see what the hell was coming up behind him when he smelled Cooper.

A moment later, the team's demo expert—also in his wolf form—raced up beside him. Remy would have thanked his pack mate for the backup if he could speak. But since he couldn't, he concentrated on catching up to the car taking Triana farther and farther away from him.

———

Triana gripped the door handle with one hand and the seat belt strap with the other, holding on for dear life as the big Cadillac swerved around the vehicle in front of them and almost slammed into the side railing of the bridge over the Industrial Canal.

"Slow the hell down," Lee shouted from the front seat as he bounced off the door. "There's no one behind us. We're fine."

The man driving didn't seem so sure of that, but as they came off the bridge into the Lower Ninth Ward, he slowed down a bit. He still kept checking the rearview mirror every five seconds though.

"Stay on Forty-Six until it crosses Thirty-Nine," Quinn said casually from his place in the backseat beside her.

The jerk had gone out of his way to cozy up close to her from the moment he'd thrown her in the backseat at the dock. Triana had tried to push him away more than once, but all he did was laugh and move next to her again.

"There's a yacht waiting for us in slip eighteen," he told the driver. "We'll be in the Gulf and beyond the reach of the police an hour after we get on board."

Triana's stomach clenched. The thought of being trapped on a boat with these men, especially Quinn, for any length of time terrified her. But that wasn't going to happen. Somehow, some way, Remy was going to find her before it was too late.

She'd almost lost that hope when she heard the gunshot down in the hold of the ship when Quinn had been dragging her away. She'd thought for sure Remy was dead. He was strung up on a chain, unable to move more than an inch or two, so there was no way he could avoid a bullet. And yet something inside her refused to believe Remy was dead. She would have felt it if he were. She knew it in her heart.

So, until she knew otherwise, she was going to believe Remy was still alive and coming after her.

In the front seat, Lee cursed. Twisting in his seat to look at her, he held up his arm. Blood had seeped through the makeshift bandage he'd wrapped around it. "My arm still hurts as much as it did when that mutt first bit me. When will the pain stop?"

Hopefully never, Triana wanted to say but didn't. She had to keep Lee believing all the crap she'd been telling him about becoming a werewolf until Remy showed up.

"Soon," she said. "The pain is a good sign. It means the change is already happening."

Lee studied her for a moment like he was trying to figure out if she was lying to him. He must have decided she wasn't because he nodded and turned back around in his seat, a small smile on his face.

Triana was still shocked she'd been able to talk Lee into letting Remy bite him. She'd been playing for time when she'd started the whole werewolf story, praying she could delay things long enough for Remy to get loose. She never dreamed Lee would agree. He must have been even more desperate for power than she thought.

She was scooting closer to the door when she felt Remy somewhere nearby. A split second later, she caught a blur of movement in the darkness to the right of the car. Pulse racing, she turned her head to look out the window as something slammed into the front passenger door so hard the window shattered. The big car rocked on its suspension, one side of the vehicle nearly coming up off the road. Crap, it was like they'd been hit with a wrecking ball.

The driver swerved the car away from the impact, crossing over a narrow, grassy median and into the double lane of oncoming traffic before ending up on a side street, taking them deeper into the Ninth Ward.

"What the hell was that?" Quinn shouted.

He pulled a large pistol from behind his back, waving it around like he thought whatever hit the car was going to join them in it any second. Triana didn't have a clue what was happening, but she knew it had something to do with Remy. She could feel him out there.

In the front seat, Lee was brushing glass off his clothes and telling the driver to get the hell back on the highway. But the streets were a little tighter in this part of town, forcing the man to slow down as he looked for a place to turn around. The Ninth Ward had been the section of the city hit the hardest during Katrina. Some of the structures had been rebuilt, but there were still a lot of abandoned and overgrown homes too. It was hard to see this part of town and not realize that a lot of people had never recovered from the storm.

Triana peered out the side window, looking for Remy, when the window in the driver's side door suddenly shattered. The next thing she knew, the driver was gone, getting ripped out of the car and disappearing into the darkness with a scream.

Quinn cursed and threw himself over the front seat, lunging for the wheel, but it was too late. Triana ducked as the front of the Cadillac plowed into an overgrown wall surrounding a dilapidated house. The car hit the brick wall doing at least thirty miles an hour and the impact was loud and violent. Thank God she'd taken the time to put on her seat belt or she would have joined Quinn and Lee in the front seat.

The vehicle ended up perched on the remains of the wall, the front tires off the ground. Triana didn't wait to see if Quinn and Lee were alive. She popped her seat belt, opened the door, and scrambled out.

She didn't get more than a few feet before Quinn caught up with her. He wrapped an arm around her neck, yanking her against his chest as he backed away from the car toward the house. His breath was loud in her ear as he pointed his gun in every direction at once. The area didn't have a lot of streetlamps and the rain was only making it worse. If it wasn't for the car's headlights, they'd have had a hard time seeing anything.

Lee joined them a moment later, pulling his pistol out as he squinted into the darkness, trying to see down the street. Triana turned her head to see a man lying there. It might have been the driver of the car, but it was hard to tell at this distance. He wasn't moving though, that much she was sure of.

Suddenly, an animal darted across the street. It was big and fast—much too big and too fast to be a dog.

Another animal followed the first, this one just as big. Whatever they were, there were two of them.

As the animals slowly came out from behind the building they'd been behind, Triana realized they were wolves. The biggest wolves she'd ever seen in her life. If they'd been standing beside her, their withers would have been level with her hips.

Triana's breath hitched as the wolves' glowing yellow eyes pierced the darkness. One of them was Remy. She didn't know how that was possible, but she instinctively knew it was him.

Eyes fixed on her and the two men, Remy and the other wolf slowly moved toward them, baring their teeth in fierce snarls.

Muttering a curse, Lee turned and ran toward the house behind them, shouting at Quinn to follow. Quinn hesitated for a moment, seemingly torn between shooting at the wolves and retreating. He must have decided discretion was the better part of valor because he lowered his weapon and dragged her toward the dilapidated structure.

When they reached the vine-covered porch, Lee was trying to yank off the boards covering the door.

"Kick in the door," Lee ordered Quinn, grabbing Triana, keeping her in front of him like a shield as he shoved his gun to her head. "You can't kill me now that I'm one of you!" he shouted into the night. "If you try to come in here, I'll execute her right in front of you. Her death will be on you, not me."

There was a loud crack behind them as Quinn ripped off the boards and tossed them aside. Lee shoved her at his enforcer, who immediately caught her and dragged her into the house. Lee hesitated in the doorway, looking out at the dark street.

The asshole never saw the wolf come at him from the side. One moment Lee was standing there, and the next he was flying off the porch.

Quinn shoved Triana outside, scrambling around as he looked for his boss, but there was no sign of Lee.

Somewhere in the yard, Remy and the other wolf howled. Muttering under his breath, Quinn quickly dragged Triana into the house again. In the glow from the car's headlights, she could see that they were in someone's old living room. It smelled like mold, mildew, and rot.

Triana struggled against Quinn, but it was worse than useless. He was simply too strong for her. He didn't stop pulling her across the room until he had his back up against the far wall.

"Come in here and I'll shoot her!" Quinn yelled, his voice laced with fear. "And after I kill her, I'll do the two of you next. I know how to kill monsters."

There was a low growl at the door as a pair of glowing yellow eyes appeared. There was enough light from the car to see the wolf clearly now. He was even bigger than she realized, lithe, muscular, and graceful. His fur was mostly gray with shades of brown and what could almost be called blond mixed in. Even if his eyes didn't give him away, Triana still would have known it was Remy.

He was beautiful.

Before Triana realized what was happening, Quinn aimed his gun in Remy's direction and fired. Triana screamed, but the sound died in her throat as she realized Remy was nowhere in sight. In the time it had taken Quinn to point the weapon and pull the trigger, Remy had darted off. A moment later, he was back in the doorway, teeth bared in a fierce snarl.

"Stay back!" Quinn warned, pointing the weapon at her now. "I'll do it. I'll pop her right in the head!"

Triana heard the growl behind the partially intact wall in back of them before Quinn did. Realizing the second wolf was there, he turned his pistol in that direction.

As Quinn moved, his hold on Triana slipped. Remy's words from the other day echoed in her head. *If you only have one chance to hit a person—and it's life or death— aim for the throat and punch as hard as you can.*

Balling her hand into a fist, she spun around and aimed for Quinn's throat, punching him hard enough for her to feel it all the way through her wrist and up into her arm.

Quinn staggered back with a weird gurgling sound.

Sensing more than seeing Remy move, Triana jumped out of the way. She hit the floor at the same time Remy smashed into Quinn, knocking him though the wall. There was a gunshot, then lots of snarling and growling mixed in with a few cries of pain.

Triana was glad it was too dark to see anything in the other room, but she knew what was happening. After the part Quinn had played in her father's death, she couldn't find it in herself to feel sorry for him.

It couldn't have been any more than thirty seconds later before Remy bounded out of the hole he and Quinn had made in the wall. He stopped when he saw her standing there, his whole body displaying how hesitant he was to approach her.

Smiling, Triana stood and moved to meet him halfway. Then she dropped to her knees and held out her arms. He was there immediately, his head towering over hers, his huge muzzle sniffing softly around the scalp wound that she'd gotten when Quinn had slammed her head into the wall of the van earlier. She'd almost forgotten about it.

"I'm fine," she said, almost laughing as he chuffed and continued to sniff at her head. "Are you okay?"

She ran her hands along the thick fur of his withers and sides. "You didn't get shot, did you?"

He chuffed again in answer. Triana sighed. This part was going to be tough. She was obviously going to need to brush up on her wolf sounds.

Not having any other way to know for sure, she ran her hands all over Remy's body. He was huge, so it took a little while, not that he seemed to mind the attention.

When she was satisfied he hadn't been wounded, she sat back on her heels and looked up at him. "I didn't know you could do this."

He sat down and chuffed again.

She laughed. "You're absolutely beautiful like this, but do you think you could turn back, so I can actually talk to you?"

An expression that looked like concern crossed Remy's furry face, but then the second wolf padded out of the other room to stand beside him. Remy visibly relaxed as the second wolf—he was the same size but with darker brown fur mixed with gray—lay down on the floor and closed his eyes. Remy did the same.

Triana watched, fascinated, as the muscles under their fur began to twitch and spasm. Then it got a little weird as their fur started to disappear. Okay...a lot weird. But as a curious science nerd, she couldn't look away, even when the bones under all those muscles started to change shape. Besides, this was Remy, the man she loved. There was no way she was going to look away.

Until they were done shifting back into their human form and she realized they were both naked as the day they were born. She certainly had no problem looking at Remy like that, but seeing some guy she'd never met before was…strange.

As she stood up and turned her back to give the man some privacy, she had to admit her mother had been right—alpha werewolves were certainly hunky.

Triana felt Remy's presence behind her even before he turned her around and kissed her. She wrapped her arms around him, squeezing him tightly as she kissed him back. Then she pulled away a little to take a closer look at the two bullet wounds on his chest. She could still see them, but they were completely closed over. She hugged him again, never wanting to let him go. But after a while, she heard the other man clear his throat.

Remy chuckled. "Triana, this is Cooper. He's one of the werewolves in my pack."

Triana went through the most unusual handshake ritual of her life with a naked guy who'd moments before been a wolf. She suddenly knew how guys felt when they met a woman. *Don't look down. Don't look down. Don't look down.*

"It's nice to meet you," Cooper said with a quirky grin that suggested he knew exactly what she was thinking. "I hate to interrupt the reunion, but we need to get out of here. The gunshots and that wrecked Caddy are going to attract attention sooner or later, and we don't want to be here when the police show up because that"—he gestured at the other room—"is going to be damn hard to explain."

Crap. Triana hadn't thought of that. She grabbed Remy's hand and started for the door. They obviously weren't leaving in Lee's car, so that meant walking. Then the problem with that idea hit her.

She stopped and turned to look at them. "You guys didn't bring clothes with you, did you?"

They both shook their heads.

Of course not. "Then we might be in trouble because I don't have my purse or cell phone, and you can't go out there naked."

Remy and Cooper exchanged looks.

"This is New Orleans, darlin'." Remy's mouth twitched. "I doubt anyone will even notice. Besides, it's dark out."

Triana felt her jaw drop as Remy gave her hand a tug and started for the door, Cooper in tow. Crap. They weren't really doing this, were they?

Well, this was probably going to be interesting. Then again, something told her everything in her life would be more interesting now that Remy was in it.

Chapter 20

TRIANA SAT AT THE PICNIC TABLE BESIDE COOPER'S WIFE, Everly, watching Remy and the other members of the Pack on the volleyball court as they kicked up sand and laughed like a bunch of kids. Running around without a shirt, sweat glistening on that perfect body of his, Remy looked good enough to eat. She had to admit she appreciated some of the other guys out there too, particularly the ones displaying that wolf head tattoo on the left side of their chests. They weren't Remy, but they were fine.

"If the Pack gets any larger," Everly remarked, pushing back her long hair, "I think we're going to need a bigger volleyball court. Between the SWAT guys, Jayna's pack, my brother, and the new betas, the place is getting crowded."

Triana laughed. Everly was quickly becoming her closest friend in Dallas. The other woman seemed so comfortable talking about werewolves, like it was the most natural thing in the world. Triana, on the other hand, sometimes still had to pinch herself as a reminder she wasn't dreaming and really did live in a world where werewolves existed. Thinking about it now, it was hard not laughing at the crazy notions she used to have. She thought she knew everything about how the world worked, but it turned out she was still learning.

Fortunately, there were a lot of people around to teach her what she needed to know. In addition to

Everly, there were the other wives and girlfriends, as well as Khaki Blake, the female alpha she'd heard so much about. Then there was the Pack doctor.

She'd spent hours talking to Dr. Saunders about werewolves. While she'd been surprised the Pack had a primary care provider, she was glad to finally have someone she could talk to about werewolves in a language she understood. As for Dr. Saunders, he was stoked at the thought of being able to do a DNA profile of the daughter of a known werewolf. The possibilities of what they could learn seemed endless.

A familiar laugh by the grill interrupted her musings, and Triana looked over to see her mother shaking her head as a shirtless Max leaned in and tasted the jambalaya they were making. Her mom was in town for the week, visiting and getting to know Remy's extended family—the Pack.

It had been a crazy three weeks since she and Remy had gotten together. In every possible way, her whole life had changed that night in New Orleans when she admitted her love for the charming werewolf. Since then, she'd quit her job in Houston, packed up everything she owned, moved in with Remy, applied for and got a new job with the Dallas ME's office, and become a member of the Pack. She'd never been happier in her life.

Remy had asked her to move to Dallas the same night he'd rescued her from Quinn and Lee. Since she'd already decided she was going to spend the rest of her life with him, it only made sense to start by moving in with him. The thought of asking him to leave his pack after what she'd seen Cooper and the other guys do for him was out of the question.

She, Remy, and Cooper had only walked a couple of blocks that night in the Lower Ninth Ward before Brooks had pulled up beside them in an NOPD vehicle, as if picking up naked pack mates out for a stroll was a common occurrence for him. She had no clue how the other werewolf had known where they were, but she hadn't been about to look a gift horse in the mouth. She and the guys had climbed in and gone back to the dock to grab Remy's and Cooper's clothes.

The driver of the Cadillac must have survived getting yanked out of the moving vehicle because he wasn't on the street when she and the guys walked out of the house. As for Lee and Quinn, no one had found their bodies for two days. By the time someone finally stumbled over them, rats had gotten to them and made a mess of everything. The police seemed to think one of Lee's enemies had killed them and promptly shelved the investigation. After seeing how quickly her father's murder had been shoved to the back burner, Triana wasn't surprised. No one really cared who'd killed Quinn and Lee. Everyone was simply glad they were gone.

Triana would have felt a lot better about how things ended if they'd been able to come up with information about the hunters who had actually murdered her father. But at the moment, all they knew about the elusive hunters was that they were dangerous, liked to kill werewolves, and were getting more aggressive.

A few days after she'd left her job in Houston, her friend from the lab there had called saying she'd found an alarming number of murder victims—twenty-two in a period of two years—that had come back with animal tranquilizers in their systems. And those were just the ones who had been found. Her friend said there was a good chance the number was double or triple that since there were a lot of cities and towns that wouldn't bother with a full toxicology screening on someone who'd obviously been shot to death.

Her friend thought there was a good chance the FBI had taken notice of these murders and were looking at the situation as a potential serial killer case. The only thing that seemed to have them hesitating was the complete lack of connection between the victims. The murders had occurred all across the country and the victims had come from every walk of life. They'd been farmers, teachers, stay-at-home mothers, college students, military veterans, even a firefighter.

When Triana mentioned her father had been killed in the same way, her friend had sent her copies of everything she'd collected. Triana and Remy had spent hours poring over the files with the other members of the Pack. There was no way to know if all the people who'd been killed were werewolves, but the fact that every single victim had been shot in the head seemed to support that conclusion. That being the case, they had to face the extreme possibility there was a large group of hunters out there doing everything they could to track down werewolves and kill them.

Triana was still thinking about what that meant for her and her new friends when the game broke up. Remy, her mother, and several other members of the Pack, including Brooks and Cooper, joined her and Everly at the table while the rest crowded around Max over by the grill. The Pack's two adorable mascots—a pit bull mix named Tuffie and a lab mix named Leo—walked around and made puppy eyes at everyone, begging for something of their own. Based on how much they got, it was obvious they were very good at it.

Remy slipped a hand around her waist and grazed his warm lips across the skin of her neck, making her shiver.

On the other side of the table, her mother smiled fondly at them. While the subject hadn't come up yet, Triana knew her mom was already thinking about whom to invite to their wedding.

She was about to ask Remy what had ended the game so soon when she saw Gage Dixon—the Pack alpha— and his wife, Mackenzie, talking to some new arrivals to the party. Their group consisted of three women, a guy, and a little girl who couldn't have been any more than four.

"Who's that?" she asked curiously.

"It's a beta pack," her mother said.

Remy looked at her mother in surprise. "Okay, I can smell they're werewolves, and I assumed they were betas from the size. How did you know?"

Her mom shrugged. "I'm not really sure. I've been around werewolves since I was a teenager, so I seem to recognize them when I see them. The same way you know someone has blond hair or blue eyes, I suppose."

Triana shook her head, both amazed at what her mother was able to do and by the appearance of another beta pack at the compound.

"That's the third group of betas that has shown up here in the past two weeks," Zane remarked as he sat down with a plate of ribs and a bowl of jambalaya. "Counting the omegas who have moved into the area, there must be close to twenty new werewolves in the city."

Her mother's gaze once again drifted to the group talking to Gage, but this time worry creased her brow. "They're trying to get close to your alpha pack for protection."

"That's a good thing, right?" Triana asked. "Strength in numbers and all."

At the next table over, Brooks nodded. "Definitely. There's no way hunters would come after a pack this size."

"You don't think so?" her mother asked, turning to look at the SWAT werewolf. "Haven't you stopped to wonder why all these other werewolves have started showing up now? Why so many members of your pack have been finding their soul mates all of a sudden? Why some of your pack, including Remy, are learning how to fully shift into a wolf when the need arises?"

Beside Everly, Cooper frowned. "Are you saying that each of us finding *The One* wasn't just random chance?"

Her mom shook her head. "I don't think so. Most werewolves consider the legend of *The One* to be just that—a legend. That's because it usually only happens once in a generation, if that. To have it happen this many times in one pack should be impossible."

"But it is happening," Remy pointed out.

Her mother nodded solemnly. "Yes, it is. Sometimes, when a pack is in danger, it will do things to protect itself, such as other werewolves joining or members finding their mates. Not necessarily soul mates, but mates who will make the pack stronger. That's what's happening now, only more extreme." She sighed. "In addition to betas and omegas joining your pack, more of you are learning how to shift completely into wolves. Not only are you finding soul mates, but each of you are finding *The One* as well. All of that means there's a major threat to the Pack, one so extreme that even a pack of this many alphas may not be able to handle it."

Silence descended on the group, worry reflected in everyone's eyes.

Triana's stomach clenched. She'd lost her father to these damn hunters. She refused to even think about losing anyone else she cared about. Maybe it was because of the bond she shared with Remy, but she already cared deeply about everyone here.

Having someone who could pick up on her emotions was a good thing in this case, since Remy leaned over and wrapped a big, strong arm around her, lending her some of that strength to help her feel safe.

"Are you regretting moving here and putting yourself in the middle of all this?" he asked softly in her ear.

"No, of course not! I love you. There's nowhere else I'd rather be than with you." She narrowed her eyes at him. "And don't even consider pulling any of that I-love-you-too-much-to put-you-in-danger crap. Because I'm telling you right now, I'm not putting up with it."

Remy pulled her close again, giving her a kiss that warmed her all the way down to her toes. "You won't have to. If there's any danger, I want you right beside me where I can keep an eye on you. I love you more than anything in the world, and I refuse to let anything come between us."

"Do you think the hunters will come here?" she asked. "Do you think they'll really try to take on the Pack?"

He shrugged. "I don't know. But if they do, we're

going to be ready for them. And they're going to learn that this pack isn't like anything they've ever dealt with before. We're used to facing bad guys, killers, and psychopaths on a daily basis, and because of that, we're a pack bound together in ways these people could never imagine. If the hunters come here, we'll deal with them together—as a pack."

Around them, everyone voiced their agreement. Max, who was still over by the grill, tipped his bottle of beer in Remy's direction. "Damn straight we will. As a pack."

As everyone began eating and laughing again, Gage walked over with the new betas, introducing everyone.

Triana leaned in and kissed Remy, smiling up at him. "As a pack," she whispered.

Acknowledgments

I hope you had as much fun reading Remy and Triana's story as I had writing it! I thought it would be fun to get the SWAT guys out of Dallas for a while, and with his background, New Orleans seemed like the perfect place for Remy and his pack mates to go for a howling good time!

This whole series wouldn't be possible without some very incredible people. In addition to another big thank-you to my hubby for all his help with the action scenes and military and tactical jargon, thanks to my agent, Bob Mecoy, for believing in me and encouraging me and being there when I need to talk; my editor and go-to-person at Sourcebooks, Cat Clyne (who loves this series as much as I do and is always a phone call, text, or email away whenever I need something); and all the other amazing people at Sourcebooks, including my fantastic publicist Stephany, and their crazy-talented art department. The covers they make for me are seriously drool-worthy!

Because I could never leave out my readers, a huge thank-you to everyone who has read my books and Snoopy Danced right along with me with every new release. That includes the fantastic people on my amazing Street Team, as well my assistant, Janet. You rock!

I also want to give a big thank-you to the men,

women, and working dogs who protect and serve in police departments everywhere, as well as their families.

And a very special shout-out to our favorite restaurant, P.F. Chang's, where hubby and I bat story lines back and forth and come up with all of our best ideas, as well as a thank-you to our fantastic waiter, Andrew, who takes our order to the kitchen the moment we walk in the door!

Hope you enjoy the seventh book in the SWAT series coming soon from Sourcebooks, and look forward to reading the rest of the series as much as I look forward to sharing it with you.

If you love a man in uniform as much as I do, make sure you check out X-Ops, my other action-packed paranormal/romantic-suspense series from Sourcebooks.

Happy Reading!

About the Author

Paige Tyler is a *New York Times* and *USA Today* best-selling author of sexy, romantic suspense and paranormal romance. She and her very own military hero (also known as her husband) live on the beautiful Florida coast with their adorable fur baby (also known as their dog). Paige graduated with a degree in education but decided to pursue her passion and write books about hunky alpha males and the kick-butt heroines who fall in love with them. Visit www.paigetylertheauthor.com.

She's also on Facebook, Twitter, Tumblr, Instagram, tsu, Wattpad, Google+, and Pinterest.

HER DARK HALF

New York Times bestselling author Paige Tyler delivers pulse-pounding paranormal romantic suspense in the X-Ops series

Coyote shifter and cover operator Trevor Maxwell has a lot on his plate. His former director was killed, and it's up to him to track down the killer. The job is difficult enough, but after his boss pairs him with Alina Bosch, a distractingly beautiful CIA operative, it's damn near impossible.

When the daughter of a DCO VIP is kidnapped, all hell breaks loose. Suddenly Trevor and Alina are thrown into a much more dangerous operation, and they'll have to trust each other to make it out alive.

"As fresh and fun as the first."

—Booklist for *Her Rogue Alpha*

For more Paige Tyler, visit:
www.sourcebooks.com

WOLF UNLEASHED

New York Times bestselling author Paige Tyler delivers action-packed paranormal romantic suspense in the SWAT series

Wolf shifter Alex Trevino has fallen hard for veterinarian Lacey Barton. Getting her to agree to a date is a lot of work—and winning her heart proves even harder.

Lacey can't deny her crazy attraction to Alex, but she has no intention of letting herself fall for him. In her experience, men don't stick around. Then Lacey's sister is kidnapped, and it's up to Alex to crack the case—and prove to Lacey that he isn't going anywhere.

*"A SWAT team of hunky werewolves?
I think I have an emergency NOW!"*

—Kerrelyn Sparks, *New York Times* bestselling author, for *In the Company of Wolves*

For more Paige Tyler, visit:
www.sourcebooks.com